Tilting Gravity

Jenn Storey

Dreamsphere Books
Winnipeg, Canada

Published April 2023 by Dreamsphere Books, an imprint of Story Perfect Inc.

Dreamsphere Books
PO Box 51053 Tyndall Park
Winnipeg, Manitoba R2X 3B0
Canada

Visit http://www.dreamspherebooks.com to find out more.

For the brokenhearted 14-year-old in all of us.

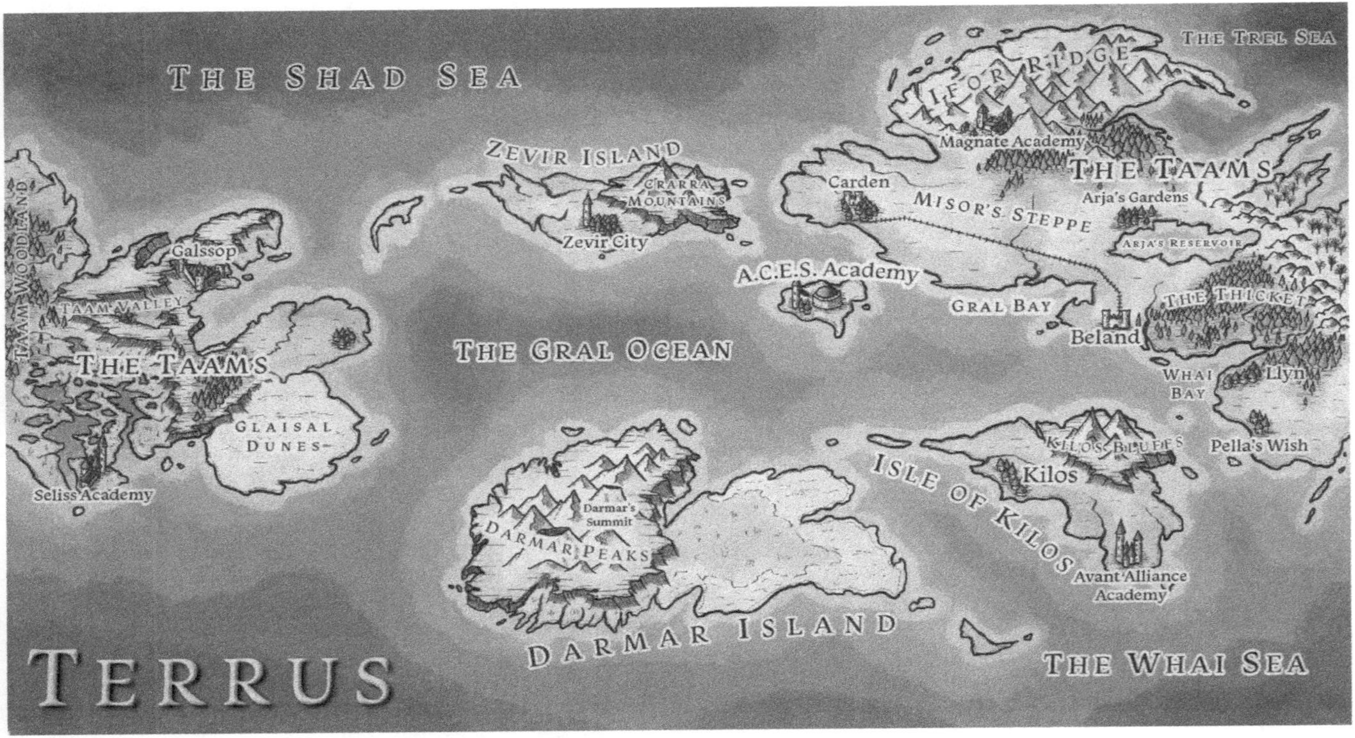

THE SHAD SEA
THE TREL SEA
IFOR RIDGE
Magnate Academy
THE TAAMS
Arja's Gardens
ARJA'S RESERVOIR
Carden
MISOR'S STEPPE
ZEVIR ISLAND
CRARRA MOUNTAINS
Zevir City
A.C.E.S. Academy
GRAL BAY
Beland
THE THICKET
WHAI BAY
Llyn
Pella's Wish
TAAM WOODLAND
Galssop
TAAM VALLEY
THE TAAMS
GLAISAL DUNES
Seliss Academy
THE GRAL OCEAN
KILOS BLUFFS
Kilos
ISLE OF KILOS
Avant Alliance Academy
Darmar's Summit
DARMAR PEAKS
DARMAR ISLAND
THE WHAI SEA
TERRUS

OVERTURE

A goddess creates a planet. The planet rebels, developing raw, unstable energy beneath its surface, and the goddess must save her creation from itself.

First, she forms the australs, elemental guardians to keep the planet's force stable. When the australs prove to be too wild, she creates giants, the Rhurgs, as caretakers. But they are too large for the task, and mold humans from their clay flesh to act in their stead. The giants perish, becoming mountains, islands, and deserts. Humans, though innovative, are too fragile for the task by themselves, and the balance tilts again. The energy of the planet's core is too great.

The goddess responds with a gift: a second moon, Nova, with the ability to transfer a sliver of her power to the humans. Every twenty years, this power passes from one woman, the Eichon, to another. In turn, the Eichon becomes the planet's ruler and serves to balance the planet by mere presence alone.

With Nova came another blessing, one that imbues some humans with innate majik upon birth. These, the Eheris, became the protectors of the Eichon.

But an Eichon is not always as benevolent as the goddess she invokes, and many have fallen prey to a more tyrannical nature.

Over the last 1,200 years, humans have grown and advanced to utilize great technology under the rule of the shifting Eichons, and the planet has found stability. However, humans are never without a natural balance themselves. There are others who would deny, even destroy, the Eichon no matter the cost.

CHAPTER ONE

Eight Years Prior

Adeline was restless. The drapery from the four-post bed cast shadows, and even though she was exhausted, her mind kept returning to the girl with eight silver clasps in her thick curls. Adeline had, just that morning, been gifted her very first hair clasp and the excitement of the day hadn't worn off yet.

Her ninth birthday had been delightful. A big trip with children her own age on a boat—a *real* boat—on the sea and everything. Adeline had never been on a boat before and was so thankful when the girl—Syd—had introduced herself and shown Adeline around.

The cabin had been squeaky, everything wooden except the popping fireplace, and the chatter of so many new people had made Adeline shy. She'd liked the porthole windows and the way the light beamed in from the deck. Everything had been aged in a way she'd never known; it had made her impatient somehow.

Momma had been busy with telling stories to the other children, ones Adeline had heard before in the sleepy haze of bedtime back when momma still had time to put her to sleep. The smell of salt and the whooshing sound of the boat gliding on the water had made her heart pound. She couldn't wait to get outside in the sun and feel the wind in her hair.

After a while, Adeline had started to feel quite sorry for

herself. It was, after all, her birthday. Shouldn't everyone be doing what *she* wanted to do? And then, Syd had tapped her shoulder, and Adeline had refused to leave her new friend until it was time to return home.

Syd had shown Adeline every nook and cranny of the *seaship*. Syd had corrected her and answered every one of her questions obediently.

Adeline liked that about Syd.

They'd traded questions, Syd explaining how sometimes she and the other orphans took lessons on the seaship, though she didn't know why. Adeline had tried to describe her home the best she could to someone who had never seen Zevir's Tower.

Like a big castle, Adeline had explained. *But instead of a bunch of different towers, there's just one and it's tall and black and pointy at the top. And there's a bunch of people living there with us, commanders and soldiers and stuff. They help keep momma and me safe when da' is gone.*

The only question Syd hadn't answered was what happened to her parents.

Just don't have them, I guess, Syd had said. Adeline worried she'd upset her new friend, but then Syd showed her something special.

Adeline played the day over again, making sure she wasn't missing any details. Momma's archivists were always praising her on how analytical she was in her lessons. Surely she could figure this out. She twirled and twisted her own silver clasp, nestled in her dark braid and given to her that very morning by momma's new commander as a gift. She hadn't liked the old commander, Commander Rhiuld. At least Commander Herf smiled and laughed, and he had given her a present after all.

She spun her new hair ornament in thought. The etchings of a bird, a bear, and a serpent glinted in the low moonslight of Runar and Nova from the window. She took a deep breath and then smiled, feeling comforted and protected by Commander Herf's warm face, deep laugh lines, and big voice.

Then, Adeline frowned and threw the thick covers of her bed aside with some effort. She hopped off and pushed through a connecting door. Rummaging through a few big and sturdy chests, she tossed out toys that just wouldn't do. Finally, she found the one she was looking for—a soft plush, in the shape of a shiny-scaled fish. She stood in the middle of the floor and took a step back. She concentrated, circling and thinking.

Adeline had begged Syd to do the trick again, but she'd refused.

It makes me tired, Syd had said, so Adeline hadn't pushed it.

But still, what a trick. Adeline had never seen majik like that before. How exciting it would be if *she* could reach out and stop a fish mid-leap from the water with only her mind! Momma's majik didn't work like that. Neither did Aunt Vi's. And what a curious person Syd was.

Adeline's frown deepened. She didn't have many friends, aside from her caretakers, momma's soldiers, and the Tower staff, and they were all adults. She sat on the floor and hugged her knees to her chest. None of the other children on the boat had even looked at her, except for Syd. The room felt suddenly big, empty, and cold. Adeline squeezed her knees a little tighter. She missed her new friend with the strange and exciting majik.

The next day, Adeline asked momma if Syd could visit. A week later, Syd arrived at the Tower, but still refused to show Adeline her trick again. *Matron Reos said I shouldn't without her around*, Syd had said.

And Adeline's curiosity only grew.

Present Day

Syd tapped the stylus on her tablet's screen and yawned. Class had only just started, and already she itched to get out of the lab and into the hangar.

Across the room, water Eheri extracted and returned moisture from the small potted plants set in front of them. She looked at her own plant, its leaves wilted. She wasn't sure what exactly she was supposed to do with it. Squash it? Smoosh it? Regardless, even if she knew, she wouldn't.

Her table partner was deep in concentration as he transferred vitality from himself to his plant's leaves and roots. Streams of green swirled around the stems. Syd scooted her quickly browning plant toward his side of the table.

Instructor Boylt paced the room, nodding in approval at each student's progress. She'd been a pain in Syd's side and vice versa since year one. Five years later, and familiarity hadn't eased their tension. Boylt hadn't taught Syd anything new, and Syd wasn't interested in whatever Boylt could have taught. Syd pocketed her tablet and, when Boylt's back was to her, bolted for the door.

"Syd Orleen!" Boylt's voice made Syd's shoulders shoot up to her ears. "I don't remember giving you permission to leave."

Syd paused but didn't turn around. The door—freedom—was so close.

"Forgot my tablet. Thought you wouldn't mind if I nipped out to grab it." She had probably used that exact excuse several times, but Syd liked to believe that Boylt had grown fond of their little back-and-forths, even if the instructor's hair had grayed at an alarming rate in their years together.

"Oh no. Not today, Syd. You sit back down and—"

But Syd's fingers were already working her majik. Gray surfaced from their tips, and she molded, stretched, and sculpted it into something tangible and strong. The gray searched and reached out, finding the molecules of the water Eheri were diligently manipulating. With a subtle twist of her wrist, the gray dissipated, attaching itself to the water, and caused a wobble in time. The molecules expanded and multiplied so rapidly, the feeling overtook Syd with sudden dizziness. She caught herself on the wall just as her majik left her body. The satisfying sound of a splash hitting the lab table signaled her chance, and she took it, bounding out the door.

The echo of her name followed her down the hall, the stairways, and to the airship hangar. The bay's giant doors were opening for the morning and letting in warmth to the otherwise cold concrete and metals. The sound was deafening, gears ground against each other to let the sun in. Light bounced from the sea outside and glinted off tool chests, fuel barrels, and the beautiful steel of a Zeppfish 150S Class A that hadn't been there when Syd had left the hangar the night before. The scent of salt, sea, and grease mingled, and she relaxed, tying her coily hair up and away from her face.

"Student ID." A voice came from behind a glass box.

"C'mon Blair, we do this almost every day."

Blair shook her head, pointed to the scanner on the corner of her booth, and returned to marking things off on her tablet. Syd tapped the black bracelet on her wrist to the scanner. It beeped twice, and Blair sighed without looking up. "You are supposed to be in Majiks Lab, Cadet Orleen."

"Forgot my tablet here the other day."

"You'll leave that thing lyin' around anywhere, won't ya'?" Jo's voice called from behind Syd.

She turned, and Jo's face was stone cold. But the crow's feet around her eyes turned upward. She tapped her beige faculty bracelet onto the scanner.

"I'll see to Cadet Orleen, Admin Blair." Jo said, and Syd followed without another word.

"You'd think she'd have given up by now," Syd said once they were out of earshot.

Jo shrugged and led Syd to the lockers. Jo put on her beige jumpsuit over her plainclothes—simple black trousers, heavy boots, and a light-colored tank top. Dog tags hung around her neck, but Syd hadn't ever asked their origin. Jo was too young to have fought in any war, and Syd figured it was best to leave the past where it was. Jo tossed a navy jumpsuit—signaling the rank of student pilot—at Syd.

"She's just doin' her job. Followin' orders an' all that."

Syd smirked. "And you?"

"I can't deny talent when I see it," Jo said. "Plus, don't be goin' around thinkin' you're the only one in this academy with Eichon Wenna's favor."

Syd's face fell, and she pulled the jumper over her Eheri uniform made of stretchy silver armor that was as tight as it was resilient. It retained heat when she needed it and cooled her when her temperature rose in combat. Though, what made her flush at the moment wasn't battling some beast in the training center. Jo had brought her directly to the 150S, and it was magnificent. Vintage in style, likely an original with a bulbous shape. The social flyer could seat six in its bay comfortably around a full-length table. Syd ran her hand along its side, fingertips slipping over rivets and bolts. She stepped over the fuel line and diagnostic hoses attached to its underside.

"So, what rich bastard brought her in?"

Jo gave Syd a look and opened the hatch. A ladder extended down for them. "Owner lives over near Galssop. Says he can't get her air pressure to stabilize."

Inside the cabin, Syd couldn't remember the last time she'd seen such an archaic system. The space was cramped and dimmed by yellow emergency lights. In front of two monitors were leather seats, cracked with age. The paneling around the controls was intact, but its shine had faded, and the riveting style along the walls, windshield, and edges dated the airship. The screens were running diagnostics, and Syd leaned closer to read them.

"Rear, passenger-side compressor. I thought I felt some extra air flow around there." *Too easy.* Syd turned to Jo, cocking a half smile.

Jo smiled, too, nodding.

"Got time for a flying lesson?" Syd asked.

Jo bent down over the dash and typed in a string of commands. "Come back after lunch."

Syd's heart sank, and she ran her hands over the cabin door's frame. "Don't let the owner take her home without me saying goodbye."

"Wouldn't dream of it," Jo said and waved her off.

The halls were quiet, and her footsteps echoed off the light tiles that lined the floors and walls, all gleamed to perfection. ACES Academy was built like a coliseum, home to the world's most elite soldiers in all things majik, combat, and austral energies. The training grounds for an army sworn to protect the Eichon.

Syd couldn't help herself from wondering what it would have been like if she hadn't grown up in the world ruler's shadow. Would she have performed better in northern Magnate Academy, hidden away in snowy mountains and known for its mech and weapon manufacturing? Or what about ACES sister academy, Avant, on sunny Kilos, assuming they'd even allow an Eheris in. How many Avant specialists hid their majik, simply for the benefit of training as mercenaries? Even Seliss must have more freedom than here.

Her boots clanged up an inner stairwell until she reached a heavy metal door. The door gave a click and unlocked when she waved her wrist over the scanner. Then, she worked her way from one side of the academy around the curve to the other. The hallways were filled with identical labs built for practicing majik and training austral specialists to control and harness cloned energies. Catwalks crisscrossed over the humongous glass dome of the training center. The whole thing opened up to the sky when the weather was good—which was more often than not. Blue skies without a cloud in sight, fresh sea air sweeping in the sounds of cresting waves and gulls. A coliseum smack-dab in the middle of the ocean; a floating marvel, or a floating prison.

At the other side, Syd took the stairwell down to level 2. She walked the dark inner halls around the training center. The cooling system overcompensated for the humidity escaping from inside the greenhouse that propagated more than just tropical plant life. She exited the tunnel and propped herself against the main hall's rounded wall. Electronic banners ran in the wall's middle, world news racing by in neon letters:

—olcanic activity on the rise. | Evidence suggests some

pets telepathic. | Seliss Assistant Director returns from South Islands. | Transference Countdown: Next Eichon still unknown. | Galssop energy suppliers concerned about usage. | Dr. Ivor Malvuk and team discov—

Syd frowned. She knew there was going to be hell to pay for dodging class again, but it's not like she asked to be here. An orphan goes where an orphan is told to go. In that way, she was trained to take commands and was primed for academy life. Something heavy swirled in her chest.

Sometimes orphans were adopted. Sometimes they were adopted by powerful people. And sometimes those powerful people sent you to places. While Syd hadn't officially been adopted by Eichon Wenna, she ended up being so close to Adeline there was never any question.

Now, Adeline and Syd were in their final year at ACES. As the Eichon's daughter, it wasn't a stretch to figure out Adeline would be next in line, regardless of what the headlines said. It also wasn't a stretch for Syd to know her own fate. She would be made into a PRISM soldier, her Eheri majik binding her to the Eichon's will. To what end—guard the Eichon or kill her enemies—was yet to be determined. The bell dinged, signaling the training center doors to slide open, the heat from within escaping. The hall filled with cadets as young as 11. Syd smiled and caught Adeline's eye from across the way.

Adeline was stripped down to her undershirt and uniform pants, heavy boots caked in mud. She glowed from the aftermath of training. Strapped to her back was the only thing more faithful to Adeline than Syd: a broadsword gifted to her by her father Matius, who also just *happened* to be the leader of Avant's mercenary forces.

No, it really wasn't a question who would be next to receive the transference—the child of Eichon and mercenary leader.

Syd watched as Adeline slipped through the stream of cadets, who parted and gave her room to walk. Syd chewed her lip. The special treatment they both received was no longer unusual, but it did leave a perpetual bad taste in Syd's mouth. That was until she smelled earth and lavender, and Adeline wrapped her arm around Syd's waist with a smile. Though a warrior on the field, Adeline's embrace was soft, simple.

"How was training?" Syd asked, smiling up at Adeline.

"They'll need to restock soon," Adeline responded and dropped her hug. Her cheeks pushed up the corners of her almond eyes. "There's hardly anything left to kill."

"I'll never know how you do it." Syd shook her head, voice almost envious.

They began walking, and Adeline glanced at Syd, eyebrows raised in concern. "Bad day today?"

"I'm sure Boylt's filing a report right about now."

Adeline's fingers grazed Syd's as they walked, then she reached out and squeezed Syd's hand.

"Not everything has to be so cut and dry," Adeline said. She tilted her head thoughtfully, then made up her mind with a nod. "We'll go see Malvuk this afternoon. Maybe he will have some guidance. In any case, he has more seniority than Boylt and can tell her to lay off."

Syd shrugged but nodded. It felt like special treatment. It felt like she didn't want it.

"Oh! I almost forgot. Keal has something new to show us." Adeline smiled again, sudden, and excited. Syd shook herself from her thoughts and followed as Adeline picked up her pace, the heaviness of self-pity replaced with giddiness.

Adeline and Syd wound their way around the academy to Keal's lab room. Adeline stopped in the door frame, pressing a finger to her lips. Syd caught the mischievous glint in Adeline's eye and grinned, staying quiet. Keal, dressed in his usual white lab coat, was hunched over in the back cabinets of his lab, no doubt still setting up for his lesson. Being the headmaster's son allowed him to start his day later than any other faculty. It also gave him the brightest, sunniest lab with a full wall of windows overlooking the endless blues.

"Y'know," Adeline called from the door. "If you do this the night before you wouldn't be in such a rush in the morning."

The white lab coat jumped in surprise. A clattering of instruments fell when Keal hit his head on a shelf. Adeline giggled, and Syd suppressed a chuckle.

"Dammit, you two!" Keal emerged, one arm full of beakers. The other hand rubbed the back of his head. His blonde hair, which always seemed to stick out at odd angles, matched the now lop-sided glasses. He readjusted them and looked to Syd.

A year ahead of Syd and Adeline, Keal graduated early

and quickly moved into his role as instructor. Syd knew he would much rather be working alongside Dr. Malvuk in the field, but even a protégé must climb the ranks. She walked over to the washing station and dug under the counters for goggles to clean before his class started. Adeline unlatched her weapon and set it by the door, then joined Keal and helped him set up the workstations.

"Saw the incident report come in a few minutes ago," Keal said. "Syd, you gotta start taking this seriously."

"Don't see why." Syd shrugged. "We're almost out of here anyway."

"Your actions effect more than just you," he warned.

Syd's lips thinned. "I don't understand why I can't choose what I want to specialize in. I mean, you two got to choose your areas of expertise."

Syd didn't need to turn around to know Keal was shaking his head. "You know that's untrue. Adeline was trained from a very early age to be a combat specialist and I was practically raised by Dr. Malvuk because Rhiuld was too busy running the academy."

It was jarring to hear him call his mother by their last name. Taking in a deep breath, Syd summoned a rebuttal that was cut off too quickly.

"—Anyway," Adeline injected, her voice pitched. "You wanted to show us something?"

"Oh, right!" Keal dashed to his podium on the front side of the room.

Curious, Syd turned and tilted her head.

"I forgot to tell you," he started. His voice was high and excited as his computer station whirred out of sleep mode.

The projector screens descended along the windowed wall, masking the blue ocean with white. "Malvuk found a new austral!"

He beamed, almost jumping from foot to foot like a child.

Syd gave a sideways glance to Adeline, hiding her smirk.

"So, you know the earth-based australs we've been cloning?" Keal asked them.

Syd vaguely remembered something about the work he'd been doing with Malvuk and nodded.

"Eichon Wenna called Dr. Malvuk back to Arja's Gardens, you know—where we last found an earth austral."

Syd grinned at Keal's liberal use of the word "we". Malvuk had only just started inviting Keal on field assignments.

A picture of pure origin austral energy came into focus on the screen, pixel by pixel. A pale-yellow sphere glistened in the middle of the planet's largest known energy epicenter, the hanging gardens of the first Eichon's resting place.

"We believe it's an air-based austral!" Keal removed his glasses and polished them on his lab coat. "Whatever it is, it sure was smart. It hid itself away under the other austral sites we've found there."

He clicked through to other slides full of preliminary notes he and Malvuk had started making. Syd sat on a nearby stool and listened to Keal go on. His excitement was a small comfort, like everything was right in the world because at least his love of australs made sense.

Syd couldn't stop grinning. "You're such a nerd."

Keal's face faltered, and his smile faded. He turned back to his computer in an attempt to hide his blushing.

"So, where's this bad boy at, then?" Adeline asked.

Keal flashed a smile and went to the cooling unit behind his podium. He dimmed the lights and sat out two clear beakers with clasped stoppers in front of them. Inside one, a soft green fog glowed and swirled inside. The other was full of the same pale yellow from the image, shimmering off any light it could find.

"Aren't they beautiful?" he whispered, leaning in closer to watch both of them glimmer in their containers.

Syd never fully understood how austral control and cloning tech worked, in the same way Keal wouldn't know his way around the 150S back in the hangar. But what she did know was his face lit up in the same way hers did when she was working with Jo, so she leaned in too.

A cold blast of air hit her face, and the glass beaker exploded, spraying shards of broken glass. Adeline gasped, and Syd raised her arms to shield herself. From the broken beaker, green fog swirled and expanded, taking up space along the floor. It rapidly moved to the door, and Adeline rushed to shut it, locking them and the austral inside. Smoky tendrils recoiled, the air filled with the heady scent of moss, and Syd's breath became heavy.

Syd moved in front of Adeline, putting her body between Adeline and the threat. Syd's mouth went dry, the air heavy with oxygen, and the moisture inside her wanted to flee. She cupped her hands in a perfect sphere, but her concentration was cut off by the sound of the second beaker breaking. Above the green fog, a shimmering yellow grew and took up its own space near the ceiling.

The two colors kept their separation, and for a moment nothing happened. Syd's breath was labored, but she refocused as quickly as she could and drew her energy outward toward the empty sphere of her palms. There, her own gray fog gathered, took shape, and grew in density. The two clouds retracted, their forms condensing into wisps of yellow and green.

The australs made the first move and shot across the room toward Syd and Adeline.

"Get down!" Syd shouted to Adeline, and she drew herself up.

Her mind faded and became lost in the gray. She twisted and kneaded her energy with her fingertips until it was something solid, something tangible and malleable. She grabbed it tight and hurtled it toward the green and yellow clouds just as Adeline ducked under a table.

Flashes of emerald, gold, and ash collided, and all Syd could see was white. Soon, her vision cleared, and she heard her breath before she could feel it. She hunched over, hands on knees, and panted. The air was coming in short bursts, but when she looked up, the australs were suspended and unable to move.

"Hey Keal," Syd gasped, waiting for her body to recover. "Why don't you put away your damn pets."

Keal moved out from behind his podium. "Oh.—Right. My—Oh. Wow."

He looked at the australs in awe and Syd gritted her teeth. Adeline came to her side and leaned down to meet

Syd at eye-level. Adeline's eyes were wide with worry. Syd shook her head.

"You ok?" Syd asked, smiling through her grimace.

"Yes, of course. Are you hurt? Do I need to get the medics?" Adeline's hands hovered, afraid to touch Syd but wanting to help.

Sometimes, Syd's majik came easy, like with the water molecules. Other times, it was hard like it was now, and she never knew what to expect. Syd supposed this was what Keal meant when he said she should take this more seriously.

"Nah. It'll wear off," Syd said, though her face betrayed her. "Keal, what the fuck, man?"

"Just—" Keal muttered to himself, the australs drawn back into new, more secure-looking containers. The look on his face was starting to remind Syd of Malvuk. Adeline must have been thinking the same thing because she cleared her throat.

"I've never seen australs respond so quickly," Keal said. "It must be in response to the upcoming eclipse."

They let that sink in. When the Great Moon Nova drew closer to its eclipse, the natural world grew in strength and hostility. Of course, they had only ever read about it because the eclipse happened once every twenty years. The phenomena also meant another thing; they were drawing closer to the Eichon transferring her power. Syd looked at Adeline.

A ding came over the PA system.

"KEAL RHIULD, ADELINE KEYLEN, SYD ORLEEN. REPORT TO THE ADMIN OFFICES

IMMEDIATELY. REPEAT: RHIULD, KEYLEN, ORLEEN, REPORT TO THE ADMIN OFFICES IMMEDIATELY."

CHAPTER TWO

Director Rhiuld's face was as unmoving as a mountain, and Syd couldn't tell if this was better or worse than the typical yelling. The Director's office was tidy, floor to ceiling bookshelves full of archaic texts, a simple sturdy desk, and the typical accessories: tablet, computer, and a metal tray for any stray papers that may need filing. No windows, no sunlight. Syd could probably recite the bookshelves from memory by now. The office felt like it was closing in with so many people in the small space.

With her dark hair captured in a severe bun at the nape of her neck, Jexa Rhiuld held herself with poise and dignity as the Eichon-appointed director of ACES. The only way to tell she was Keal's mother at all was the nose he'd inherited—narrowed and pointed. She stood, eyes seething with severity, next to Dr. Malvuk. He, with his bald spot, white hair, and slight hunch, every bit her polar opposite. For as long as Syd had known him, it was impossible to tell if he was 60 or 600. He'd always looked squat and leering.

For their part, Syd, Adeline, and Keal stood at attention during the pause before the reprimand. Their hands clasped behind their backs, faces forward, eyes focused on some middle distance.

"Typical behavior aside," Rhiuld started and looked at Syd. "We're not here to dole out Cadet Orleen's weekly punishment."

Syd's eyes moved to Malvuk. He'd taken Keal under his

wing some time ago, recognizing Keal's interest and ability in all things austral. It was how Keal graduated early and took up residence as instructor and researcher. Syd stopped herself from chewing the inside of her cheek, worried at the presence of the man rumored to lead human experimentation in his off time.

"Director Rhiuld, I can assure you Adeline and Keal did not—" Syd started.

"As much as it pains me, Cadet Orleen," Rhiuld cut Syd off. "Whatever is about to come out of your mouth must wait. It has come to my attention that the australs Dr. Malvuk's team discovered have gone missing from his lab." She turned her head to Keal and arched an eyebrow.

"Er," Keal started. "Yes. I was hoping to run some tests…?"

Keal had always been a terrible liar. Honest to a fault. Syd caught herself from reacting at his fumble.

"What Keal means to say, Director, is I had asked to see what the team had been working on," Adeline said, and she spoke with the grace of an ambassador. Though, Syd knew, that was what Adeline had been groomed for all these years: a representative of her own mother. Syd suddenly felt small, unsure of her place in this room. She squeezed her hands tighter together behind her back.

"I hadn't meant to unleash them," Keal said.

All heads snapped to him, and Syd suppressed a groan. That was Keal in a nutshell, brilliant but great at saying the exact wrong thing at the exact right time. Syd let her composure go and sighed just as Rhiuld unhinged, the swollen tension in the room collapsing.

"You did what?!" Rhiuld shrieked. Keal winced. "You let an unknown austral energy lose in the academy?!" She was just winding up, a move Syd had seen countless times. "What in the Great Moon's name were you thinking? You could have injured cadets, or worse!" Her eyes going to Adeline.

"Director Rhiuld, we are fine. Syd was able to control the situation," Adeline explained, breaking her stance now, too, and talking with her hands.

Now Rhiuld let out her own groan and rubbed her face before taking a seat. "Yes, of course she was. Can't do a damn thing in the classroom, but can somehow control a crisis."

Syd would be lying if she said she didn't take some gratification in Rhiuld's exasperated look. For six years, all she and her administration had wanted to do was find a way to analyze Syd's majik. Along the way, they told her it was to help her grow and control it, and she'd believed them. But, by year three, it had become clear that all their measuring sticks were too short. Syd didn't need their help in training or mastering her majik, and since then she'd refused to be some specimen under their microscope.

Instead, she'd focused her mind elsewhere, specifically with Jo and the airships in the hangar. That was something measurable, something that made sense in diagrams and metrics. And it pissed Rhiuld off to no end because they both knew how powerful Syd's majik could be, especially under pressure. The guilty pleasure that spread across Syd's lips spoke louder than anything either of them could say. She may be forced to live within the academy's walls, but they couldn't force her to comply. Especially not at their command. Not yet, in any case. Maybe that would change once she was assigned to PRISM and actively protecting the Eichon. Until then—

"Well?" Syd jumped out of her thoughts at Malvuk's ancient voice. "What did the specimen do when loose? I have not been able to get it to perform since bringing it back from Eichon Wenna's excavation."

"Wait, that was an excavation?" Keal asked. "You told me it was research funded from Zevir."

Everyone grew silent when it was clear that Malvuk had said too much this time. Eichon Wenna had been dispatching teams for excavation since before Syd was born. Rumors had been going around lately that it had something to do with Wenna's powers, but even Adeline had been kept in the dark. No matter how much she'd tried to get answers from either of her parents.

"Why did my mother order you to an excavation site, Dr. Malvuk?" Adeline asked, making the first move. And there it was again, that assuredness and command.

Director Rhiuld broke in before Malvuk could say another word.

"As unfortunate as it is that the ACES disciplinary actions must be postponed," she said and eyed Keal. "We received a communication a short while ago. Eichon Wenna has requested the presence of the three of you. Cadet Orleen, you will pilot one of our airships to Zevir City as soon as possible."

Syd glanced to Keal and Adeline, and they exchanged a look. Unsatisfied and left without answers, they excited the office when dismissed to gather their things for a short stay in Zevir City's Tower. As Syd changed and carelessly stuffed her academy-issued suitcase with an extra uniform and a change of clothes, she couldn't shake the feeling that something—maybe even something big—has happened.

"See? Promised you a flight lesson today," Jo said.

Keal and Adeline joined them in the hangar while Syd completed her walk-around inspection on the small academy airship, painted in navy and yellow. It was built for surface skimming with four seats and a moderate cargo hold in the back. Syd finished ticking off the checkpoints on Jo's tablet and handed it back.

"Hm? Oh. Yeah," Syd said, her attention drawn away when Adeline walked up. "Be back before you know it."

Keal and Adeline saluted Jo who returned the salute, nodded, and walked off. Keal loaded the luggage, and they boarded quickly, Adeline's forehead in knots.

"So, what else did you find out?" Syd asked, taking the captain's chair and hitting a switch. The hatch door let out a satisfying hiss as it closed.

Adeline and Keal took their seats behind her, buckling in.

"Rhiuld was no help," Adeline sighed, distracted.

"Didn't have much luck with Malvuk either," Keal added. "Was able to get him to confirm the excavations are linked to Eichon Wenna's power, but not much else."

Adeline crossed her legs. "Well, that's something at least."

The airship's engines idled for a moment before Syd pulled it out of ACES' bay and into the reflective blue outside. The airship handled easy, tracking synced nicely, and the radar was alert and ready. Not that they needed to worry. These were friendly waters; Seliss knew better than to come so close to either the academy or Zevir City.

They skimmed along, an easy glide with clear skies that reflected a bright cerulean below. Syd set the airship to autopilot and swiveled her chair around.

Keal glanced at the controls nervously. "Shouldn't you be watching the proverbial road or something?"

"Calm skies and currents out there, course set to Zevir. Stop being such a worry-wort. I'm not a trainee anymore. Jo signed my cert."

Keal gave something between a scoff and cough. He and Adeline had been subjected to quite a few rough landings during Syd's training. Still, sitting in a flight deck had always felt more natural to Syd than slouched over a table or desk or stalking beasts in the faux forest of the training center. Or, laying under the bright lights of examination chairs.

Syd looked at Adeline who brushed her dark, wavy hair behind her ears. Adeline's dark brown eyes had become increasingly laced with worry lately.

"Think we're being summoned for the transference? How many days until Nova's eclipse now?" Syd asked.

Adeline leaned back in the seat when Syd said what she had been thinking, and Syd gave an encouraging smile. Maybe, just maybe, when Adeline became Eichon, she wouldn't use the Eheris as her mother had. Even if she did, there was always a chance Adeline could make an exception for her, and Syd wouldn't have to become a soldier, a weapon.

"Seventeen, give or take a few hours. Wouldn't make sense to have us along though. They'd probably just send a proper escort, wouldn't they?" Keal asked.

"Not if they wanted to keep it quiet," Adeline said, staring off.

"Yeah." Syd considered. "I just can't believe they waited this long to say anything." She was trying to get Adeline to open up, but this had always been one thing Adeline kept to herself. Syd's lips pursed, and a soft pang hit her chest. She wanted to be there for Adeline, but even after all these years, she hadn't broken through. "Do you have everything you need should you—they—"

Adeline nodded at Syd's stutter, and she came back from whatever distant place she had been with a smile. "I have you two, don't I?"

Keal relaxed into his seat then, but Syd titled her head.

Adeline waved off Syd's concern. "Whatever is going on, we'll find out soon enough." She pointed beyond Syd's shoulder, and Syd swirled back around.

The flight was always shorter than she expected it to be.

If the Gral's blue waves weren't enough, flying into Zevir was a sight unto itself. The island practically sparkled, floating in the middle of the ocean's expanse. The newest and most technologically advanced city was a shimmering beacon of blues and greens. Seven circular rings stacked on top of each other, made of translucent sea glass. Each ring was a thoroughfare for foot traffic. The seven levels seemed to float one above the other, perfect circles around a single, dark skyscraper rising in the center. The Tower's base was almost as wide as the first ring, and it stretched toward the sky high above seventh circle. The gray Crarra Mountains only made the city's brilliance stand out more.

Zevir had been an experiment, constructed over 400 years ago by Eichon Ilith. Its efficient and practical design quickly made it the most advanced and most desirable city. Zevir had been locked down for almost half of its operational years, inaccessible to the outside world; an unreachable haven that has housed each Eichon since its creation. Residency was granted only under an Eichon's permission or command.

If there was one thing Syd admired about Wenna, it had to be her transparency in most things. Her first order had been to open Zevir's borders, which set the tone of her reign. But the secrecy of the excavations had been overtaking that gesture. Even in the halls of ACES, an uneasy tension had been growing toward Wenna over the past few years, and that tension had extended to Adeline. Fellow cadets had started to avoid Adeline, and faculty and staff had never been as severe with Adeline as they were with others.

As history had proven, it wasn't rare for an Eichon to begin her rule peacefully and end in complete Madness. Randomly poking holes in the planet isn't exactly normal behavior even to her moon-worshipping Novari followers. In fact, those who thought themselves the planet's guardians—the Terians—found the action to be downright hostile, and that included Seliss.

A voice clicked over the flight panel's comms, instructing Syd to dock in the northern hanger. On Zevir's fifth-level, dedicated solely to the transportation industry, airship bays stuck out at each cardinal direction, and Syd followed the flight control center's directions automatically.

They exited onto the streets of Zevir. Syd's eyes watered and adjusted from the darkness inside the hangar. The inner ring of the level was jammed with businesses, mostly industrial. Around them, people went about their lives. Residents dressed in light silks strolled leisurely, workers in varying dark-colored uniforms jogged to one business or another, jacketed representatives from other levels negotiated and bargained with storefronts, and even some low-speed hover tech mingled among the pedestrian traffic. Zevir was a busy city, shining and glistening within the city's hazy blues, and its people were just as diverse and vibrant as the science and majik the city held within itself.

And it felt safe, mostly. Syd could blend in and be part of the masses, as if she wasn't unique, or rare, or given special treatment—and if not treatment, then interest. It was one thing to be an Eheris; it was another thing entirely to be an Eheris with gravity majik, and adopted, more or less, by the Eichon. She could hide among these crowds and never be noticed, and a wave of comfort overtook her. That was until, of course, she caught a glimpse of a dark figure with a pure black visor in the crowd.

There were three specific populations in Zevir that caused the most controversy. Firstly, the Novari, who worshipped the Great Moon Nova and followed the Eichon unquestionably. Syd thought they were fanatical in their ways, but who was she to judge?

The second were the residents of the Zevir Sciences. Made up almost entirely of Rhurgari—the religious group that wasn't really a religion at all, but the absence of one. They were equally fanatical in their interest in australs and thirst for knowledge. Malvuk was their unofficial leader, and the Rhurgari scientists were a force in and of themselves.

And finally, the third population: the black-visored PRISM. This third group was made up of Eheri that had graduated from ACES. While PRISM were mostly still human, their black armor connected to and grew with their skin over time, eventually tapping into and syncing with their neural pathways. This meant that if Zevir was ever under attack, PRISM would receive their commands over Zevir's Veral network and removed the need for any relayed, and therefore delayed, instruction.

After graduation, Eheri were given a choice to join PRISM. Though, choice was a strong word. Not many places accepted, let alone wanted, Eheri. The Terians had been growing in numbers over the past few centuries, and they thought Eheri to be abominations. It made finding and making a home outside of Zevir difficult, to say the least.

Syd chewed the inside of her cheek and turned away.

They made their way through the crowd to a central bank of elevators before anyone recognized Adeline. As much as she disliked them, it was strange there weren't any PRISM to greet them when they landed and ushered Adeline home. The hair on the back of her neck stood up, and Syd looked around when realization clicked.

A few years ago, they were asked to keep close to and protect Adeline at ACES, should there be the need. At the time, Syd had thought that was an overreaction. But the buzz of the entire world not knowing who would lead them next had been leaking into the halls of the academy as of late. Adeline could handle the few pointed questions from fellow cadets and even some instructors, but a larger crowd would overtake her without a proper escort. Now they were here on their own suddenly. Syd and Keal *were* the escort; they were Adeline's Guard.

Adeline keyed in her codes after swiping her black ACES band against the receiver, and they stepped in. The opposing side of the elevator was made of clear glass. From it, Syd could see all the way up or down inside the city. Interior stairwells, wired gangways, ladders, and bulkheads all spiraled and wove together.

The compartment moved forward toward a bulkhead immediately ahead of them some twenty yards away. Two PRISM stood at attention when they exited the elevator. Of course, there were main entrances on each level to the central building, but this way was quieter.

Syd tried to not stare at the black visors, but she couldn't help it. The fact she couldn't see their eyes, unable to know how much of them was still human, made her skin prickle. Adeline gave them the command, and automatically they twisted open the bulkhead and stepped aside wordlessly.

The group wound their way from the side entrance to the fifth-floor lobby. The space was sparse, save for a Zevir scientist identified by their white robes, and a PRISM soldier lounging on the open seating. They stopped their conversation immediately. Footsteps echoed off the dark, marble floor and walls of the Tower. Syd looked up, taking in the sheer height of exposed, interior walkways that encompassed each floor above: the exact inverse of Zevir's design.

The soldier moved in response to their entrance, and all Adeline needed to do was raise her hand. The black visors scanned for facial recognition. Or something like that. Adeline explained it all to Syd once, but Syd tended to tune out whenever the topic of PRISM came up.

Keal and Syd followed Adeline to a large, circular couch with a small podium at the center of the floor. Adeline placed her hand on the screen and entered the code for Wenna's suite. The hover cushion activated and began their spiraled ascent slowly, following the interior circle. In any other building, an elevator would have done just fine.

"It's good to be home at least," Adeline said, sinking into the cushions and closing her eyes.

CHAPTER THREE

Eventually, the hover cushion docked itself at the eighth floor. Adeline led them around the circular walkway to Wenna's offices, and the doors slid open. The room expanded with floor-to-ceiling windows that overlooked the blue city. Wenna was at her desk, in conversation with three of her Council members, and all eyes turned to Adeline, Keal, and Syd when they entered. Not a unusual sight. Council members have flurried around Adeline's family for as long as Syd had known them.

Whatever was being discussed stopped immediately. Wenna smiled patiently, and the Council members each bowed their heads in greeting to Adeline.

"There you three are. I was almost beginning to worry." Wenna waved over to the couches in the center of the room. "Come in. We were just finishing."

"Hello Mother, Aunt Vi," Adeline said with an easy breath and smile, making her way to them immediately. She looked to the others. "Reth, Saaviana, you both are looking well. It's nice to see you again."

"Hello, Eichon. Thank you for the invitation." Keal followed with a nod. "And Director Torok and Consul Torok! What a nice surprise!" Keal called with a little too much enthusiasm. He clearly hadn't forgotten his role in all things as Rhiuld's son. He served as ambassador for his mother as much as Adeline did hers.

"Ah! Adeline, Keal!" Consul Torok said in reply, opening his arms in greeting.

Consul Reth Torok, in blue and yellow Council robes, was a sturdy man built by his years as a blacksmith in the valley of the Ifor Ridge. His light eyes contrasted his deep auburn beard and copper skin. Rumor had it, he was a fire Eheri and, at some point, had managed to dodge being recruited into PRISM and secure a spot as Wenna's consulate for the Ifor region.

Director Saaviana Torok, on the other hand, was a small woman who led Magnate Academy. Appointed, like Rhiuld, by Wenna. Saaviana's black body armor was decorated with the orange triangular symbol of Magnate. The armor was so well suited that even the cuffed neckline just under her chin looked to be a natural part of her skin. Comparatively, her eyes were a dull green and less than impressed when she looked at Keal.

From what Syd knew of their personalities, the pairing of Reth and Saaviana made little sense. Politically, though, it was a match made in heaven.

Their presence was a reminder that Syd had been destined for Magnate before meeting Adeline, and guilt slid around in Syd's chest. Those who were not adopted by age 11 were sent to the northern mountains, and if Wenna hadn't taken her in, Syd liked to believe she would have made a decent weaponsmith or mechtechnician.

It was no secret that Magnate sold its mechtech to the highest bidder, especially in times of civil unrest. Maybe it didn't matter where Syd ended up; maybe she'd be just as unhappy under Torok's thumb as she was Rhiuld's.

Regardless, both Directors needed to supply something to remain valuable in the eyes of the Eichon, and in that way, they were the same. ACES simply produced something more organic in nature.

Syd shuddered at thinking of herself as something manufactured and folded her arms.

Wenna's sister, Villette, stood beside the Eichon's desk, a blue shawl draped over her thin shoulders. She lowered her dark eyes, and her chin-length hair slipped around her face. She smiled at Adeline who was busy greeting her mother, and she bowed her head to Syd. As Wenna's twin and Adeline's blood aunt, Villette also served on the Council. In fact, the only one missing Council member was Matius, Adeline's father, who was likely busy running Avant. *Talk about high conflicts of interest.* Eichon Wenna had made sure to position those closest to her in almost every leadership role on the planet. Most transitioned power peacefully, though Syd never did hear what happened to those who were less than willing to give up their post.

Syd scoffed to herself, almost forgetting her place. She kept quiet but returned each greeting with a blank smile and nods of her own. She straightened her back to attention while they held court. She didn't like the idea of being a soldier, but it was an easy role to fall into when she didn't know what else to do.

Wenna and Adeline embraced, and the room's temperature shifted warmer, an attribute unique to Wenna's powers. The world didn't understand much about the Goddess gift bestowed on a single woman every twenty years from Nova, but what they did know was that Wenna could amplify auras and energies. Anyone holding space with her was affected.

"Syd," Wenna said. "It is nice to see you again. Adeline seems to be taking good care of you."

Her voice was measured, steady, and just slow enough to know each individual word was carefully thought out. She then broke into a smile, the joke settling. The fine lines around her dark eyes crinkled, and she offered a hug. Her bracelets clanged together in Syd's direction as her arms extended, and her pale-yellow gown flowed from her arms to the floor. Syd accepted and relaxed her shoulders.

Eichon. PRISM leader. Unofficial guardian. Girlfriend's mother. It was hard, sometimes, to know how Syd was supposed to act around Wenna. Walking on eggshells more and more these days, Syd was an outsider in more ways than one. Orphan. Eheri. Destined for servitude. As quickly as the disparity rose within her, Syd's nose was filled with sharp spices. It was the scent of Wenna from days past when she would join Adeline and Syd in play. A small comfort in the grand scheme, a fleeting familiarity, but one Syd gladly took.

"So, how is everyone?" Wenna asked and returned to sitting at her desk.

Adeline moved to the room's seating, the same plush fabrics from the lobby three floors below. Keal stood with the Toroks, a silence overtaking their chitchat about Magnate and ACES. Syd joined Adeline and leaned against the couch's arm. She looked to Villette who had yet to take her eyes off Syd. Villette smiled again, and Syd averted her gaze, growing uncomfortable at being watched so intently.

"We are well," Adeline said. "But Director Rhiuld didn't send us here to tell you about our day."

"No, she did not," Wenna confirmed.

Wenna straightened her back and placed her hands together on the desk diplomatically. "I sent for you because—" She paused, taking longer than necessary to continue.

Villette stepped closer. "If I may?" Her voice was honey dripping through a sieve.

Wenna nodded.

"You'll forgive the abruptness in calling this meeting." Villette looked around the table. "And the lack of pleasantries. It's likely just as well we dive right in. We've called you here to discuss Project Nova."

Impatience prickled up and down the back of Syd's neck, and she took a deep inhale. She'd never heard about any Project Nova, but if it was important enough to pull her, Adeline, and Keal from ACES, it meant this could be good news. For her at least.

"Part of Project Nova are the excavations, like the one Dr. Malvuk and Keal were sent to recently," Villette continued. "They are part of a larger hypothesis the Zevir scientists and the Council have been exploring. We understand the powers of the Eichon are linked to Nova, and the transfer of power that happens once every 20 years when the Great Moon is in eclipse. But, something else has been taking place as well. It appears that with each transference, the gravitational pull of the planet is, quite literally, pulling Nova closer.

"As you might imagine this is quite a problem for— everyone. We see it in the rising temperatures of the southern islands, the increase in tremors and earthquakes, volcanoes erupting. Project Nova has been searching for a way to reverse Nova's trajectory, hoping to find some answers inside the planet itsel—"

"What?" Adeline interrupted.

Her forehead was knotted, and Syd realized hers was too. The casual tone of everything forced restlessness in Syd, and she stood simply for something to do. Nova was simply growing larger, not moving closer. Something to do with the power swelling with each transference, like a wet sponge. At least, that's what they'd been taught. That's what everyone had been taught. Hadn't they?

Adeline shook her head, and Syd looked to Keal for some hint on how to react, but his eyes were distant in the same way he took to when calculating risk during combat training.

"Why are you telling us this? Why have you called us here?" Adeline broke the silence. The confusion in her voice was thick, but Syd recognized something else: disappointment.

Villette looked to Wenna, and they exchanged a worried glance.

"Because, without going into the finer details," Wenna took over. "The long and short of it is that if we can successfully change Nova's course, there's a high probability it will also alter, if not fully eradicate, the power of the Eichon."

The room filled with a silence that swelled with each passing second. The pressure built; the air paused. Everyone was holding their breaths. And then, the tension bent, and the air released. First, like a cool breeze.

And then, like a tornado.

CHAPTER FOUR

Seven Years Prior

"Mom's building a new school for people like me and you," Adeline said, and pointed between her and Syd. She'd been waiting to show Syd, and hadn't wanted to put it in a letter. Something so thrilling just had to be shared in person.

The two young girls poured over a map on a large table inside the Tower's library. Bright lights illuminated the vast circular room. Shelf after shelf entirely full of recorded history. The lower floors were old stone carvings and parchments; the upper levels, digital tablets whose memory chips were full. Adeline loved the richness of the library.

"We'll train like Da does, with real weapons and everything!" Adeline grinned, pointing to a spot on the map. "And you'll be trained in your majik so that you can become a Zevir soldier! It's being built in the middle of the ocean. Isn't that cool?"

Syd looked at the map, to where Adeline's finger hovered. "How will it float?"

Adeline shrugged. "How does anything float? C'mon, aren't you excited?"

Syd looked away and shook her head. "I like the orphanage. I like Matron."

Adeline's face fell, and she put her hands on her hips. "It's like a big orphanage, just better!"

"What if I don't want to go?"

"Don't you want to get better at your majik?"

Syd took a step back and shrugged. She peered between the shelves that surrounded them.

"I like the warm sand."

Adeline groaned at her friend in frustration. "I thought you'd be happy, getting away from that crummy building on that stupid island!"

She stormed off, and Syd chased after her. They ran through the stacks, up and down the stairs, until the frustration and hurt turned into giggles and laughter again. Adeline ducked behind an unsuspecting stack and jumped out to scare Syd. Instead, she jumped out in front of one of the archivists, their face shielded under a hazy blue veil.

"Your mother has requested I escort you and guest Sydney to her," the archivist said.

"Oh…" Adeline said and looked around for Syd who ran around the stack at the opposite end only to stop at the sight of an adult.

The air inside Eichon Wenna's office was heavy with fragrance of spices; Adeline always felt held here—safe and comforted. She ran to Wenna and hugged her mother who sat behind an imposing desk. Wenna brought a caring arm around Adeline, squeezing her in close.

"That will be all, Archivist Larew."

Without a word, the archivist and their blue veil exited. Wenna stood and walked to the center of the room to a circular couch. She sat and patted the spaces next to her, making her many bracelets jingle. Adeline and Syd hopped onto the cushions.

"Well then, has Adeline told you all about the school I'm building?" Wenna asked Syd, who nodded. The air in the room thinned, but the temperature stayed the same.

Adeline relaxed into the couch, happy to listen.

"Do you know why I'm building it?" Wenna's voice was patient.

Syd shrugged, looking at the floor. "Ad said it's so people like me can train."

Wenna leaned in closer. "People like you, people who can manipulate the natural world like you can, are special, Sydney. There's so much strength and power inside you, you just don't know it yet. I want to help you find it. Don't you want to be strong and powerful?"

Adeline peeked out from cuddling against Wenna when Syd didn't immediately answer.

"I guess…" Syd said, but didn't look up. She kicked her legs a little. "It's just… I won't know anyone there and I know everyone at the orphanage."

"You'll have me!" Adeline chimed in cheerfully.

"That's right," Wenna said. "Adeline will be there with you. And, I have a very special task I'd like to give you."

At that, Syd looked up. Adeline grinned at the curiosity on her friend's face.

"I'd like you, specifically, to look after Adeline at this new school. Watch out for her."

Syd's eyes widened. "Me?"

Wenna smiled, her earrings dangling and swaying as she nodded. "Who better than Adeline's very best friend to keep her safe?"

Syd looked between Wenna and Adeline, then back to the floor.

"Well," she said. "If it's for Ad… How bad can it be?" And, thinking it through in her own time, Ad saw Syd smile.

Present Day

The tension in the room collapsed, and Syd gripped the couch to steady herself.

The implications of the Eichon power stopping were unfathomable. Questions formed like rapid fire as her brain caught up to what her ears had just heard. No more Eichon, no more PRISM, right? How *much* was Nova being pulled? How soon would it enter their atmosphere? Why had she— they—all of them—been lied to for so long? The questions came like a spray of bullets. Syd reached out and grabbed one.

"But what does this mean for Ad?" Syd asked.

Why that was her first question, she did not know. She should be more concerned about what it all meant for her, shouldn't she? A project that could end the Eichon power? *Wait. Screw what it means for me. Nova is on a crash course.* The questions piled on again, a fast-moving train and at the end of it all: *how?*

Wenna stood slowly, and the temperature in the room cooled. "There's so much to explain here." Her voice strained, fingertips resting on her desk. She lowered her eyes.

Realization dawned on Adeline's face, a look only seen

when she felt hurt or betrayed. A lump in Syd's throat tightened.

Villette shuffled quietly. "We didn't know until recently if Project Nova would be accomplished. We couldn't, in fact," she said. She clasped her hands in front of her, and the blue shawl trailed down her slender, pale arms. "We needed to wait until Nova was in position for the transference to begin. The excavations were...are...our attempt to confirm our hypothesis that the core of our planet is, indeed, creating greater gravitational energy during the weakened orbit of Nova at the time of transference."

Villette moved closer to Adeline and placed a gentle hand on her shoulder. Adeline looked up and stared at her aunt and mother. Syd's heart pounded in her ears.

"If we allow that to continue, Nova will, eventually, collide with the planet and destroy it completely. Any effort we make to correct this may disrupt the link between Nova and the Eichon power, therefore sacrificing the future of the Eichon lineage."

Adeline looked to the floor and collapsed into the back of the couch.

"So, everything—the training? ACES?" Adeline locked eyes with Villette, then with her mother. "And you had me groomed as if I'd be the next Eichon even though you had the intention of—" Adeline's voice cracked. "It was all for nothing?"

"Not necessarily. Again, there is so much to explain here, Adeline," Wenna said.

"So, explain it." The words escaped Syd's mouth before

she could control them, the heat in her chest rising instantly.

The cooled atmosphere of the room no longer mattered. Adeline's face, her voice small and pained, caused the back of Syd's neck to sweat.

The Toroks shared a glance but remained silent. Speaking out of turn, to Wenna of all people, wasn't exactly proper etiquette, even for Syd. But, just as Adeline had been groomed to be Eichon, Syd had been groomed to be Adeline's guardian. When Adeline was threatened, Syd stepped forward.

"You called us here to tell us the plan, right?" Syd's heart was in her throat, but her voice was steady. "So, tell us. Why are we here?" *Cut the bullshit. Give us answers.* Syd clenched her hands into painful fists.

The silence was suffocating. Villette slowly turned her head to Wenna.

"We want to recruit you, Adeline, and Keal to help Project Nova," Wenna said simply, her face indiscernible, and Syd couldn't tell if Wenna was pissed or sobered by the outburst.

Villette raised a hand. "Perhaps we should let the information settle in a little while…"

"Yes," Wenna agreed. "I think we could all use some time to process." Her eyes moved to Syd. "We'll continue this at dinner," she said with the tone of dismissal.

Adeline stood in a flurry of emotions. She exited the room without a word. Syd's mouth dropped, the weight of something this big being denied any further discussion only caused more heat in her chest. But Syd knew an order when she heard one.

Outside the room, Adeline was already punching in the code for her private quarters on the hover cushion. Syd jogged to hop on before it left with Keal at her heels.

"Ad," Syd moved to put her arms around Adeline and pulled both of them down to sit.

The cushion took them to the top floor in silence, the tension building. Keal sat with his arms bent on his knees. Syd listened to the whirr of the hover craft. The future Eichon and her guardians. Possible future Eichon. *Maybe future Eichon.* Syd rubbed her face and pressed her palms against her eyelids until she saw stars.

They exited the hover cushion, and Keal went to his quarters with a shake of his head. Seeing Keal deep in thought was usually a comfort, like all was going on accordingly. He was the thinker of their triad, the calculator, the processor. But now, it was off-putting and made the back of Syd's throat gummy.

Adeline and Syd retreated to Adeline's room automatically. The familiar sight, decorated with childhood toys, was a time capsule. They used to play here, endlessly, locked away from the rest of the world. Syd supposed they were still locked away at ACES in most ways. Maybe not anymore, though. Guilt built in her mind as a trickle of what could change sparked Syd's imagination.

Syd sat on the edge of the over-sized bed, elbows on knees and face in hands. She stared at Adeline who had immediately started unpacking her luggage brought in from the hangar by some nameless Tower staff. Her movements were sharp, quick, as she threw her clothes around and stuffed them into her old wardrobe. Syd straightened her back but didn't interrupt. Adeline was thinking, and it was all Syd could do to watch her quick, effortless movements. She was graceful even when she was upset. Adeline retrieved her old leather journal from her bags and slammed it on her bedside table.

"It's not like we can say no," Adeline finally said.

Syd's brain caught up as the truth of her statement sank in. As Eichon, Wenna was going to do whatever she pleased, even so close to the transference. And, if what her scientists said was true, then something had to be done. Adeline collapsed next to Syd on the bed, and Syd lay back to join her. She stared at Adeline's jaw, sight trailing to the sharp angle to her chin. Porcelain skin punctuated by pink lips and deep, dark eyes. Eyes that had started to well with tears as she stared up at the bed's canopy.

"We don't have all the facts yet," Syd said.

"What facts do we need?" Adeline turned her face to Syd's. "One of our moons will collide with our planet and the Eichon wants us to help stop it. Nothing else—not me, not my future, not who I am or who I will be—even matters."

"All of our futures are in question now." Syd's brows came together, a defensiveness rising in her throat and a pit forming in her stomach.

Adeline turned her face back toward the ceiling. She closed her eyes, taking three deep breaths.

"You're right," Adeline said after a time. "There are still so many questions that need answered and all we can do is wait."

Adeline's jaw was set, and she sat up in one easy motion, slumped forward. Syd reached her hand out to rub Adeline's back, and Adeline let her hair down, the natural dark waves spilling onto her shoulders.

"What if Project Nova succeeds? Wouldn't that be something…" Syd said, her lips tugging into a smile.

Adeline's back muscles tensed and Syd sat up. Their eyes met, Adeline's full of shock.

"What? Why?" Adeline asked.

Syd shrugged. There were so many reasons why, and finding the loudest one floating in her head was difficult when they were all shouting for attention.

"Because," Syd struggled for a moment and looked away. Her eyes focused on some distant point on the wall. "Because we don't want to be pawns any longer?"

Adeline leaned away.

"Think about it, Ad," Syd tried to reason. "This could be an opportunity for us, both of us, to change everything. If you're not going to be Eichon, and I'm no longer to be PRISM…" She splayed out her hands, trying to find the words. "We'd be free to live a life we want." Syd's voice turns upward, almost pleading for Adeline to understand.

Adeline shook her head. "I *want* to be Eichon. I *want* the future that's been laid out for me. I'm no pawn."

Adeline stood again, moving to the vanity on the other side of the room. Syd stood, too, and her stomach turned into a mess of knots. Pressure built under her eyes. *What about what I want?*

"Well *I* didn't want to become PRISM. And now I just might have a chance to be in control of my life for once. I don't know if you realize, but while your path led to becoming the most powerful person on the damn planet, mine had me following orders until the day I die. I mean what kind of future is that anyway?"

And there was that heat in Syd's chest again. This time it grew, engulfing her and spilling out through her mouth. An uncontrollable growl of frustration. They didn't fight often, and when they had, it was never about something so big: what to do during their free hours, where to travel for breaks, whose room they'd be sneaking to on any given night. Syd would default to Ad because it was easier, because it made more sense eventually, because Ad had always been the leader. Those blow-ups seemed like fizzles and false starts compared to this one now—a deep, burning ember finally being stoked. Adeline looked at her, confused, and Syd shook her head.

"Seriously," Syd said. "How can you only think of yourself right now when a chance for us, you *and* me, to do whatever the hell we want opens up?"

"And how can you see this as something *good*. Exciting, even? If Project Nova succeeds, it all changes. Everything changes, Syd."

The pressure behind Syd's eyes increased, but she squinted to hold back the tears. Another groan escaped her throat, and she threw her hands up. "Yeah. Exactly. It *does* all change."

Syd took a deep breath and turned to the door. She grabbed her luggage, waiting there. "I'll see you at dinner."

When Adeline didn't respond, the boiling inside Syd quickly turned to cold fear.

Only the clanking of silverware to plate drew Syd out of her thoughts. Thoughts about what it meant if she and Adeline weren't on the same page. She stared at the table. A long, formal affair, made of dark wood probably from the middle of the Taams somewhere—the Thicket or its sister forest, the Woodlands.

Out of Syd's peripheral, yellow-robed staff refilled drinks in silence, replaced some platter or another from the center of the spread without a word. Fruit salads were switched out for mushroom dishes, then switched out for seaside fish and mainland meats.

The blue backdrop made Syd dizzy, and she pushed her plate away. Blue marble floors, blue marble walls, two blue marble staircases with a single yellow runner each framed the head of the table where Wenna sat. Above, more ringlets of floors, all encased in half walls of the same sea glass that made up everything else in Zevir.

The seven of them sat huddle to one end of the table: Wenna at the head, Villette and the Toroks to her left, and Adeline, Keal, and Syd to her right.

Villette signaled for the final spread to be switched out with Adeline's favorite dessert—a Galssop treat made of thin sheets of fried dough, layered with chocolate mousse, and topped with a tart, fruity syrup. Keal nudged Syd and offered to serve her. When she didn't say anything, he did so anyway. Syd chanced a glance at Adeline who made a good show of moving the dessert around her plate.

"Well," Wenna cut the silence. "Now that dinner is coming to a close, I suppose it's time to fully discuss."

Syd felt Keal stop eating before she heard him put down his fork. Wenna nodded to Villette who quickly wiped her mouth with her cloth napkin, and the Toroks leaned back in their chairs. It was as if the entire room relaxed at once. Everyone except Adeline.

Villette spoke first. "We know the three of you, and the world if we're being honest, have been increasingly curious about the excavation sites that Wenna has commissioned over the years. Keal, your involvement in these research projects has been vital to our discovery. The tasks, as they were, that Dr. Malvuk put you on were, in fact, dig sites to find the best ways of accessing Terrus's core. When we started to discover australs at these dig sites, we knew you'd be the perfect person. Passionate and hungry enough to push the efforts forward to help grow your own research at the academy. It was a win-win, so to speak."

"Wh—" Keal started, but Wenna raised her hand to silence him and Villette.

"Thank you. I'll take it from here," Wenna said. "Finding ways to the planet's core has been part of a larger hypothesis, and project, Zevir's scientists have been working on. Our scientists have kept meticulous records over the Eichon legacies. It's a good thing these men and women are more loyal to the name of science than to any particular Eichon, to be frank. They have spent their time, either under command or in secret, tracking Nova's movements and have discovered that with each transfer of power, Nova moves closer in orbit. I took an interest in this early on in my reign, and understandably if I do say so myself. If one of our moons is on a trajectory to break into our atmosphere, it could mean something as vast as complete destruction of the planet.

"But, what was pulling Nova closer? The planet itself. Every twenty years, at each transference, Nova's power is weakened—hypothesized, though not confirmed—because of the energy exchange it must perform for the transference itself. The gravitational pull from our planet to Nova is drawing the moon closer in its weakened state. We knew something needed to be done, but we also needed a way to confirm all this activity, hence the dig sites. Since being able to access more of the core from multiple points, we've been able to confirm increased gravitational energy emitting from below the surface as we continue to draw nearer to the time of transference."

Syd's face betrayed her finally. Her lungs too. Her entire body, in fact. Impatience was getting to be too much, and she took a deep breath before leaning back. Out of habit, she crossed her arms.

"So, that explains the excavations!" Villette's voice popped suddenly, and she clasped her hands with a smile. "Now, back to why you three are here…"

The Toroks, Syd noted, had been very still and silent through all of this. How much did they know?

"Yes, thank you Vi," Wenna said, the informal nicknaming accompanied a warm calm that swept the room.

"It's clear that something must be done. By our estimates, we have five, maybe six, more reigns before Nova reaches the top layer of our atmosphere and even that may be enough to—" Wenna stopped suddenly, as if lost in thought, and Villette reached her hand to Wenna's forearm. This brought Wenna back from wherever she had gone. "As I mentioned earlier, we are aware that anything we attempt could greatly alter not only the planet, but also the Eichon power, the transference—all of it, really. But, we believe any alteration we could do pales in comparison to the complete devastation that will happen should we not act.

"There are many reasons we have called you three here. The main one being that we would like your assistance in our efforts. We see each of you playing critical roles in Project Nova. Adeline, your battle prowess and upbringing will likely put you in a place of influence, should our work fall short of complete before the transference. We'll need to ensure you're positioned correctly. Keal, your focused research on australs and energy, and direct mentorship from Malvuk, puts you ahead of almost any of Zevir's generalists. We'll need someone to lead them in their work. And Sydney, your unique Eheri majik, if honed correctly, could be exactly what we need to succeed."

All heads turned. All eyes on Syd.

"What?" she said, finishing Keal's interruption from earlier.

"While your performance at ACES has been sub-par," Villette said, and the corners of Syd's mouth twitched. "Malvuk's best hypothesis is that your particular strain of majik could be harnessed in our ultimate goal: to stabilize

Nova's orbital position. Based on records, we know of only a few other Eheri with gravity majik, and they were all before Malvuk's time. Through the Doctor's recent research, we've been able to extract majik from individuals to study and, possibly, expound upon the natural source. This could very well be, in the correct magnitude, the exact energy we need to stabilize Nova and combat the pull from the core at the same time."

Villette's eyes turned hungry, the corners tightening. Syd's mouth gaped.

"You want to poke and prod me more, is that it?"

"Not exactly," Wenna said, and the room cooled off. "We don't know how long it will take for Dr. Malvuk's process to work. It's still very experimental. Instead, we *can* better estimate how long it takes for an Eheri to master their majik *if* they train properly."

Syd's jaw clenched. *Unbelievable.* "So, you had us come here just to tell me to do better in school?"

The temperature continued to plummet. Syd tightened her folded arms against the chill. She looked around the table at the worried faces around her, and she sighed, letting the anger go.

"We'd like to send you to train with Villette at her home. It's clear the academy setting is not doing you any favors, and we have very little time before the transference. Keal and Adeline are as trained as they're going to be, and Vi has her own unique majik that she learned to control by herself as we were growing up. Maybe her guidance will serve you better than the walls of a classroom."

Syd relaxed a little and lowered her head. The twang of

being a fool filled her chest. What they were offering wasn't freedom necessarily, but it wasn't a classroom, and it certainly wasn't PRISM. But was it an offer at all? Without being able to say no, it was just another command. Was that truly better? And if not better, was it different?

Reth stood, breaking Syd from her thoughts. His forehead was lined with worry, but his eyes were wide with kindness.

"Eichon," he said. "This has been quite a lot of information to digest in one sitting. Perhaps a night's rest is in order and we can return to the matter in the morning."

The temperature of the room reheated as Wenna looked to Reth. She held his gaze for a moment, but eventually nodded, and the room itself exhaled.

"Yes, you're right," Wenna agreed. "We'll all meet back here in the morning for breakfast and continue our discussion."

Syd's neck prickled at another command-not-command, but she and Keal left in file, Adeline guiding them up the stairs in silence. Only once outside on the stair landing did the three look at each other and breathe.

"Stop looking at me like I have three heads," Syd said.

"Sorry, just...what do you think?" Keal asked, looking between Adeline and Syd.

Syd shrugged, and her shoulders felt heavier than they should. Adeline exhaled sharply.

"I think Reth is right," Adeline said. "Let's just get some sleep."

CHAPTER FIVE

There was one thing Syd always enjoyed about visiting Zevir: the beds. For all its technological prowess, the city enjoyed old-fashioned canopies cascading around four-posts.

Her legs slipped and slid under layers of fabrics gathered from all over the world, finding the most comfortable to be the silk sheets. She rolled over and stared at the wood grain in the nearest post, lighter than the wood from the dining hall. She rolled over again onto her back and stared at the ripples of blues that draped from one corner post to the others. Layered, entwined. As light as soft waves stretching onto the shore and as deep as the indigo that hides in watery shadows.

Flipping onto her side, the restlessness growing like a squall, she scanned this side of the guest room. Adeline had *thought it best* if they slept separate tonight, and who was Syd to argue? She had clearly wanted to do enough of that at dinner. The glass vanity's mirror reflected the bed's drapes with a tall white wardrobe next to it. Shelves hung on the walls with fresh sea flowers arranged in blues and yellows. A few books sat stacked here or there with no discernible titles, just more shades of blue that she'd swum through her entire life.

Her favorite had been the sea that bordered the orphanage. That was a rich and depthless blue they weren't ever allowed to swim in. The attendants had said that it was too cold, but Matron Reos once confessed that it was because there were vicious fish who dug their homes just below the sand and would attack anything that entered their territory. That might have been the first time anyone had told her about beasts, now that she thought of it.

It hadn't frightened her enough to keep her away from the seashore, though. All she had wanted to do was catch a glimpse of those fish, their homes buried deep under the froth of the tide. But it never failed. An attendant would find her throwing rocks at the water's edge and usher her back to the safer meadow, closer to everyone else. Closer to the other kids who either ignored her or ridiculed her for being Matron's favorite.

Heat rushed to her cheeks at the memory. Special treatment had always followed her around, and it was no different now than before. All she had ever truly wanted was to be left alone, to do whatever it was she pleased. Now, the empty room mocked her.

She rubbed her stinging eyes. It wasn't like she didn't want to think about training with Villette, about the mission, about Nova. She just couldn't. She wanted to think about what to say in the morning, to Wenna and Villette. To Adeline. She kept her eyes closed and listened to her breath, the rhythm, a tide of its own, washing ashore and receding. Over and over and over.

Her eyelids popped open again, and she groaned. *Fine.* Her legs swung over the edge of the bed, and she stood to stretch. The floor was cool on her bare feet as she walked to the door and put her wrist band to the scanner. The door whooshed open to the 9th floor carpeted hallway. She listened for any noise, but it was all eerily quiet. She peered over the half-wall all the way down to the 5th floor lobby. Her toes flexed against the walkway's plush, navy carpet, and her feet carried her to the stairs that spiraled the height of the Tower. She hoped the walk would tire her out.

Floor 8 looked identical to floor 9. Floor 7, too. Same blue carpet. Same marble walls. Same sea-glass barriers. Floor 6, though, had a red horizontal line in its carpeting that followed around the curve of the hall. Syd followed it, making a game of balancing on the red strip. Identical door after door, though these seemed sturdier than others in the Tower.

Every so often, red-cushioned benches or tall, twisted trees in red pots sat inside alcoves like sentries. One tree looked browner than the rest, and Syd was bored enough to stop and prune it.

A thumping caused her to jump and stand up straight, alert. The sound of hurried footsteps just beyond the hall's bend came towards her. Startled, and feeling like a kid out of bed, she wedged herself behind the tree, which was easily big enough to conceal her. For a half-second, she considered how ridiculous it would be to get caught like this.

Her heartbeat matched the speed of the footsteps, and the sound rounded into her view from behind the leaves. Two PRISM soldiers and one commander, their visor an opaque yellow instead of black, flanked Wenna in the center of the group. They hurried by, stopping at a door as identical as the rest only a few down from where Syd hid. Wenna waved her hand at the door's sensor, and the group sped in.

Curious, Syd quickly slid out from her spot and quietly

closed the distance. Before the door could close, she triggered the sensor with her foot to keep it open. She pressed against the cool marble wall outside and peeked beyond the door frame.

The room was dark with thick steel tile work covering the floor in a reflective metallic sheen, and the walls were lined with computer stations. Lines of blue-on-black lettering flittered across the unoccupied terminal screens. In the center, a semi-circle control panel blocked the rest of the room from Syd's view. Large, hologram images cascaded more code above the intricate circuitry of the central terminal. The soldiers and Wenna crowded behind one image flashing red.

Syd's heart pounded so loudly and fully she could feel it in her mouth. *What am I doing?*

"There's been another attack on the Veral System," the commander said.

"Seliss?" Wenna asked.

"Yes, and they seem to be making progress."

Wenna folded her arms, then jumped as the door emitted a high-pitched alert. *Shit.* Syd removed her foot, but it was too late. Gloved hands grabbed her and yanked her inside the room. She fell forward onto the cold floor and heard the unmistakable sound of a weapon being drawn before she could look up to confirm. She froze, her gasp caught in her throat.

"At ease, Commander Herf," Wenna said.

The commander returned his weapon to his side, and the soldiers released their grip on either arm. Syd stood, massaging her biceps where she'd been grabbed.

"Difficulty sleeping?" Wenna asked.

To Syd's surprise, Wenna's voice was kind. Syd nodded, and the air in the room warmed.

"I used to have trouble, too, my first few years here, sleeping alone in those impossibly huge beds."

A strange, but not wholly unwarranted comment. Ever since they were little, Adeline and Syd shared a room. It was clearly odd that they hadn't tonight.

The door slid shut finally, and the soldiers posted themselves to either side of it. *Trapped.* The flashing red from the hologram reflected off Wenna's pale face and the commander's yellow visor. Syd stood, a calmness spreading through her, which was more likely Wenna's doing than anything. Knowing this, Syd took a step forward.

"What's...wrong?" The words stuck in Syd's mouth, but she needed to fill the silence.

Wenna took Syd in, eyes scanning up and down as if searching, judging.

"I suppose, one way or another, you'll need to know this," she said. "This is our central command. It hosts the three main systems that run Zevir." She pointed to each of the three central screens individually. "PIMA, which oversees Zevir's trade and industry. Azur, the shield technology that was disabled soon after I came into power. And Veral, the brain of Zevir. It controls, among other things, the PRISM network. Seliss has been trying to breach it for a few days now."

The hair on Syd's neck stood on end. Seliss was the reason the Eichon needed PRISM at all, the reason for academies that train kids to be soldiers. It all came back to the long history of attacks on Eichons—as small as individual assassination attempts and as large as full wars that lasted years, draining resources from both sides. These were the lessons Syd had actually paid attention to, knowing she'd probably come face to face with Seliss one day. An engaged enemy was predictable. A quiet enemy was dangerous. And Seliss had been quiet since before Wenna became Eichon.

"Why?"

"War is no longer waged solely on battle fields. It's in trade, and industry, and especially in security networks. Seliss has been planning an attack on me and Zevir since I came into power. They just now figured out a better way in. If they can get into Veral, it would completely disable our best means of any defense of a physical attack."

Wenna was incredibly calm and patient as she explained to Syd. Her words were thoughtful once again, slow and processed. Or maybe it was her majik filling the space; maybe Syd was finally finding composure. Maybe both.

"As favorable as my reign has been compared to some before me, Seliss has always been the natural enemy of any Eichon. From their point of view it makes sense; a single person with unknown power and control? We are targets to anyone who fears that."

Syd looked at the red screen. A jumble of letters, numbers, and characters cascaded down endlessly. This isn't what war looked like in her texts or lessons and her brain strained to connect dots it knew were there.

Syd looked at her hands. "Wenna, I apologize for my outburst at dinner. I didn't—I don't know what to do with everything. And now this. Are you asking something of me?"

Syd tried to make her voice bigger than it came out. These attacks, the project, the recruitment. It was all leading somewhere she couldn't see. Yesterday, Syd knew what it looked like after graduation. Now the picture was fuzzy and confused, and the only thing that could help the sinking feeling inside her was sleeping four floors above where she stood now.

Wenna searched Syd's eyes, and Syd felt like a child again, something small that could be molded.

"There's more Villette and I haven't shared. We wanted to wait, but we might not be able to now," Wenna trailed off again. Her face turned to the screen once more, but her eyes were focused somewhere beyond it.

Syd shook her head. *What more could there possibly be?* Her eyelids drooped, and her head was getting heavy.

Wenna snapped out of her thoughts. "For now, Commander Herf will escort you back to your room."

Too tired to argue any of it, Syd followed the yellow visored Commander out the door.

CHAPTER SIX

Rapid knocking woke Syd up from a dreamless night. She bolted upright, heart pounding, and it took her a moment to focus. The beating at the door came again, and when she opened it, Keal smiled at her. Syd yawned in return, eyes squinting into the brightness of the hallway.

"What time is it?" she asked.

"Early enough to get some austral training in before breakfast," Keal said.

"Since when are you an early bird?"

Keal flashed his belt at her, an upgrade from the one given to him at ACES. Arranged on its clips were a number of silver canisters. Syd's eyebrow perked, teasing a lack of amusement.

"C'mon," Keal continued undisturbed. "ACES sent over the new specimens with a comms that said I'm to give a demonstration to the Council. Guess Mom forgave me pretty quickly, eh? Reth thought it would be a nice way to blow off steam after dinner last night."

"Reth? On first name-basis now?"

Keal shrugged his shrug and grinned his grin, a gesture she knew intimately when he was feeling particularly proud of himself.

"New belts aren't the only privilege around here," Keal said. "Adeline's getting dressed. Meet her in the lobby when you're ready. I need to go on ahead and prep."

Syd rolled her eyes but couldn't help grinning back at Keal.

"Alright. See you soon then," she said to his expectant face.

As promised, Adeline had been waiting for her in the lobby. They took the inner elevator down to the first ring, full of cerulean houses for Zevir's citizens, and took the northwest exit toward the training fields. Only after they were through the gates did Adeline move closer to Syd. Though silent, when Adeline's knuckles brushed against Syd's hand, she interlaced their fingers together instinctively. Both their shoulders relaxed.

"Whatever is ahead of us," Adeline said. "I want it to include you and me. Together."

Syd looked off to where they were heading and squeezed Adeline's fingers. "Thanks, Ad."

They walked an old path, unpaved and dusty in the Crarra Mountains' dry valley. This side of Zevir opened up to an impressive amount of unused land that served as the training fields for PRISM. Metal fences created the boundaries for different sparring areas, and even though it was early, the sun beat down. The barren terrain alone was enough to test a soldier's will after a few hours, and the looming gray of the Crarras made Syd dizzy. A steadfast reminder of one's place in the world.

Before humans existed, the Goddess Eher created australs and their keepers, clay giants known as the Rhurg. Rhurgs, like Crarra, created humans from their flesh and the land from their bodies. People like Keal and his family were direct descendants of the Rhurg, and they were gifted with an affinity to austral energy. To a lesser degree, that affinity could be taught to anyone as all bloodlines eventually traced back to the Rhurg.

Syd thought she and Keal were not so different, really. The Eheri with their majik, named after the Goddess herself; and the Rhurgari with their ability to manipulate australs, named after those first giants from which all was made.

Every so often, a PRISM soldier was posted, machine weaponry held loose. Syd tensed at each one they passed.

"Relax. They are here to protect against any monsters coming down from the mountains," Adeline said.

Ahead, a group of people came into view in one of the sparring sectors.

"Ad," Syd said, trying to make sense of last night. Was the conversation with Wenna a dream? Does Adeline know about the Seliss attacks? "You know I want a future together above all else. I'm sorry. Let's just…remember that when we get to breakfast. Something tells me there's more to all this."

Adeline stopped. She turned to Syd and smiled. Still half-asleep, Syd blinked and smiled back. Before she knew it, Adeline's lips were on hers, the smell of lavender heavy. Catching up, Syd's hands moved to Adeline's waist and returned the too-quick peck. Adeline leaned back, playfully.

"Yeah, that may be. But first, guess what?"

"What?" Syd said, still lingering in Adeline's touch.

"You're it!" Adeline laughed.

She slapped Syd on the arm and bolted off in the

direction of the group. Syd snapped out of it and laughed, her feet slow to start.

"Ugh! It's too early for games!" Syd groaned playfully, but she ran and tried to catch up.

They neared the group, their feet kicking up dust in their game of chase. The Council—Wenna, Villette, Reth, and Saaviana—were looking to Keal. In front of them, Keal commanded the earth austral as it swirled and grew. The austral's green haze swelled. It curled, its mass moving and bending, and took a humanoid shape. Keal clapped excitedly and said something to the group.

Adeline neared them, her footsteps pounding loudly against the hard earth. The austral changed form quickly, and its color deepened, thickening. Syd gasped, and a wind bellowed from the green mass as it shot into the air, coiling up in front of Adeline. Syd realized too late what was happening.

"Keal!" Syd shouted. "Tell it Ad's not a threat!"

The raw amount of energy pooling above Adeline was greater than anything Syd had seen in the training center, let alone the confines of Keal's lab. Syd pushed through the soles of her feet, willing them to be quicker. At the same time she steeled herself, seeking for that perfect eclipse of adrenaline and anxiety. Syd cupped her hands.

Her gray mist trailed behind her, and she struggled to keep her majik dense and formed. It gathered and eventually combined to grow—to mold—and she stretched it with her hands. Her lungs caught fire, though from running or from the majik she didn't know. Just a little farther and she'd be in range. *Just a few more yards.*

The majik spilled from Syd's fingers all around her just as the austral released, unleashing onto Adeline in a single, swift movement. The ground shook, and Syd lost her footing by a half step. The austral swelled again, rearing for a second attack.

"Ad!"

The gray ball in Syd's hands turned solid, malleable, and she stretched it carefully. She controlled it, the small, dense ball of gravity between her palms, but only just. Her arms rose above her head, and she came to a halt, using the momentum to launch the ball at the austral. It hit, and Syd tumbled forward onto her hands. The gray majik sizzled through the green austral, slowing its movements. Syd's nose filled with static, her sight blinded.

Syd picked herself up, doubled over. When her sight returned, she jogged the rest of the way to Adeline's limp body. Syd collapsed to her knees, gums aching, but could think of nothing beyond willing Adeline's chest to rise and fall, her panicked breathing filling her ears. *Please, please, please.*

Cutting through the group, Wenna knelt next to Syd and held her hands a few inches above Adeline's ribs. Syd gasped for breath, struggling to keep her head upright, and watched through hot, blurred vision.

A brilliant white flashed and poured from Wenna's fingers. Try as Syd might, it was too bright. She closed her eyes, and her head sagged. Everything was quiet. Not even a breeze. Not even a breath. Syd's lungs burned and screamed at her, her breath caught in a moment of time. Then, a single thunderous clap. A gust knocked her back, and a painful thump caused her to suck in air. The light faded as quickly as it had appeared.

Syd scrambled to Adeline, muscles protesting every inch of the way, and grabbed for her hand. She looked to Wenna. *Is she ok? Please say she's ok.*

"Vi," Wenna said. "Call the medics to take Adeline to the infirm."

Villette did as she was told, and Wenna looked to Syd finally. Syd's arm threatened to give out, but she didn't dare waver.

"Adeline is healed. Her body remains unconscious from the impact."

Syd's mouth went slack, and her neck bent again to relieve the built-up tension. Somewhere around her, feet began to shuffle.

"The austral thought it was protecting me," Keal explained to no one.

The medic craft arrived silently, and Wenna said nothing to Keal. Instead, the Eichon whispered her orders to the medics. They saluted before lifting Adeline's body up and away. Syd strained to stand. An audible grunt escaped when she straightened her back and stepped to join the medics.

"No," Wenna said. "Let them tend to her."

Syd stared at the medic's blank face. He didn't seem much older than her, and he stared back, waiting for her. Stuck between the commands of the Eichon and her own desire, Syd stopped and simply watched as the rear door of the medic craft shut in her face. The craft drove toward the blue blur of Zevir.

How many times had Syd watched Adeline spar and

train? How many beasts had been felled by Adeline's mastery of her blade? Early on, when they were younger, Adeline had gone to the infirm plenty for minor wounds. In recent years, she hadn't needed to go at all and only sometimes complained of muscle fatigue. But this austral was unlike anything the academy had ever stocked, and Syd had been completely useless in stopping it before it hurt Adeline.

Syd blinked. Wenna's healing majik surpassed anything she'd seen in labs too. Equal parts breathtaking and frightening. Syd watched the craft disappear in the wake of its own dust and turned around. The crackles of her majik filled the silence as it held the suspended austral.

"Keal," Wenna started.

Keal shook his head, his eyes widening and focused again. He swallowed. "...Right, yes."

He called the energy back into its canister through a series of intricate, swooping gestures.

"Forgive me, Eichon." Keal lowered his eyes. "I've never felt such strength in an austral before. It's greater than what I've studied with Malvuk."

"You'll take the austral to our labs immediately for study," Wenna said plainly. "We've all underestimated the power demonstrated here today."

Her eyes flashed to Syd before nodding to Reth and Saaviana. "You two will accompany Keal back to the city."

The three left without another word, boarding one of two hover crafts Syd only now noticed.

"Are you alright? Shall I call another medic?" Villette asked.

It took Syd a moment to realize she was being spoken to.

"I'll be fine." It's all Syd had the energy to say before they rode back to Zevir in a deafening, weighted quiet.

CHAPTER SEVEN

Six Years Prior

Adeline leaned back into her seat, putting her stylus next to her tablet. She kicked her leg out, foot resting on the attached desk's leg, and swiveled herself back and forth slowly. Year One History lessons, so far, had been nothing but repetitive, boring facts she learned years ago from her schooling in Zevir. Today wasn't any different.

A digital image of the moons Nova and Runar emerged on the screen behind the instructor, a pudgy man with an even voice. "Gifted to us by Eher herself over 1,200 years ago, Nova appeared in our sky."

Adeline peered around the chair's wings to Syd seated next to her. Syd scribbled notes on her tablet and Adeline huffed louder, but not loud enough for the instructor to hear.

Syd looked over to Adeline in question. *What?* Syd mouthed.

Adeline turned back to her tablet and began typing. Syd's tablet vibrated, followed by a message:

Ugh. I can teach you all this stuff later. How do we get away from Instructor Snooze?

Syd made a show of tapping her stylus to her chin thoughtfully.

The screen at the center of the classroom changed to an image of a timeline. One end was labeled "1st Era: Hunters & Gatherers". At the other end was "10th Era: Majik".

A large red bar hovered above the timeline, stretching from "4th Era: Cohabitation" mark to the 10th Era mark.

"Early writings show signs of humans with majik in the beginning years of this era here—the 5th era." A black dot appeared in the bar.

Adeline's tablet vibrated.

Follow my lead… The message said and Syd grinned over to Adeline who grinned back.

"However, Eichon Arja is the first Eichon on record, seventy-five years after Nova's appearance." Another black dot popped up close to the first.

"Stop it, Adeline!" Syd shouted out.

The rest of the class turned their attention away from the instructor, all eyes on Syd with her face scrunched up in annoyance.

"What? I didn't do anything?" Adeline gasped and looked around.

"You did so! Stop throwing paper wads at me!"

The instructor looked between the two of them, impatient.

"I did no such thing!"

"Did too!"

"Did not!"

"Both of you!" The instructor called, his voice still even but just louder. "If you continue to disrupt my classroom, you'll be sent to Director Rhiuld." He gave them each a stern look. "Now, if I may have everyone's attention once more, you'll remember we were talking about the first Goddess Power theory in which—"

"Seriously! Adeline, knock it off!"

At that, Adeline couldn't help herself and giggled.

"—OUT!" The instructor yelled. "Take your tablets and get out. I won't stand for disruption again."

Adeline and Syd slid off their chairs, taking their tablets with them as instructed. Adeline tried to quiet her giggling while Syd just grinned, and they left the room.

"Hah!" Adeline exclaimed when the door whooshed closed behind them.

"Too easy," Syd boasted. "Probably won't be able to use it again, though."

"Won't be able to use what again?" A woman came from around the hallway's bend. Her uniform was the same beige color of all faculty, but it was a jumper instead of pants and jacket. Goggles sat in her graying hair.

"Uh—" Syd started.

"We were…" Adeline talked over Syd.

"There's only one reason you wouldn't be in class right now. Between you an' me, Harolde can be a bit too sensitive," the woman said, looking at the classroom door. "But, I suppose you're bein' sent to the Director? Let's go."

Adeline didn't move. Neither did Syd.

"Um, excuse me," Adeline said, jutting out her jaw. "Who are you?"

"Technically, you should call me Instructor Playnar, but I prefer Jo. Look me up in your third year when you're choosin' your secondaries. I'm Head of Transport, which means I teach 'ship piloting and repair."

They started following Jo, who didn't skip a beat. "So, what he get you for? It's always somethin'."

"Well…" Adeline tried to explain.

Syd jogged next to Jo and looked up, "Actually, we just really wanted out of there. It's *so* boring."

Jo looked straight ahead, leading them to the elevator bank. "It might be boring now, but it's important. Probably." Jo winked down to Syd and, when the elevator dinged its arrival, they stepped in.

"You're Adeline Keylen?" Jo asked.

Adeline nodded.

"Hm. Thought so. And you?" Jo looked to Syd again who looked to the floor.

"Syd Orleen," Syd replied.

Jo pushed the button for the administration floor. "Well, I'm supposed to call you Cadet so-n-so, but it's nice to meet you both. Know what you're goin' to say to the Director?"

Adeline and Syd shook their heads in unison. Adeline wasn't sure what to make of Jo, but if she was staff, she was trustworthy. Momma would never let Rhiuld hire someone who wasn't. The elevator dinged up one floor. Two floors. At the third floor the doors opened.

Jo leaned down to whisper, "Could use some help in the shop."

Adeline wasn't sure who Jo was talking to, but without another word, she nodded and held the door open with her arm. The three exited into a bright, half circle room. The elevator door closed, and a man behind a desk called over.

"May I help you?"

"Cadets Orleen and Keylen to see Director Rhiuld," Jo said and led them to a set of oversized, red chairs.

"Ah! Yes, the comm just came through. I'll let the Director know."

Shortly after, a door swung open. Director Rhiuld held it with one arm, her navy uniform crisp, hair kept tight and low. Without hesitation, Jo stood and brought them inside the office. Small and plain, the room had minimal natural lighting. Rhiuld took her seat behind her desk, neat stacks of paper all around. She tapped into her tablet. Adeline and Syd sat in the hard-back seats provided.

"Thank you for escorting the cadets, Instructor Playnar. You are dismissed." Rhiuld waited until the door closed and pursed her lips. "Class disruption?" She looked between Syd and Adeline.

"We were just trying to—" Adeline said, her heart in her throat. She knew she was at fault, but the fire in her belly made her nostrils flare. Why was it her fault the lessons were so boring?

Rhiuld shook her head and locked eyes with Syd instead, "There is no excuse for this type of behavior."

Syd's eyes darted to Adeline and then back to Rhiuld. Adeline's heart went to her stomach suddenly, and she stared at the tips of her boots dangling above the beige flooring.

"We have a no tolerance policy for misbehaving," Rhiuld said. "ACES Academy only accepts the best. And if you aren't the best, we might as well send you back to your family now before you become more of a menace."

Syd shifted in her seat and Adeline heard her friend's breath quicken. Tears started to well in Adeline's eyes as she sat quietly, frozen in place at the harshness of Rhiuld's words.

"Director, I don't…" Syd's voice was small, and Adeline hated it.

"Yes, I know. You don't have any family so we have nowhere to send you back to. Which means you're stuck here with us, and we're stuck here with you." Adeline didn't have to look up to know she was sneering. "As such, you'll be given different disciplinary actions. We have several facilities that need assistance. I'm feeling generous today, so I give you a choice: Cafeteria, Airship Hangar, or Training Center."

Syd took a moment to answer, and Adeline looked sharply to her friend. Syd moved her head to the side, away. It was then that Adeline saw Syd was crying too, silently.

"Your answer, Cadet Orleen? I don't have all day."

"Um," Syd said, blinking away more tears. "Hangar?"

"Very well. You will spend your free evening hours after dinner cleaning the hangar for three months. Dismissed." She tapped something into her tablet and, when she said nothing more, Adeline and Syd slid off their chairs and left.

Jo stood outside, waiting, arms folded. She crouched, bending at the knees. Syd brushed any wetness away from her cheeks quickly. Adeline did, too.

"I can expect you to help me clean later tonight, then?"

Syd nodded up to Jo and Adeline turned around to see Rhiuld closing her office door.

Present Day

She couldn't help it. Syd was starving by the time food was brought out. She knew she should have fought against Wenna, fought to go see Adeline in the infirm. But Syd was still recovering from using her majik, and by the time she had blindly followed Villette to the Tower and met up with Keal, they were being seated at the long, dark table again in the dining hall. Food was put in front of her, and she did what you do when food is put in front of you. She ate.

A fork fell and hit the table.

Syd's head jerked toward the sound, and she met Keal's stare, his light eyes filled with shock.

"Hm?" she said.

The table had clearly been talking, discussing something. Had she really not been paying attention?

"Sydney?" Wenna asked. "Are you alright?"

"What?" Syd repeated and looked to Villette for a hint.

"I said, the Council has decided who will be the next Eichon," Wenna tilted her head at Syd, her words impatient.

"Wh—" Syd stared around again, landing back on Keal. He raised his eyebrows at her.

Pieces of conversation came flooding back. *Not Adeline*, Villette had said, and Wenna had explained that, while it was the obvious choice, she would not pass her powers onto Adeline. *We've chosen* you *Syd*, one of them had said. That was when Keal's fork had dropped.

Shit. What? Syd's inner voice rang in her head. *How?*

"Wait." She scooted her chair away from the table,

something cold slicking up and down her spine. "Okay, just wait. Me?"

Wenna's patience was visibly wearing thin, which, in turn, made the atmosphere wear thin around the table. The air was a little less than it had been a moment ago.

"The Council thought it best that an Eheri become the next Eichon," Wenna explained with her hands.

"So? You have plenty to choose from," Syd choked out. *Why me?*

She looked at her plate, heart pounding at everything and anything this could possibly mean. They were quiet for some time, while the air around them was slowly sucked away by some invisible force.

"We prefer someone we're familiar with," Villette said, cautious. "If Project Nova disrupts the transference, or the goddess gift, we will need someone with a naturally high level of majik."

Syd swallowed hard and squinted between Wenna and Villette.

"As to not cause panic, you understand." Villette placed her utensils down on the table with precision. "The potential of a disruption of that magnitude could cause mass chaos, hysteria. You have such untapped potential. Of course we know you keep it hidden, mostly. That was demonstrated quite nicely this morning. But, because you've never truly shown what you can do—having you in place could at least buy us some time to—"

"To what? Lie? Cover up? You believe my majik is strong enough to literally push our moon from our surface, right? How long do you think it will be until people start noticing Nova is suddenly smaller? A day, if that?"

Syd flung her fork down with a loud clink. She wasn't some pawn to be played and put on display before the world.

"It doesn't work like that," Villette said.

The hell it doesn't. "You don't even know if this scheme will pay off. What if it doesn't? What if I'm suddenly stuck being Eichon; the *real* Eichon?"

Syd stood, and her chair knocked against the back of her legs, threatening to tip over. "And you tell us this without Adeline here?" Her breath was labored, struggling against the heat of her anger. Panic tingled up her arms to her throat.

"We were waiting until the three of you had more training. Until the mission was underway. But with Seliss's attacks, and we're so close to the transference—"

"Wait, Seliss attacks?" Keal interrupted, and everyone turned their attention to him. "Uh, right. Later."

"Does Adeline know?" Syd asked, jaw clenched.

Wenna shook her head and opened her mouth to speak but closed it just as quickly. There was barely any oxygen left in the room. Syd's ears rang, and she rubbed her face before she finally realized: no one was prepared for this. Not even the Eichon herself.

Shit.

The medical wing of the Tower faced the shores of the island, though it was still several stories above sea level. The staff all pointed her in the direction of Adeline's room without so much as a word. Whether it was because of the look on her face or because they knew who she was, she didn't know, and she didn't care.

The heat in her cheeks and the pressure on her chest were almost unbearable until she opened the door to the one-bed room. Its space was bright, sterile, and didn't match the rest of the Tower. It didn't match Adeline, surrounded by white walls with two thin, red stripes running through the middle around the room.

There was no medical equipment. No tubes or wires. Just the rise and fall of Adeline's chest. It all meant she only needed rest, and Syd let her breath go easy. The air was metal, antiseptic, and bandages, nothing remotely natural until she leaned down close to Adeline and took a seat on the stool next to the bed.

Of course, she looked beautiful, peaceful and asleep. When didn't she? No strain on her face, her hair taken down for comfort. A dark crown for a princess in slumber. The wheeled, yellow seat squeaked under Syd's weight, and she took Adeline's hand in her own.

"Ad..." Syd whispered, not knowing what to say or where to start. She hung her head, trying to find the words. "What are we going to do?" *You're going to wake soon and then we have to figure out this mess.*

On the hurried walk out of the dining hall, Syd hadn't allowed herself to think. She couldn't. But now, in the stillness, in the quiet of only their breaths rising and falling, together, thinking was all Syd could do.

Maybe she could just tell the Council no. Refuse to accept the transference. Was that even possible? She felt so small, the questions swimming around her so fast she might drown. Syd squeezed Adeline's hand and brought herself back to the surface. She looked up again, hoping to find Adeline awake. The thought was sudden and dreadful all at once. Syd's stomach flipped, and something hardened in her throat.

And what were the damn odds anyway? Of any possible outcome truly working? All paths led to Syd becoming Eichon, no matter what. She chewed the inside of her cheek, but these thoughts were drowned out by something larger. Something darker and looming. Something heavy.

"I guess we have no option but to see the project succeed before the transference," she said, more to herself. Then Syd added, "See it succeed together."

She closed her eyes and took in the stillness of the room.

Footsteps sounded from beyond the door. Syd replaced Adeline's hand to her side. Staring at the floor, Syd fought back tears. The footsteps ended just outside the room, and the door silently pushed open.

"Wasn't sure what to do after you left," Keal's voice was soft, though strained.

"If you're here to unload more on me, don't. I can't handle that right now."

Keal shuffled closer, and Syd looked at him, seeing a hurt on his face as he glanced between her and Adeline.

"Sorry," Syd mumbled.

"I wanted to check on my friends. Plural. Both of you. The doctors said she'll wake up in her own time later tonight. Wenna's healing magic did most of the work."

Keal leaned against the far wall, his hands deep in the pockets of his dark trousers. He still wore his white lab coat. *Almost like a status symbol.* It hung loose, undone, on his tall, slender frame. Its lapel sported the academy's colors: blue and yellow threads twisting up around the collar. Another symbol: the ties between the world's most elite academy and Zevir. Syd rubbed her forehead, the bridge of her nose, and finally stopped to cup her chin. She took a deep breath.

"I have no idea how to handle any of this. Do you—do you think this is the right decision?" Syd asked.

Keal moved closer, peeling his back off the wall. His forehead wrinkled, eyebrows raised in question, and then he let it all go. His eyebrows, his cheeks, his shoulders let go into a slouch.

"Does it matter?" He shrugged. "If it's you or Ad or my great aunt Parlla, I mean. Does it really matter? Each Eichon has left their mark on history. They've raised cities, destroyed others, won and lost great wars, and still none of that comes close. Not a single one has tried to do what Wenna is proposing. Eichon or not, wouldn't you want to be a part of that?"

Syd dropped her gaze to watch the rise and fall of Adeline's chest. Even. Measured.

"Knowingly or not, I think we already are. I think we always have been." Syd sighed, trying to exhale that thought, the one that kept lurking behind corners in her mind. "In any other circumstance, if someone uttered even half of what we've learned in the past day I would call them insane. I'm still inclined to think that."

"But..." Keal edged, his voice rising.

"But," Syd shrugged. "I slept like shit last night. I'm exhausted from going against that damn austral, and we can't really do anything but go along with this because, at the end of the day, the Eichon commands it."

She kept the image of puppet strings to herself, imagining lines from her arms and legs stretching ever skyward. Keal nodded and stepped back to the door.

"C'mon," he said. "We don't know when Adeline is going to wake up, you need rest, and I need to figure out why that austral was so strong."

If anything, she could count on Keal to keep things practical to the point of pragmatism. That consistency was a comfort and Syd smirked at him.

She was facing away from the door when the knocks came, on her side and staring at the wall. She couldn't sleep, and honestly, how could she have been expected to. Instead, she'd let her mind go numb, blank, and stayed that way. The knock came again. And again. And again.

Then, the keypad beeped, and the door opened.

"Syd?" Adeline said.

Syd leapt to the door. She grabbed Adeline tight, pressing into her and, after a moment, Adeline's arms squeezed around Syd too. Syd buried her face into Adeline's neck until Adeline let go and moved to sit on the edge of the bed. Syd stood there, watching her glide from one spot to another.

"How are you, are you okay?" Syd followed.

"Yes, I'm fine. More tired than I thought." Adeline

gave a weak smile and folded her hands in her lap. She fiddled with her nails, and Syd ached to hold her, but Adeline was nervous. Worried.

"What is it…?" Syd asked.

"My mother told me. She told me about Seliss." Adeline paused. "And you."

"Oh." The word fell out of Syd like a sigh.

How long had Adeline been awake? How long had Syd been in this room? Syd jumped when Adeline took her hand.

"I heard you. When you came to visit me in the infirm. You and Keal," Adeline said. "And you're right. It is a mess."

"Ad, I…"

What Syd wanted to say was that she knew Adeline's world had just crashed down around her in one mighty tug. What she said, instead, was nothing, because no words felt big enough.

"It's unfair," Adeline said quietly. "The whole thing. I want to be upset, angry even, at my mother. Villette. You."

Adeline's shoulders gave, caving in around her, and Syd was afraid to look at her.

"Not like we have a choice," Adeline continued. "But I think we should go. The three of us. Go to Llyn, train there with Villette, follow the plan however it morphs and changes. What else would we do?"

The truth sank in. She was right. How could Adeline or Keal or Syd go back to ACES now, knowing what they knew? How could any of them just sit in a classroom, watching a clock tick? Syd exhaled and looked at Adeline finally.

There was a tenderness around the edges of Adeline's eyes, her cheeks glistened, her lips were chapped. Syd reached out, cupping Adeline's face, drying any leftover tears, and she kissed her. She kissed her cheeks, her chin, her neck. She took as many as she was allowed until Syd collapsed, face buried against Adeline's chest, blanketed in the scent of lavender. Shielded by it. Protected. Then, she let everything go. And it all poured out of her in violent, heaving gasps.

CHAPTER EIGHT

The next morning, the three seemed to have a new air about them, but whether that air was good-new or bad-new was hard to tell. They were given drab, plain clothes because while they would be mostly—relatively—safe, they were still going to the Taams and closer to Seliss. Adeline had protested the wardrobe almost as much as she had protested moving into enemy territory. Even though it wasn't the first time they'd been to the Taams, those visits had been when they were younger and more reckless. Seliss had been quieter then, too, and hadn't been posing an active threat.

Hiding in plain sight is the best way to keep an ear to the ground, Villette had said before leaving to make preparations.

Adeline's disagreeing surfaced the most by taking her frustration out on the tailor. As the daughter of the Eichon, the closer one got to Seliss, the bigger the target on your back became. Blending in was key. Keal's clothes were left untouched, and Syd wasn't quite sure if that was an insult or not.

The uneventful ferry ride from Zevir to Carden had set them all in a better mood, though. One transport down, one to go. As they boarded the train to Beland, Keal took them directly to their private cabin.

"We'll have an escort when we get to the last stop in Beland. It's the nearest town to Llyn," he said when the cabin door shut.

The cabin itself was roomy, although full of muted colors that matched their outfits. Adeline went to the couch and pulled out her journal from the inner pockets of her beige coat. The journal had been the only thing couldn't be convinced to leave behind in Zevir. Keal took his place on the top of two stacked beds. The door to the private bath squeaked a little on its hinges as the train began to move and the low hum of vibration settled.

"Isn't it suspicious we're in such an expensive cabin for only a half-day's ride?" Adeline asked.

"Nah, the station was running a special. Any tourist would jump on it," Keal explained.

"I thought we were supposed to be *from* The Taams," Adeline tried to argue.

"We are." Keal made himself comfortable on the mattress. "We're kids from Galssop looking for a weekend away from the city. Wenna's strategist told me it happens all the time. Apparently, Seliss relaxes its control on small towns and city folks will go there to vacation."

He sprawled on the bunk, leg dangling. Adeline relaxed on the couch. Syd picked up an outdated copy of *Beland Chronicle* left out for guests. It fell open to an article about an old research facility in the southern Whai Sea, and she couldn't help but be reminded of the stories the older kids would tell at the orphanage. Her favorite had been about a sea serpent locked away in an underwater castle.

The story eventually devolved into what other types of monsters might lurk there. Descriptions of razor-sharp teeth thrashing, deadly fins slicing through any obstacle, and cutting scales armoring in defense masked by the dark of the deep unknown. She would lie awake and imagine which beast would be the highest on the food chain, and the lowest, and where they would all live, or hide, in the watery fortress.

According to the article, this research center had been constructed by the mad Eichon Larke. The journalist didn't go into that part of history, but they did consider that the research facility, URCHIN, had been built as a means to catalog sea creatures, friendly or otherwise. The editorial ended with a general recognition that no one knew for sure what once inhabited the research center, which was decommissioned not 60 years later by another Eichon. No record existed of any person finding this fabled underwater bestiary since, and, apparently, whenever anyone tried, all mechanical instruments would fail.

The train gave a jolt, and Syd put the magazine down. "How long until we arrive?" she asked.

"We just started moving," Keal complained at the question.

Answers like that only made Syd feel even more uncomfortable. She stood, stretched a little, and nudged Keal's dangling leg. He was supposed to be their guide until they met the escort at the rendezvous. She had questioned why only Keal was given the details, but Wenna had explained it was for security should Adeline or Syd run into trouble. *Your escort will know if something is amiss and come searching for you should you not arrive safely*, she had said. Seemed stupid to Syd.

"If we're supposed to be kids on holiday, I don't think

we'd hide in our cabin the whole trip," Syd said and looked to Adeline.

Adeline had busied herself with scribbling in her journal. Syd's nose turned up, not understanding why she used such old technology. Keal swatted at Syd from above.

"*This* 'kid' is tired," he said. "And *that* 'kid'," he thumbed over to Adeline, "is under strict order to stay put as much as possible. The rest of the world is still under the assumption that Adeline is the next Eichon. If anyone recognizes her, we're done."

Syd folded her arms at him. "Just trying to *enjoy the vacation.*"

But a sinking feeling swirled in her stomach. Should she be taking this more seriously? Most likely. Out of the three, Keal was the most sensible. Maybe that was why he was entrusted with the details instead of Syd.

"We at least need some food, right?" Syd asked. "I'll go check the dining car."

Keal threw his forearm over his eyes with an annoyed groan and handed her a keycard for the cabin.

Outside, each train car looked similar—long, narrow halls with dark, automatic doors. The other side of the hall was wood-paneled halfway under large window panes. A lazy yellow haze full of prairie grass opened up to the Steppe just outside Carden, and they were making their way through it at a pretty high speed. Not as quick as an airship, though.

Syd squeezed past several other passengers socializing and staring out the windows. It felt strange to blend in, so easily unnoticed. A hint of guilt mixed with something else. Something similar to those few times Adeline and Syd ventured off to Carden or Galssop on actual holiday. Something like freedom.

She turned sideways, allowing room for another passenger to pass by. This could be one of the last times she was completely anonymous, completely unknown. Sure, she had been a novelty for the first couple years at ACES, but eventually the faculty and lab assistants fell into the ease of familiar-by-proximity. Now, one way or another, she would soon be known the world over no matter what happened. No matter if she was, actually, going to be Eichon. No matter if Project Nova succeeded or failed. Things were about to get very public, very quickly. Was this what Wenna felt all the time: vulnerable, open, exposed? What about Adeline? Syd had never thought to ask. Adeline always seemed to enjoy the spotlight.

The next connecting door had a neon sign that flashed the word "Cafe" above it. *Finally*. Sliding the door open and moving through, the dining car was even more packed. *Looks like Keal was right. Again.* People were snatching up those travel packages back at the station and now they sat, stood, or leaned, around every square inch of the dining car, all self-involved in their own thoughts or chatting over the sound of a smooth percussion tune coming from the speakers in the car's corners.

A booth along the opposing wall was packed, too, full of bodies turned toward a bartender. Above them was a menu that boasted of handmade pies and cakes, but the bakery display case was empty, save for a few crumbs

The floor shifted beneath her feet suddenly. A piercing screech rattled through the room, shaking the windows, and spilling glasses—empty, full, or some gradient in between. Syd was pummeled by something knocking into her, and she knocked into the person standing closest to her. The train had stopped, and a moment later, she was pushed off the person she had slammed into. Syd scanned around quickly; confused voices overtook the musical ambiance still playing. *Adeline.* Her legs launched her out of the room, careful to dodge the disordered mass of people.

She walked quickly through the cars. Sprinting, though she wished she could, would attract too much attention. The other travelers talked in low, concerned mumbles that quieted when she neared them, but she kept moving on to the next door, the next car, until she reached theirs.

A crackling emitted from the train's PA system, "Apologies for the interruption..." There was something muffled in the background before the microphone clicked off only to click back on. "Yes, ehm. Would all passengers please return to their cabins or seats. We are conducting a, uh, routine check of our...passenger list?"

The mic cut out again at the same moment all cabin doors flew open and were held there automatically. Syd moved to their door and relaxed when she saw Adeline still sat on the couch with only a concerned look on her face. Keal jumped off the top bunk and pulled Syd inside the cabin. His eyes were wide, and his face made her heart thump hard in her chest.

Keal huddled them, his body and Syd's shielding Adeline from view of the door. *Smart.* It was so easy to forget that underneath his lab coat and glasses, he was trained in combat too. The first thing they learned in training was to protect.

Syd's mouth dried up at the sight of Adeline's eyebrows rising higher and higher in worry. She looked between Keal and Syd and twisted her hands together. All weapons had to be left behind with the promise they'd receive new ones upon arrival. Whereas Keal's weapons were concealed in his clothes, Syd's lived inside her. Adcline's hands typically needed to be holding something sharp in order to be deadly, and it was hard to blend in with a broadsword strapped to your back.

"I don't suppose my mother's strategists told you what to do if the train is stopped and searched, did they?" Adeline hissed.

"Not…exactly," Keal whispered back.

Syd looked at Keal, his eyes darting back and forth at some distant point on the floor, and she knew he was thinking, calculating.

"Well," Syd said and strained to keep her own voice quiet. "We can't cause alarm *and* we need to hide Adeline somehow."

"They have a passenger list. They know there are three of us in this cabin," Adeline said.

Shouts came from the next car over, barely audible. At least two voices.

"Okay. Okay, look…" Syd pushed her brain to have an idea. None came.

"Adeline, get in bed and toss up the sheets." Keal ran

into the bathroom and grabbed the rubbish bin. He placed it bedside. "Fake motion sickness. Hide your face."

Syd stared at him blankly. "You can't be serious. Why can't she just hide in the bathroom, then?"

"Don't you think that's even more suspicious?"

It was a long shot either way, but it was all they had. "Fine."

Syd helped Adeline mess up the lower bunk and ruffled the sheets around her. Adeline rolled over, facing away from the door. Keal grabbed Syd's arm suddenly.

"Remember," he said. "We're three kids on holiday from Galssop to get away from the city. Our friend has terrible travel sickness."

He led her out to the hallway. Other passengers were huddled by their doorways too. Keal shook out his arms, and Syd rubbed her face to get some of the tension out. Maybe the worry on their faces would pass for general concern. *Maybe.*

Moments later, the car door swung open with a bang that made Syd jump. Three Seliss soldiers passed over her and Keal, the lower half of their face—the only part of their face visible under their helmets—emotionless. The maroon cloth of their uniform bunched under heavy armor plates on their shoulders, elbows, chest, hips, and knees. Black boots thudded in half-time to the rhythm of Syd's heart rate and breath, both of which climbed by the second. Each of the soldiers had a green, electronic screen attached to a bracer on their left arm. Something touched Syd's shoulder, and she jumped again.

Slow your breath, Keal mouthed to her.

She took in a single long inhale and breathed out a single long exhale to reground herself. Heavy footsteps came up behind her, and she turned around. A larger, fourth Seliss soldier came through the door. His uniform was exactly the same as the others except the fabric beneath was a dark green, likely signaling a higher rank. He barked his orders for the soldiers to search the rooms.

"Look in every closet!" he shouted. "They could be hiding anywhere!"

The commander turned to Keal. If Syd focused long enough, she could just barely see his eyes under the helmet's dark visor, its design similar to the visors PRISM wore. He parted his lips in a half-snarl before checking the screen on his arm, and she caught a glimpse of his right canine, chipped and jagged from years of neglect. It felt familiar somehow. She scanned what she could of the rest of his face. Badly shaven stubble with young taunt and tanned skin underneath. An old scar, just barely visible, above his lip.

"Cabin 4F," he barked, breaking her stare. "Passengers Birel, Nestat, and?" He listed off their fake names and leaned close, peering into the room, and Keal and Syd stepped aside.

Something burned and bubbled inside Syd. Not her stomach, not her chest. It wasn't anger. It wasn't the cold heat of fear, either. It was something deeper, denser.

The commander spotted the lump under the sheets. "And Shaqui."

There was an almost unnoticeable stutter in his voice. Something someone wouldn't catch unless they knew to look for it. Keal pulled out the keycards for him to confirm his and Adeline's fake identities. Syd automatically reached for hers, and her hands shook, but her eyes were unable to stop staring at the commander's face.

"Getting a break from the city..." Keal tried to sound conversational.

From underneath his visor, Syd saw light eyes look from the keycards to Keal and back to Adeline's body on the bed. *Eyes like...*

"Gaav?" Syd whispered before she could stop herself.

Keal coughed and started to sputter some kind of apology. Syd held her stare as the commander's eyes reached hers for the first time. It had to be. She was sure of it. She'd know those eyes anywhere. They belonged to the boy who had been a couple years older than her, at the orphanage. The one who became her friend so easily, and was just as easily adopted. An ally among the bullies, ripped away from her.

The commander was silent for a long moment. His eyes squinted more and scanned her face until they relaxed. Their edges unwrinkled into something of recognition.

Syd's face spread into a smile. How many extra chores had they done together as punishment for playing hide and seek in the hung laundry, for splashing each other with too many bubbles while doing the dishes? How many free hours had they spent playing, chasing, laughing? She'd know him anywhere.

But Gaav only scanned the cards across the screen on his forearm in silence. He kept his eyes fixed on his work as each scan produced a beep that signaled their clearance. He handed the cards back to Syd and leaned in again to the room to take a look. Syd's breath stalled. On his way back out of the door frame, he stopped by her ear, towering over her.

"Keep out of trouble."

Syd's shoulders heaved in relief.

"ALL CLEAR!" he shouted to the other soldiers, and the group thundered off to the next car.

Syd turned to Keal, his mouth slack. He shook his head but no words came. Adeline remained motionless. Syd sat at the edge of the bunk and stared at the floor. Wasn't there something about allies in their training? Keal sat on the couch in silence too.

When the train resumed service, their cabin door shut on its own. Syd's heart finally left her stomach and Adeline sat up and flung the covers off. "What happened?"

Adeline's hair was a frizzy mess, and Syd combed through it with her fingers. Keal hopped back up to the top bunk.

"I think...I have an old friend, a very old friend, in the Seliss army," Syd said.

There was a tickle in her throat, but when she went to cough, it expanded and turned into a laugh. It was a little too deep, a little too loud, but a laugh all the same, and the tension left the room.

CHAPTER NINE

At least there hadn't been any more random searches by the time they arrived at the last stop in Beland.

"That was weird, right? That's not normal," Adeline said as they descended the steps from the train platform. She stopped and stared at the station's aging schedule with mild interest.

"The only thing I can think of is word has already spread that you're in the Taams. How, though, is beyond me." Keal shrugged. "We won't know until we can meet with your mother's strategists again."

"The *strategists* won't be in Llyn, Keal. We don't know when we'll see my mother again," Adeline said in a low voice.

The platform opened to a colorful cobblestone street, wide and bright with the early evening sun. The stones reflected blues and greens, sea glass mixed with some shells. Something about it felt off. Beland butted up against heavy woods, not a shoreline. The buildings on the main street were short, squat rectangle variations with sharp lines and neutral, muted colors. Syd looked up, and the sky felt closer than before.

"Keal, didn't you say we would have an escort?" Syd asked.

"Yeah, we need to find the TV Station."

"What?" Adeline squinted her eyes at him. "Why do we need to go to a TV station?"

Adeline looked at Syd as if she was in on some joke. Syd shrugged.

"It's the name of one of the bars here," Keal said.

A bulletin board littered with papers sat a few feet away. Getting closer, it seemed to be a map of the town. An old one, but a map nonetheless.

"We're doing a pretty good job at being tourists," Syd said.

Adeline and Keal moved closer. Above the map read: Historical Media Tour of Beland—Self-Guided. Below the title was a grid with certain buildings enlarged as points of interest and small blurbs about places like the TV Station, a lively pub erected in the spot where a transmission satellite tower used to stand, or the head offices of the *Beland Chronicle*, the Taams' largest print magazine (factory now closed, tours offered on certain days. Offices still functional and required a reservation in advance to visit).

Keal pointed down the main street to a T intersection.

"The bar should be down that way and a right at…" He double-checked the map. "The Radio Dial Hotel."

This town was corny to the point of grating. Themed names? Syd couldn't remember any lessons on what happened in Beland for it to be considered historic. "Hey, Keal, you're on the curriculum planning committee, right? Why aren't we taught anything about Beland?" she asked.

They walked past a row of small shops selling wind chimes and trinkets made out of tortoise shells. *Where the hell are they getting tortoises around here?* Through the windows, the shops were empty, even though their signs said they were open. Syd shivered. It just didn't feel right here.

"Probably the same reason Beland doesn't know anything about Darmar or Kosh. People are only taught the big things in the basic history classes. Our primary curriculum is built around the struggle between Zevir, the Eichon, and Seliss," Keal said. "If you'd taken any interest other than airship tech, you could have taken classes that would have taught you Beland used to be a city of influence."

Keal's voice took on the tone he used in lecture, and in the lazy heat of the evening, Syd's eyelids started to grow heavy.

"At the end of the Seventh Era, Eichon Berlene came into power. She was from Beland and commissioned the city to become the world's greatest telecommunications hub. Obviously, that's no longer the case. The tele-technology fell out of favor around the time of Eichon Stedda in the Ninth Era."

Syd made soft snoring sounds which made Adeline smirk. Keal threw his hands up.

"The Council will bore you with all of this soon enough, I'm sure," Keal said, a little too loud over her miming.

Syd and Adeline stopped in their tracks.

"Weren't you the one telling us to take this seriously on the train?" Adeline hissed. "Keep your voice down."

Keal looked apologetic but said nothing before they started walking again. Adeline was right, Syd knew. They needed to be careful about what they said, even in a mostly barren town like Beland.

They rounded the corner at the Radio Dial Hotel, and the street turned into cafes and bars with neon lights advertising local drinks and food. The large pedestrian square was vacant, just like the rest of the town, except for an older couple enjoying themselves at the outdoor seating. Tables and chairs were placed between trees encircled by concrete and mosaic tiles of turquoise.

Keal led them to a bar whose sign buzzed off and on: TV Station. It looked dated on the outside and, as they stepped in, it was even worse. The dark bar was littered with old leather seating cracked with age. The carpets were deep red and, with the lights so low, it was hard to tell what exactly made certain spots squish beneath Syd's boots.

A stout woman, hair hidden beneath a sand-colored bandanna, greeted them with a wave from behind the bar in the center of the room. She stood in front of an impressive bottle selection, backlit and mirrored to give the appearance of there being more than there actually was on the shelves. Syd took a seat, fully ready to decline any offer of a drink. Adeline followed her lead, but Keal remained standing.

"The plains of the Steppe are quite breezy these days," the woman said to no one in particular. She busied herself with a futile attempt at wiping a stain on the counter's surface.

Syd raised an eyebrow to Adeline, uneasy with people who talk to themselves. Adeline returned the eyebrow with an unsure smile.

"Wh—" Adeline started.

"But the bears sleep soundly," Keal said.

Syd looked between the barkeep and Keal. The pause

lingered between them, and Syd slowly stood, putting herself between Keal and Adeline with one eye on the door.

"Yer escort's in the back," the woman said.

She waved them off behind her in the general direction of a dark door hidden by the poor lighting. Keal nodded his appreciation.

Still cautious, Syd followed Keal and put Adeline behind her, but the back door led out to an alleyway with boxes, crates, and barrels. On one of the crates leaned a familiar face with salt and pepper hair, the figure decorated in dark leather, a scabbard on each thigh. Syd relaxed and stepped aside for Adeline to see too.

"Dad!" Adeline rushed to wrap Matius in a hug.

Matius smiled and took his time with the hug before letting go. Syd and Keal stood back, giving them their space. Adeline had always been closer to him than Wenna. He was, after all, the one who trained her to fight before being sent to ACES, and their bond never had the same tension Adeline and Wenna could sometimes have.

Matius then walked to Syd and hugged her as well. An embrace just for her, and her shoulders fell away from her ears.

"Syd," he said in greeting. "How's my favorite guard?"

She caught the scent of something smoky on him, burning even, before it was covered up by the smell of leather from his jacket, belts, and boots. It was always safe to assume that Matius knew what was going on, but if Wenna kept such a big revelation from Adeline, would she have kept it from Matius too?

Syd caught a glimpse of his crooked smile as he pulled

away. *Ah, of course he knows.* But he didn't look at her any differently now than he did when she was little. There was a deep quiet about him that was as commanding as it was calming. Safe. Another thing he and Adeline had in common.

Matius turned to Keal, and they started exchanging pleasantries, speaking in trained code about Avant and ACES. Adeline joined them in a circle, and Syd stayed back, leaning against a pile of crates. She looked up and down the alley. It was much shabbier than the main walkways. Instead of stylized quiet tones, the backsides of the businesses were all the same sandy color, left untouched and unfinished. The ground, too, was unfinished. No sea glass here. No tiles of turquoise to catch the sun's light. No tall buildings to provide any shade.

Syd tried to catch Adeline's eye to give her the signal she'd like to get moving. It was a small thing between them, but it meant so much. When either were ready to leave a situation, all they had to do was look at the other in a certain way. But now, Adeline was too busy trying to be part of the conversation with Keal and Matius.

"Llyn's about an hour's walk to the southwest through the Thicket," Matius said and pointed off behind him.

Keal nodded and opened his mouth, "I—"

"Villette is expecting us," Matius cut Keal off. "Llyn is under some light Seliss occupation after having to contract monster patrol to keep the increase in population out of town. They shouldn't give us any trouble. Just some locals close to retirement."

Keal deflated. Syd thought he'd been enjoying being

head of the expedition so far, but now that Matius was here... *Sorry, Keal. You're outranked.* She smirked and walked up to him, nudging his elbow.

"Are we ready then?" Syd specifically asked Keal.

"Oh! Uh—Yes. I think so, yes." Keal nodded, his shoulders straightening again.

"Going back the way we came would be suspicious. Three go in, four come out." Adeline said.

Keal opened his mouth again.

"There is a fence down the way we'll use to exit Beland on the other side," Matius said and started to walk off.

Adeline quickly followed, leaving Keal and Syd to trail behind. Syd studied the picture of father and daughter, matching step for step. Keal huffed, his thunder stolen again.

"Hey. If, y'know, I do actually become Eichon or whatever," Syd waved her hand. "You can be my head strategist."

Keal smirked at that but shook his head. "Nah, I'd rather be your impulsive scientist."

That sinking feeling, the dense one, returned. Swirling, reaching, and expanding. She kept a smile on her face as they walked, trying to stomach the new sensation. A mix of embarrassment for even letting her mind go there, and the tiniest sliver of desire for it to be true.

CHAPTER TEN

Five Years Prior

In the middle of the main hall, the second-year cadets stood together facing the looming doors of the training center.

"Welcome to the first day of your combat training here at ACES!" Instructor Cervet spread her arms wide in front of them in greeting.

Adeline squealed excitedly with a number of others and adjusted the straps of the starter sword's sheath on her shoulders.

"As a reminder, you'll be paired with one of your cadet mates and with a third-year cadet who will guide you inside the training center." Cervet pointed to the door behind her.

Butterflies filled Adeline's stomach. She looked around at who she might be paired with. This is what she's waited a whole year for! Actual combat training! Adeline caught Syd's nervous eyes and her smile fell, but only slightly. She gave Syd what she hoped was an encouraging glance and Syd eventually smirked back.

"There will be one combat specialist, one austral specialist, and one Eheri per group. Only three groups allowed in the center at any one time. There are instructors inside to provide any aid should you need it. However you will be docked in your grading depending on how often and what type of aid you receive. Best marks will be given based on what type of beast you're able to overtake, if any."

Sharp footsteps sounded from around the hall's bend

when Cervet paused for a breath. All heads turned to see Director Rhiuld approach. She ignored the cadets and whispered something in Cervet's ear. Cervet nodded and immediately tapped something into the tablet she cradled in her left arm. Director Rhiuld turned sharply and Adeline followed her stare directly to Syd. Syd averted her eyes to the floor. Adeline shuffled her feet a little, moving closer to Syd. The hallway remained silent until Rhiuld walked away again and out of sight.

"Well, then," Cervet said with a friendly voice. "Let's get started, shall we? The first groups are… Cadets Jori, Long, and Perroux; Cadets Delesense, Faroque, and Cristae; and Cadets Keylen, Orleen, and Rhiuld."

Adeline gave another small squeal and hugged Syd as the cadets all found their way to each other. She teetered back and forth on her feet, and her dark ponytail bobbed along.

"We're sure to get good marks," Adeline whispered as the others started to talk amongst themselves and prepare. "We're with the headmaster's son and he's the best austral specialist in his class. Let's go say hi."

Adeline led Syd over to a skinny boy with uncombed blonde hair and glasses. Easily a foot taller than both of them. He didn't notice their approach as he checked his belt full of silver canisters. Adeline gave a small cough. She'd seen him around before, and of course momma had told her Director Rhuild had a son in the first cohort of ACES students. The boy jumped and Adeline raised an eyebrow.

"Oh…hey," he said absently and finished his checking.

"I'm, um. I'm Keal." He pushed his glasses up by scrunching his nose.

"I'm Adeline. You can call me Ad, though. This is Syd." Adeline extended her hand, an impressively formal move for a twelve-year-old.

Keal looked at it for a moment and shoved his hands into his pockets, shaking his head. "I know who you are. Everyone does. Don't think it's a coincidence we're grouped together."

Syd shifted her weight from one foot to another and Adeline looked between them. She chewed the inside of her lip.

"And you're her shadow?" Keal asked abruptly. "The Eheri? What type?"

Adeline didn't like the way Keal talked to Syd, but was cut off before she could say anything.

"If you don't already know, then you'll just have to wait and find out." Syd said simply.

"Not very good at this teamwork stuff, huh?" Keal replied. "Hopefully you won't kill us in there."

Before Syd could answer, Keal turned and walked toward the door. "C'mon. Let's get this over with."

Adeline didn't follow right away. She stopped to look at Syd, held tilted. Syd gave a little sigh.

"Do you think there will be monsters like the orphanage?" Syd asked.

They both watched the automatic doors slide closed behind Keal. Adeline thought about the question and then grabbed Syd's hand. She didn't like when Syd asked questions like that.

"Whatever's in there we face it. Together," Adeline said. She watched her friend carefully while her heart thudded with excitement. "Right?"

Syd looked away from the door to Adeline with a grin. "Right."

Inside, the air was thick. A carved stone path led through the heavy vegetation, tall with leaves as big as, or bigger than, their heads. Adeline looked around and spotted an instructor stationed at a nearby tree. She opened her mouth to call to them, but then remembered that any aid, even probably just asking where her teammates were—maybe even especially asking where her teammates were—would cost them points. Syd took a deep breath and Adeline looked through the moss, vines, and ferns closing in the farther along the path they walked.

Then, Adeline giggled. She tugged on Syd's hand and bringing them into a small clearing where Keal waited, crouched.

"What did you catch last year?" Adeline asked Keal in a whisper.

Adeline's ears perked at some rustling nearby. For a brief moment everything stilled for her, the leaves suddenly greener, the calls of birds inside the training center's dome carried louder. The sensation subsided when the sound quieted again.

Keal interrupted Adeline's focus. "My group was able to take down a Yellow Spinnard—it only had six legs, still a youngling. We were docked points for that but finished second overall. As far as I know, the more legs, the more points. And even higher marks for no legs."

Adeline looked up at the canopy of leaves. Syd followed her gaze. Birdsongs in here were different from the seagull sounds that echoed in the walkways of the academy.

"And wings?" Adeline asked thoughtfully.

Keal shrugged and then shook his head. "You've got a toy sword and the australs they gave me aren't strong enough for long distances."

Adeline thumbed over to Syd, whose eyes widened, looking between them. Syd shook her head and Adeline frowned. Syd had barely used her majik at all, and she'd only do it when there was no other choice. Adeline wished Syd knew just how much she, Adeline, would give to have such a cool gift from Eher.

"C'mon Syd. You can do it." Adeline chewed on her lip.

"It doesn't work like that." Syd's voice was quiet, distant.

"All you have to do is grab it and bring it closer." Adeline reassured her friend. "Keal and I will take care of the rest." Adeline shot him a glance.

Keal's eyebrows rose. "Wait. You're the gray Eheri, aren't you? Mom told me about you. Well, her advisers were talking about you and I overheard, anyway. Can you stop time? I mean, actually?"

Syd's jaw clenched again and she glared at Keal. Overhead, a bird called again, closer this time. Syd looked to Adeline whose face shot up into a smile. She nodded at Syd.

"Just try," Adeline said.

Syd looked up to where the chirps were coming from. Slowly, she walked closer to the sounds, eyes darting at any movement to catch a glimpse of the bird. Adeline and Keal followed, bent over low. Stalking.

As quietly as she could, Adeline unsheathed her sword, her mouth drying up. She took a steady breath, the hair on her neck raising. Keal unhooked a canister from his belt, thumb on the latch.

Following Syd, Adeline stopped when she stopped and looked up, spotting pure white in the sea of green up above. The bird calls stopped too. Feathers spread, a sharp beak peeking through. Even from this distance, Adeline could tell the bird was at least her size.

"Uh, ok..." Syd said, barely audible. "Stand back, I guess?"

Keal and Adeline took a step back, and Syd shook out her hands. Adeline straightened her shoulders, lining up her stance like da' had taught. She rolled her neck carefully, eyes never leaving her mark. The edges of Adeline's vision began to blur while Syd tried and tried again to get her majik to spark. In the back of her mind, Adeline gave a small prayer to Eher.

Keal sighed and shifted his weight. A twig snapped. Adeline blinked.

Ad's eyes flashed open to where the bird had been. White feathers and beady, red eyes flapped in the trio's direction all at once. Ad counted four wings before she was forced to duck under her arms at the beast's attack. A quick gust of wind hit them, kicking up debris. The beast retreated, and the three looked up to find it hovering just out of reach. Its wings flapped in unison to keep it aloft.

It readied its next attack, head turning from one side to another, and Ad saw the beast lock its eye onto Syd. Fire surged through Adeline's veins in that moment as she drew her strength to draw the beast away from Syd.

Without warning, it made another swoop directly for the group, letting out a cry and showing its double row of tiny, pointed teeth. It snapped at Syd, going for her arm. A moment too late, Adeline watched as a burst of gray flew out from Syd's hand. Running to put herself between Syd and the beast, Adeline collapsed knees-to-ground, protecting her and Syd from the strike with her left arm and side body. Adeline imagined the tearing of the skin, the searing hot pain, the warm blood before she felt it.

When it didn't come, she jumped up and looked around. The beast was pinned, one wing held under an imaginary weight. It screamed, bellowing more wind in their direction. It flapped its three free wings to get airborne again and cried out. To them, or the other beasts in the training center, Adeline didn't know. But the sound pierced her ears and just as Syd had captured their prey, it was Adeline's turn to perform.

She left Syd crouched and out of breath. Keal unleashed a fog of sage and the air smelled of moss and earth. The fog searched and encircled the winged beast, confusing it and making Adeline's job even easier.

She almost smiled when the beast's cries were cut off at her toy blade; at the satisfying tear of metal into flesh.

Present Day

Syd felt more relaxed the deeper into the Thicket they went. The forest's canopy was shady and cool, even though a bit humid. A small breeze kept the air moving through the trees, causing the leaves to shake every now and then. They followed a hidden path over fallen trees, the dead bark full of moss. New life teemed around, under, and inside.

"When was the last time anyone took this route?" Adeline asked.

"Infrequent foot traffic to Llyn. It's a dying town," Matius said. "If someone wanted to visit, they would take an airship from Carden. Villette, in particular, likes that type of solitude and the people there like her enough to give her the old mayor's house because she's able to protect them from any monsters by hiring patrols. No one else there can afford to."

"So, what you're saying is we could have taken a 'ship," Syd said and swatted at some gnats.

"Someone as young as you knowing how to maneuver an airship is a dead giveaway you're not local. Folks from Carden hire pilots and we couldn't risk that either. You three are supposed to be at ACES right now."

I guess, Syd thought but said nothing.

"I think I read somewhere that Eichon Larke was born in Llyn," Keal said to no one.

"Read where?" Adeline asked. "Larke did her best to keep her life a mystery."

Keal smiled. "You don't only find australs during research trips. There are usually historians and archaeologists on those digs too. You'd be surprised what you find out about people, hidden in tombs or written in cast-away diaries. Once we found a locke—"

Leaves rustled loudly, and twigs snapped around them. They quieted immediately, and Matius raised his gloved hand to focus attention on him. Adeline did her best to center among the group, still unarmed and the most vulnerable. They circled around, backs to her.

Silently, Syd drew up energy through her chest and expanded it down to her arms and fingers. Eyes open, alert, she followed the sound of moving foliage. Out of the corner of her eye, Keal quietly lifted the edges of his coat to access his belt. Syd's breath waited, and energy pulsed in her fingertips.

In a single motion, Matius reached and unsheathed his short swords with a deadly silent precision. Syd's eyes darted from him to the tree line again and back. Matius's face was emotionless, his eyes focused, and he moved without a sound. Syd cupped her hands and forced a gray mist to swirl and dance with itself, growing in weight.

A roar rang out, and a black mass shot toward the group. For a moment, all Syd could see was rippling muscles and matted black fur. The smell of the forest was a thick musk. The beast closed the distance in the time of a single heartbeat, and Matius shoved Keal out of the way. Keal fell to his hands, and the bear missed him, but only just.

Adeline took cover behind Matius, and the bear reared onto its back paws and thrashed its head. It towered over them, as tall as it was wide. This wasn't an ordinary bear, Syd knew. Beasts and creatures of all types changed under the influence of Nova's eclipse. Or so her lessons had taught. This was the first time she'd actually seen it.

She looked down, and the mist in her hands spilled over itself before she felt it. Heaviness on her shoulders pushed against her while something deep inside threw her off balance, as if being pushed over a ledge. She caught herself on the ground. But the world was suddenly tilting, turning sideways. Gray majik seeped from her, not just her fingers, but her hands, her wrists, and her arms. It curled onto the forest's floor. Syd tried to look up to see where the bear was, where Matius and Keal and Adeline were, but her neck wouldn't move. Her elbows locked against an invisible force pushing her down, and her majik crawled up her arms, her shoulders. It slithered over the back of her neck, up her cheeks, and static filled her ears.

Barely able to breathe, Syd's elbows shook. White seeped into the edges of her vision, closing in fast. She tried to say something, to scream for help, but her lungs were too tight, her throat too clenched. Her body jolted with each tiny breath she was able to take, getting smaller and smaller with each inhale. An electric haze filled her mind, and her vision faded to white. Everything was buzzing static. One elbow gave out, then the other. The grass was cool against her cheek, against a fire searing her skin.

She thought she heard Adeline call her name, but Syd couldn't move. Pinned with the smell of grass and moss choking and inescapable. Her lungs burned through her chest, her jaw so tight her teeth creaked. She gasped for another breath, and somewhere in the distance, a scream rattled in her skull.

Syd slipped—fell—spilling open in every direction, and the white turned black.

Something tapped Syd's forehead. No, something dripped onto her forehead. She didn't want to open her eyes just yet. She couldn't. But she wished the dripping would stop. Her back was against something hard. The edges of it tickled her skin. She tested her fingers. Grass, and a crunching sound of something being stepped on. Leaves. Something was stepping on leaves. Then, birdsong and some buzzing too close to her ears. The smell of something purple. *Lavender.*

"Ad!" Syd bolted up.

A flash of black fur and gray mists forced her eyes open, and they immediately watered and shut at the brightness. Syd leaned back onto her elbows and used one hand as a visor against the light. Her head pounded and ears pulsed. Something thumped next to her, and before she could respond to the sound, Adeline pulled Syd to her. It was all Syd could do to stay upright, and she gave Adeline more of her weight than she normally would.

"I'm here," Adeline said.

Syd's mind tried to focus, slumped against Adeline. *Gray. Heavy.* "What hap—" Syd whispered.

Syd sunk, eyelids closing on themselves. *No.* She took a sharp inhale and forced herself up again with a grunt. An ache rattled her vision, and the world blurred in shades of green.

Where's Keal? Matius? Syd's head jerked before she

could think about what she was doing. She swayed at the sudden movement, and she grabbed onto Adeline again.

"Hey, hey…" Adeline soothed. "Easy. We're all here."

Syd breathed slowly and relaxed.

"Well," Keal said from a different direction. "Almost everyone. The bear has—is—"

Syd forced her neck to turn her head toward Keal. Through the tiniest slit, her eyes finally focused on something other than green. The white blur of Keal's coat flooded her with comfort.

"Good…" Syd breathed out. "Job."

"N-no, Syd. We didn't—" Adeline said cautiously.

The crunching sound came again, and heavy boots walked up to Syd. Matius crouched down in Syd's line of sight, and thunder pressed against her temples at the quick motion. "Syd," Matius said calmly. "*You* took out the bear."

"Flattened it," Keal said matter-of-factly.

Syd turned her eyes away from Matius to Keal. Focus came in and out. His face was downturned to a heap of dark fur. He nudged it with the toe of his boot.

What? Syd tried to say, but her voice wasn't working. *No. No no. I hadn't wanted it dead. I hadn't meant—*

"Whatever you unleashed," Adeline said. "It completely—the bear is gone."

"What?" Syd repeated, and this time made the sound.

"Just a pile of fur and skin. No bones, even…" Keal picked up a fistful of fur a foot into the air and let it drop. It sloshed when it hit the ground.

Something hot threatened to come up Syd's throat, the acid bitter in the back of her mouth. She turned away, hiding her face against Adeline's shoulder. She swallowed through the gag.

"We need to get her to Villette," Matius said.

Keal and Matius lifted Syd to her feet, and Syd did her best to help. Adeline led the group out of the clearing without another word.

Between each step, Syd slipped back into that dark, expansive place.

"What do you think happened?" Adeline asked.

Syd's neck lulled, and she was jolted back into consciousness.

"I don't know. It was like a shell or a shield," Keal said.

Syd rode a wave of darkness, pulled back again by Adeline's voice.

"Protection majik doesn't work like that. It doesn't..." Adeline struggled. "Shoot off the body like that." Another slip and Syd fell into black. Then up again into white. "Syd doesn't have protection majik."

Then, silence. Footfalls in between her dips. She tried so hard to raise her head. To make sense of their conversation. *Why was my majik pinning me down?*

Another voice surfaced from a corner of her mind, a spot in the darkness. Quiet at first, but strong and calm. *Because you don't know how to control it,* it said.

I've been controlling my majik for years now.

That wasn't your *majik.*

A sharp, cold breath brought her back to Adeline, Matius, and Keal. The ground below her half-stepping feet changed from rocks and twigs to soft soil. Syd groaned, and the group stopped.

"Syd?" Adeline said. "We're almost there. Can you keep going?"

Syd gave a small nod, finally able to lift her head and open her eyes. They focused enough to make out the wheat fields around them and the gray shapes ahead that must have been Llyn.

The sunset filled the sky with red. She took a few steps, easing her grip on Matius and Keal until she could stand on her own. They continued on in silence, meeting the only road into town. Dirt and dust kicked up under foot, and wheat swayed on either side in soft whispers.

Adeline led them into what was once the town square where Villette's house stood. A three-story mansion, its façade peeled and bowed. It was easily the oldest thing amongst its neighbors: an inn, a desolate cafe, and a small store front that said it was a library, but its windows were so filthy with soot that it looked like it might have suffered some kind of fire. Overhead, a small flock of birds called out. Tiny black specks shaped into a V and headed directly for the setting sun.

CHAPTER ELEVEN

Villette was waiting for them at the front steps with her hands folded in front of her. To her left, a soldier in a maroon Seliss uniform stood and stared directly at them. The mansion was framed by thick columns that led the eye up to a balcony in disrepair. The paint on the columns was chipped almost beyond recognition, and the floorboards of the wrap-around porch splintered.

Villette smiled as they neared. Syd stopped walking when her brain registered a Seliss soldier was present. Matius turned, placing a gentle hand on her shoulder and nudging her forward. She looked to Adeline and Keal. Their faces mimicked her own confusion and concern. She was too weak to fight against Matius's guiding hand. Was she wrong to trust him? To trust any of them? Are they going to take Adeline? Matius wouldn't give his daughter to the enemy, would he? Maybe. Maybe as trade for some kind of cease-fire bargain against the hacking attempts. Syd's feet continued to move forward against her will. It was only one soldier. Surely, they could take him. But not if Matius was against them.

Syd's breathing became more rapid the closer she got. At the front steps, Villette bowed her head. She turned to enter the house wordlessly, and they followed. The soldier remained outside, turning his gaze away as they passed.

Inside, the windows of Villette's home were boarded up. The dim light from the spaces between the boards illuminated a foyer that was more an art gallery than an entry point. Numerous masterpieces crammed against each other on the walls, barely giving each other enough room to breathe. Thick, dark strokes mingled with delicate landscapes. Most were crooked, fighting for space against the mix of silver, bronze, and wood frames. In the corners were pedestals with vases and crumbling statues. Syd's head spun, and she reached to steady herself on the door frame.

Matius moved, catching Syd swiftly. Keal helped to bring her to a couch in the next room, her vision blurring before finally giving out.

Birdsong, chirps, squawks, and a melody crept into Syd's consciousness. Something was over her eyes. She ripped away whatever was sealing her vision, a brief moment of panic subsiding when she stared at the damp cloth in her hands. She scanned the room, recollecting the string of events last night.

Light streamed through boarded windows. Boarded windows. *Llyn. Villette.* There had been a Seliss soldier outside. Everyone helped her to the couch. After that, it was all black. She sat up on the small bed made with pastel sheets and blankets, a soft mattress. No headache or muscle aches. No dizziness.

She tested her balance by standing. All seemed to be good there. She then leaned over and grabbed the shoes someone had removed and made for the door after putting them on. The floor creaked under her boots, and she winced at the sound. Everything beyond the door was quiet. The brass doorknob, worn with age, mocked her.

Okay, she said to herself. *If the door is locked, you're in real trouble.*

She reached out, gripped the handle, and twisted. The door swung open freely. Not like she knew what she would do if it had been locked anyway. Break through the boarded windows? And then what? The paranoia was a real hangover, adrenaline rising fast and falling faster.

The darkened hallway outside smelled musty and unused, but was otherwise neat and plain. Syd crept along the narrow hall that led to a banister, an identical hall was on the other side of the stairs. Below was the entry way. The art on the walls, from this angle, almost made more sense. There seemed to be a rhythm to it, at least—a gradual progressive style and then sometimes not so gradual. Only now did she notice they were all landscapes.

Something moved out of the corner of the room, and Villette's pale face smiled up to her.

"Good morning, Syd," she said lightly. "How are you feeling?"

She returned to dusting a vase, without waiting for a response. Syd's forehead knotted. *Come to think of it I'm...* "Fine." No sensitivity to the light that was coming up from below. She felt her heart beat steadily. Her breath was even.

"Where's everyone?" Syd asked as she descended the stairs that emptied into the drawing room off the foyer.

"Matius and Adeline are patrolling. They graciously agreed to take over for the time being. I'm glad I was able to call the soldiers off or we'd have very little privacy. Locals are loyal, but they are still trained enemies. I think Keal is helping Mrs. Hersh pick some flowers."

The idea of Keal holding a basket and frolicking in a field somewhere in this tiny town lightened Syd's mood for the moment. She reached the bottom step, and Villette rounded the corner to greet her. The sudden movement made Syd jump. She kept her distance, and her mind automatically started calculating all the possible ways to the exit, including launching her body off the rickety banister. Her hand gave it a little test for sturdiness.

"Did you rest well?"

Syd nodded slowly, face and body following Villette's movements.

"I'm sorry if you're feeling a little edgy. The side effects of my healing can do that." Villette moved to place her hand on Syd's arm, and she instinctively dodged the move. "Ah. It will wear off soon, I promise."

Patience dawned on Villette's face, and she smiled. Syd released her grip on the railing. Villette was rarely around when Syd would visit Adeline. Now that she thought of it, she knew very little about Adeline's aunt, other than she was the Eichon's twin sister. Syd hadn't even known Villette was Eheris until recently. *If she was going to harm me, she would have already,* Syd reasoned. Might as well not waste the opportunity to ask questions.

"You're a healer Eheri?"

"Yes and no." Villette raised her eyebrow. "Wenna and I share in our healing abilities, but mine are far more acute in comparison since her transference."

Syd studied Villette's face. She wasn't exactly identical to Wenna, but their looks were close, and they shared many of the same features that had also passed on to Adeline. When she smiled, Villette's eyes crinkled in the same way Adeline's did.

"But surely you didn't travel all this way to talk about my majik, did you?" Villette asked.

Even though she knew it was a leading question, Syd couldn't help herself.

"I mean, sort of, right? I know we're here to train or whatever, but do you really expect us—me—to blindly buy into all this? I'm not exactly used to the idea of being an Eichon when it was supposed to be Adeline."

Villette raised her hand to object. She shook her head and motioned for both of them to sit. Not really knowing what else to do, Syd took a seat in an aging armchair, its deep mahogany chipped so badly that it gave way to the tender beige and tan underneath the veneer. She looked at the floor. Villette folded her hands in her lap.

"What happened in the forest, Sydney?"

Syd's mouth ticked to the side. *Guess we aren't talking about what I want to talk about anymore.* "Didn't the others tell you?"

"Yes, but I'm asking *you*."

Syd leaned back into the chair. Her leg bounced, and she chewed at her lip. *Fine.* "I don't…really know. It was like my majik was…crushing me. Pushing me down. Trying to harm me. I couldn't control or hone it in any way. It took me over completely. And by the time I came to, the bear was dead."

The words rushed from her mouth at the same time she realized, "I thought it was going to kill me." Syd's throat tightened at that, cold and damp fear flooded her palms suddenly.

Villette sat attentive and patient. "Wenna believes I have something to teach you," she said plainly.

"Can you?" Syd asked. Her voice sounded more desperate than she had intended. The thought of losing control again, of her majik taking over, of not being able to stop it made Syd's eyes sting.

"Wenna sent you to me because she believes you aren't training and mastering your majik at the academy. She thinks I can give you something different. A different way *in*, so to speak."

Villette wasn't answering the question. Syd looked up from the floor. She scanned Villette's face again for anything, any hint of what the hell the woman was trying to say. Nothing. She was placid as ever with that stupid, gentle smile on her face.

Syd's jaw clenched. "Villette, I don't know what I'm supposed to do here. At all. With any of this. With being chosen as Eichon. With Adeline *not* being chosen as Eichon. With the fucking moon falling." She pressed her palms against her eyes and rubbed her forehead, sighing out. "And now this." She motioned to herself. "My majik? It's never done this before. I don't know what's supposed to happen now."

Villette raised her hand again, and Syd shook her head, annoyed by the silencing gesture. "Whatever is supposed to happen, will," she said.

"Will what?"

"Happen."

Syd's face flushed with heat immediately. "That's it? That's all you're going to give me?" She stood, and the backs of her knees scooted the chair back a few inches. "How is *that* helpful?" Her voice rose, and she didn't care. "With any of this?"

"Syd," Villette said calmly. "It's the most helpful thing I possibly could give you. I know it may not seem like much now, but this is what I teach. If there's one thing my sister's gift has given me, it's the simple truth that we can only accept what is and act accordingly."

"Take that soldier outside my door yesterday," Villette said. "Of course, I do not *want* Seliss occupying my town. But, the monsters outside are aggressive and Llyn doesn't have the manpower it once did. I knew I was putting all of us at risk by having them here, but I was also putting the residents of Llyn at a greater risk by not. I concluded that a few lazy soldiers would have been no match for you, and accepted everything would work out the way it should. Now, the soldiers have gone *because* the four of you arrived, giving everyone what they wanted. A little faith can go a long way."

Unbelievable. Syd splayed out her hands. "Faith? Now we're talking faith?" Her throat burned.

"No," Villette's voice turned stern. "We're talking about what *is*." She quickly brushed some of her hair behind her ear and took a breath. "Now, let's go back to the beginning. Please tell me what happened in the forest yesterday."

I did! Syd clenched her fists to keep herself from

screaming at Villette. *I couldn't control my majik and it killed. It killed completely, without my permission, without my say so! It came without my calling, and it pinned me down. I was an afterthought, an inconvenience. It did whatever it wanted.* Syd's eyes widened with understanding. *My majik acted on its own accord.*

She shivered, trying to shrug the chill of realization. *If I'm supposed to be the damn Eichon, real or fake, that's a fucking problem. If I can't control it, no one can and no one can help me.*

"Look," Syd said through a clenched jaw. "I need answers, not more questions."

Syd rounded the chair and headed for the door. If Villette wasn't going to help her, then at the very least she wasn't going to make this easy for Villette. Syd heard Villette stand behind her. *Fine. Let her follow me.* The door gave a satisfyingly loud smack against its frame as Syd left.

CHAPTER TWELVE

Syd's pace slowed only once she was out of the pathetic town square. Syd passed a few shops and crossed over a stone bridge that overlooked a mostly dry creek. The crumbling cobblestone quickly turned back into a dirt path. Wheat fields to either side, the hazy browns and tans danced in the breeze. Judging by the sun, it was probably just around lunch time back at the academy. She stopped, catching her breath a little and letting the openness settle in around her.

Her shoulders dropped only after she realized they were reaching for her ears. She rolled her neck, wiggling tension out of her arms. Looking out to the horizon, the clear day gave her breath an expansiveness she hadn't felt since leaving ACES. As frustratingly opaque as Villette was being, Syd's mouth twitched with a moment of guilt. She inhaled. Villette was the only person who seemed to know what the hell was going on, even if she wasn't saying exactly what it was. Even Matius, to some degree, didn't carry the same certainty as Villette. *No, not certainty. Something else. Understanding.*

Syd stared out at the fields until she felt herself calmed down from her outburst, her inner self silent. The whispers of the fields around her slowly, quietly, started to harmonize into a static. A bubble of anxiety formed in her belly at the sudden solitude. She tried to ease the rising energy, but it came too quickly—a wave cresting and dragging her into its undertow before she could even gasp.

She looked at her hands, wisps of gray starting to trail out from her fingertips. She shook them, trying to get rid of it. When that didn't work, she tried rubbing them together, but that only made it worse, and the gray became denser.

I didn't call you out! A panicked voice rose in her head.

And then that calmer voice, a lower tone, a second-self chimed in. *No*, it said, *you didn't.*

She stared, frozen in place. A pressure building once again on her shoulders, behind her eyes. They started to bulge, and she became unable to close her eyelids. Locked in place. The mist continued to pour, cascading down and mixing with the breeze all around her. She slumped forward finally, the hold releasing, and her lungs began to tighten as they had in the forest. The pain increased with each breath, shards of ice and heat stabbing her insides.

We could flatten this place, the second-self said. *Eventually, we could flatten everything. All of it.*

"Wh-why?" She heard herself say out loud to only herself. *Am I losing my mind?* The pain radiated down to her stomach, and she bent over fully with her hands on her knees. The streams of majik started to envelope her legs. She steadied herself, locking her elbows against the weight piling on her back.

No... She echoed this over and over in her mind, her eyes locked open and looking at the ground, at the dirt. The edges of her vision blurred. Her breath shortened before she felt it, a million tiny stabs over and over with each inhale. At the edges of her sight, she saw desolate fields instead of the lush ones she knew were there, and tumbled buildings ahead and behind her. *No.* There were no birds. No breeze. No sounds. Complete silence. In the center of it all, she saw herself, standing all alone. Terror shot through everything, the image darkening. She braced for the black. *No.*

"No!" She forced her lungs to carry her voice over the waves of yellow in the fields and through the white clouds in the sky that she knew was there, even if she couldn't see them.

She waited before taking her next inhale. Her vision slowly started to sharpen back in. She tested a breath, the pain subsiding. She drank the air in steady deep gulps against her erratic heartbeat drumming in her ears. She tried to stand up. No resistance. Finally, she looked at her hands and turned them over. The last of the majik dissipated and was carried away in the wind.

No, she thought one more time and headed toward the far end of town in search of anyone but herself.

At the other end of the village, Syd stopped at a church. Banging, metal hitting metal, and an occasional chitter or yelp rang from the spire that doubled as a clock tower. She looked up, shielding her eyes from the mid-day sun, to see light hair peeking out from the open clock face. Confused why Keal would be here, she walked through open oak doors into the vestibule. The doors gave easily without a single squeak. Grease pooled at the edges of the door frame and onto the floor. Someone had recently oiled the hinges.

She turned in the direction of louder yelps coming from

above and moved inward toward the gray stone pews and the massive altar at the far end of the room. Whatever Rhurg these people worshiped here, their faces carved into the walls, had long been worn down with age. The yelps continued and led her to a spiral staircase made of the same cracked and chipped stone as the pews.

In the attic, Keal sat hunched over a pile of gears that were two times his size. Lingering dangerously at his heels was a tawny ball of fluff. When it noticed her, it quickly scampered and ran to hide inside a bundle of lesser clock cogs.

Syd coughed, startling Keal on purpose. "Villette said you were helping someone with their flowers?"

Keal jumped. "Dammit, Syd." He inhaled, inspecting his work. "I was, but the old bat turned me away. Said I'd be more useful trying to fix this clock." He sat aside an ancient hammer. "I have no idea what I'm doing, but I think I'm making a good show of trying, right?"

The tawny fur ball reappeared at Keal's feet, and something like a paw scuffed at his left boot. He bent down to pick it up. "And this little guy is very confused. I found him up here hours ago, by himself. He hasn't left my side since and I can't find his nest, or any of his litter."

He held the cub under its front legs for Syd to see. A small snout, with large ears and black eyes looked back at her, and Syd's cheeks pulled her lips up into a smile. Then, it gave out a sudden cry, and Keal returned to cradling the floxling.

"Motherhood looks good on you." Syd's smile grew wider at Keal's upturned face.

He rolled his eyes half-heartedly, never fully taking his stare away from the small thing in his arms. Then, he turned to place it on the floor, but not without a quick kiss on its head. A chuckle tickled Syd's throat, and she couldn't contain it. Keal gave a smirk, ran his fingers through his hair, and motioned for her to sit next to him on the giant gear.

"I see you're feeling better," he said.

Syd found an uncomfortable groove to adjust into. "Did you know the plan was to leave me alone with that woman?" She pointed off in the direction of Villette's house. She propped her head in her hand, elbow on knee for support. She looked at him, then to the floor, and let her gaze grow distant while it followed the grains of the shoddy wood. "I woke up convinced you all had led me into a trap."

Keal nodded. "Yeah, Vi said that might happen. Did she talk to you this morning?"

"Vi? We're calling her Vi now?" Syd's temper flared, but she stabled it with a sigh. "If by talk you mean ask me the same question over and over and never answer mine, sure. We talked."

"Ask what question?"

"She wanted to know what happened in the woods yesterday, even after you all had told her."

Keal took a moment to reply and let the floxling back into his lap. It plopped down and nestled in for a nap in his body heat. "I don't think she wanted the details of the attack Syd. What you did yesterday was—"

"I don't know what I did yesterday!" Her cheeks flushed with heat, and she rubbed her face. "I don't want to talk about it."

"But Vi does," Keal said. "And, she probably has her reasons."

Syd turned her face from him and stared out the opening of the clock. "I said I don't want to talk about it."

"Ok. Then *I* will." His tone shifted into teacher-mode. "Do you know why I'm here, Syd? Why I didn't just go back to ACES where I could continue my research safe inside a lab?"

She shrugged lazily at him, leaning back onto her hands and turned her face up to him. "The *adventure*?" She let the sarcasm drip heavily from her mouth.

"Please. You know I'm happiest curled up with my books in my room. I came along because *Malvuk* asked me to. Specifically. Once all of Wenna's people got wind that you're to be the next Eichon in the midst of everything else, he came to me immediately and told me I needed to watch you, to look out *for* you.

"No one knows what you're capable of, Syd, not even you because you never pushed yourself at the academy. You kept your majik safe, mastering some of it, sure. We all noticed. It's why Boylt was always on your ass. They all wanted to ease you into your powers because we can only guess at how great they can be. But you stayed safe and fought everyone every step of the way, so we never could get a measure of what you could do."

He paused only to catch his breath, as if all of that had been bottled up and ready to explode. "And now? Now you're stuck in a place you've never been with only a handful of people who know *what* you are, and you can't control your power. I'm here for the same reason *you're* here. To figure this out. What happened yesterday was only a taste of what you can do. And, frankly, I'm scared of it."

Keal quieted finally, his chest rising and falling rapidly with a look of shock on his face as he realized what he had just said.

"You think I'm not scared?" The guilt that came with his words made Syd's voice small. "I didn't ask you to come, you know. Remember that. That was Malvuk. But, you're right. I can't control this, and I don't even know where to begin. And yes, it's my fault, alright? I don't want any of this though. I don't want my gravity majik and I sure as hell don't want to be the damn Eichon. I don't want to think about Nova crashing into Terrus. I don't want to think about the transference and what it'll mean for Adeline and me.

"And yet here I am! In the middle of fucking nowhere, with a girlfriend who is trying not to hate me for overshadowing her entire future, a woman who talks in riddles, and the town's new handyman and-slash-or zookeeper! Not to mention Matius who, I'm sure, is here to make sure everything goes according to plan...whatever the hell that is."

Syd's chest felt like it was going to explode, and she stood so fast the floxling jumped and ran into a pile of gears for protection. She clenched her fists, ready to fight something, anything. Even Keal if she had to.

"Four days ago, we were all doing what we do: training, teaching, and dodging," Syd said. "That was the beat of life I liked. Everything is out of control. We have no clue what we're doing!"

Keal didn't stand to fight. He didn't even raise his

voice. "I think what happened yesterday was exactly because we're so…out of our element. Confused. We were all afraid, but you have something far more terrifying inside you. You can't control it. It's kind of like australs, you know? You can't control what you fear."

Syd's fingers slowly release from their curl, lessening the pressure of her nails digging into her palms. The lump in her throat ached.

"It's okay to be afraid, Syd. It's natural," Keal reasoned. "But it's only when you can give a name to what you're afraid of can you then start to control it. Once you accept that, then we can start to work with it instead of against it."

Slick heat spilled from her bottom eyelid, and she blinked the tears away before more could come. "Where's Adeline?" she asked.

Syd then jumped at the feeling of something grazing her leg. The floxling had reemerged at her boot and raised a paw to her.

"It's around midday," Keal said. "I suspect Adeline and Matius are headed to the pub for lunch." He scooped up the creature into his arms. "Maybe we should go too. I got to find this little guy some grub anyway."

He started to walk away, but Syd lingered behind. When he reached the stairs, he turned back to look at her.

"We're all here for you, no matter our reasons." Keal stared at Syd. "You can yell and swear at us, threaten to fight us, but we're here. And we're not going anywhere unless you do. You know, like in combat training? When they tell us supports to watch after our fighter? You're the fighter now.

The battle hasn't changed, just the roles. Use your supports well and we all reap the rewards."

She said nothing, and he left. She listened to him make it down the stairs to the ground floor. Her ear followed the thud of his footsteps as he walked away, and the almost-silent swing of the church doors, and then, outside, on the dirt road below, she heard the floxling chitter.

Keal chittered back.

CHAPTER THIRTEEN

Four Years Prior

Adeline could tell in the way Syd clenched and unclenched her fists that she had been pushed too far today. She watched from afar, minding the hangar's painted lines indicating where it was safe for visitors to stand. Syd shouted over to Jo, her voice muffled by the loud engines. Syd had been spending every spare minute in the shop lately, and when Adeline couldn't find her, looking here first was a safe bet. When they noticed Adeline, they both walked over to her.

"Syd…" Jo said in warning. "Take a lap with Adeline. If anyone gives you two trouble about it, tell 'em to come talk to me."

The crease in Jo's forehead made Adeline's eyebrows raise. Syd's shoulders collapsed, and she shook her head, but without a word, allowed Adeline to lead her out of the shop and into the bright, clean hallways with air full of salt and sea. They both took a breath.

"So, what happened?" Adeline asked.

Syd shoved her hands in her jumper pockets. Adeline looked at the floor as they walked around the main hall's bend, past the cafeteria.

"Told Boylt to fuck off. Rhiuld is going to lose her mind."

Adeline stopped, mouth in a gasp, and she couldn't help but laugh.

"Really? Why?" Adeline asked with a grin and resumed their pace.

"Yeah..." Syd shrugged. "I just—being here, doing what's asked. It's easy for you. Everyone's able to do what's asked no problem. And I'm just left feeling tired with bad marks. Moons, I don't want to face Rhiuld right now."

Syd groaned as they pass the infirmary, following the curved hall.

"Mother wouldn't have put you here for no reason. What if..." Adeline paused, an uneasiness coming over her. "What if we see if Dr. Malvuk is in? I think I heard Keal say something about him visiting yesterday."

"That creep? What would he do?"

"Well...he is Terrus' best scientist." Adeline reasoned with herself. "Maybe he knows why you're having trouble?"

Syd sighed but nodded. "Anything's better than going to Rhiuld."

Dr. Iver Malvuk's satellite offices were located at the bottom-most floor of ACES, under sea-level. Syd and Adeline walked the gray halls, in a fishbowl with open ocean on either side. The water's surface reflected and magnified the sun, light dancing on the gray, cement floors until they got to the door they wanted and knocked. There was a crash, something like glass shattering within, but no answer. Through the goosebumps that ran up and down her spine, Adeline squared her shoulders and knocked again.

"Dr. Malvuk?!" she shouted through the door.

There was some mumbling, and the doors swung open.

An old, gaunt face greeted them, eyes hidden and distorted behind goggle lenses of differing strengths. Adeline tried to smile.

"Oh what is it now?!… Oh! It's dear little Adeline and who's this…?" Dr. Malvuk peered around Adeline to Syd. "Ah, the little gray Eheris is it? Hm. What could they want?"

Adeline gave a cough; a heady, sour smell was coming from the open door now. She looked past him to a lab table, tinctures of varying colors smoking or billowing.

"Well," she started. "Syd has been having some trouble in her majik classes and… Um. We were wondering if maybe you could help."

Malvuk lifted his goggles from his face and stood at his full height, which was still hunched. The last time Adeline had visited him was when she still lived in the Tower. The persistent rumors of human experimentation that followed Malvuk's work ran rampant. His bright blue eyes shone in the hallway's reflecting lights, a sparkle or hunger; Adeline wasn't sure.

"Ah yes. Well, come in."

Adeline looked back to Syd and gave a reassuring glance. Inside, the sour stench was almost suffocating. Adeline's nostrils flared, and her eyes tried to blink away the sting. He took them to the back of the plain lab, past a few rows of metal tables with individual overhead lighting. Computer terminals lined the walls every so often, numbers and letters scrolling quickly on their screens. A quiet, dripping noise was coming from somewhere indiscernible in the dark corners of the room. Adeline's arm hair stood up on its own accord.

Malvuk retreated into one of the dark corners and flipped a switch. A light fizzled on, revealing a reclined chair with metal arm-like attachments of varying instruments: mirrors, magnifiers, sharp silver ends. He patted the seat, looking at Syd, and wheeled a stool out from the darkness.

"Come now. Let's have a look at you."

"I'm fine, really," Syd insisted.

Syd looked to Adeline for help, but Adeline's mouth was dry. She gave Syd a shrug and a nod, encouraging her to be a little more honest. A couple days ago, Syd had shared she was having trouble finding her majik and momma never had that trouble. Adeline then looked to Dr. Malvuk as he brought up Syd's physical charts on a computer terminal. If momma trusted Dr. Malvuk, maybe they should too.

Syd did eventually obey, and when Malvuk brought something sharp to her inner elbow, she reached for Adeline's hand and squeezed. Adeline squeezed back.

Present Day

As much as she did want to see Adeline, Syd found herself avoiding the pub when she reentered the town square. She even avoided glancing in the direction for fear Adeline would be in the doorway. Guilt crept up again, and she forced her feet toward Villette's house. As always, Keal was right. Syd knew she shouldn't have stormed off, and that she should apologize.

It made her feel special to know ACES faculty had

been looking after her all these years, even Malvuk. Maybe even specifically Malvuk. Special, in the worst possible way. All the time, energy, effort, and she repaid them by what? Slacking off, making a mockery of it all. And now, it—everything—was all too real, too heavy. Whatever was causing her majik to act out against her would need to be sorted. She needed to get a handle on it, and as much as her jaw clenched at the idea of giving in, she knew it was true. It—she—was suddenly too dangerous, and it would only be a matter of time before someone would get hurt.

She may not want to be the next Eichon, real or fake, but everyone else—*all the adults around here, anyway*—seemed to want her to. So what if she'd allowed herself to daydream a little on the walk back? There was no harm in that.

Maybe she would even enjoy it. But right now, it was all too much, and she couldn't do anything, really, but play her part in whatever plans she'd been recruited to. That's what good soldiers did. They took orders, and they acted on them. She could, at the very least, do that, and right now, her order was to train.

She came back from her thoughts and found herself at the front of Villette's house.

"Villette?" she called loudly. No one answered. "Hello?" Nothing.

She took in the pieces of art in the foyer again, this time not in a rush or the haze of recovery. There was still only a hint of organization, but the more she looked at the varying styles, the more they seemed to complement one another and tell a story. Of what, she didn't know, but some were grouped together in like colors, some by theme. Most were landscapes, but there were a few abstracts too.

She walked over to a painting of a meadow, the paint so thick that it created a landscape of its own. The scene was an open field, dotted with the yellows and blues and pinks of wildflowers. In the background was a blurry, unfocused forest, likely a vantage point somewhere nearby in the Thicket.

It was a simple scene. The sky was a clear blue. The tall grass and blooms seem to sway gently in the wind, paint strokes leaning toward the right edge of the frame. What caught the viewers' attention the most, though, was a single white feather floating just off-center and just above the swaying grasses. It seemed misplaced, as if it was transposed into the scene after the fact. There wasn't any indication of where the feather had come from, even though it was in a perfectly natural place for it to exist. And yet, it was foreign. It had no reference.

Syd frowned.

"That's one of my favorites," Villette's voice came from behind.

Syd jumped instinctively and turned around. "Villette, I'm sorry for how I acted. There isn't really any excuse. I know I need your help and, I think, more importantly, I want it," she said.

Villette smiled widely, "It's quite alright. I've taken much worse, I can assure you."

Her eyes focused behind Syd. "My curators tell me the artist was an Eheri from Darmar, like you. When she made this one, she'd never even seen the Thicket, only read about it in books. This was her rendition. When she became famous and traveled to Carden, she would add bits of herself to her paintings before handing off a bought piece. Something about wanting to play with expectations. It became her trademark."

Villette shrugged and let her smile fade.

"But, enough about art history. You probably have quite a few questions by now?"

She led Syd out of the room and to the backside of the house that butted directly against the tree line. The rotting porch overlooked a small stream below and down a hill. Syd peered over the edge, not daring to trust the railings with her weight. Below there was a small cluster of skarpines by the water's edge, their red scales glinting off the afternoon sun and their poisonous tails always positioned and ready to attack. From up here they looked no bigger than the average scorpion, but these were likely half Syd's size and not yet fully grown.

Villette took her seat on an old porch swing. She motioned for Syd to join her. She adjusted her shawl once, and Syd turned her eyes downcast. A small beetle crawled confidently toward the edges of the warped floor.

"So," Syd started, trying to find a way to not sound needy, ungrateful, or just plain stupid. *Always leave room for what you cannot see*, Boylt had said during her first year. Back when she had paid attention. Back when she had cared. There really was no delicate way to ask this.

"You can really help me?"

Villette took the question in thoughtfully. "Only time will tell, but I do believe so. True, you were sent here to train, but given the recent developments, I have a working theory of what may be happening, at the very least. You know about the Madness?"

Syd nodded and said, "A few years ago, we started learning about it in our classes. Well, I guess more about which Eichons it affected and what happened."

"Yes, I suppose they wouldn't need, nor want, to cover more than that," Villette said. "The Madness is our, frankly, poor way of describing what we believe to be the cost of using powerful majik. It's why we see it in Eichons and not the general Eheri population. Up until now, like all Eheri, the balance is maintained through physical fatigue. But, your powers are growing and it could explain what is happening, is what I'm saying. It looks very similar from my perspective."

Syd grew quiet and reflected on any lessons she could recall. Eichons who went Mad did things like commission questionable experimentation and new technology. It's how scientists like Malvuk came to be, and how the bioengineered PRISM soldiers were created. Others, more thirsty for power and conquest, destroyed cities only to raise new ones in their own honor.

"And you can help me get rid of it?" Syd asked.

"I've been known to be able to, yes. Syd." She leaned closer. Her voice quieted, but not fully a whisper. "Do you know how Wenna came to be Eichon?"

Syd searched through what little information she'd gathered over the years in majik history and theory classes.

"Um, Malvuk discovered her and presented her to Eichon Ashe."

She knew there was more to it than that, but she couldn't remember. She looked at Villette, into eyes like Adeline's. But they weren't actually like Adeline's now that Syd was closer. They weren't brown with deep streams of varying shades. They were black, fully black, surrounded by stark white. Villette lacked irises entirely. Syd's eyebrows lowered in question, hiding her shock.

"That's the short version," Villette said. "The longer version includes a lot more sacrifice. Of which, I was one, and Wenna, to a different degree. But that's not my story to tell."

Syd's jaw went slack, and Villette shook her head. "I thank you for whatever sympathy you're going to give, but it isn't needed. I tell you this so that maybe you'll understand why I choose to accept things as they are and not fight against it for something different. That's the key to not only mastering your majik, but conquering the Madness as well.

"At age thirteen, Zevir's research labs became my home. Wenna's too. Under Eichon Ashe's guidance, and as part of the peace agreement between Zevir's Novari and Rhurgari citizens, the recruitment for the Eichon's army began. The negotiations stated that the Novari were free to begin recruiting young Eheri for the army if the Rhurgari scientists were allowed a 'pick of the litter', so to speak. What they likely left out of your lesson was that during the reign of Ashe's predecessor, Eichon Herana, Malvuk was a rising star. Herana provided much of Malvuk's initial funding, in fact, and quickly promoted him and fast-tracked his experimental research, growing his team far and wide.

"Anyway, the two of us and Reth were part of the hand-selected Eheri and that's when we all first met Malvuk. He wasn't always so…" Villette's voice trailed.

"…Creepy?" Syd suggested.

Villette gave a half-shrug, "I was going to say 'intense'. It came to light eventually that the Rhurgari scientists in charge of, well, rounding up the most talented young Eheri were acting under Ashe's orders directly. She had become obsessed with finding the most *worthy* to become her successor. She called it 'progress', a way to a better future, and had great support among the people. Malvuk, however, was not one of them.

"On a good day, Ashe wanted the best and brightest by her side. But the good days were few and far between. More often than not, her intentions were seized by vengeful jealousy of any majik user whose powers showed promise. When Ashe ordered Malvuk to run experiments to see who was the strongest of our group, he tried to protect us. He feared that bringing such a concentrated amount of Eheri to Zevir would end in genocide. So, he locked us away in various research labs his team were using at the time, outside of Zevir."

Villette paused, taking in a breath long enough for Syd's mind to start filling with questions. Why hadn't she heard about any of this? She knew about the negotiations, sure, but only that they had ushered in a sort of peace between the two warring religious sects at the cost of Eheri freedom. And things were, at least, better now. Recruitment was no longer mandatory, and families of a young Eheri were given what appeared to be a choice, however slanted that choice might actually be.

Villette continued, "At the core of his mission, Malvuk still had to report findings to Ashe and couldn't very well come up empty handed. It was Wenna who volunteered. She wasn't the strongest among us, but she was still talented in her healing majik. Talented enough to attract the attention of Ashe, anyway. No matter how much I protested and begged her not to, afraid of what might happen to her when out from under Malvuk's protection, she refused to listen. Even Malvuk was reluctant to agree but eventually he had to submit *something* to Ashe, and that something, in the end, was Wenna.

"While Wenna grew up in Ashe's shadow, Reth and I grew up in Malvuk's. Not that we were immune to his own special brand of Madness. While we waited for Wenna to transcend, Malvuk grew more and more hungry for a way people could defend themselves against mad Eichons and stop something like this from ever happening again. It's this research that lent him Seliss's ear over the years, and his resulting privileges between both Seliss and the Eichon.

"Six years we were subjected to Malvuk's experiments while he attempted to replicate a way for normal folks to harness energies like the Eheri. Six years, torn apart and sewn back together in almost complete isolation by a man we must now work alongside to help save the planet. All in the name of progress, all in the name of changing the course. Again.

"I've found the strength that comes from discovering peace in one of the most inhospitable circumstances. Strength over the voices of rage, of despair, of the depths at which one so young can sink to when put on operating tables over and over and over again. Once Wenna and I were reunited after her transference I taught her this too, after she confessed her own fears about a Madness she felt holding her captive.

"Based on what your comrades told me of the incident with the bear, you have an uncommonly powerful amount of majik in you that will only expound should a transference be necessary before we're able to correct Nova's course. As I said, powerful majik comes at a price. I imagine that price is already starting to be paid."

Syd stared at the floor in silence once Villette finished, her mind filled with so much new information it was unable to make any of her own thoughts.

"I suspect," Villette said eventually. "You will want to ask me if there's a way to change the Council's mind on choosing you."

Syd tried to swallow, but her mouth was dry. "Is there?"

"No." Villette turned her face away from Syd's staring out at the trees. "For all of Ashe's Madness, there was a shimmer of brilliance in her initial idea. We will need someone powerful enough to either calm or intimidate—likely both—the people once the project is complete."

Syd's stomach sank, and her posture sagged helplessly. The will to fight drained from her. Even if she fought, where would she go? Where would she hide? The only people she ever knew to trust were all right here. The world suddenly felt tiny, and she was nothing more than a speck.

"That's it, huh?" Syd gave a long, slow sigh. "I have no say whatsoever?"

"There are some things larger than you, me, Seliss, and

even Wenna. You will be a very fine Eichon, once we understand your majik a little better. But, I'm not here to convince you. I'm here to teach you."

Syd leaned back and stared up, the faint white of Nova and Runar set against the blue afternoon sky. She closed her eyes. At some point during the silence, the swing started to rock, creaking in both directions.

"So, what happens now?" Syd asked.

"Really, that's up to you," Villette said. "But, at some point, we do need to talk about what happened in the forest."

"Oh."

And that's all Syd could say. The quiet surrounding the two of them gave Syd's mind space to think. The words were trying to form, but they kept coming up in the wrong order, in a way that wasn't quite right. They weren't fully explaining what happened. Every so often, Syd took an inhale as if ready to say something but would promptly shut it down again when no words came. It all felt like some kind of test. The kind that gave only a single chance to get right.

"I," Syd's mind raced to simplify as much as possible and focus on a single, accurate point. "I was unable to control my powers."

Her shoulder slouched forward again, and she found herself not worried, but disappointed. Keal's words rang in her head. *No one knows what you're capable of, Syd, because you never pushed yourself at the academy.*

Now it all felt like a responsibility she didn't even know she had to begin with. Was it really her fault if she never knew *how* special she was? She was just an orphan from

Darmar with *unique* abilities, but not special. Surely not this powerful, in any case. But had she known? Or wished? Somewhere deep inside herself something stirred, rolled, and tumbled around, as if restless. Should she have tried? Should she now?

Villette broke Syd's thoughts. "This next question, I don't want to hear what you think you should say. There's no sense in hiding any longer."

Syd nodded and braced herself.

"How does it feel to know you're capable of more?"

You mean aside from: afraid. Like I was going to die, crushed and suffocated, and terrified. She kept these thoughts to herself with a deep inhale. They swirled around together in her mind until they tired of being the loudest voices, and gave way to something else. A sense. A feeling. She exhaled and wrapped her arms around her middle, hunching over and searching for...something. Anything. The truth. A small surge of adrenaline hit her chest and slowly expanded. Blood rushed to her face and turned it hot. Her heartbeat pounded in her ears.

"Powerful," Syd whispered. "I feel...powerful."

CHAPTER FOURTEEN

They sat in the quiet for some time. Syd took in her words, drank them up, as they lingered between her and Villette. The breeze rustled the leaves of the trees. The swing's rusted chains creaked. The sun reflected off the stream below. Finally, Villette stood.

"We'll start training tomorrow," she said.

Syd's heart plummeted. The last thing she wanted was to be alone right now. Alone with so many questions. With so few answers. With herself.

"Where are you going?"

"I have some business with the people here. I don't get to live in this house for free." Villette paused before going inside. "Don't worry. What you're feeling is completely natural. The key is to harness it. That kind of confidence can, yes, be dangerous. But, it can also be one of the most valuable assets a person can have."

She walked off, leaving Syd to her thoughts again. What had she even meant? *Powerful.* The word tumbled around in her head and in her mouth. She clicked her tongue to try to get rid of it. How could it be that she felt powerful at the same time she felt so...*helpless*?

Helpless that it was her, Syd, who took Adeline's future from her. Helpless that she didn't have any say in the matter. Helpless that Wenna and Villette and Reth and Matius, the whole damn Council, have it—her—and what to do about Nova all planned out. Helpless she didn't even have the option to say no. Did she really think this was going to be any different? That she and Adeline could start a life of their own, one that wasn't orchestrated by anyone else?

Helpless and *foolish*.

She collapsed her body forward, chest on knees, and looked down at her boots. Helpless as in unable to decide for herself who and what she was to become. Foolish for ever thinking otherwise. She'd always gone with the flow, but even in that, she'd been lying to herself. It was never her choice. She followed Adeline's every wish, first out of gratitude for such a loyal friendship. Then out of gratitude for such a loyal love.

But was that what it was, truly? Or was it just another coordinated effort? And if that was true, how long ago had they actually chosen her to be Eichon? How long had they kept it from her? How long had they lied?

Syd pressed the palms of her hands to her eyes until she saw stars. Until the questions stopped coming. Until all she could hear was her breath and her heartbeat. Until a trail of goosebumps trickled up her spine to the back of her neck, and down again along her arms. She stood up, a pit in her stomach.

The inn's sign said it was already closed for lunch. But when she tried the handle, the door was unlocked, and she went inside anyway. The receiving room was empty and full of old-world charm, like the theater houses in Carden. Dark wooden floors, aged but meticulously kept, gave a soft glow where the light came in from stained-glass windows. The haze from the colored glass, and the stillness of the air were stuffy and warm. High tables were decorated with small vases of fresh wildflowers.

Along the far wall was a bar, and a set of stairs to its left led up to a closed door. The bar itself was unassuming and made of the same deep wood as the floor. Four seats, a few shelves of miscellaneous bottles, and the walls were painted a rich sage.

Grunts came from another door behind the counter. Syd felt she should go, but before she could turn, the door swung open with the help of a booted foot. A large man with skin deeper than Syd's, his long hair pulled back and decorated in golden beads, huffed. Tall and imposing, he lifted a barrel half his size and turned to set it under the bar. He didn't seem to notice Syd, fully concentrated on his work.

"Excuse me," Syd called and walked over.

No answer. He didn't even seem to notice her.

"Excuse me!"

Bright honey eyes looked up at hers from his crouched position. They were stern but curious. He notched an eyebrow at her in response, but quickly resumed his work.

"Did a girl around my age come in here for lunch? She's with an older guy, looks like her dad?"

He made no reply. Not even an effort to acknowledge her. She folded her arms.

"Hey! I asked you a question!"

The door flung open again, and this time, Adeline emerged. Her hair up in a high ponytail and her muscles tensed as she shimmied a barrel through the door. She wiggled it into position before catching her breath and smiling at Syd.

"He's deaf," she breathed, sliding onto the stool next to Syd.

It was only then that the man stood up and signed, "Thank you."

Adeline nodded to him, and he left them alone, returning to whatever was behind the bar door. Syd stared after him, expecting the man to reemerge.

"Good to see you up and about," Adeline said easily. "Sleep ok? Do you need something to eat? I think Poole's got some olives somewhere around here." Adeline stood and leaned over the bar.

"I'm fine."

"Oh? Well, okay. What have you gotten up to? When you didn't come in for lunch with Keal I figured you were busy with Villette. Did you see that floxling Keal found? It's adorable, don't you think?"

Adeline came back down to the stool and fidgeted with her hair. Her eyes darted from Syd's to just beyond her shoulder and back again. Syd sighed, shaking her head.

"Where were you this morning?"

Adeline stopped fidgeting, her eyes snapping back to Syd's. "What do you mean?"

"I mean, when I woke up, I was all alone in a place I didn't know. Why weren't you there?" Syd's heart thudded, and she swallowed. It wasn't exactly what she had meant to say, but there it was, and she found herself suddenly overcome with a feeling of betrayal and her words laced with suspicion.

Adeline's face reflected Syd's hurt. "I—Villette asked dad and me to go patrol. I didn't think it would be a big deal. Villette was there to tend to you, wasn't she?"

"That's not the point," Syd muttered.

Adeline's eyes grew sharp, and she drew herself up. "Okay, then what is the point? You're fine, aren't you?"

"No thanks to you. The point is you should have been there to—I don't know. Watch over me? Protect me? Right? Like I would have done for you? Isn't that what we agreed on? To do this together?" The edge on her words shocked Syd.

Adeline stood and threw her hands up. "Hey! I don't know the rules. I thought you could handle yourself with Villette there to look out for you! And maybe I wanted to spend some time with my dad, Syd. Ever think of that? Maybe I needed some time to process this shit too."

Adeline made to leave, and Syd stood up, annoyed.

"No, wait." Syd strained her voice.

To Syd's relief, Adeline stopped walking. But she didn't turn around.

"I'm sorry," Syd said slowly. "I didn't mean to snap at you. I didn't—of course you should spend time with Matius. Of course you should have time to think about all this." Syd rubbed her forehead. "Villette just—I just don't know her that well, is all. And she unloaded so much on me all at once." She leaned back on her stool and slumped.

Adeline turned around and folded her arms. "Like what?"

As Syd began to relay everything, Adeline seemed to soften. First, her arms loosened. Then, she came closer.

Finally, she sat back down and leaned her head in her hand to listen. When Syd was finished, she nodded, drew in a deep breath, and looked down. With her free hand, Adeline scratched at the smooth surface of the bar. Syd retreated into her own thoughts.

"It's amazing what they all keep from us," Adeline said. "Even I only got a watered-down version of how my mother became Eichon. It wasn't that much different than what we learned in the academy." She sighed. "It sounds like they had their reasons, though, right? To keep it from us?"

"Do you think—" Syd hesitated, unsure of herself, her question, and, even more than that, if she wanted to know Adeline's answer. "Do you think they kept other things from us too? I mean, they groomed you all your life to be Eichon. How long do you think they knew it...wasn't going to be you?"

Adeline's silence was heavy, and Syd stared at her hands.

"I don't know," Adeline's voice was small, and she coughed as if trying to clear away a frog. "And honestly, I don't think I want to."

There was a bite in Adeline's voice that Syd didn't like but chose to ignore. She didn't have it in her to pry or to start another argument. She forced a smile, because deep down, she knew that even if she had wanted all the weight and responsibility that came with being Eichon, it actually wasn't hers to be had. The Council would be the ones truly pulling all the strings, and she would be a figurehead. A cool wave of relief came over her, quick and sudden. It wouldn't be anything near freedom. But the burden of being Eichon wouldn't be on her either.

"Yeah," Syd said. "I guess you're right."

That night, everyone sat around Villette's house, even the little floxling. It hadn't taken much convincing to let the thing inside, and it immediately curled up in Keal's lap once they'd all settled in for the evening. Syd, Adeline, and Keal listened over drinks as Villette and Matius recounted days from Adeline's childhood. Or times before Adeline came along, early in Wenna's reign, when they were all trying to find their footing and clean up the mess Eichon Ashe had left behind.

Most Eichons, especially the mad ones, chose to end their lives after the transference in what was called the Resting Ritual. Over the eras the transference had started to account for the practice, and Eichon Ashe was no exception. So, after the late Eichon was laid to rest, the new Council had very few to help guide them and maintain peace among the religions.

It was all so normal, so easy. The chatter quickly gave way to laughter. And while Syd couldn't speak for everyone else's, hers was a laugh at the pure absurdity of it all. At the power running through her, at the inconceivability of her ruling anything at all, let alone the known world. At the Madness she would have to tame and the training she had to begin.

At Wenna, and Matius, and Villette. At Adeline and even Keal. At everything she knew now and everything she had only begun to question. And especially at Nova, at the impending doom, should they—she—fail. She laughed along with everyone because there was nothing else she could do.

When morning came, she awoke as she had so many mornings before, and everything felt right in the world. Adeline lying next to her, still asleep, a crown of dark curls floating around her face. Birds, just as the morning before, chirped, and sunlight crept in through the boarded window. The difference was the calm, the sureness, the comfort of familiarity in the midst of so many unknowns, so many questions, and so much that lurked just beyond where her mind could reach.

Before she knew it, Villette had given everyone their tasks for the day: patrols for Adeline and Matius, odd jobs for Keal.

"Alright then," Villette said. "Ready?"

Ready for what, Syd didn't know. She nodded anyway, feeling more like herself after a good nights' rest, and followed Villette out of the house and to a secluded clearing just on the outskirts of town behind the inn.

"Ah, we should be able to get on well enough here. Matius cleared this area yesterday. Now then, let's begin."

"Just like that? No warmup or anything?"

"Do you need one?"

"Well, no," Syd admitted. "But at least buy me dinner first."

Villette tilted her head, and Syd was sure the joke missed.

"Sorry," Syd said. "I mean, I still have questions like—

like about the transference. What actually happens? Don't I at least get to know what to expect should it come to that?"

"I see," Villette said and drew her hands together to make a triangle. "Assuming you were still paying attention at that point, your texts and lesson should have covered the basics at the academy. When Nova comes into position, the Eichon draws the energy down from it and into herself. She then uses herself as a vessel to guide the energy through her and to the receiving entity, connecting them to Nova and severing any further connection she may have."

"Yeah, got that. But how does—what happens if, I don't know, an Eichon decided to just keep her powers instead?"

"Nova will transfer the power no matter what. The gift seeks a woman physically closest to the Eichon at the time of transference. It's *easier*, we'll say, for everyone if the Eichon channels the energy. Which is why choosing a successor became common practice."

The emphasis caused Syd to swallow hard, and Villette's hands fell back to her sides. Syd wanted to ask about Ashe's ending, about the Resting Ritual. What was it like? How was it done? Was it painful? Was it *expected*? What Wenna's plans were, if she was going to Rest. Surely Wenna would have told Adeline those plans, wouldn't she? Maybe not, given everything Wenna hadn't told Adeline. Still, Syd couldn't bring herself to ask it. Not fully at least.

"And the ceremony takes place in Zevir? Why did we have to come here just to go back?"

"Seliss grows restless. Better to keep Adeline, and you especially, hidden."

"Aren't you a Seliss target, though, too?"

Villette shrugged at that. "It's easy to get lost in the shuffle after you've been hidden for so many years. The Council is rarely a target for them, and the idea of a twin likely never crossed Durac Sevnior's mind."

Syd raised her eyebrow at how casually Villette said the Seliss leader's name. "You sound like old friends," she said.

"When you spend a majority of two decades playing defense against a sitting army, waiting for one of you to make a move, names tend to lose their power."

She mulled that over long enough for Villette to take advantage of the pause.

"That's enough questions for now." Villette pointed to the other end of the clearing, and Syd followed her silent command, walking to the spot. "I only know what I've seen in reports from ACES, and what we saw with the austral in Zevir. I'll need a little preview of what you can do so I know where we begin."

"Where do I start?" Syd conceded.

"Wherever you'd like."

Syd looked around at the trees and quieted her mind. She took in the subtleness around her. The birds in the distance, the soft breeze rustling through branches, the deep greens and browns encircling her. She focused on the flicker of sun dancing through the leaves and reached for one not with her hands, but with her mind. With her whole body. Gray mist poured out from her fingers, and she worked it carefully in her palms. All her cells took hold of the leaf, and with a swooping motion, she latched on. Her majikal grip on the leaf expanded to the stem, entwined into the bark, seeped its way into the tender pale wood underneath. Down it grew while Syd's breathing became labored. It searched for the tree's depths just as her lungs searched for air.

She quickly snapped her wrist, and a top branch broke off, falling and getting caught in the lower branches. She snapped her other wrist, and more fell away. One by one, falling away. The motion rapidly increasing, a dizzying flurry that sent her into vertigo. But she gritted her teeth and held on, all muscles tensing.

Until something pulled at her. It started small, distant, in the back of her mind. A faint light, or sound—she wasn't sure which. But it expanded with such speed and ferocity, it overtook her before she realized. Her palms seized and pooled her magic at the base of the tree, plunging into its roots. She gasped, unable to stop it. Her fingers clenched, gripping her majik around the roots.

Something pulled hard and fast, with a strength bigger than her own. Larger than herself. It ripped at the roots, full of vicious hunger. *Fall*, a voice said. But it wasn't Syd's, and it wasn't whatever had come to her before. It was soft, gentle, and honeyed. It poured over her mind slowly, dripping. *Down*. Then like a passing breeze, whipping through her head and was gone as soon as it came. *Ground*. And this time, the voice was clear, big, and full. A boom that expanded in all directions. Syd's majik was held tightly, she felt her heartbeat everywhere. Her skin fizzled with heat, and her chest felt like it was going to crack, her breast bone wanting to snap as easily as the branches had.

She gave a cry, and her body threw itself to the ground

with a final thud, her scream splitting her open. When she opened her eyes, the tree laid upturned

"What the hell was that?!" Syd gasped, doubled over on all fours.

"That," Villette said. "Was me."

Syd gulped the air, wincing at the pain in her ribs. She spat, gums aching, and looked at the ground. No wonder Malvuk wanted to keep Villette from becoming Eichon.

"You can read minds," Syd said.

"Not exactly. But I can, let's say, sway them."

CHAPTER FIFTEEN

Syd fell back onto the ground, letting her body recover from expending so much of its energy. She shook her head. It was starting to get pretty crowded in there. Another voice? She let out a sigh and flinched, unsure how much more room she had. Villette approached and placed a hand on Syd's shoulder. Her body was flooded with a warmth that came as quickly as it went, ending with a jolt in her stomach that set her on edge. She tried to ignore it and failed.

"Mind control?" Syd said, disbelief creeping into her tone.

Villette shrugged. "Not mind control—"

"Whatever. Ever heard of consent? Even a warning would have been nice."

"The Madness won't wait for permission."

Syd drew up her knees and rested her arms on top of them. She squinted up at Villette, backlit by the sun, knowing she couldn't argue with that. But she didn't have to be happy about it.

"And this is how you helped Wenna? By getting into her head and screwing with things?" Syd scoffed.

"More or less," Villette said patiently and withdrew her hand.

Syd unclenched her jaw and flexed her fingers, feeling good as new. The swirl in her stomach turned sour. She stood up and took a few steps back, away from Villette.

"So you'll just do this whenever you want then? Just," Syd waved her hands around, "take over?"

"No. I can't use my ability without another Eheri using theirs. If it helps, think of it like mining. I need a vein to tap into first."

But Syd only shook her head, her eyes growing wide. Her feeling of control slipping away as uncertainty crept up her throat and made the back of her mouth bitter.

"I know it can be quite jarring," Villette said.

Jarring doesn't even begin... Syd thought and inhaled, the sharpness of fresh soil from the upturned tree rushing through her.

"But it is the best way we know to strengthen your majik and your mind. I'm what Malvuk calls a Synthis. We're rare. Just like gravity Eheri. You and I make quite the pair, honestly." Villette gave a small chuckle. "I can amplify your majik to where you'll be strong enough to see Project Nova succeed. And, I can amplify your mental fortitude until it's like second nature whenever the Madness creeps in from your naturally high majik energy."

But Syd couldn't find the humor in any of this, nor the logic. Her suspicions warped into a dark place—a place where not only Villette was lying, but Matius and Keal, maybe even Adeline. She backed up even further, feeling cornered. Violated.

"It's alright Syd. I know it's quite a lot to take in."

You're damn right it is. But Syd could only shake her head, trying to make it make sense. When it didn't, her shoulders hunched forward. There was something there, something just out of reach. The back of her neck itched in frustration. Some connection she wasn't quite making and couldn't quite see. She folded her arms around herself and looked to the ground once again, feeling defeated. What else was she to do if this is what it took to—to—she could barely even think it. *To save the planet.*

"It gets easier with practice," Villette offered, voice gentle as ever.

"And you expect me to master this in time? Isn't the eclipse, like, tomorrow?"

"Fourteen days," Villette said plainly.

"And this is the only way?"

"The only one we know of."

Syd didn't answer. She didn't have to. She wanted to make herself small, tiny. She wanted to hide from everything and everyone. But she knew that was no longer an option. She questioned if it ever, truly, had been in the first place.

"Okay," Syd said. "Let's try again."

The afternoon was full of Syd attempting to rid her mind of Villette's influence. When that failed, she tried to ignore it. When ignoring it clearly wasn't working, evidenced by the chaos of broken twigs, felled branches, and toppled trees that encircled them, she tried frustration and annoyance and complaint. Unfortunately, nothing seemed to work against Villette, and Syd sagged in relief, sweat tickling the sides of her face, when Villette eventually, finally, looked up to the sky and ended training for the day.

Syd's body had been through the ringer, and after a cold

meal and a hot bath, she promptly fell asleep in the guest room before anyone, not even Adeline, could ask her how the first day of training went. She slept hard, and deep, dreaming of a blood red moon pouring itself into the sea.

When morning came, she was hungry for more. More training, more pushing, more majik, and more control. But the spot next to her was as empty as it had been when she went to bed, and when she went downstairs, she only found Villette, Keal, and the floxling in the sitting room.

"Where's Ad?"

"Off patrolling," Villette said. "Breakfast is in the kitchen. Get your strength. Today I'll be amplifying your majik, and Keal has kindly agreed to spar with you using his australs."

Syd's forehead bunched. "First you want me to try to get you out of my head and now you want me to keep you *in* my head?"

"We're still getting to know each other," Villette reminded her, and her tone was almost playful.

"Plus, it's been ages since we sparred together," Keal added with his own pep. The floxling yipped excitedly.

Syd frowned, but stopped herself from reminding Keal they'd never actually sparred *against* each other before. Yesterday's training had been a failure, and today probably wasn't going to be much better. By the end of it, Villette's voice rang even louder in her mind, not softer. She retrieved her breakfast of cold sausage and eggs, feeling sheepish. It was one thing to fail in front of Villette. It was another thing entirely to fail in front of Keal.

• • •

"Didn't really hold back yesterday, did you Syd?" Keal said as they entered the clearing. The floxling had followed them all the way and took the chance to romp among the debris and trees.

Syd grinned against the growing fear in her stomach that hopped and scampered even more than the yelping fluff of fur. She eventually lost sight of Keal's new pet behind a tree trunk.

"Having second thoughts?" Syd asked.

Keal gave a *pfft* sound and took his place across the clearing from her. The floxling came bounding up with a mouth full of leaves and dropped them at Keal's feet. It yapped at Keal who only shrugged and ran his hand through the back of his hair. Villette coughed, grabbing everyone's attention.

"Based on yesterday's performance, it's clear Syd can focus well on single, immovable targets. Now, let's see how she does with quick-moving opponents. Keal, I assume you have something like that?"

Keal nodded eagerly and checked his belt lined with canisters. Their metal glinted in the morning sun, unsettling Syd. She shook out her nerves, masking the movement by stretching her arms and neck.

"Good. Syd, I'd like you to replicate what you did in Zevir, please."

Syd pursed her lips. She hadn't even really thought about what majik she'd used to protect Adeline that day. If protect is even what you call it, considering Adeline had ended up in the infirm.

"Ready?" Keal broke her thoughts.

She nodded, easily calling her majik from her veins to her palms and fingers. The rush at how easily it responded gave her a little bit of confidence, and when Keal unlatched the lid to his chosen container, she felt a tickle in the back of her mind. Something dense and sticky, and not entirely unwelcome.

A dark cloud poured from Keal's canister, quickly obstructing Syd's view of him. Dark blues and purples swirled, and the cloud expanded. A soft, distant, thunder engulfed the space, growing in intensity and rattling Syd's skull as if it, too, were in her head. She flicked her wrists in annoyance, urging her majik to gather faster and become whole.

The air around her cooled, gusts from seemingly nowhere lifted her hair and whipped at her face. Electricity sizzled through the dark space in front of her, its buzz vibrating the backs of her teeth. Then, a blinding flash of light, followed by a cracking boom that sent a shockwave up and down her spine and made her jump. Syd dove within herself and drew her hands together, concentrating. Another splitting echo, and the cloud lifted. At first, she thought Keal had called it back, but when she looked up, the austral loomed overhead. Its energy pulsed, and with every roll of thunder its lightning threatened to strike.

Syd crouched, eyes not leaving the blanket of storm above the clearing. She turned one palm facing up, and with her other hand, she made a swirling motion. The gray mist responded, creating a small tornado of gravity in her palms. She felt herself sink into it, losing herself in the swirl. The ground swayed, and she was at once something of pure destruction and herself. When she breathed, the majik expanded. *Duck!*

The clearing lit up, an ear-piercing crack shattering her concentration. Syd's body threw itself to the side, and her majik landed on a nearby tree. When she looked to where she had been standing, only a black spot remained, the ground scorched where the lightning had hit. *Jump!*

Syd's legs pushed her out of the way again as another bolt of lightning hit where she'd just been. She let out a frustrated grunt, getting to her feet against already protesting muscles, and tried to gather her majik once more. She searched the austral's body for vulnerability or weakness. *What stops a storm?* The thought consumed her. At a loss, she simply kept moving while the thunder kept sounding, giving no sign of letting up.

She wove further into the thicket of trees, taking care to step over fallen stumps and branches. The extra cover only gave her enough pause to panic. She tried, again, to swirl her gravity into something useful, something that could slow or stop the austral long enough to figure something out. But Keal was relentless, the storm clouds chasing her. She felt them searching for her through branches and leaves. *Roll!*

But Villette's command came too late, her grip too distant. Syd gave out a cry as a searing pain caught her calf when she tried to dodge the brilliant flash. Her majik shot off in a different direction from her hands, and her body sizzled, the shock radiating through her bones. Her jaw flexed, her teeth biting together sharply. She needed to move, fast. Get under more cover. When she tried to move her leg, a wave of fire overtook her, and she cried out. The clouds above crackled, as if mocking her sound, and she used every protesting muscle she could to drag herself closer to a nearby evergreen. She broke through its needles and assessed the damage to her leg, grinding her teeth against the pain.

Then, she heard a yapping, and a small ball of fur appeared. The floxling's ears were low, its eyes wide and scared. It trotted up to Syd as fast as it could and laid itself on Syd's burnt leg. Syd gasped, ready to throw the animal off her, but where she expected another wave of fire, she only felt a calm of cold. The floxling closed its eyes, and its body relaxed. The coolness spread, an invisible sheet of ice enveloping her entire leg, and a peace overtook her. It took her several moments to comprehend. The creature was healing her.

Thunder clapped above, and they both jumped. She tested her leg, inspecting it first with her hands, and then she tried moving it. It was practically as good as new. And then, she realized so was the rest of her.

Syd and the floxling stared at each other for some time. The moments stretched, the noise of the storm dimming. The floxling laid itself down on its paws, and its ears drooped. Syd moved closer to pet it, but it didn't respond to her touch at all. The sky above cleared, and Syd jumped again when she heard Villette and Keal calling her name.

"O-over here!" Syd called, still in awe.

Animals having special powers wasn't strange; the academy's bestiary studies had talked about creatures having majik. But Syd had only ever interacted with the ones in the training center. The ones held captive. The ones forced into defense.

There was a rustling, and Keal and Villette pushed back the branches to find Syd.

"Oh good, you're not hur—" Keal started, but stopped and rushed to the pup.

Villette came and inspected Syd's leg. Finding nothing wrong, she raised her eyebrows. Syd shook her head, her throat suddenly too dry to explain.

Keal scooped up the floxling. "What happened?"

Syd stood, anticipating more pain with a wince. But she stood to her full height, her leg fully recovered and the exhaustion she knew she should have gone. She swallowed and tried again.

"It...healed me," Syd said.

Keal pressed his ear to the creature. "It's weakened. I can barely hear its heartbeat. We need to get it back so it can rest."

Villette gave Syd a look, but Syd was already on the move, leading them back to town.

CHAPTER SIXTEEN

The floxling took a few days to recover fully, and Villette had agreed it best to not include Keal in training. Syd only saw Adeline in passing and during evening meals on the days she had the energy to stay awake. Syd suspected Matius and Villette were keeping them apart. But even when she was able to catch Adeline's glance, there was a distance where she'd expected longing and her heart began to ache in the same deep way her body did during training.

Hands on knees and doubled over, Syd wheezed and looked at Villette.

"Break. I'm calling a break."

"The Madness won't care if you—"

"Yeah, yeah. I know. Won't care if I need a rest. Got it. But you're not the Madness and I need to ask you something."

Villette quieted, adjusting her shawl, and Syd took that as a win for the day. She straightened and tried to walk out her tense muscles, gathering her thoughts. She rolled her tongue around her dry mouth and swallowed mostly air as she tried to catch her breath.

"Growing up, did you and Wenna ever…Was there ever any…" Syd searched for the words, feeling Villette's patient eyes as she circled. "Resentment? Between you two?"

Syd stretched her arms and twisted at the waist, covering up her clumsy question. The pit in her stomach had been growing over the past few days, larger and heavier each time she had tried to spend time with Adeline. But Adeline had been busy patrolling, or helping Poole, or with Matius. It seemed she wasn't able to get a single moment alone with her. And Syd was starting to worry she was pushing Adeline away somehow. "Or, Wenna becoming Eichon and you not?" Syd finished, chest deflating.

"Hm?" Villette said, absent-mindedly. "Oh. Well, Wenna and I were apart for so long that when we rejoined after her transference, we were almost...strangers. We'd both been through so much—" She cut herself off. "Ah, this isn't about us, though, is it."

The question came as a statement, and Syd suspected Villette could read minds more than she admitted.

"Wenna and I have a very different relationship than you and Adeline. You were like sisters from such an early age, true, but that's blossomed into something else over the years. You have managed to hold all three—friend, lover, guardian. That's a lot of weight for anyone. Even for you. Even for Adeline."

Syd shivered and folded her arms even though it wasn't cold. She disliked it when Villette got like this—knowing too much—and it seemed to be happening more and more these past few days. Of course, they'd never kept their relationship secret, but they'd also never talked about it with anyone. It was their own space to belong in. Together. If she thought about it, the two of them had always existed in their own little bubble, in their own little world. Uninterrupted and undisturbed, until now.

Even the day they had met, they were left alone on a crowded seaship. Syd chewed her lip. Guarded, protected.

Whatever it was that had been lurking out of reach tugged at her again, finding its way into her memories.

"Matron," a young Syd said. "How long until we can go up on the deck again? You never keep us down here for this long."

Matron Reos took the girl's hands, petting them reassuringly.

"My child, the seaship is usually anchored. We don't want you to fall overboard. Besides, you see that girl over there?"

The older woman looked back to a circle of children, sitting around the cabin's fireplace. The boat creaked and strained against strong currents outside. A young couple were playing and talking with the other children. Next to the man Syd would come to know as Matius sat a pale, dark-haired girl.

"It's her birthday today," Reos said. "We're going on a trip to Arja's Gardens to celebrate."

Syd scrunched her face, playing with the metal clasps in her hair. "But, we have plenty of gardens back on Darmar."

"Yes, we do. But Arja's Gardens are much nicer. The air is cooler, lighter. The water warm and refreshing. There's plant life and animal life you've never even seen on Darmar. The gardens almost shimmer with energy as the final resting place of all Eichons."

She patted Syd's hand once more.

"Now, why don't you go say hello and make a new friend?"

Matron had never forced Syd to interact with others before. This was strange, but so was everything else about the trip. Having nothing else to do, and being a polite child in general,

Syd nodded and walked over to the circle of kids. She tapped the girl on the shoulder from behind.

"Um. Matron said it was your birthday...Happy birthday!" Syd said.

The other girl stood up. She was a couple inches taller than Syd, her complexion a contrast to Syd's darker hues. She immediately smiled, jumped up and down a little, and gave a small bow.

"Thank you! I'm so excited for the gardens, aren't you?" she spoke quickly. "I've never seen them before! I've never been on a real seaship before either. Are you one of the ones that live on here? Everyone tells me about the stuff you learn on this boat. Oh! Can I see where you sleep? I've always wondered what living on the sea would be like! Oh hey!" The excited girl barely took a breath, pointing at Syd and then the metal clasp in her hair. "I have one too!" she beamed.

Syd's face fell a little flat. She liked to absorb what people said before answering, but this girl was simply going too fast for Syd to keep up. A black-gloved hand scooped the other girl into a soft hug.

"Adeline..." Matius said quietly. "One thing at a time." His voice was kind and full. Syd had liked it greatly.

"Oh, sorry!" The girl released herself from her father's embrace. "I'm Adeline." She stuck a hand out to Syd.

"I'm Syd." Syd followed the strange greeting.

Adeline grabbed Syd's hand, her face full of pure delight. "So! Do you live on the seaship?" she asked again.

"No, but we do have sleeping quarters..."

"Oh, good! Can you show me around? Da'," Adeline turned her face up to Matius. "Can Syd show me around?"

Syd watched as Matron Reos and Matius exchanged a glance, and gave Adeline a silent nod of approval.

Knowing there was no other choice, Syd clasped her hand around Adeline's and took her through the cabin doors. As Syd shared about the seaship and the orphanage, Adeline shared about her home in a big, dark tower made of majik.

An hour later, everyone was on deck to stretch their legs as they neared land.

"What happened to your parents?" Adeline's voice was quiet, her eyes wide.

"Just don't have them, I guess." Syd shrugged, never having thought about it. She'd always been here, with Matron Reos. And she'd always stayed here, as everyone else was adopted to their new mothers and fathers.

Adeline shook her head. "That's silly, you have to have a ma' and da'."

Adeline was the first new kid her own age that Syd had met in almost two years. She wanted to keep this friend of hers and worried Adeline would go back to her palace of blue and green, with its dining room the size of seaships, and forget all about her like all the rest of her friends who left to join their new families. She'd have to think of something—something that wouldn't make her so different for not having a mom and dad like everyone else.

"Hey, Adeline…watch this!"

Syd pointed to the wave crests that had become slower and less harsh the closer they were to land.

"It'll be quick, so pay attention!" Syd added.

Syd opened her hand, her palm facing the waves. Her eyes narrowed in focus on one wave in particular. Not too big, not

too small. One that, if someone else was watching, they'd proba-
bly not notice it. She took a deep breath, closed her eyes tight, and
opened them quickly with intense force. The unsuspecting wave,
for but a half second, stood still among the others before joining
the rest again to be swallowed by a larger wave.

Adeline searched the waves. "What?" she asked.

"The wave! Didn't you see it stop for a second?"

"Oh…no." Adeline looked off to the other kids.

Syd searched the water for something else. A couple fish
swam next to the hull. They jumped in and out of the water,
playing and dancing with the waves, in something like a
rhythm. If Syd really concentrated, she might be able to capture
one.

"Okay, I'll try again. Watch the fish this time."

Again, Syd held her palm out. Again, she focused her eyes
until they started to glaze over. Again, she tensed, closed her eyes,
and opened them quickly. She held the smallest fish in place for
but a moment, almost able to feel it in her palm. It then promptly
plopped back, slipping from her grip, into the water, though its
jumps were now slightly off beat with the others.

Adeline gasped and brought her hand up to her mouth.

"Oh!" she said earnestly. "You did that?"

Syd nodded, unsure of Adeline's reaction. The only other
person who had ever seen her do anything like that was Matron.
Well, Matron and Gaav, but he was gone now. Matron had
warned her to not show the other children. But Syd figured Ade-
line wasn't like the other kids she lived with. After all, they were
going on a whole trip just for Adeline's birthday, and they'd
never done that for anyone else before.

Adeline quickly broke out into a smile which turned into a laugh and then quieted back down into a giggle. Syd giggled too.

"Syd?" Villette's voice broke Syd out of the memory.

"What? Sorry." Syd stopped chewing on her lip and squinted at the ground, trying to recall something. The ease at which Adeline had liked her, the quick friendship that had ensued first as pen pals, then they had started to visit each other, and finally to the academy together.

"I was saying, it's reasonable that you both are experiencing some tensions. This is an abnormal circumstance, after all."

Syd didn't like the way Villette said *abnormal*. And she also didn't like a few new things in that memory she hadn't noticed before: the only trip the orphanage had ever taken on the seaship, Reos encouraging her to talk to Adeline, Matius's looking to Reos for permission. She swallowed, shaking her head.

"Yeah, I guess you're right," Syd said. "Sorry, I'm just hungry. You've been running me pretty hard." She grinned, hoping she sounded genuine.

"Well, it is almost lunch time. Let's head back," Villette said.

Syd followed her out of their ever-expanding circle of destruction, her mind clawing at all the little dots that had suddenly started to circle each other.

Keal gave a sharp whistle as they entered the pub, and the

floxling clomped up from somewhere else behind the counter. It clumsily found its way back into Keal's arms, so small it fit into Keal's lab coat pocket. Syd's shoulders relaxed at the smell of the aged wood and dusty windowsills that had quickly became familiar and comforting during their short stay in Llyn. Poole stood behind the counter, looking more and more uneasy at an animal having its way with his supplies. He wiped the counter silently, keeping an eye on Keal's pocket.

"How was training?" Keal asked, turning in his seat.

Syd shrugged.

"I think we're just now starting to understand the weight of things," Villette said evenly.

Keal perked his eyebrow at Syd who perked hers back with a little shake of her head and a small shrug.

"Where are Ad and Matius?" Syd asked.

"Not back yet," Keal responded.

"I'll go tell them it's time for lunch, then," Syd said, turning abruptly for the door before Villette could stop her.

Syd shuddered when she heard Keal jumped from his seat. "I'll come with you, I could use the walk."

She had wanted the walk alone to think. To form her thoughts clearly, succinctly. To gather her confusion and make questions out of it all. Whatever was creeping along her spine extended through her body now, an eerie anxiety. She chewed her lip but didn't protest. Whatever was going to come out of her mouth, Keal should probably be there for it.

They headed for the eastern edge of town, across the square, and followed a very beaten path down and around

Villette's house. The sound of metal versus metal was an easy giveaway they were heading in the right direction. Matius and Adeline had taken care of any monster control in the first few days. Now, they used the time to spar together. Upon seeing Keal and Syd, they immediately disengaged.

"Who's winning?" Keal asked, friendly. He leaned down and let the floxling out of his pocket to roam. It gave a tired yelp before catching the scent of something and wandered off.

"Who do you think?" Adeline's voice was a little harsh, and she sheathed the broad sword she'd been training with. "This new blade is weighted differently than my old one."

There was that word again. Weight. Syd shook her head, trying to pry her eyebrows apart. Impatience tickled her jaw, and her teeth clenched.

"That's the third one we've given you," Matius says with an edge of warning in his voice. "You're an agile fighter. Being able to use differing weapons is a must."

Adeline gave a little groan and walked to Syd with her arms out to embrace, eyes shifting away from Syd's stare. Syd stepped away and folded her arms.

"Syd? Are you alright?" Adeline asked.

Syd gave some distance between the three of them and herself. She took a deep breath, feeling her forehead knot even more. Her throat tightened around the yet unknown question stuck in her suddenly thundering chest. Adrenaline spiked, and the tips of her ears went numb for a half second before—

"Why were you on the boat when we first met?" Syd blurted.

As a group, they looked at her with various faces of confusion that mirrored her own. The reflection was too much, and she looked away.

"What?" Adeline asked, eyes shifting.

"On the boat, when I was at the orphanage. Why were you there?" Syd began pacing, carefully watching her feet, finding a rhythm in her steps. Her brain was like rapid fire, loud and spattering, and she was having trouble holding it all together in her head. Heat rose in her chest, stomach bubbling with fear.

"It was my birthday, Syd. You know—"

The heat in her sparked and caught flame. "Why was there a boat at all?" Syd's locked eyes with Matius now. "Why the orphanage at all?" Then her eyes went to Adeline. "You had birthdays safely in Zevir up until that point, right? And I don't remember you ever having any other birthdays like that after, either."

Adeline showed her palms, shoulders reaching for her ears. Her eyes grew wide as she looked between Syd and Matius.

"Syd, I…what are you asking? What's going on?" Adeline stepped forward, trying to close to gap between her and Syd.

Syd searched Adeline's face. The familiarity dulled her edge, if only a little. Eyes deep as chocolate turned down in worry and concern. Adeline's lips twitched into a frown.

"I have no idea what you—" Adeline stammered and moved closer still.

Syd didn't back away. Instead, she turned her fire on Matius.

"You set up that Adeline and I would meet, didn't you?"

He remained silent and busied himself with sheathing his own weapon, a long, fine saber.

"You made sure we'd become friends, didn't you? You and Wenna? Villette?" Syd's voice rose in her ears. Adeline turned to look at Matius too.

Matius sighed and turned his face to the sky, eyes closed. "I suppose you and Villette have had a chance to talk," he said.

"This I figured out on my own," Syd spat her words. And her ears rang when she realized he wasn't disagreeing with her.

"Let's head back. We can talk at the house."

"No. We talk now." The command in Syd's voice would have shocked her, if she could have heard it over the piercing ringing.

Matius dropped his face finally to meet hers. His eyes, so much like Adeline's, edged on Syd's empathy, and she took a breath, following the cool air trail from her nostril down to her belly. She blinked, refocusing, and the ringing stopped.

He took his time to find his words. "What do you remember of your parents?"

"What does that have to do with anything?"

"It has a great deal to do with everything. Any memories at all?"

"No. I only remember the orphanage."

Matius nodded, setting his jaw. He took a deep breath of his own, letting the words spill out of him like a sigh, like a confession.

"Shortly after Adeline was born, the Council started the excavations for Project Nova to try to learn as much as we could about the magnetic pull of our planet and Nova. Even with Reth and Saaviana's support, we didn't have the resources so early on to begin in the north, so we went south to Darmar where it was easier and cheaper to dig. Your parents were…part of a team on the first excavation site; local laborers, a small group from towns along the shorelines. We weren't expecting it to be a big dig, so we outfitted camp with enough for workers to bring their families. Your parents chose to bring you."

As he started to explain, he clasped his hand behind his back and walked the length of the clearing. The sun danced in the leaves, shaping patterns of lace with their shadows on the forest floor.

"You were at such a young age that, whenever they would leave you, you would scream and cry all day. We even had a matron, Reos, there to watch over any kids on the site. About three or four days into the dig, you were having a particularly bad tantrum. Reos walked you over to where it'd be safe for your parents to say goodbye before starting their days' work. After they left and entered the work pit, you stopped crying entirely. And, not a minute later, the mine collapsed. It trapped and killed everyone inside.

"Reos was still holding you when it happened. You had stopped crying because you fell unconscious after '*a cloud of smoke*', Reos had called it, shot from your body and then into the mine's entrance. Just like your majik did on the way here, to Llyn."

Matius stopped abruptly, as if that explained

everything, and Syd wanted to respond, wanted to stomp her foot and demand an answer to how that explained anything at all. But she couldn't move, couldn't feel the breeze in the air, nor the sun on her skin or Adeline's hand when it grabbed her.

She saw Adeline's lips move and couldn't hear anything but the birds and insects in the trees, quickly overtaken by static that started in her ears and spread through her skull. She blinked. Adeline's face told her she was supposed to respond. Instead, her body lurched forward as if it understood something her brain couldn't. Adeline steadied her, gently helping her to the ground. The two knelt together, and Syd saw Adeline mouth shape her name, but the sound didn't reach her ears.

She whispered to Adeline, stomach dizzier than her mind. "Did you know?"

Adeline shook her head, eyes wide. The soft thud of footsteps approached. Keal crouched down with them. Through the static, she heard Matius say something before he walked off in the direction of town. She still had so many questions, and this only brought more. But her body refused to let her call after him. The heat inside drained, leaving her to float in the lukewarm space between confusion and comprehension. The fight in her fled. The ground fell away, and pressure built under her arms as Keal and Adeline lifted her up.

The rush from standing made her vision fuzzy for a moment, and it was all she could do to trust her feet. Somewhere deep inside, something swirled and slithered.

"Why?" she finally heard herself say.

Adeline and Keal stopped.

"Why what, Syd?" Adeline asked, her face full of the same worry and concern from before.

Syd shook her head and found herself again. Or at least enough of herself to stand on her own. She released her grip on her friends and rubbed her face harshly, redirecting her attention away from the tension building behind her eyes. Keal called the floxling back with a high whistle that made Syd's jaw flinch. She reopened her eyes to watch the dark figure of Matius grow smaller and smaller on the trail ahead of them.

"N-nothing," she said.

The wind whipped suddenly. Her hair bounced and waved in it, and that something inside her, the something made of wisps and onyx and age, said, *Because look at what it gave us.*

CHAPTER SEVENTEEN

Adeline and Keal helped Syd back to Villette's house. She retreated to the guest room she and Adeline had been sharing, and her friends stayed with her. Adeline sat on the edge of the bed, and Syd joined her in silence, leaning against the headboard and hugging her knees. Keal put his hands in his pocket and looked to the floor. The floxling found a pile of dirty clothes to curl up in.

"Syd I'm so sor—" Adeline turned to her.

"Don't," Syd said and laid her head on her arms. She sighed and closed her eyes. The darkness spun, and her stomach churned. She inhaled before it could overtake her. "Please," she added with a hint of pleading.

"You couldn't—"

"Ad, not now." Syd clenched her eyelids tighter, squeezing until she saw stars.

"But you didn't—"

Syd's jaw tightened, her neck tensed, her arms held onto her legs, pressing them as close as she could. She made herself small, trying to feel something.

"You were just a baby," Adeline finished and flung her arms around Syd, crashing into her.

Syd was immediately engulfed in lavender and moss, and she sank into it. For a moment, she felt protected under the cover of Adeline, held by her strong arms. The softness of the dark space, Adeline's body shielding out any light in the embrace. Syd was safe here, in her shadow. *In her shadow.*

A knock came at the door. Syd shook herself out of Adeline's embrace, and Adeline released. Syd coughed, wiping something wet from her bottom eyelids. She gave a nod to Keal who opened the door.

Matius stood in the door, his shoulders square and his face set.

"May we have the room?" he asked Adeline and Keal.

Before either could move, Syd shook her head.

"Whatever you have to say, you can say it to all of us."

Syd couldn't figure out why she was so upset with Matius. *He* hadn't killed her parents. But he had kept it from her all these years. He, and Wenna. Villette. Reos. They all had. Something that *big,* that *important...*What else had they kept secret? Syd started to shrink again, feeling little and insignificant at remembering Project Nova. She turned her anger at herself for forgetting something so much bigger, so much more important, than herself, her troubles. They all must be so tiny in the eyes of Eher. A speck, a blip. Syd's eyes began to well up once more.

"I am sorry you found out this way, Syd. All of you."

"And there was a better way?" Syd shot him a glare, forcing the tears back.

"That day, the day your majik manifested, changed everything. We hadn't planned—" He cut himself off. "It doesn't matter."

"No, it doesn't matter, does it? Whatever you had planned, whatever you are planning, doesn't really matter at all if, say, any of us knew anything about it either I guess, huh?" Heat surged through Syd suddenly, her mind picking up speed. The wave of sadness gone to a distant shore somewhere.

Matius remained calm as ever and cleared his throat. The floxling perked up as he stepped into the room.

"The plan was to adopt you," Matius started. "Once we understood what had happened. Keep you close, safe. Raise you two as proper sisters. Reos convinced us to wait a few years, to see how your majik grew. So, we dispatched some of our own Eheri to become attendants and keep you guarded, safe, at an orphanage near the village you were from.

"During that time, we continued our research of Nova and were able to bring Dr. Malvuk on board. When he found out about you..." Matius sighed. "When he became aware that an Eheri with gravity majik existed in his lifetime, he knew you would play a role. He wanted to bring you to Zevir to study, like Eichon Ashe had. Villette fought against that, and Wenna listened. Still, we knew we couldn't find a solution to Nova without Malvuk's help. When he threatened to leave the project, a bargain was struck: an academy, a way to formally train Eheri for the Eichon's army—PRISM. Malvuk would have access to study and train you—and others if he so chose—under Council supervision."

Matius finally paused, looking to the three of them. There was almost something of an apology on his face, but it disappeared as quickly as it had come. Syd's nostrils flared, the ache around her eyes begging to be released.

"The birthday trip was special, yes. Planned." Matius looked directly at Syd. "We wanted to introduce you and Adeline in a way that was more natural than simply adopting. We hadn't expected you two to become so close. We let the world, including the two of you, believe Adeline would become Eichon because it kept *you* safe, Sydney."

A stunned silence filled the room, but Syd's heart raced, and her palms were sweaty. Anger radiated from her so hot, she thought she might set the bed on fire.

"So, when were you going to tell us any of that? Huh? Ever?" She leapt from the bed to meet Matius's eyes, putting herself between Adeline and him. "We're just a bunch of pieces in your plan, pieces you have to keep rearranging? So, tell us, all of us, what's the next step? What happens now?" she seethed, making her body nearly vibrate in rage. She never wanted to be special. She never wanted to take Adeline's future. She never wanted to cause so much pain, so much destruction.

The tears fell now, big and hot, but she fought against her tightening throat and the echoes surfacing in her head. They whipped around her and filled her ears, calling and tempting her majik. Syd's skin prickled at the mere thought.

"If we're just your pawns, what's the next move?" Syd set her jaw.

"That's the thing," Matius said. "You changed everything, and you kept changing it. We have to keep adjusting to you."

Adeline stood. "I've heard enough." Her voice choked. She gave a single glance to Syd and left the room in a hurry.

It was enough to break Syd from her anger, and she cast Matius an accusatory glance before following.

"Adeline, wait!" Syd scaled the stairs and chased her out into the square. "Stop, *please.*"

Adeline rounded on Syd, her eyes wet and full of hurt. The stare caught Syd off guard, and she staggered back.

"Must be something to be so prized," Adeline said, venom lacing her words.

"What?" Syd gasped, her chest swelling and unsure.

"How does it feel to be so cherished?"

All Syd could do was shake her head, unable to understand. Last thing she knew, she'd killed her parents. Then, they were being told that everything had been orchestrated for her—*Oh.*

Guilt fractured Syd, and she stepped toward Adeline who only clenched her fists and stood her ground. Through squinted eyes, Adeline glared and watched Syd's movements like she was under attack, like Syd was the enemy.

"Ad, I'm not—"

But the words left Syd and were replaced by a hurt, an ache so deep, it tore at her breastbone. Dull at first, it expanded, ripping. The way Adeline was looking at her, the way her jaw lifted and her nostrils flared, the way her shoulders set back and her arm muscles flexed. Syd choked on her breath, a fear radiating up and down her body so hot that it was cold. She felt paralyzed when she realized there was no softness in Adeline. No space for Syd to fit into.

Her words evaporated in the air, and when Adeline walked off toward the other side of town, Syd was still unable to move. All she could do was watch as the echoes of Adeline's receding steps rippled through her.

Syd rolled over and found Adeline's spot in the bed empty again. Yesterday had been a blur of walking on eggshells, of Villette and Keal trying to console Syd while Matius checked on Adeline. A day of holding her breath and never fully exhaling until she finally went to bed and fought the thoughts that kept bubbling up until exhaustion found her. Through the closed door, she heard commotion downstairs. Heavy steps pacing and Villette and Matius arguing.

She opened the door to listen, but the only words she could make out were *Adeline* and *gone*. Immediately, Syd rushed to the top of the stairs.

"What's going on?" she called.

Villette and Matius halted their conversation and looked up. Keal's door creaked open as he joined them. His face was full of sleep still, but Syd suspected he'd been listening too.

"Have either of you seen Adeline?" Villette asked severely.

Keal and Syd looked to each other, eyes growing wide.

"No," they answered in unison. "Could she have gotten an early start on patrols?" Keal added.

Matius just shook his head, heavy boots starting to pace again.

"I've surveyed the patrol spots early this morning," he said.

Villette placed a hand on Matius's arm, but he didn't stop.

"Neither of you heard anything last night? Any sounds of her leaving?"

Again, the two shook their heads, and Syd gripped the banister railing. A weight built in her skull, thudding behind her eyes.

"She's run away," Syd said quietly, and her shoulders slumped forward.

"I've dispatched four of Villette's scouts to Keld and Pella's Wish," Matius said. The command in his voice, devoid of any emotion, was unnerving.

"We're waiting on word from them," Villette said.

"Keal," Matius interrupted, "get dressed and meet me outside. We'll run the parameter again. Villette, Syd, you will stay here. Come find us should word arrive."

There was no time to question or protest. Matius left the house immediately, and Keal, giving one glance to Syd, left to ready himself.

"I've made tea, if you would like some," Villette said finally.

Syd, not knowing what else to do, her mind dumbstruck and head aching, descended the stairs and followed Villette into the kitchen.

The morning passed slowly, each moment unbearably longer than the last. Syd sipped tea until she felt waterlogged. Villette fluttered around the house until she had to step out to help Poole with something. Syd had simply nodded, not paying attention and lost in her own thoughts.

Alone in the house, she found herself in the guest room Adeline had been using. Outside, the light was dim and gray, barely able to stream in through the boarded slats on the room's window. She caught her reflection in the dresser mirror, touched the puffiness under her eyes, ruffled some of her kinks, and searched the drawers for something to tie her hair up and out of her face.

The drawer's runners gave a loud squeak when she pulled on the old wood. The sound hit her bones, and she shivered. The first drawer was empty, but in the second, she found a leather-bound book. *Adeline's journal.* Syd's eyebrows shot up her forehead. Why would she leave her journal here if she was running away? What lay next to it made her gasp, a bitterness at the back of her mouth sudden and sharp. Adeline's ACES cadet band, identical to Keal's and Syd's, sat off to the side.

Syd took both items in her hands, running her thumbs over the smoothness of the leather and the silkiness of the silicone. They were trained to only ever remove their bands when bathing—and even then, it was looked down upon. The bands tracked them, and Syd's had been how Rhiuld always knew she was dodging class. A rush of tears suddenly brimmed Syd's eyes as an emptiness opened within her, hollow and gaping, and she'd never in her life felt more homesick for a time and place she could never, ever go back to.

She pocketed the band and fanned the edges of the journal. Whatever was in here was sacred, secret. Adeline had kept journals for as long as they'd known each other, and it was the one thing that was ever truly hers. Syd's heart beat faster at the thought of invading that privacy, but she knew she had to. Adeline was missing, and if finding her meant prying, it didn't matter how mad she'd be when she found out... Right? Syd's mouth dried up when her thumb caught on a page on her third fan through bookmarked by something. She opened the book, and a letter fell out.

Swallowing hard, she picked up the paper and opened it, folded neatly in thirds. Inside was a page of sharp, quick strokes in heavy black ink.

Dear Adeline,

I have begun the requested research and secured facilities by-way of E.F. We will owe them for the risk they are undertaking, but further negotiations can wait. I will meet you at your requested location.

-I.M.

Syd flipped the letter over in her hands. Adeline had been receiving mail? Here? Who but the Council knew of their location? Syd stared at the initials I.M. and E.F., and her forehead knotted. I.M. could be Ivor Malvuk. In fact, the lettering looked like what she'd seen in his labs before. But E.F.? And, what research? What facilities and location?

Her head swam, and she felt she would drown under all the questions, new and old. The room spun, and she reached out to grip the dresser. A loud slam from the front door broke her out of the dizziness.

"Syd?!" Villette's voice rang up through the house.

Syd ran out of the room. "Yeah, what is it? Any news?"

Villette's face was pale, and she was out of breath, as though she had been running.

"My scout," Villette said. "He's returned. Adeline bought a train ticket to the midlands—Hartell."

"When does the train leave?" Syd met Villette on the first floor and looked to the door.

"It's already departed."

They met Keal and Matius on their way back from searching for Adeline. Matius's face flashed fury for only a moment, and then returned to the commander he was trained to be. They walked to the inn and took their usual seats around the space, empty except for Poole who had somehow been talked into pet sitter duties. The floxling jumped into Keal's lap as soon as he sat.

"Why Hartell?" Keal voiced the thought on everyone's mind.

Hartell was a small town that bordered Seliss territory. It didn't make sense. She was going *closer* to the enemy? Why? Syd had left the journal and band in her room for safe keeping, still unsure what to do with either. Of course, it could hold all the answers, but something protective bubbled inside Syd whenever she thought of handing them over. She had brought the letter, though.

"I found this in Adeline's room," she said relinquishing the letter.

Matius read the letter in silence. Anger lingered at the edges of his squinted eyes and thinned lips, and he slid the letter to Villette.

"It has to be Furlong," Villette said after she finished reading.

Matius nodded knowingly. Syd looked to Keal, but his eyes were focused elsewhere, thinking.

"What?" Syd asked.

Villette tilted her head to Matius who nodded.

"E.F. is Elena Furlong," he said. "She is a ranking commander of Seliss. Recently, she has seen rapid promotion. We only know this because of our inside intel, of course. Once she started climbing the titles with speed, we began to keep an eye on her. She has ties similar to Villette's to Malvuk, the *I.M.* signed here." He pointed to the letter on the table, and there was a small jolt of pride in Syd's belly that turned sour. Matius shook his head. "Regardless, Furlong is unofficially considered the second in command now for the Seliss training campus and if she and Malvuk have made negotiations for some facilities…and this research…"

He trailed off, losing the thread. Villette reached out to him again and gave his arm a reassuring squeeze. He gritted his teeth but slouched forward.

"Wenna feared telling you the truth for this very reason," Matius said, voice low and ashamed. "She feared Adeline would retaliate in some way. And"—he took a deep breath—"It seems she was correct."

"Malvuk has arranged facilities in Seliss for some type of research," Keal brought the conversation back to the facts. "And that is somehow tied to Adeline." His eyes were distant again.

"Yes," Villette confirmed.

Something boiled in Syd's veins. "So, we go after her. We know where she's going. We know who is helping her.

We don't know where she is, and we don't know where Malvuk is. But we do know where Furlong is."

"We can't just barge into Seliss," Keal countered, his jaw dropped at the idea.

"...No," Matius said slowly. "But, we do have a way in."

Villette shook her head urgently. "Do whatever you will, but Syd stays with me. Her training isn't anywhere near complete and we're quickly running out of time."

Syd turns sharply to Villette. "The hell I will. Adeline is *gone*. Out there somewhere, going straight into enemy territory, backed by a madman. That's a little more important than you messing with my head at the moment, don't you think?"

"Syd, you won't—"

But Matius cut Villette off with a wave of his hand. "We do not know what Adeline is getting mixed up in. There's advantage to having Syd on our side."

Impatience flared in Syd at being talked about as if she weren't there. Once again pawns being played.

"I'm going too," Keal said, and everyone turned to him.

Keal had never been one to stake claims in anything but his own research. So when Syd tilted her head at him to ask if he was sure, he cut her off at the chase.

"I'm the only one of us who has worked closely with Malvuk recently, right? I might be helpful. Besides that, Adeline *is* my friend and I *am* a trained as a soldier too. The lab coat just comes with the job title."

Keal puffed his chest out a little, and Syd found herself smirking at him despite how awful she felt. She was grateful for his friendship. Grateful she wouldn't have to do this alone. Grateful he was by her and Adeline's side.

Through minor protests from Villette, Syd packed whatever she could carry. They were to walk to Pella's Wish to secure water transport to Kilos and Avant Academy, where Matius said they could plan better. She tucked the journal deep into a backpack she'd found in the closet of her room. She slung the bag just over her shoulder as Keal came to get her, the floxling at his heels.

"It's not coming with us, is it?" Syd asked, worried about the small thing making a sea trip.

"Matius told me it'd have a good home in the estuary at Avant. There are plenty of human attendants and animals to play with while we're gone."

Syd frowned, thinking it had plenty of humans and animals to play with here, but Keal's hopeful voice caused hers to keep quiet. "If you're keeping it as a pet, you should probably name it," she said, pushing past him and making her way out of the house.

"Been thinking about that. What about Keeraw?" He followed her out.

"...Like *Eichon* Keeraw?"

"Yeah, she had such great healing majik. Greater than Wenna's even. What do you think?"

Syd stopped, turning around to Keal and the floxling. She bent down, chittering at it. It tilted its head at her but stayed behind Keal. "Having a pet is a big responsibility," she teased Keal and stood up.

She smiled at him, and he smiled back in a knowing sort of way. Keal had always had a way with talking to things that weren't necessarily human. She'd seen it time and again with australs and the beasts in the training center. It became so frequent, Syd and Adeline had started teasing him about keeping so many 'pets'.

"I like it," Syd said, trying the name out and calling to it. To her surprise, Keeraw trotted up to her obediently.

CHAPTER EIGHTEEN

Three Years Prior

Keal took his typical seat at their table for mid meal.

"So, how was class?" he asked.

Syd gave a shrug, leaning over her bowl. She wolfed down the thick, fish stew and rice by the spoonful. Adeline went for the bread instead. She chewed thoughtfully, dusting her finger and thumb together to rid them of crumbs,

"Y'know," Adeline said. "You'd think mom's advisors would have taught me more about Seliss, but for once… classes aren't a waste of time. Like, I knew Seliss was a threat, but I didn't realize just how much. I always thought they were some little academy in a swamp."

Keal finished slurping his broth directly from his bowl.

"Yeah, strange huh? Apparently they're twice the size of Magnate, but they don't recruit like the rest of us."

Adeline quieted again, wondering how in Nova's name Seliss Academy recruited more than ACES, Magnate, and Avant Academies combined.

"Anyway," she interrupted her own thoughts. "How's advanced austral training going? You started private lessons with Malvuk today, didn't you?"

Syd coughed at that, pointing her spoon at Keal. "Something's wrong with that guy. Be careful."

Keal shook his head. "You'd find something wrong with every instructor here if you could. He's fine. In fact, he just started showing me how to bond with the austral energies for better control. He says I'm a natural."

Keal puffed out his chest just as two other cadets came up and knocked the wind out of him with a sharp slap on the back.

"Natural suck up more like it," a tall girl with light, blond hair sneered at him.

Adeline glared, eyes focusing on the girl. Her ears burned hot.

"Must be nice having Mommy make all the arrangements for you, huh?" Another, beefier boy folded his arms, staring down at Keal.

Syd made to stand, pushing her tray away from her loudly, and clenched her fists.

"Oh? And what're you going to do, Eheris?" The girl said, bringing her fists up into a fighter's stance.

Adeline jumped up and slammed her shoulder into the girl's side, knocking her off balance and onto the floor. She reached behind to the training sword always strapped on her back, hand on hilt, only stopping when she realized she was about to pull her weapon on another student. She swallowed hard. The tables around them all stared, silent. The boy turned to Adeline, putting his hands up in peace.

"Easy. No harm meant. Just having fun."

Adeline said nothing, but stared him down as she read his lips. The thunder in her ears was deafening. When she didn't move, he helped the blonde girl up, and they walked away without a word. Adeline and Syd sat back down, looking to Keal. His face red, he stared at the table. They each waited until the tables around them started to chat again.

"What was that about?" Adeline asked, trying to keep her voice low.

"You really know how to make friends." Syd smirked, and Adeline pursed her lips.

"Those two are the only other advanced austral cadets...they're upset that I was chosen to work directly with Malvuk," Keal said quietly, looking up and in the direction the two had wandered off in.

"But, I mean, you are the better specialist, right? You deserved it." Adeline asked.

Keal shrugged. "Maybe. There wasn't ever really a contest, just an announcement."

The three quieted down and slowly went back to their food, Adeline looking off over Keal's shoulder.

Present Day

When it came time to say their goodbyes to Villette, Syd was at a loss for words. Should she thank her for all she's done? For all she helped reveal? Instead, Villette embraced her.

"I'm sure we'll meet again soon and pick up where we left off."

There was a glint of knowing in Villette's black eyes that set Syd on edge, but she nodded. And before she knew it, her feet followed Matius out of town.

The walk was quiet, and they kept a steady pace. Every so often something would rustle in the bushes under the increasingly pink sunset sky. Keeraw would leave the group to go chase a bird or squirrel and then come trotting back triumphantly.

"How long are you going to keep him?" Syd asked to fill the silence and shake off the drone of anxiety. Walking helped, but it wasn't enough.

Keal bent down to pick up Keeraw. "Aw, is Syd trying to get rid of you already?"

Syd didn't understand what place a floxling had in their future, but she also didn't understand her own place until very recently, so she kept her mouth shut.

Ahead, Matius guided them to Pella's Wish. Once a thriving port town, it had been the site Eichon Pella used as her home base during her expeditions at the end of the fifth era. Syd's texts had said Pella was a fire Eheri before her transference, and had used her majik to burn down the forests around the shoreline to build Pella's Wish. Many types of fire breathing salamander had since been named after her, and she was credited for discovering the isle of Kilos.

And still, Syd thought to herself, that was nothing compared to what she was supposed to do. But she couldn't think about that now. She could only focus on the next thing because any time she tried to think of the past, or even much further into the future, her head ached, her stomach twisted, and something protective roiled under her skin in a way that made her uneasy. She still had the Madness to deal with, and Nova beyond that, but those things would just have to wait because the next thing was to find Adeline.

"Our contact in Pella's Wish will get us to Kilos by morning," Matius interrupted her thoughts.

"Why didn't we just get a 'ship?" Syd asked.

"This is quicker than sending a message to Avant without having my comms specialists. Seliss controls the airwaves in this region. It's too dangerous without the necessary precautions."

That would explain why Malvuk had sent an old-fashioned letter, Syd thought. *It would have passed through a network of Council contacts. Much safer than anything else.*

"So, we get to Avant. Then what?" Keal asked.

"I'll first need to meet with my officers. You two will take the additional time to rest," Matius said, ending the conversation flat.

Syd bit her lip but said nothing. She adjusted the straps of her bag and felt the heaviness of the journal there, tucked away, and the ACES band in her pocket. A breeze danced off the calm sea waters as they approached the shore. She stayed quiet; whatever burden she carried would be her own for now. The wind danced through her hair, and she squinted at the purple haze overtaking the horizon. Nova and Runar illuminated everything from high above.

The last time Syd and Adeline had been to the Taams was about a year ago, during break from ACES. There'd been a new club opening in Galssop. And even though political tensions never seemed to reach the electric city, they still disguised Adeline as best as they could. They'd caked on her makeup, closer to a clown than anything, and she'd laughed, touching her face in the mirror—an even melody of hiccups from somewhere deep in her chest.

Syd's heart ached at the distant echo of the sound. Now that moment felt so long ago, so far out of reach. Her yearning yo-yoed, snapping back and slamming her into the present again. Syd glanced to Keal, her stomach in knots. She opened her mouth to say something, some form of thanks for him being here with her. But Keal only nodded.

"That looks like the dock," he said, scooping Keeraw and picking up the pace.

Syd had been daydreaming so long she hadn't seen the tiny village sprout up right in front of them. A small, creaking dock took a rather brutal beating from even the laziest of waves. At its end was a small vessel whose sides were patched with scraps of metal.

They approach a man who seemed to be more bushy gray beard than anything else. He wore a rain hat and old fisherman waders. He puffed on a pipe and only removed it when they drew near. His piercing, blue eyes scanned them, and the smell of tobacco overtook Syd. It was similar to the heady scent of Matius's leather jacket and boots. It mingled with the sharp smell of sea salt and sour, rotting seaweed. Her stomach churned.

Matius waved in greeting, and the two shook hands. Syd looked past them down the path into the village. Only a few lights glowed in the last glimmers of sunset.

"Nollan, it is good to see you again," Matius said.

"Sir," Nollan responded stoutly. "Ready to go back then, aye? And with more cargo?"

Nollan looked over Matius's shoulder to Keal and then Syd who averted her eyes to the ground. Matius coughed, and that ended any line of questioning.

"Ah none of my business. Payment though?" Nollan's voice turned up.

"Of course," Matius said.

The two discussed specifics, and Syd's eyes floated back to the seaship. She nudged Keal with her elbow and nodded to the patchwork with a perked eyebrow. Before Keal could say anything, Nollan pointed to Keeraw in Keal's arms.

"I don't take beasts aboard."

Keal looked to Matius with a start. "What? We can't just leave him here. Not after what he did for Sy—"

Matius cut him off before he said too much. "We'll pay extra."

Nollan grunted, but eventually nodded, and they each made their way onto the deck. It was a small ferryboat, though by the smell, it was more used for fishing than crossings. They each followed Nollan to the helm's cabin. Keal closed the door behind them. Yellow light illuminated a worn cloth bench and a metal floor with missing rivets. Some loose wiring hung precariously.

Unknowingly, Syd found herself ready to sit in the captain's chair until Nollan gave a grunt and moved his pipe from one side of his mouth to the other.

"Oh. Sorry…" Syd said, distracted by the shape of the boat. "Force of habit."

"Syd's the best pilot at ACES," Keal said.

Syd and Matius shot him a glare, and Keal quieted, taking his seat on the bench.

"Of airships," Syd mumbled, punctuating and killing the conversation.

She joined Keal on the bench, and something in the

back of her mind hissed. Matius sat on the bench across from them, and everything felt…

Off, Syd thought.

Keal was a renowned austral scholar. Matius was the leader of the most elite mercenary force in the world. And she was the next damn Eichon. What the hell were they doing buying passage on such a rickety boat?

The awkward silence continued, and when Nollan started the engine, the cabin shook violently. The boat jolted forward, and Keal lurched into her. Keeraw gave a disgruntled yelp, climbing from Keal's lap into his coat pocket.

Eventually, they all eased into the steady, rhythmic vibrations of machine and sea, and Syd watched Nollan scan the expanse from his window. The confined space of the cabin and the vast darkness outside made her chest constrict, and the silence made her mind wander. Neither of which she was ready for. A metronomic beep came from the control panel scanner, signaling they were the only ones on the waters.

"How long did you say until we get to Kilos?" Syd interrupted whatever was about to creep into her mind next.

"We'll be there before mornin'" Nollan replied in a voice that was almost comforting if it hadn't been so noncommittal.

She looked over to Keal again who just shrugged and relaxed into his side of the bench. Matius stared at the floor harshly, lost in his own thoughts. With nothing else to do, Syd closed her eyes and leaned back. She matched the rocking of the boat to her breath, inhaling and exhaling as though she were the ocean, the watery depths, and everything that lived below.

Syd's head snapped and jerked her body awake. The sounds of alarming yelps were coming from inside Keal's lab coat. Keal tried to calm Keeraw, but that only made the yelping worse. She looked to Matius who stood hunched over behind Nollan's seat.

"Lil' beast must know there's a storm headed our way," Nollan said.

He nodded his head toward the window, at a cluster of clouds shooting lightning across the sky. The only things brighter were Nova and Runar, hanging low and heavy on the open sea.

"We're gonna have ta divert a bit," Nollan concluded to no one.

The boat gave a wild shake, and winds created bigger and bigger waves as they slowly veered off and away from their main course. Syd kept her eyes on the clouds, jaw tight and hands gripped on the bench below her to keep her steady.

"I know she's not much ter look at," Nollan continued, "But this little beauty of a boat has fared much worse. We'll be through the storm before you know it."

Syd's nerves shot up, annoyed and a little frightened. Sea travel was so much less efficient than airship. Voyages took longer, you were at the mercy of the weather, and there were too many variables to account for.

Keeraw's yelps turned into whines. The wind increased,

and the metal floor creaked against the few bolts holding it in place. Thunder grew louder, closer, and more threatening with each passing second. The electricity in the air made Syd's skin crawl.

Over the howling outside, she heard another boom of thunder so close that it made her jump to her feet. She gripped an overhead railing to steady her legs and stood on the other side of Matius behind the captain.

We're not moving fast enough.

The thought was interrupted when she was slammed to the side, her grip lost and her body colliding with the cabin's wall painfully. She righted herself and looked to make sure Keal and Matius were okay.

"What the hell was that?" Keal asked.

But Nollan didn't answer, and Matius only clenched and unclenched his jaw, his arms braced against the control panel. The screens flashed, beeping their own alarms, and the sounds rattled Syd's mind. She looked back to Nollan and followed his bright, blue eyes as they gazed out, his mouth slack and his pipe barely hanging on.

Stormy nights had been her favorite at the orphanage. While the older kids would stay up late telling ghost stories, Syd would anxiously wait for everyone to fall asleep. She knew that, in the morning, the beach would be filled with new creatures washed ashore by the storm. Shells, sea flowers, even some new wayward fish would be there, waiting for her. A new world to explore.

One story the kids used to tell was about the most fearsome sea creature, Argodana. The myth said that deep below the seas, the mother hydra waited. She had six heads, one for each of the oceans she ruled over. Argodana was the only hydra left in the seas; her mates and children had vanished at the hands of humans. On nights when she felt particularly loathsome—or lonesome—she summoned electric squalls to vanquish any man seeking passage in the cover of night.

How lucky then to be those men.

Syd's eyes turned up, growing big at the sight of six eel-like heads towering above them. The beast's necks whipped around as if calling more thunder with each cry. Dark water covered Argodana's body, glimpses of her black-scaled enormity only visible in the half-second flashes of lightning.

The boat jolted again, and even though she had been better prepared, Syd found herself flying over Nollan's chair. Keal and Keeraw landed somewhere on the floor behind her, and Matius's face threatened to go through the window. Nollan's face was white, and Syd wasn't exactly sure how much longer the tiny ferry was going to hold up. She gave a frustrated growl, her body already sore from being tossed around. Keal was only just righting himself, and Matius looked to be calculating something on the control panel. She gripped her way through the cabin past them, water seeping in everywhere.

"Syd?!" Keal called over the noise of the seaship's strain and the storms blasts.

"Wait here!" she shouted back, jamming her elbow against the door and letting in the deafening roar from the outside deck. She squinted against the water hitting her from all sides, drenched from the ice-cold sky and sea. Another tidal wave came for them, and she hugged the nearest railing with all her might.

For a moment she saw stars and felt her side snap. Her entire body screamed at her, but she didn't have time. Keal yelled something from behind her, and before she had time to process, he appeared next to her, grasping and clinging to the railing. She gritted her jaw so tight that her teeth threatened to break, and lightning flashed again, illuminating Keal's hand. In it, a canister, and he flicked it open.

Syd's vision filled with bright blue. It swirled and enveloped her and she shook her head violently, knowing she'd be useless if she couldn't see. Her muscles tensed, readying for the next impact and unsure if she'd be able to withstand another. But it never came.

The vapors faded, and a blue, transparent sheen was all around her. A protection barrier was being built by small blue energy sprites. Keal mouthed something again, but he was muffled, everything dulled inside the circle. Then, something primal, hungry, surged.

Enough, it said with a voice that gripped her mind like tar.

She dug into herself, Keal's austral providing some cover from the outside. She closed her eyes, searching for her gray mist, calling for it somewhere behind, beneath, this other, darker force. *Find the strings of yourself,* Villette had said. *Pluck them.* But the threads were distant, and when she reached for them, they retreated.

The deck beneath her quaked with another blast from Argodana, and Syd's eyes shot open with panic. Debris flew past her, and Keal retreated for cover. She didn't know how long she had, how long the protection austral would last. She closed her eyes and tried again.

This time, she was met with a strike of searing pain that sent her to her knees.

Where are you? she called inward and listened outward at the continued wail of beast and sea. The sound of the protection austral whooshed around, repairing the damage done to the barrier. She smelled the storm, the salt so sharp it stung even in her shield. Thunderous claps interrupted her searching, and she cried out, digging her fingernails into the deck. Unable to concentrate, unable to search, unable to find her majik.

In the distant, inky black of her mind, a silver light came to her, and she reached for it, desperate. It retreated, and she followed.

Wait! she called out. *We need you!*

Confused, Syd began to plead. The light stopped, swiftly coming into view and forming itself as a floating ball. The voice that came forth was like her own, but hollowed— all echoes and imitation. It radiated through her body more than it spoke, questioning and doubting.

Dread flooded her, threatening to pull her away from the silver light, from her majik, from herself.

"No!" she gasped a sob in the surrounding storm.

The orb faded then, visions drowning her senses. For a moment, all she could hear was her breath. The deepest black, closed in. It restricted, confined. It grabbed her and held her down, pinned under its force, it's weight. She struggled, crying out, pushing and twisting against the dark.

She heard it before she felt it, a resounding crack.

Then, searing, a blistering as scalding as it was true starting at her chest and ripping out. The smell of iron and earth. She was on fire; she *was* fire.

And her light buried her before the pain.

First, there was the sound of an infant crying and crumbling red rocks and stones. Dust came for her, filling her eyes. She heaved, choking on it. She plucked at the string, suffocating.

Then, there was the smell of a beach, bright and sunny with children playing on the shore. She grasped for them. Their faces turned to taunts and their eyes filled with fear. Her hand outstretched, mist trailing up her arms, her neck, and she screamed before it reached her mouth.

The space reset, and the children avoided her, laughed at her, and abandoned her. She moved toward them again, and they recoiled. Their laughter cut off abruptly, swallowed by the sounds of a creaking seaship and the sight of a young Adeline, giggling and smiling at Syd.

Warmth engulfed her body, wrapping her in soft comfort and safety. She was covered in gray majik, and Adeline didn't retreat like the other children.

Somewhere beyond Syd was a violent roar, and the visions faded. The orb shimmered from behind it. She sank into the blankness around her once again, sticky and slow. Then, there was nothing but the silence of herself, bold, and strong, and true. The threads of herself burned into the back of her mind. Impressions buried in forgotten valleys and groves.

The orb returned to that dark space. It waited, pulsed. She focused all of herself on it, refusing to let it out of her sight again, refusing its tricks and distractions. She threw its diversions aside. With each in-breath, she found more and more resolve, more and more clarity. With each out-breath, she stayed steadfast, heavy, planted. She was unmovable, untouchable in this place.

Help, she called to the orb and reached to the back of her mind.

There was nothing but the silence of herself.

You've spent too long hiding, denying yourself of who you are. You are a piece of Eher's brilliance. Of their light. You shine as bright and reach as deep. You cover all. You are all. You are everything. The orb pulsed again. *You do not need help.*

Thunder roared, and her vision was pierced with white light that sent her tumbling back into time. A wave of sounds shook through her, her nose once again filled with storm and salt. She took in the sight of Argodana and listened to her cries. When Syd stood, the movements of the seaship, of the beast, of Keal and Matius and Nollan—it was all so easy to calculate. She knew where each blow would land, where each wave would crash. Reality resumed before her, because of her.

"Syd?!" Keal's voice came to her over the chaos around them.

She looked at him, his face a foil of confusion. Staring up at Argodana, Syd forced her mist to curl around her extended arm. It met her fingertips and concentrated there for a moment. Her other arm came then, forming a circle. The majik expanded into a perfect sphere. Her body moved on its own accord, but she didn't fight it. She couldn't. The movements, the steps, the dance took her over as if it was the only one she'd ever known.

With a final, knowing thrust, she pushed her majik out, and she found herself flying, curving around Keal, Matius, and Nollan. Shooting through the metal and wood and wire of the boat. She swelled higher and higher until she was looking down on Argodana's heads.

And then she unleashed, slipping into the peaceful surrender of her expanse.

CHAPTER NINETEEN

The calls of seabirds filled the room, and the blackness behind Syd's eyelids turned to a deep red. A faint breeze touched her face. Cautiously, slowly, she opened her eyes and instantly hissed at the brightness.

Yellow curtains swayed on the window above, and the bird cries came again, louder. She wiggled her fingers, her muscles tight and aching. With a grunt, she moved her arms and checked the rest of herself. Everything seemed to be in order, though her right ribs were sore. She froze at the sound of footsteps approaching.

A woman in a coat similar to Keal's entered the small room, which appeared to be an infirmary. A read out of numbers displayed on a screen to Syd's left, and a single stool and side table were on her right. The woman leaned over Syd and squinted at the screen. Her dark hair was pulled back tight and face emotionless. She lifted back one of Syd's eyelids suddenly and flashed a light into her eye. Syd recoiled at the bright pain.

"How are you feeling?" she asked.

The woman moved to repeat the motion on Syd's other eye, and Syd dodged the motion. Something glinted off the woman's coat. A name tag with the familiar navy-blue signet. Two scripted *A*s, one flipped upside down to form a diamond shape. *Avant.* Still, Syd's jaw remained clenched as the doctor finished her checks.

"Well, aside from a few cracked ribs you seem fine," the

doctor said and walked out of the room without another word.

Syd closed her eyes again and listened to the birds outside. *Avant*, she repeated. Where were Matius and Keal? Were they okay? Did Nollan make it? And Keeraw? She thought about calling for the woman, but her vocal chords protested the mere thought, her eyelids too heavy.

"Hey, Syd…" another voice jerked her out of falling asleep.

The familiar slip of the *s* in her name shook her awake fully, and she blinked at the hulking figure in the doorway.

"Gaav?" she whispered, and he moved closer.

Syd forced herself to sit up, confusion swarming her again. She braced against the pain in her ribs, jaw tight. This didn't make sense. Gaav was a Seliss commander. Had Syd read the name tag wrong? Dreamt it? She gripped the bed under her.

Gaav chuckled nervously, "I told Keal I shouldn't be the one to keep watch in case you woke up."

Keal? He's okay? Syd glared at him.

Gaav's hands shot up as if to prove he was innocent. "It's ok. Keal's ok. He's with the Director."

Syd shook her head, closing her eyes as they started to cross, and her mind played catch up. *Director? Which Director? Avant's or Seliss's?*

"Where…" Syd licked her lips, testing her voice again. It was dry and whispery. "Where are we?"

"Oh. Heh…" Gaav moved closer. "Avant."

"But you're…Seliss? The train?"

"Not…exactly. It's probably better if Director Keylen

explains this, but…" His voice was a deep, comforting gravel, and now that she could look at him—*really* look at him—she saw he'd grown into a handsome man with a strong jawline. Tanned skin and thick, brown hair that fell easily over his forehead and off to the side. A glimpse of dark stubble on his cheeks. Such a difference from the chubby boy who had always won at tug of war.

Gaav's eyes darted to the door, and he lowered his voice. "I was on assignment, undercover, when Seliss caught wind that Adeline Keylen was traveling the Taams. Imagine my surprise to see you there, too, of all people. You three were lucky I was in charge of that search." He paused, jutting out his bottom lip just like he did as a kid when he was in thought. "We'll have to teach you to lie better."

"Yeah…" Syd trailed off, distracted.

Assignment. Undercover. *Spy*, was what he meant, and Syd very much doubted him being there had anything to do with luck. The rumored spy network led by the Eichon's spouse wouldn't just *happen to be in the neighborhood* as their daughter traveled into enemy territory. Regardless, Syd couldn't help but be impressed at just how far Gaav had come since being adopted.

"How long have we—have I—" She cut off, sudden flashes of memory coming to her. The storm. Argodana. The silver orb.

"About three days now. You've got good timing too. Director Keylen was about to go ahead without you."

Syd inhaled, looking at her lap. "I guess…you know, then? About everything?

Gaav nodded, and to her shock, Syd was filled with

relief. She let out her breath, slow and careful. At least she wouldn't have to explain.

"First chance I got, I cut my mission short to get back here. I'm *technically* on recruitment leave from Seliss."

Syd didn't exactly know what that meant, but she had bigger concerns. She tossed aside the sheets and made to leave the bed. Gaav was at her side in an instant, offering to help her move.

"Doc said you cracked some ribs."

She felt her wrappings under the infirm gown, then gratefully accepted Gaav's help.

"The healer did a good job. I can barely feel anything."

Gaav tilted his head but said nothing. Syd flushed, embarrassed. She'd almost forgotten that Avant didn't staff Eheri, let alone train them. Something to do with the local Terian sect outnumbering the Rhurgari and Novari both. How they'd ever allowed Matius on the island at all was beyond her, but that was a question for a later time. This explained *why* the doctor had been so rude, though. Eheri weren't allowed on Avant campus, not even as visitors.

The door opened, and Matius, followed by Keal, stepped in. Syd was flooded with so many emotions; her eyes teared up at the sight of them both. Gaav held a salute until Matius nodded to him and then looked to Syd. Her watery eyelids dried up when she saw indifference where she had expected kindness. Dark circles had started to form under his aging eyes, his facial hair thick with speckles of salt and pepper.

"That will be all, Slait," Matius said to Gaav, who exited at the dismissal.

"Are you well enough to walk?" Matius asked, his eyes blank. "Dr. Yowri has administered restorative aids. You should be feeling the effects of them."

"I think so," Syd responded.

"Good. Keal, you'll escort Syd to my offices after she's fully recovered. You're free to catch up until then."

Matius exited without another word. Keal waited until his footsteps faded completely before he hugged Syd, quick and sudden. She winced against the embrace, her side crying out.

"Oh, sorry," Keal said, pulling away. "I'm just—I'm glad you're ok. And awake. I thought you—" He stumbled over his words, and, instead, he grabbed her clothes off the hooks on the wall and placed them near her on the side table. He turned around and waited, embarrassed.

Syd had so many questions, but she did feel silly in the medical gown. She changed, slowly working her way back into her clothes again. She checked her pants pocket for Adeline's ACES band and came away empty-handed. Her stomach lurched. Had it been lost at sea somehow? Where was her backpack? The journal?

"Okay, I'm finished," she said to Keal. "So what... happened?"

Keal offered his arm, and she took it. They left the infirm and exited out into the greater parts of Avant, taking deliberate steps as Syd felt her muscles finally loosen. The smell of sea hit her first, but not sea like ACES, or even Pella's Wish. Sea like sandy beaches and palm trees, like warm breezes over salty ones, and lapping waters instead of tidal waves. Sea like how she remembered the orphanage and the long, bright days full of exploring, and curiosity, and hope.

Avant was laid out in four quadrants, all surrounding a central elevator bank, three stories high. Each quad was closed off by glass walls and sliding doors that spilled out into grassy courtyards, open to the outside. Young cadets—*No. Mercenaries,* Syd corrected herself—in dark blue uniforms socialized and laughed among the tables and manicured lawns, outlined by shrubs. Syd could almost hear the trickle of the white stone fountains that decorated the outer hedges.

"It was…incredible," Keal started. "You—your majik—held Argodana in place long enough for us to get away. You didn't just slow her. You actually *stopped* her, Syd." Keal waved his other arm excitedly. "I have to ask…how did you do it? I mean, you were unconscious. How were you able to—"

Syd shook her head at him, unable to recall anything but the feeling of release, of surrender, and then nothing again, nothing at all, until she woke here. Before that, there had been the silver orb and Adeline's young face. The kids from the orphanage and Keal's austral. Syd stopped in her tracks.

"That austral!" Syd turned to him. "Keal, thank you. I couldn't have…You risked your life coming on the deck like that."

"I mean," Keal's cheeks turned a few shades pinker, and he ran a hand through his hair. "All our lives were at risk."

Syd threw her arms around him then, hugging him close through the pain.

"Still, thank you," she said, muffled into his collar.

"Uh…don't mention it?" Keal said, and when she pulled away, he gave her a smile. "You act like we haven't trained together before."

But this was different, and they both knew it. They'd never been in the field together, in a controlled setting or otherwise. The deck of a ferry being attacked by Argodana wasn't a scenario they planned for inside the training center at ACES.

She decided to change the subject. "Where's Nollan?"

Keal rolled his eyes. "Probably drunk in Kilos town by now, bragging about his grand run-in with the most feared of all the sea creatures. He passed out as soon as you went on deck. Missed the whole thing. Probably for the best, though. Don't really want word getting out that you—"

"And you?" Syd interrupted before he could say too much, suddenly embarrassed she hadn't asked sooner. "Were you hurt?"

"Nothing a little sleep couldn't fix. We've all just been kind of…waiting for you to wake up."

"Yeah…Gaav mentioned that."

"But look, Syd, things—," he stopped, searching for his words. "Tensions are high. Matius found Adeline's journal in your backpack. He's not happy you didn't turn it over. That, and her ACES band."

Syd's chest flushed with defensive heat.

"What do you mean *not happy*?"

Keal shrugged. "You withheld possible evidence to where Adeline went or what might have happened."

Syd forced her anger aside, but cursed herself for not reading the journal sooner, "And? Do we know more?"

"I don't know. Matius hasn't shared any of what was in it with any of us."

Syd chewed her lip. "Us?"

"He's put together a few of us for—to—" Keal sighed. "At the very least, you'll be happy to know we *are* going after Adeline, and soon. Like, really soon. Like, tonight. But, hey, Matius will probably do a better job than me explaining all this."

People kept saying that, and Syd folded her arms in thought, but she didn't protest. A slick fear slid through her, and she didn't know if the new pain in her chest was from the healing aids wearing off or from panic. Frankly, it was probably better if she didn't know which. They walked up the stairs leading to the elevator, framed by a winding ramp, and stepped in. The door shut silently, and Keal swiped his band to be taken to the top floor.

Syd coughed nervously. "Is Keeraw okay?"

"Oh!" Keal grinned. "Yeah, little sprout is doing just fine in the estuary. Already made some new friends and he's taking well to the handlers. They may not like Eheri here, but they don't seem to mind creatures with majik." Keal shrugged.

In no time at all the doors reopened into a lavish hall. Dark marble floors met the edges of white walls, lined with knotty potted plants that reached for the glass ceiling. A thick, navy rug ran the length between the elevator and another set of doors. Above them, an intricate, fan-like mural was carved into glossy redwood. The space felt sturdy, ornate, and precise.

The doors gave way into another light-flooded room. A large table took up most of the space with a singular desk at the opposite side. Behind it, the walls were mounted with monitors that showed halls and stairwells from the first and second floors of Avant. There were no papers, nothing askew. Everything was sterile and intentional. Gaav and another woman sat at the table when Syd and Keal entered. The woman was short and lithe. Her hair graded from blue to purple to pink and cascaded down the right side of her pale face.

Before anything could be said, the doors opened again, and Matius came trailing in. Gaav and the woman stood immediately at attention, holding their salutes.

"At ease," Matius said, and they both relaxed back into their seats.

Syd and Keal followed suit, and without a word, Matius tapped a panel at the head of the table. A hologram keyboard projected onto the surface, and he typed something that caused a holographic image to float and render in front of them.

"Syd," Matius finally said and motioned. "You already know Gaavin Slait. He is our lead Intel commander for Avant, and this is Widjette Onna. Widje leads our Comms."

But they're both so young. Gaav couldn't be more than twenty or twenty-one, and this blue-haired Widje, she couldn't be more than seventeen. Probably younger even. How had they reached such ranks so soon?

"Ah, I'm just a tinkerer," Widje said, smiling. She leaned forward on the table and watched the hologram come to life. She placed her elbow on the table and cupped her chin in her hand.

"Be that as it may, it seems the only system Widje can't break into is Zevir's," Matius said severely.

Widje's eyes gleamed, and she mumbled to herself, "Bastards're gonna beat me to it..."

The image finished rendering and produced a 3-D blueprint of a spider-like structure. Syd instantly recognized it. *Seliss.*

"While you were recovering, we fleshed out our reconnaissance and infiltration plan. Assistant Director to Seliss Academy, Elena Furlong, *is* somehow connected to Adeline's disappearance. I've convinced the Eichon to hold off on a direct attack for now. Instead, we will have the four of you enter into the campus as part of the Seliss training forces and find out what you can."

Syd's chest tightened with anger and hurt. Matius was acting like this was any other mission. That he could just send his mercs and spies out into the world to fix the problem, like this wasn't Adeline they were talking about. Syd blinked away her emotions and adjusted in her seat to refocus, but her eyebrows came together, and a deep impatience flushed from her chest down to her toes. *No, not impatience,* she thought. *Rage.*

"Our evidence," Matius continued without much of a pause. "Suggests that Seliss may not be at the root of this. Malvuk, Furlong, and Adeline may be working alone and using Seliss resources right under Director Sevnior's nose.

Even then, it's only a matter of time. Should Sevnior find out, we cannot account for what he may do.

"Malvuk has continued to secure funding for his laboratory sites near the campus, as much as the Council has attempted to dissuade him. He is, ultimately, a free agent to the highest bidder—" Matius cut himself off and leaned back in the chair. "We suspect him to be operating out of one of those sites." He then nodded to Gaav.

"Adeline's safety is the first and foremost concern," Gaav continued. "Our greatest fear is that, should Sevnior discover what Furlong has been up to before we do, he will use Adeline to his advantage. We can only imagine what that might look like.

"There are numerous buildings surrounding the outer regions of the Seliss Academy campus," Gaav explained and pointed to a number of scattered structures on the image projection. "The northeast and northwest buildings are mainly used as supply holds. I have not yet been granted access to the others."

"But!" Widje chimed in and reached out to spin the image. She zoomed in on a particular building with her fingers. "This building here? The heat map scans have come back and there's a great amount of energy reported in this area. I haven't been able to crack that part of the system *yet*, but if there was a lab for, say, a mad scientist in Seliss, I'd put all my DaCs on that one."

She zoomed in more, and the image repopulated the scan of the T-shaped building to show four underground levels, entrances, doors, and an elevator shaft. Syd glanced from the image to Keal and back again, skeptical.

"Ah. Lucky for us, Seliss is terrible about securing their digital model databases," Widje smiled and clapped her hands.

"Isn't that a little...convenient?" Syd asked before she could stop herself, and the room went silent. Widje's face dropped, but Syd refused to feel bad. This wasn't any other mission. This wasn't a drill. This wasn't even a field trial. This was *actually* going directly into Seliss. This was *actually* acquiring a target. This was *actually* all about Adeline, and that seemed to keep slipping from the forefront. Syd's jaw tensed, but she stood her ground, staring blankly at the rotating model.

"Be that as it may, it is our best course of action at the moment," Matius's voice was testy. "I will be requesting aid from Magnate should we need it. Zevir cannot, and should not, expend its resource due to the continued Seliss cyberattacks.

"Gaav's position as a ranking Seliss commander has yet to be compromised. Widje has altered his personnel file to have him on recruitment leave, returning tomorrow morning. The three of you are to pose as Seliss cadets while I manage the Magnate negotiations."

Matius tapped a string of commands into the keyboard. Three profiles appeared and replaced the blueprint.

"Widje has input your new identities into their system. Seliss cares less about security and more about war. They are bigger than the other academies combined because they recruit anyone. You will simply be another number."

Matius clicked a button and the image dissolved

suddenly. He stood, and Gaav and Widje jumped to their feet.

"You leave in 6 hours. Widje will fill you in on anything else at that time." Matius looked to Widje and Gaav then. "You will meet Syd and Keal at the Kilos docks. You are dismissed."

The two saluted Matius once more and immediately vacated. No questions, no hesitation. The blind loyalty of it all sent shivers down Syd's spine. She couldn't imagine ever saluting Rhiuld like that. But Seliss and Avant weren't so different from one another. Their students and cadets followed their leader's blind passion. Seliss took anyone—they came on their own free will. Avant, on the other hand, didn't necessarily recruit, though they did seek potential cadets from less fortunate families and provided them with a better life. Syd's lips pursed.

Matius moved to his desk and opened a drawer. He flung something book-shaped onto the table in front of Syd with a thump so loud, it made her jump out of her thoughts. He returned to his seat and ran a hand over his mouth, as if trying to choose his words carefully. Syd instinctively slunk back in her chair.

"Now this," he said. "Why did you hide it from us?"

Syd's stomach flipped, and she felt like she was going to be sick. *Hide it?* She wasn't hiding anything. Staring at the journal, she shook her head.

"I didn't—" She started and was cut off.

Matius tossed something else onto the table. Adeline's ACES band. The dull black of it mocked her in the swelling silence.

"And that?" he asked.

All Syd could do was stare at Matius. He slouched now, the wrinkles around his eyes seeming to deepen with every passing second. He rubbed his face again.

"Syd, if you are hiding anything else from us, we will find out. You do understand that, don't you?"

Something like embers ignited in her, and she gritted her teeth when she spoke next.

"I'm not hiding anything from you." *What the hell are you accusing me of?* Her fist clenched. She looked at Keal who avoided her gaze.

"...You too?" She spat at Keal. "You think I'd keep something like that on purpose?" Then back to Matius. "I found it while you two were off searching for Adeline. What else was I supposed to do? I didn't even read it, I—" her voice stalled again, and she stammered. She didn't actually know why she kept it. To feel closer to Adeline? To hold onto a piece of her? She'd convinced herself it was because she wanted to protect Adeline and whatever was written on those pages. To help keep that small part of her safe. If she could do that, then maybe Adeline would—The tears welled up suddenly, and her chest burned.

"Does it say anything about her plans?" Syd eventually asked.

"No," Matius concluded, and Syd felt a weight drop from her.

"But," Keal said, "If you truly haven't read it, you probably should. There's—Adeline— Her writing grows hostile toward the final pages. It starts a few weeks before the date of Malvuk's letter."

"So? She was irritated by the situation in Llyn, in general. We all know that." Syd shrugged.

"No, Syd, she becomes aggressive in her writing towards...you, in particular."

Syd's nostrils flared, and she took in a deep breath. Her eyes squinted to Matius who stared at the journal, and then to Keal who perked his eyebrow at her and waited for a response. Instead, she looked up at the glass dome, to the sky overhead, to the clear blue with fluffy, white clouds. The room started to feel small, started to sway as she held back, held on, preventing the embers from igniting into flames. Betrayal, she discovered, tasted like bile and felt like burning flesh.

"If it doesn't help us locate her, I don't need to read it."

Matius stood. "I need to prepare for my meeting with Magnate. Gaav is your mission leader," he said. "He knows how to navigate Seliss. Follow his instructions carefully. I suggest you two rest before leaving. I've arranged two rooms at the Harbor Inn in Kilos town for you."

Keal grabbed the journal, and Syd found her footing as they were dismissed.

CHAPTER TWENTY

The air outside the academy was hot, just like it'd been at the orphanage. The sounds of waves in the distance brought Syd back to peaceful mornings, when she'd wake up to the same sound. Those quiet moments to herself, all on her own, she had fantasized about what spanned the sea surrounding the island, what else was out there. Now, everything felt so much smaller, explored and conquered.

"Keeraw will be ok at the estuary?" Syd asked.

Keal frowned but nodded. "He'll certainly be safer there than trying to smuggle him into Seliss with us."

They matched pace along the walking path from Avant to Kilos town, which followed the shoreline. Students and townsfolk took their leisure in the easy breeze under a bright sun. Syd looked up at Nova's ever-present face, waxing closer and closer to the transference. A constant, pale reminder that was so much heavier than before.

"I guess there's really no going back now, huh?"

Keal followed Syd's gaze. Syd wasn't sure how much guilt she should feel for putting Adeline first, but it felt as large as a moon. She sighed. In Kilos's open valley, ocean on one side and mountains on the other, the clear sky with Nova's haunting reflection was sobering.

"Eh, never say never," Keal said. "Maybe you'll be the great Eichon who spends her legacy fixing up old airships."

He grinned, and Syd grinned back, but her heart wasn't in it. A group in Avant uniforms jogged passed. She watched them, heard their labored breathing. The soft vibration from their thudding feet reverberated in her chest, and she found the pain from her ribs had all but vanished. Her eyes followed the group on their way to the town's simple archway.

Passing under the stones felt strange, unwelcoming. Syd had wanted to visit Kilos with Adeline but had never been allowed. It was the one thing—well, the one thing besides the journal—Adeline had kept from her, and Syd was beginning to question just how much of that was truly circumstance, or if Adeline had preferred it that way. She filled her lungs with air, breathing out the guilt.

It didn't work. Questions of what and how much she could have done to stop all that led to Adeline's search and rescue. That was, of course, if Adeline even wanted to be rescued.

Kilos's small market plaza was located at the entrance of town. The weapons shop, windows full of last year's leftovers from Magnate, and a few cafes greeted them. Students enjoyed the free afternoon, sitting outside at tables surrounding a large marble fountain whose water spouted from giant, gaping fish heads. The low chatter of conversation, the soft trickles from the fountain, and the distant calls of seabirds made Syd forget herself for a brief, fleeting moment.

"We should take Matius up on his offer," Keal said and pointed to a signpost directing them to the Harbor Inn.

They followed the gray cobblestones of the streets until they found a rotund building with a blue and gold dome. It shone in every direction under the bright sun, and flags of all major city-states, even Seliss, hung on poles attached to the façade.

The maroon-and-white-striped flag cracked in the breeze, distorting the golden emblem: a circle sliced down the center by a black line. Below it, the line split off to form an upside-down Y shape. It was a symbol for forking paths, for questioning the greater knowledge, for the followers of Terianism and those who considered themselves the planet's guardians. At least, that was what ACES taught, and Syd's thoughts turned critical.

Look at me questioning, while heading straight into the belly of the beast.

A beast who, she knew, opposed those who follow the Eichon and Nova's gift. A beast that existed simply because the first Eichon's misor, Misor Seliss, turned on her and gained a following for his anti-Eheri rhetoric. A beast that would eat her up the moment they knew what she was.

What will happen when they learn about Project Nova?

Syd rubbed her hands together and chewed her bottom lip. Keal stopped before heading into the Inn and followed her gaze to the flag.

"Don't worry. Matius knows what he's doing," he said.

The doors chimed at their entrance. A small man shuffled out from behind the back-room door and took his place behind the half-moon counter. The lobby was empty and spacious with a simple blue rug and evenly spaced floor-to-ceiling windows that let in the light. Above, exposed walkways showed the dark, ornate doors to the rooms.

"Ah, sorry folks, no vacancy at the moment. Lots of families visitin' for Avant's final exams, y'see," the man said.

Syd's thoughts wandered to what she and Adeline would be doing right now to ready for their own final field tests and exams leading to their ACES graduation.

Keal spoke when Syd didn't, "I believe Director Keylen has reserved two rooms for us?"

"Oh! Ah, Director Keylen. Yes. Apologies to you both for the assumption." The man bowed, disappearing behind the counter for a moment. "Right then, if you'll follow me," he said.

They were shown to their rooms on the third, top-most floor. Both suites were decorated lavishly with fresh flowers, dusted rugs, hung tapestries, and adjoining balconies.

"Let me know if you need anything else." The man bowed again before taking his leave.

"You grabbed Adeline's journal?" Syd asked.

Keal reached into his coat and handed it to her.

"I'll come get you when we're ready to leave. I'm right next door if you need anything," Keal said without questioning, and Syd was grateful for it.

And why should I even have to explain? she rationalized to herself.

She nodded without another word and latched the door behind her. The silence of the space was soft, comforting, and instantly made her eyelids droop. She sat on the bed with a little bounce, promptly fell asleep on top of the covers.

Syd's eyes fluttered open sometime later. Through the glass doors leading to the balcony, she saw the afternoon sun was still up. She lay still, listening for any other sounds from the room next door. Only when she heard nothing for a while did she roll over to find Adeline's journal.

She traced the grooves and nicks in the leather cover with her fingers. It was the closest thing she had to Adeline now, the lifeline tethering them together still. Adeline felt so very far, and so very close as Syd stared at the wrinkled pages.

Staring at the ceiling, she took the journal in her hands and held it against her chest.

Everyone else has by now; there can't be much harm in me reading it too.

Still, she hesitated and fanned the water-stained pages with her thumbs. Something bubbled in her rib cage, a melting pot of every emotion she hadn't had time to feel yet. Worry surfaced for a single moment and was replaced by sadness, replaced by anger, replaced by worry, replaced by sadness, replaced by—nothing. Which stayed long enough to hold on to, and the cycle made her numb.

And yet, there was something else there in the rolling boil. Excitement? No, that wasn't right. What if they get to Seliss and were discovered before getting to Furlong? What if she was captured? What if she was killed? Something acidic hit the back of her throat. Does this replace Project Nova? Does Wenna still need her? But it didn't matter if Wenna needed her. Or did it? What happened to Project Nova if she didn't make it out of this alive?

Her stomach felt like a stone, growing as the moments ticked on. Fear washing over her, at first gentle, but quickly shifting into a violent tide.

The cries of the seabirds outside brought her back from drowning, and she resumed fanning the pages. The small breeze they made cooled her, and she opened the page still bookmarked by Malvuk's letter. The sight of Adeline's handwriting blurred her vision, and she blinked away the tears.

I am upset with myself and upset with Syd, my mother… Villette. It feels guilty to admit, even egotistical. I have failed and I cannot seem to reconcile this. Has all my training been for nothing? No, I suppose not. Syd as the Eichon would only naturally mean I'd be at her side as Zevir's Commander. I should be excited for her, but I feel empty.

Syd took in a steady, measured breath and skipped along the next pages. She scanned, and the heat in her chest crept up to her neck and face. Words started to jump out at her.

…Why? It is unfair. Am I to sit around and bide my time as Syd trains? Isn't there something we should be doing?…

…What makes her so much more worthy? Meeting with Villette has proved useless. The woman talks in riddles…

Syd's eyes unfocused and her breath caught. Why hadn't Adeline come to her? Talked about things with her? The sob in Syd's throat disappeared and turned to tears, and they overtook her. Only the feeling of wet trailing from the edges of her eyes, only the tickle of the tears running through her hair, only a sick curiosity propelled her forward.

…I need to go to Zevir, to help mother with Seliss and Nova. Father won't allow it, no matter how much we argue. He says my place is here, to help and support Syd. I love her, but this is becoming monotonous and intolerable…

...Maybe they were wrong. Made the wrong choice. Maybe they just need to see it. There has to be another way to be sure...

The heat inside Syd made her skin crawl. The tears slowed and dried, a soft pounding in her head started to replace them. Her eyebrows knotted together, and her fingers acted on their own accord, greedily flipping just to get to the last page and end this.

...I am sure I, too, have some power inside me. I am the Eichon's daughter, after all. It flows through my veins...

...Malvuk must know something more about Nova and the Eichon succession. He has worked with my mother her entire reign, and the two women before her...

...But we cannot meet in plain sight. Syd and my mother would find it a threat and though I could pacify Syd easily, mother is too much for me to go against alone...

...Do they not even care about me? Did they ever?...

...Everything for her, everything because of her...

...It makes me sick...

Syd slammed the book shut and threw it to the floor. The pounding in her head grew fierce. She rolled onto her side, the pressure behind her eyes clouding everything, every judgment she could possibly have made. Tears came when her mind could process no longer. Her body, shaking and gasping, curled tighter and tighter at each unstoppable, unfair, cry.

A loud knocking woke Syd from a dreamless black. The room was decorated in the lattice work of the setting sun, signaling it was time to go. The headache throbbed dully behind her swollen eyes. She swung her legs from the bed and made to open the door.

"Time to go rescue a princess, sleepy head!" Keal chimed, smiling.

"You must have had a great nap…" She muttered and went back to collect the journal from the floor. She caught his gaze when she handed it back to him.

"You read it," he said.

She nodded and shifted her weight.

"She's still Adeline," Keal said. "There's plenty of other stuff in these pages. Good stuff. We just need to be aware. Well, more aware than one usually is when going straight into the enemy's lair anyway."

He returned the journal to the inside of his lab coat.

Heaviness sat in her chest, threatening to cut off her air at any second. Syd tried to remember the last time she smelled lavender. It hadn't been so long ago, had it? But it seemed like forever. Forever since she had seen Adeline smile, full and brilliant and true, pushing her cheeks up in blushing apples and crinkling the corners of her dark eyes. And her laugh, Syd could barely remember the echo.

Pining cascaded through her, from her fingertips to her toes, at once hollowing and overwhelming. She missed Adeline. Not the Adeline from those journal pages, but the Adeline from before. Before they had met with Wenna, before they'd learned of Project Nova. She missed the giggling Adeline that snuck through the halls of ACES late at night with her; the fearless Adeline, always ready for the next fight; the bold Adeline, who would move mountains for the ones she cared about; the curious Adeline, the bored Adeline, the Adeline who propelled everything forward.

It was time for Syd to do the same. Keal was right. There was still plenty of the real Adeline in those pages.

"She's still Adeline," Syd confirmed.

They exited the hotel, and the air outside was thick with the smell of salt and seaweed. The birds were quiet now, and the lights that illuminated the town created a hazy, orange buzz. The sounds of music and chatter echoed from the plaza, and a vast orange-pink sunset greeted them when they rounded the Inn to the docks. A sunset like that took up everything, so massive it could have swallowed Syd whole.

Her heart sank as a full-sized transport seaship bobbed into view. It was painted maroon, fully enclosed and big enough to carry a dozen soldiers. Through its midsection ran a thick, white line of paint. The colors of the Seliss Academy and Army. The hatch opened with a faint hiss.

Gaav and Widje waved them over. They were already wearing Seliss uniforms, Gaav in the green from the train and Widje in the lesser-ranked maroon color. Syd looked at her own clothes, then to Keal's coat.

"Ah, don't worry. Your uniforms're inside!" Widje said and ducked back in.

The liner was decorated in redwood features and tanned leather benches that seated up to fourteen. The low lighting of the room made the seaship look like a lounge. Doubts and second thoughts crept into Syd's mind.

"Won't this be weird? Four of us creeping up in a liner in the middle of the night?" Syd asked.

Gaav waved his hand, "Don't get ahead of yourself. Widje will brief you on that once we get rolling."

Syd tilted her head at his aloofness. Like this was any other day. Then she remembered, *It probably is.* Gaav had to be about twenty now, and Seliss didn't recruit anyone under the age of sixteen. He'd been at this for at least the last four years.

Widje opened a cabinet and pulled out two more maroon uniforms. The captain and co-captain chairs sat empty at the helm. Syd walked over to the control panel.

"No weapons?" she asked.

"It's a transport, not a warship." Gaav grinned.

Keal followed and took the co-captain's chair.

"What are you doing?" Gaav asked.

"Co-piloting. You're a representative of Avant, I'm a representative of ACES. Makes sense we'd work together to steer this *ship*, literally and metaphorically."

Widje joined the conversation, head wagging between Keal and Gaav.

"Sorry, instructor. I don't think your qualifications pass as pilot credentials," Gaav said.

"What I lack in traditional credentials, I assure you I make up in tactical training."

Gaav shook his head. "That's Widje's seat. She needs it for the comms overrides we'll have to do."

"Oh, I don't mind! I can do that stuff anywhere; blindfolded in a cave, really." Widje smirked, egging the two on.

Syd shook her head. The bigger concern was being on a vessel without any weapons. Unless, of course, she was meant to be the weapon. She walked away and took a seat on the bench, eyes fixed on the floor. Keal eventually conceded and joined her there. The hatch door shut with a hiss of finality.

Widje coughed. "Alright! We have business to discuss!"

Gaav started the motor and spun his chair around to face the back of the cabin. Widje pressed a button on the wall. A screen descended from the ceiling at the rear of the cabin and flickered to life with similar images to the hologram from Matius's office. Seliss Academy's insect-like campus came into focus, the southernmost building highlighted in red to remind them of the target.

"As Director Keylen already said, Gaav has been working undercover for quite some time as a Seliss soldier. Last year, he graduated early with high marks which promoted him to First Commander," Widje explained with ease.

"Right now, the records show Commander Ragnor," she pointed to Gaav, "is on recruitment leave, due back in the morning. The three of us are acting as new recruits. Cadets Arlos," Widje nodded to Keal. "Verant." She inclined her head to Syd. "And Pleyt." Widje placed her hand on her chest.

"Your personnel files are stored in your synctron." Widje lifted her left arm and showed the metallic bracer with a screen in the center. "This little doodad is your lifeline to navigating Seliss campus and is programmed to get you clearance to most areas. Gaav's file has been altered and, upon returning, he is meant to begin recruit—that's us—onboarding. As long as we keep a low profile, we should be fine."

Widje nodded to Gaav, clasping her hands behind her back.

"Seliss isn't the well-oiled machine it likes to present itself to be," Gaav said. "Their general strategy is in numbers, not in training. Like Widje said, lay low and we'll find out what's going on in no time. We have three days until we rendezvous with Director Keylen in the woods to the East of Seliss."

Syd calculated the time in her head. They were cutting it close, and the weight of the transference hung on the shoulder opposite of the one that carried the weight of Adeline.

"If we aren't at the meeting point by that third night, Avant's forces, with Magnate reinforcements should the negotiations go according to plan, are set to attack Seliss. That's the last resort, obviously. Meanwhile, the three of us will be keeping our ears to the ground and working mainly at night to search the campus. By my estimates, we'll complete our search by night two."

He nodded, indicating he was finished.

"And what are we expected to do during the day?" Keal asked.

"You're Seliss recruits!" Gaav smiled. "You'll be attending orientation and running your first drills."

Keal frowned.

"You're telling me an Ace is afraid of a few drills?" Gaav said. "You'll be fine, and if we do run into trouble, Widje here has altered your uniforms a bit. You should have enough inside pockets, though Austral use is a last resort."

Keal inhaled sharply to retort, but Gaav swirled his seat

around. The sunset beyond the cabin window shaded the sky a deep plum.

"We'll arrive while it's still early morning," Gaav said. "Get changed and acquaint yourself with the synctron and your file. The more you know about your new identity, the better."

The seaship lurched forward and away from the docks slowly. The motors rumbled below Syd's feet while they increased speed.

"Oh! And we're all stocked up on food, *courtesy* of Seliss. Help yourself!" Widje grinned and hit the button again to retract the screen.

CHAPTER TWENTY-ONE

Two Years Prior

Adeline, Syd, and Keal sat in varying stages of uncomfortable in the meeting room. Adeline's spine was straight, her eyes and ears on the door. Syd slumped a little, picking at her fingernails. Keal fiddled with his tablet and pushed his glasses up his nose. Adeline looked to Director Rhiuld at the head of the table.

"Are we…in trouble or something, Director?"

Director Rhiuld looked up from her own tablet for a moment. "No. Nothing of the sort. Just waiting on Eichon Wenna."

Adeline nodded, even though they'd never all met together, and certainly never at ACES like this. The windowless room was becoming stuffy and suffocating with anticipation. Before the academy was built, Director Rhiuld had been the military commander of Zevir, replaced by Commander Herf when she was put in charge here. Could it have been something to do with that?

The door whizzed open finally, Wenna stepping in gracefully. Adeline smiled and walked the table length to greet her, gasping when Matius walked in too.

"Mom! Dad? Both of you?!" She hugged them fully, taking in comfort from their embraces. "But why? What's going on?" Adeline looked to her friends for help.

Syd nudged Keal's leg with her foot under the table to get him to stand when the Eichon and her spouse entered.

Wenna looked to them before nodding to Director Rhiuld, signaling for everyone to sit down again.

Adeline searched her parents faces, but they gave nothing away. "Is something wrong?" she asked, trying one last time.

"No, nothing like that, Adeline," Wenna finally said, and the room became cooler and easier to breathe in.

"You requested an appointment?" Matius leaned back in his chair. He folded his leather-gloved hands on the table and looked to Director Rhiuld.

"Yes," Director Rhiuld nodded. "I was the one to call this meeting. Eichon Wenna, Director Keylen, I know you both are busy and so I'll get to it. I believe it's time we discuss the matter of the Guard."

There was a slight pause, and Matius spoke first. "They're a little young, Jexa." He looked to Wenna, his face giving away that he already knew he was outnumbered. A look Adeline had seen plenty of times before. Her shoulders eased.

"Keal has become quite a loyal friend to Adeline and proven himself in both classroom and training as a capable austral master," Director Rhiuld continued, almost undisturbed. "Syd, though lacking in the classroom and majik studies, I must admit is showing great potential in her piloting skills. Not to mention, her friendship to Adeline is unlike anything I've seen in any of the students here yet."

Adeline listened carefully, unsure why her friends were being spoken about in such a formal context. She looked to Wenna who nodded thoughtfully and her dark eyes casting a glance to Keal.

Adeline scrunched her face. "What?" She then looked to her parents, eyes darting between them both.

"Every Eichon has a personal Guard," Wenna explained. "They are close friends or loved ones sworn to protect the Eichon, and are part of her Council."

"But, isn't that what PRISM is for?" Adeline asked.

"It's true that PRISM exists for my protection as well, but their first priority is protecting Zevir and her citizens from any threat. A personal Guard protects the Eichon from others…" She trailed off suddenly, her hands moving to her bracelets. A soft clinking filled the room. "Or herself."

There was an atmosphere that filled the space, the air thinning even more. Adeline tried to concentrate on what was being said.

"An Eichon's powers can come at a cost," Director Rhiuld explained when it was clear no one else would. "Too much power deteriorates the mind and causes Madness and corruption. Great destruction and great wars have happened as a result of a Eichon succumbing to the Madness."

"…Why haven't we learned about this in our classes?" Adeline asked.

"You will," Keal interrupted, his face unmoving and gaze distant. "Next year. My course is just starting." He looked to Director Rhiuld, "You're asking Syd and me to protect Adeline?"

"The administration can't be everywhere all the time," Rhiuld said.

Adeline glanced at Syd, then at Keal. Her chest gave a

sudden ache. "I can protect myself. I have the best marks in combat out of anyone."

Matius shook his head. "Addie, a personal Guard is more than that. Your mother has me, Director Rhiuld, Commander Herf, Consul Torok, your aunt Villette. She never travels without one of us; she's never without one of us within earshot. We can notice things she may be too pre-occupied to otherwise."

Adeline quieted and sat back in her chair, under-standing this was never up to her or her choice to make. Her eyes unfocused while she listened.

"Keal, Syd." Wenna looked to them both in turn. The air in the room turned warmer. "Do you understand what is being asked? For the years remaining that Adeline attends ACES, we are asking you to be her eyes and ears when she is unable. You are to report any odd or threatening behavior directly to ACES staff and use your natural skills and talents to keep her safe, should that be necessary."

Adeline turned to Keal, her eyes wide and watery. How could they think her so weak, so useless that she couldn't protect herself? When Keal nodded, though, she felt a sense of relief. Then she turned to Syd who smiled and shook her head. Syd's curls bounced, and she rolled her eyes, forcing Adeline to smile as well.

"Sounds like a free hall pass to me. I'm in." Syd said.

"Absolutely not!" Director Rhiuld started.

Adeline came back to herself then and stifled a giggle behind her hand, the gleam in her eye catching the glimmer in Syd's.

Present Day

Seliss wasn't the most advanced army, but it was the biggest, and the irony of finding comfort in being a faceless soldier was not lost on her. Syd stared into the green glow of her synctron. The screen on her forearm was warm on the itchy, cheap material of the Seliss uniform.

VERANT, TRIYENA. 17. FEMALE.

A pixelated photo of Syd rendered onto the screen. She looked to Widje whose cheeks were full of snacks.

"Questions?" Widje smiled.

Syd shook her head and looked back to the screen. *From Doineron.*

Widje plopped down next to Syd on the bench and peered over.

"Remote little forest town in the Northern part of The Taams. Pretty isolated so people won't ask questions," Widje said.

Syd gave a small nod and looked over to Keal. "And who are you today?"

Keal flourished his hands and stood to give a low bow. "Mr. Xaviere Arlos, eighteen, from the streets of Galssop, at your service."

"Really getting into it, huh? I thought the goal was to blend in and not bring any attention to ourselves, *Xaviere.*" Syd teased, trying to release the tension in the cabin.

He grinned to himself and sat back down. "Xave for short, please."

Syd swiped to the next screen and scanned more details.

Only child. Mother died young. A pang hit Syd's chest, and she rolled her shoulders. *Elderly father is a bear trapper.*

It all seemed straight forward enough. The next screen had another photo of a middle-aged man with a long face and light eyes. The right side of his face was scarred, his dark hair streaked with gray.

Major General Durac Sevnior. Director and Military Head of Seliss.

Syd studied the image. His long cheeks, his flattened nose bridge, proportionate forehead, five o'clock shadow. This man was supposed to be the single, most dangerous person on the planet. And yet, nothing stirred inside her when she stared at the picture. No fear, no anger. She hit a button, and the screen faded.

Widje moved to the co-captain's chair and poked at a few things before yawning and stretching. Gaav sat silently at the helm.

"So, how much longer?" Syd asked.

"Couple hours still. Have to go the long way."

Syd sighed, catching Widje's yawn. She looked around and stood up to stretch her legs, pacing the length of the cabin.

"So," Gaav said, not turning around, but his voice was jovial. "How does someone go from Darmar orphan to Ei-chon?"

Syd's sudden panic subsided when she remembered they all knew, even Widje.

"The same way someone goes from orphan to Seliss Commander," Syd chided back, and Gaav chuckled. She wasn't sure how much he knew, but it wouldn't be so far of a stretch to assume he'd also been part of some Council plan. Her heart jumped.

"What happened after you were adopted?" Syd asked.

Surprisingly, Gaav opened up immediately. "Lived in Kilos town for about a year until it was time to go to academy. Avant was the easy choice. Stayed in the dorms until graduation. The couple had two other boys. One went to Magnate. The other moved to the outskirts of Carden."

"And your parents?" Syd hesitated. "They know of your position, right? Wouldn't that…put you in jeopardy?"

Gaav shrugged, "Never got close. Not even sure why they adopted me in the first place. We stopped contact as soon as I moved onto campus."

Syd considered this and frowned.

"Enough about that, though," Gaav said. "You somehow managed to woo your way into the most powerful family, and you got a prodigy sidekick to boot."

"Hey!" Keal piped up, and Syd smirked, though she shot him an apologetic glance.

"Yeah…something like that," Syd said and looked to Widje.

But Widje shot up her hands with a shrug, "Just a punk from Galssop. Went to Magnate and transferred to Avant when the recruiters came."

Syd suspected there was more to it than that. You don't just become the leading comms specialist of Avant. But she left it alone.

They passed the time with Syd and Gaav recounting stories from the orphanage, and what it was like growing up in Darmar. Gaav recalled the time Matron Reos had taken all the kids to the open market. When it came time to go home, he and Syd had gotten so lost playing hide and seek among the hanging rugs and stands that they were never allowed on group trips together again. Syd had almost forgotten that memory, and even as Gaav retold it, all she remembered were flashes of bright reds and earthy tans and the smell of spices rich in the air.

Eventually, Widje shared a little more about her childhood in the electric city too. Galssop had an entire subculture built for comms hackers, and Widje had been heavily active in it.

"Augmentors," Widje said. "I got pretty involved with the scene and my parents sent me off to the mountains as soon as they could. Don't blame them though. I wasn't the easiest kid to raise and I think I spent more time in the shops scavenging for parts than at home."

Syd wanted to ask more, but Widje stood suddenly and found the button on the wall again. The screen dropped from the ceiling, and the image of Seliss reappeared. The picture zoomed in on the northern halls.

"Final part of the briefing before we arrive," Widje said.

Cold anxiety stirred in Syd's stomach for a fleeting moment. She ran the objectives through her mind like a mantra. Infiltrate. Lay low. Gather Intel. Meet at the rendezvous.

"These two halls are the main barracks for training soldiers," Widje interrupted Syd's train of thought. "But they function more like dorms we're all used to. Five stories each, men in the Northwest Hall, women in the Northeast Hall. New recruits get the first floor, which should make it pretty easy to get to our meeting point here."

The image zoomed out and a small, red circle appears in the Southwest Hall.

"I've disabled the emergency exit alarms to this door, giving us easy access to the hot spot without using any main entrances."

Widje clicked to the next screen. Smaller red dots began to move, trailing up and down the hall to the main building structure, and around the outer building.

"Patrols are light at night, but we'll still need to time things precisely. Private Arlos—the patrol changes for the Northwest Wing is at 0100. Private Verant, ours is at 0105. Commander Ragnor has been set to patrol the Southwest Wing and will be waiting for us at 0120. This gives us plenty of time to avoid any other patrols."

Widje nodded. "And that's it. The plan is we get in tonight, catch as much shuteye as we can, and start our first day as new Seliss recruits in the morning. We bide our time until we meet with Gaav tomorrow night. Any questions?"

"Yeah..." Keal ran his hand through the back of his hair. "What happens if we get caught?"

Gaav grunted. "If you blow my cover, Private Arlos, I'll personally see to your punishment."

Keal mouthed to Syd, *Is this guy serious?*

"Cut with the drama, Gaav," Widje said in a way that made Syd question who was actually in charge of this mission. "If we're caught, we are not to engage in combat. If they're not completely stupid, they'll take us prisoner. Otherwise..." She trailed off. "In any case, if we're not at the rendezvous by the designated time, Director Keylen and crew will come looking for us. They'll do the heavy lifting of getting us out of there in the worst-case scenario. Essentially, if we're caught, our commands are: Do not engage. Say nothing."

"And Adeline? If we're caught, what happens about Adeline?" Syd asked.

Widje shifted her weight but held Syd's eye contact. "If we are caught, Adeline is the lowest priority."

Syd squinted. "And Matius is just…fine with that?"

"These are Director Keylen's mission orders," Widje said, her expression blank.

If he's so quick to abandon Adeline, how quickly would he abandon us? Doubt swirled in Syd. Were they set up to fail? Her stomach flipped, and she looked out the window to steady herself. In the distance, a hazy shipyard was coming into view in the darkness. Beyond that, Seliss loomed—a black shape against flood lights that swept the perimeter.

"We're nearing," Gaav said. "Get your helmets on. We'll be able to get in and to your rooms by using the door Widje disabled…You're sure it's off, right?"

Widje slammed the visor of her helmet down, covering everything but her mouth. She put a hand on her hip and shook her head. "Yes I'm sure."

Syd slipped her helmet over her ears. She wiggled it until it felt a little less claustrophobic and closed her visor. Keal gave her a crooked smile, and his visor fell over his eyes.

"I've rigged these helmets to have a private line just for us," Widje explained. "The design of these things doesn't allow for much privacy, but if you get in trouble you have a direct way to reach the rest of us and call for help. There's a small button near your left ear. Tap it three times to find the line."

"Private Arlos, reporting for duty!" Keal's voice filled Syd's ears. "Eh, what do I do if my helmet smells like sweat?"

"Grin and bear it, soldier." Gaav's voice was becoming a deeper, rougher gravel the closer they got to Seliss. Syd assumed it was all part of the cover, and that thought settled her stomach for the moment. *Gaav's been at this for years and hasn't gotten caught.*

"Now," Gaav said. "If we run into any trouble, let me do the talking. But, I can't help you when you're on your own. Keep your mouth shut and obey orders."

Syd, Keal, and Widje nodded in unison, taking their seats when they entered the shipyard. Gaav turned on the seaship's communicator and talked into the open air.

"SEL 5310 requesting dock clearance."

The silent pause made Syd's gums itch.

"SEL 5310, you're clear to dock in Sector 73." The line clicked off for a moment, and then back on. "Welcome back Commander." The voice on the other end was friendly. "How was your leave?"

"Keep the lines clear, Private!" Gaav barked, and the line went dead.

Gaav navigated the yard and docked with ease. No crew met them to tie off.

"Waters here are so still, the anchor's enough," Gaav said when Syd asked.

"Not like anyone's going to, y'know, steal from the

Seliss shipyard anyway," Widje said with a knowing half-grin.

They disembarked and walked along the concrete paths, footsteps hushed by a low, hanging fog and a soft rain. It was so humid here that it was suffocating, and the sheer size of Seliss's campus baffled Syd. It towered overhead, taller and wider than anything she'd expected. Bigger even than Avant and ACES combined.

They wound though the smaller, outer buildings they'd studied in the briefings. The building exteriors were painted a reflective black to mimic the central structure. They dodged floodlights and stuck close to walls, following Gaav's lead.

They stopped, Gaav going on to check for patrols and open the entrance, and Widje demonstrated the map function of their synctrons. The three hung back, assuming that if the door had reactivated, it would be better for Gaav to get caught red-handed trying to sneak in than three new recruits.

"Seems to be in order," Gaav's voice came through Syd's helmet. "Hurry before someone notices."

Inside, the bright hall was a blinding contrast to the night cover outside. The floors and walls were made of similar marble as the other academies, but a maroon and white stripe ran the length of the floor and led to a central hub further ahead. Indiscriminate doors were spaced evenly along the corridor, each labeled with its own number. Syd shivered at the similarities and swiftly walked on toward the hub.

The hall gave way to an open core with seven identical

halls shooting off in each direction, walls high and blank. In the middle of it all was the Seliss symbol, maroon stones inlayed with the marbled masonry on the floor. It was quiet. No soldiers or patrols walked this central space, and the echoes of their feet set Syd on edge.

Gaav guided the group to the two northernmost halls. A tall soldier quickly approached the group from the northeast. Syd held her breath.

"Commander," the woman said and held her salute.

"At ease," Gaav grunted.

The woman lowered her salute and continued her patrol without another word. Gaav said nothing and motioned for Keal to follow him. Syd bit at the inside of her cheek and watched Keal walk away.

"We're in room 139A," Widje whispered over the line and led Syd off in the other direction. "Be sure to scan your synctron when we enter. That's how they log everything around here."

The room was small like most dorms would be. It consisted of two identical beds on either side, with two identical bed stands, and two identical desks and chairs. Everything was some variation of beige, except for the maroon sheets and white pillowcases, lit by harsh white bulbs from the ceiling panels. No windows. No escape.

Widje picked the left bed and laid down with her helmet still on. Syd sat on the edge of her mattress, waiting for something to go wrong.

"Keal?" Widje said over the line.

"Doesn't look like I have a roommate! Good job, Widje," Keal said, and Syd's shoulders relaxed.

"Let's get some quick rest, yeah? Recruits are expected for orientation at 0600 in the central grounds. We'll meet in the atrium at 0530. Over and out." Widje killed the line, removed her helmet, and ruffled her matted, colorful hair. Syd did the same, unsure what else to do.

"Nervous?" Widje asked with a smile.

"I think I'm more concerned for Keal, being alone," Syd admitted.

"Ah, he'll be fine. And if not, well…" Widje eyed Syd up and down.

Syd folded her arms and looked away.

"Sorry. I just mean if what Director Keylen says is true, you should have no problem taking the whole damn army, right?"

Syd beat her pillow a little and relaxed onto the bed. What had Matius told her? Everything, she assumed. Maybe more. He would have needed to brief his own soldiers as much as possible to keep them safe from Seliss, right? But would he lie to them, too?

"Let's just get in and out as quick as possible," Syd said.

Widje moved to the light switch near the door. "Sweet dreams," she said.

The room went black.

Syd lay in her bed, unable to sleep. Maybe it was from the itchy uniform, but Widje hadn't removed hers, so Syd saw no reason to remove hers either. Which was probably for the best. They wanted to be able to quickly move should something happen.

The fabric scratched at her arms, and the stiff bedding rustled under her tossing and turning. A short while later,

Widje's breathing steadied in the silence. Syd curled up, moved onto her side, and hugged her knees.

How much didn't Widje know? *How much don't I know, still?*

Syd closed her eyes and searched for her majik. It coursed there, steady currents just below her skin and through her veins. It was a part of her, from her toes to her crown. She knew that now. How could she have ever denied it? It was a steady and strong river inside her. The river turned a bend, and the waters rushed faster, deeper. Here they were in the belly of the beast, and she was supposed to sleep now.

Syd took a breath and controlled it.

Behind her eyelids, she was standing in Llyn's wheat fields again. In front of her, the village was a cloud of dust. Syd looked on as horror seized her chest. She tried to move, to make sense of what happened. Had there been a storm? She couldn't get closer no matter how many steps she took.

Whatever was holding her released its grip when the dust settled. She broke into a run toward the leveled chaos of the town. It was nothing more than a wasteland of flattened brick and wood that opened to an endless, expansive orange and pink sunset. She begged her body to move closer, running as fast as she could.

Her body seized again suddenly, and she cried out, paralyzed on the spot. Something held her, kept her from moving, breathing, blinking. Her eyes watered against the pain, forced to look on.

The cloud of dust rose again from the earth, swirled to great heights, and swarmed into a towering funnel. It reared itself above her, controlling her every movement. It allowed her to tremble, and to follow its mass skyward.

A blast of wind knocked Syd free finally, and she was thrown backward. She scrambled back to her feet. Her breath was fast—too fast. She tried to run away, but her lungs wouldn't give her the oxygen she needed. She looked behind her just as the dark mass descended, swooping down and pinning her wrists and ankles. On her back, helpless and mute, the dark cloud filled her nose and mouth. It filled her ears and eyes. It leaked from every part of her and dove into her lungs. The windstorm inside her pushed and pulled, ripping and tearing through her violently. Her vision faded, and everything blurred into a brilliant bright light.

CHAPTER TWENTY-TWO

The alarm woke Syd from the nightmare. It blared from every corner of the room, and she squinted into the blackness. Widje was laying on her back, one leg over a bended knee as she fiddled with her synctron. Another three-second blast, followed by five of silence. And another round. Syd held her breath for the next. When it didn't come, she sat up.

"Ah, mornin'. Time for showers and some grub. The life of a soldier!" Widje chimed.

Syd tilted her head and followed the sound of Widje moving to the light switch. Syd shielded her eyes just in time. It was odd how carefree Widje acted, like she was truly excited to start her first day as a Seliss recruit. And then Syd remembered the way Gaav's voice started to change into something deeper, more gruff, the closer they got to Seliss.

I suppose this is what Avant's spies train for.

Widje tucked her hair into her helmet and clicked the visor down. Syd did the same. They confirmed Keal was awake over the private line, and Widje repeated the orders from last night.

They waited for Keal where the two halls met in the atrium after the showers.

"Recruits are allowed free time when there isn't anything scheduled," Widje explained quietly.

A commander brushed past them without even a glance. Syd rolled her shoulders and tried to relax, muscles aching from poor sleep. Not thinking about the dream was useless, yet she fought to focus on the crowds of uniforms moving into and out of the atrium like schools of fish. Almost all their faces were hidden under their helmets, just like hers. They could have been anyone. *She* could have been anyone.

Keal came around the corner with his helmet wedged under his arm.

"Good morning. Sleep well?" He puffed out his chest.

Widje gave a low hiss. "Put your helmet on. We can't risk anyone recognizing our faces, now or in the future."

Keal's chest deflated, but he obeyed. His carefree attitude grated on Syd, but she said nothing.

"Much better," Widje said over the line.

"How secure is this, anyway?" Syd asked, looking at her synctron to make sure it wasn't detected.

"As secure as the person wearing the helmet." Widje's lips smiled, but without being able to see her eyes, Syd didn't know what that meant.

Widje turned, and they followed her into the mess hall. It was a cafeteria like any other, jammed full of soldiers of varying ranks. Maroon, black, green, blue, and white uniforms all mingled and mixed. It was all so familiar. Recruits, soldiers, and commanders chatted and laughed over breakfast. These people could have been students anywhere else.

Not people. Enemies.

Syd scanned the crowd, searching for any weak links. A large commander emptied his tray and returned to his green-clad group. Behind them, the back wall of the hall was decorated with maroon and gold tapestries that depicted battle scenes between Seliss and the Eichons over the eras. The threads told stories of The Battle of Faith between the Novari and Terians in the fifth era and spanned to the Zevir civil war in the eighth. It had been two eras since the last great Unrest, and the buzz of the mess hall matched the low-level anxiety of a world that held its breath for Seliss's next big move. Syd wondered how many here knew about the cyber-attacks.

"You okay, Verant?" Keal nudged Syd with his elbow.

She shook her head and relaxed her face. "Yeah," she said.

"It looks like finding a seat will be a problem..." Keal trailed off, staring at the long lines for food and over-crowded tables.

A wave of heat flashed up Syd's neck, fear settling in her throat. Her majik coursed, pulsed. *All these people...*

"I'm not feeling well enough to eat," Syd said. "I think I need some fresh air."

"Good timing. Orientation is about to start anyway," Widje agreed and looked up from her synctron. "C'mon."

Keal mumbled something that sounded like protest, but followed them out to the training grounds.

Syd's boots squished into the soft, muddy ground on the walk across outer campus. They met up with a small group of new recruits who were doing their best to line up under the barking instruction of the commanders. Syd exhaled when she saw one of the commanders was Gaav.

Widje naturally fell in line, and Keal and Syd followed

suit. Back straight, feet shoulder-length apart, knees slightly bent, hands clasped behind back. The group faced an exterior side of the main building where a stage, surrounded in glass, protruded from two stories up. The clouds overhead threatened more rain, gray, and weighing everything down. Syd looked around to find everyone else's eyes fixed on the stage above.

"Loosen up," Gaav's voice filled her helmet. "You three stick out like sore thumbs."

Syd's eyes shot over to Gaav, but his back was turned. She stretched and returned to attention with a slouch. Silence rang in her helmet, and the sound of her breathing filled her ears. Somewhere in her core, a soft tremor rumbled. She stared hard at the back of the helmet in front of her, and, try as she might, it was impossible to not humanize the person in the uniform.

Why would someone willingly join the Seliss army?
Did they have nowhere else to go?
Maybe they had no choice.
Maybe they had every choice.

Sympathizing with the enemy was dangerous, beyond dangerous. With every new transference of power from one Eichon to the next, Seliss had consistently found reason to seek and destroy. They would find reason again. Syd gave herself a mental shake. Her attention was brought back by barked orders and the shuffle of a salute around her.

She did her best to follow. Left hand clenched into a fist and swooped behind, held at the low back. Right hand clenched into a fist and held tight at the right shoulder. Feet shifted together, and the sound lingered in the air until two people came onto the overhanging stage.

A tall woman with sharp features took the podium first. She wore a white uniform, its chest plate decorated with gold metals and cuffed neck up to her ears. The epaulettes on her shoulders were fringed with white feathers, and all of it matched her short, white hair and light eyes. Syd couldn't be sure from so far away, but when the light caught just right, she swore Furlong had honeyed eyes.

Is Furlong an Eheri?

Syd would have to worry about that later, mesmerized as Furlong took the microphone.

"Welcome, new cadets," her voice boomed strong, carrying over the grounds and bouncing off the surrounding buildings. "Today, you join the ranks of the world's oldest and most resolute warriors. You have freely chosen to fight on the right side of history. The side that ever-continues to bring freedom and autonomy to the people of our world, trapped under the tyrannical rule of a single person with unchecked control and power.

"Through the eras, our people, all people, have been forced to live their lives without a say in what or who leads us on. Without a say in what or who decides the economical, societal, and political constructs that make up how our villages, towns, and cities operate. Without a say in what or who decides each and every one of our fates.

"You have freely chosen to seek an end to such autocratic power by being here today. A choice that, likely, did not come easy to some, especially those few of you who saw past the veil of your native homes so intrinsically blind to the will of the Eichon. To each of you, each brave and noble person standing before me, the people of The Taams applaud you for the selfless sacrifices you will make from this day forward. Past and future historians applaud you for the courage, the truth, and the faith that you carry in you as we continue the fight to free our brothers and sisters of the world from the devastating reality we live in.

"Before you begin your training here, on this very day, on these very grounds on which so many have trained before you, General Major and Director of the Seliss Army and Academy, Durac Sevnior, has prepared a welcome of his own."

Furlong stepped aside and made way for Sevnior. She saluted, and the cadets followed the salute. Syd caught on a half-second too late. Sevnior wore a gray suit, its black lapel large and decorated with a single pendant. From Syd's angle, his cheeks were hollowed, and the shadows of the overhang highlighted his scar that ran from mid-cheek to chin, across his lips.

"As Assistant Director Furlong so eloquently stated, we are proud of the wisdom and truth each of you have shown by joining Seliss and committing your lives to the single, most important *cause* our civilization has ever known." His voice was calculated, full and thick, like he tasted each word before letting it pass from his mouth. "A cause that is coming into effect sooner than you realize."

He paused, and the tension around Syd heightened. Breaths were bated, hanging onto this man's words. He shook his head and smiled. Behind her helmet's visor, Syd searched for what to make of him, and of Furlong. Could she really be helping Adeline?

"But, for now… Welcome!" His tone changed from calculated to warm as if a switch had been flipped. "Your training commanders have been assigned to you. Today, you will start with drills to test your physical abilities and, later, you'll be given your schedules.

"Be proud. Be empowered by truth. Be fearless as we venture into a new era of liberation."

He saluted again, and the crowd saluted back. Most of them cheered. Even Widje added to the sound. Syd watched as Sevnior left the podium and paused to whisper something to Furlong. The assistant Director scanned the crowd again before she retreated from the stage.

The drills were easy. Physical training at ACES was similar; the difference being Ace cadets enrolled at age eleven and started physical combat and defense before they were placed into austral, combat, or Eheri specialties. From there, each tract continued their specific battle training as part of the curriculum. ACES was the Eichon's elite academy, after all. All cadets needed to know how to move in the field, should they be called. Syd felt a small spark of pride ignite in her belly.

Keal, Widje, and Syd ended up in the same training group, and Syd assumed that was Widje's doing. Though, Gaav was not placed as their training commander. In some kind of unspoken agreement, they each held back during the physical aptitude tests. Syd even allowed for a few clumsy tumbles during relays. Mainly, though, she just tried to keep her mind focused on the task at hand and to not show too much or too little competence. By mid-day the trainers uploaded the schedules to their synctrons before they were released for lunch.

"I'm starving!" Keal complained and followed the crowd back toward the mess hall.

"Don't tell me that took it out of you." Widje grinned behind her helmet.

Syd kept quiet and trailed behind the two of them to an empty table. The cafeteria was emptier than it had been in the morning. Every hair on Syd's body stood on end. She tried to shake off the uneasy feeling, absent-mindedly picking up a tray of food with the rest.

"Where is everyone?" she asked.

"They stagger the mid- and evening meals because of numbers," Widje responded and looked at her synctron.

Syd pushed potatoes around with her fork, then moved to the other green vegetables on her plate. Keal devoured his completely.

"If you're not going to eat it…" He reached his hand out, but Widje quickly smacked it away.

"She needs to eat," Widje said.

She tilted her head in Syd's direction, and Syd complied. Fork to mouth, fork to mouth. It's all she could do. Her mind roamed, and she barely tasted the food, barely heard the banter between Keal and Widje. Her eyes fell again to the tapestries on the walls.

"What did Sevnior mean today? 'A cause that's coming

into effect'?" Syd interrupted their minor argument over who had the best worst performance of the morning.

Keal shook his head. "He probably says that all the time. Those speeches seemed pretty rehearsed. Just a way to get his new troops riled up."

"Something isn't right…" Syd muttered.

"Nerves," Widje said. "I have them too. It'll be alright."

She reached across the table and patted Syd's forearm. In that moment, Widje seemed much older, much wiser. Whatever confidence Widje had, Syd wished it was infectious because something was building inside her, pulling her in two separate reactions. Equally, Syd fought the urge to fight and the urge to flee.

CHAPTER TWENTY-THREE

The afternoon schedule was even less taxing than the morning drills. They sat in lecture halls that assigned study of world histories Syd had learned in her second year at ACES. That made it hard to focus on anything but the growing anxiety in her belly, and she spent most of her time staving off the call of her majik.

At evening meal, she gave Keal her entire tray. Widje, from under her helmet, huffed in disapproval but said nothing. They were able to get open seats but had to share with others, strangers. Syd eavesdropped on surprisingly typical conversations—who liked whom, plans for next break, complaints about training and drills. It was all so plain and commonplace. Conversations she and Adeline and Keal would have.

They headed back to the atrium after dinner, and Syd stared hard at the floors, counting the dark speckles in the marble.

"Right," said Widje in a low voice. "Lights out is in about three hours. Cadets are free to roam the campus until then. After that, patrols start."

Widje played with her synctron. "I'm sending you both the patrol schedule. Remember, we're to meet Gaav at the Southwest entrance at 0120."

Syd looked at the green and black screen, and it flashed the times when the halls would be under monitor.

"Wait, don't they have security cameras?" Keal asked.

"Nah. Seliss focuses much of its resources on hacking technology these days," Widje explained. "They're pretty old school when it comes to protecting the campus. No one has ever tried to attack or infiltrate before. No one ever thought to."

"Until now…" Syd said.

"We should try to get some more rest. We have no idea what's actually in those buildings; only best guesses. We don't know how long it's going to take to search them."

Looking into each of their faces, Keal nodded. "See you at 0120, then."

Syd laid in the bed, staring at the ceiling. Widje had found a desk lamp and positioned it against the wall so they wouldn't be in complete darkness. The lazy shadows deepened across the ceiling panels. Widje's breathing steadied and deepened its way into a soft snore, and Syd tried to drift off.

At each attempt, her eyes would fling open in a panic at visions of the worst possible outcomes. Surely, if Adeline was here, they'd know already, right? Someone would have seen her, rumors would have spread. It would have been all anyone could talk about at dinner… Wouldn't it? Seliss was, at the end of the day, an academy too. More or less it functioned like the rest: full of bored teens and young adults. Boredom bred gossip.

A cause that is coming into effect… Sevnior's voice rattled in Syd's skull.

The cause was easy to guess at. It's been Seliss's mission

since day one, since Misor Seliss himself defected after Eichon Arja's death: eliminate the Eichon and stop the transfer of power. What would happen if Project Nova gave Seliss what it wanted? Syd's throat tightened. They were two enemies working toward the same goal.

She swallowed hard. The world didn't know *why* Wenna had commissioned so many dig sites and the reason for Nova's growth. Stands to reason Seliss wouldn't know either, no matter how powerful they were. Why wouldn't she just tell them?

Why wouldn't Syd?

She felt empty and angry and confused and scared, and above all, she missed Adeline. She missed the one person who kept her grounded and even. Without her, Syd couldn't make sense of any of this. It was all so much bigger than her, so impossibly huge. The ceiling started to shift and swirl, and the shadows from the lamp danced. She rolled on her side, and the crisp bedding crinkled at her movement.

"Yeah," Widje said suddenly and sat up. "I can't sleep either."

"I heard you snoring…"

"Pretty convincing, yeah? That was just so you'd feel comforted. Truth is I haven't slept much at all since Matius put me on this mission."

Syd sat up, too, and the spinning worsened for a moment.

"What was his mission brief, anyway?" Syd asked. "I know why I'm here and what I'm meant to do. I can understand Keal's reasoning too. But besides following orders… Or is it just that? Another in a series of orders from Matius?"

Widje stood, stretched, and joined Syd on the other side of the room. She made a shooing motion, and Syd scooted to give her room on the edge of the bed.

"The mission brief was pretty straight forward," Widje said. "Get in, conduct the search, then get out. Similar to yours, but I suspect that's not what you're actually asking. Gaav has been here long-term ever since he graduated Avant. Matius saw his potential, as did Wenna, and together they set in motion a sort of safeguard for the Eichon. A man on the inside.

"When the question of my retainer came up at my graduation, I agreed to stay on. Not sure what I'd do otherwise—I'm not really the settle-down-and-have-kids type, y'know? I like gadgets and tinkering too much. Matius saw that too. While I'm no Zevir scientist, I'm a skilled fighter with a specialty. So, after the initial attacks on Zevir's systems, they saw a need for another safeguard. Me.

"But this new safeguard would be for the future Eichon. A sort of protector for this new type of warfare. After you came to Avant, while you were recovering, it all kinda came together. A special Guard for you because, truthfully, we know very little beyond the evident risks of Project Nova. Anyway, after Adeline went missing, Keal was adamant on joining the mission, it was only right to add him to the roster. When Matius suggested the idea, Keal already considered himself part of your Guard, like he had when we all assumed Adeline would be the next Eichon."

Syd searched Widje's face. Her intense eyes shone brightly, earnest under thick eyebrows. Her mouth dimpled on either side when she spoke. Syd wanted to be angry at yet another someone choosing all this for her, but try as she might to find the flame, she was too exhausted to argue.

"We're both sworn to you, Keal by friendship, and me by duty. Regardless of who, I knew this was something worth doing." Widje nudged Syd and smiled. "I'm glad you're not some tyrant."

Syd looked to the floor. "But what if I end up a tyrant? Would you protect me then?"

Widje tilted her head and pursed her lips. "You thinkin' of going that way?" Her voice was light and playful.

"Look, Widje. I don't know what I'm thinking. I just want to find Adeline. Then I can figure everything out." The room started to spin again, and Syd rubbed her face in irritation. "But why would you blindly agree to something like that?"

Widje remained quiet for a long moment. "Because… Okay. Say you were a tyrant, right? And you had this group of people sworn to your side. If you were me, don't you think it would be worth it to help guide the hand in a better direction if you were able? And, knowing you're not one, means I get to help create something better. Honestly, it's a win-win either way for me. I get access to the planet's best tech and I'm helping to do some good."

Syd leaned back on the bed and closed her eyes. The darkness behind her eyelids was nice, but when the room stopped spinning, her thoughts took over. She tried to hold onto one.

"Who's to say what's good?" she heard herself say. "Sevnior thinks what he is doing is good, and we think he's the tyrant."

Widje tapped on her synctron. "At the end of the day, we just have to follow what our inner compass says. And my inner compass says I'm hungry again."

Syd slid one eye open to stare at Widje. *At a time like this?*

"As does yours," Widje said. She leaned over to show Syd her screen. "While we're having this heart-to-heart, you should know I've been monitoring your vitals."

This caused Syd's other eyelid to fly open. She sat up, slower this time, to look at the screen. Sure enough, numbers that monitored her heart rate, breathing rate, and blood pressure were all there. She stood up—a little too quickly—and folded her arms once the dizziness faded. Anger flared up her body, but the exhaustion took over, and the edges of her vision darkened.

Another thing she couldn't control. Another thing done to her without her consent.

"I know…I know…" Widje said, standing as well. "I didn't want to do it. It's incredibly invasive. But, given the circumstances, we needed a way to check that you're taken care of until we can get you safe. Right now, it looks like you're about to pass out because you haven't really eaten in Nova knows how long or gotten a good night's sleep. Let's go back to the mess hall and see what's left."

Syd tried to think of arguments against all this, against being here and having a personal Guard, against tyrants and the greater good. They were all there, those arguments, floating with thoughts of Adeline and the future and what it meant to have such a great source of power in a world so divided. But she couldn't hold on to any of them long enough to form a sentence.

So, she nodded, took her helmet when Widje handed it to her, and followed out the door.

They made it back to the dorm just before curfew. Syd had managed to eat some leftover bread rolls with the scrapings of a thick stew. The meal made her tired enough to promptly fall asleep.

Until she was jolted awake by a rapid pounding on the dorm door. Her body jumped upright before she could grasp what was happening.

"Cadets Verant and Pleyt!" A voice shouted on the other side of the door. "Present yourselves!"

Widje leapt from her bed, grabbing her helmet and putting it on in one motion. Syd did the same.

"Remember," Widje whispered. "Say nothing. Do not engage. Wait for rescue." Then, in a louder voice, she said, "At this hour?"

Syd thought stalling for time like that was a little bold, but she was left with no other choice than to trust Widje knew what she was doing. Syd steadied her breath because steadying her heart was out of the question. She clenched and unclenched her fists, feeling her majik beginning to pool at the heightened danger.

Widje opened the door, and Furlong pulled her lips into a smile. Two commanders stood on either side of her.

"Oh, ladies. The helmets are no longer necessary, but if you insist…"

Furlong turned and walked off, the commanders waiting for them. As they passed down the hall, neighboring doors closed, and the sound of hushed whispers followed the group into the atrium. No words were exchanged as they were led to a single-shaft metal elevator door. Syd's mind raced, but she held onto Widje's words. *Say nothing. Do not engage. Wait for rescue.*

The elevator ride was longer than anticipated, and the elevator panel did not have any buttons. Tension pulled tight in Syd, as if something would soon explode, though she couldn't tell what would go first: her mouth, her heart, or her majik. *Say nothing. Do not engage. Wait for rescue.*

She resisted the urge to look up and search for an emergency escape panel, ignoring all her screaming instincts to find an exit, to plan and strategize. Even though she'd been trained as a soldier at ACES, she was still an Eheri. The academy left advanced battle training to those students better skilled in physical combat; advanced battle training like what to do if you're trapped without weapons and outnumbered in a damn elevator.

Could she control her majik enough to not kill Widje and herself at the same time? And then what?

Say nothing. Do not engage. Wa—

The elevator dinged open, and Syd's heart rate increased two-fold, electric adrenaline stirring just below her ribs. But it slowed again when the doors revealed a brightly decorated lounge. A tan and maroon rug took up much of the floor. The walls were decorated with gold-framed paintings that depicted the same scenes as the tapestries in the mess hall. White sofas gathered around a glass table. It would have been a very welcoming space, if not for the circumstances.

"Wait here," Furlong said and disappeared into the only other door in the room on the opposing wall.

The two commanders took their stations on either side of the elevator door. Syd looked to Widje who gave a very small shrug. They both watched the door while Syd tried to hold on to her breath. She knew if she lost control of it now, she would risk her majik exploding outward. Her palms itched, her majik begged, and her breath was her only tether. Something tugged at her mind, and she gripped the back of the couch at the feeling.

Say nothing. Do not engage. Wait for rescue.

Syd stared at her hand. Tiny gray wisps flickered in and out on the surface of her skin like steam. Another tug in her mind. *It would be so very easy to destroy them. In fact, you could destroy this entire building with a single thought if you wanted.*

Syd blinked hard, repeatedly, trying to shake this other voice and not draw attention to herself at the same time. She was saved from her own depths by Furlong reentering the room, this time with Sevnior.

The commanders held their salute until Sevnior nodded. Furlong sat on the couch facing towards them, back straight and legs crossed. She folded her hands in her lap and stared between Widje and Syd silently. Sevnior gestured to them.

"Please, have a seat. Can I get you something?" He then motioned to the bar along the wall and stepped toward it.

They said nothing, though Syd admitted sitting would be nice. Her legs were growing weak from fighting with herself. She made her way around the couch, and Widje followed.

"No? Alright. Assistant Director Furlong?"

Furlong shook her head. "No, thank you Durac," she said and locked her eyes on Syd. "I really do wish you'd take off your helmets. There truly isn't any need for them."

Sevnior turned around from the bar with a drink in hand and sat next to Furlong. Syd studied his face close-up. Deep lines creased his forehead and gathered around his eyes. His scar was thick, meaty, a shade or two lighter than his already-light skin. But what stood out to Syd was how kind his blue eyes looked.

"Ladies, please," his voice was cordial. "We know who you are. Since arriving here, you've hardly been able to shut up, talking through your helmets to each other. It's rather embarrassing to admit it took us almost an entire day to catch you. Whoever programmed your communication line is very skilled."

Sevnior took a sip of his drink and leaned forward with a grin. "Was it you, Widjette Onna? You're the best communications specialist to come out of Avant, after all. We could use someone like you here."

He turned his eyes to Syd then. "Or was it you, Sydney Orleen? Being so close to the Eichon's family must provide some unique training opportunities." He leaned back and crossed his legs.

Furlong continued to grin and said nothing. Her face giving nothing away. Syd's body nearly vibrated with tension, sitting straight, clasping her hands together tightly in her lap. Furlong's light eyes *were* a honeyed yellow. Did that mean Seliss was working with Eheri now?

No one seemed to notice the gray smoke faintly trailing from Syd's hands. Widje removed her helmet, and Syd did too, using the movement to shake off the little bits of un-formed majik that she couldn't control. The tradeoff was that Syd felt vulnerable and exposed. She did her best to keep her face neutral and relaxed her muscles one at a time. Her eyes trailed back to Sevnior when he spoke again.

"Ah, much better," he said and took a sip of his drink. "Now, it's come to my attention that we all have a common goal in being here."

Syd's mind immediately raced. Did he find out about Project Nova? How much did he know about her? She looked around carefully, making sure her eyes didn't dart in panic, and finally noticed something she had overlooked. Where was Keal? Had they found him too? Why wasn't he here?

"Another embarrassing oversight on my part is it seems I missed the perfect opportunity to lure Eichon Wenna here. While I was wasting almost all my resources on infil-trating Zevir's technology, Adeline Keylen was right under my nose!" Sevnior slammed his glass on the table, all kind-ness drained from his eyes. His hand shook slightly.

"I have to give it to him, though," he said quietly. "Ivor Malvuk is one clever bastard."

So, Adeline was here... Syd tried to piece together the information while focusing on Sevnior's snarling lip.

"And no sooner had she left do you show up," he said,

and his body relaxed from the outburst. "It would be safe to assume you're here to rescue her? Ah, but you're too late.

"It's true I had given Malvuk access to a building off-grounds. He's never been one to choose sides, really, but I thought the favor might grant us some of his brilliance. By the time I realized what he was doing, they'd already left."

He sighed, waving his hand in the air. "I had the perfect opportunity snatched right out from under me. I feel a fool. But," Sevnior leaned further across the table to Syd, speaking low and barring his teeth. She could smell his breath, laced with alcohol. "I suppose Adeline Keylen's lover and her comrades will just have to do for now..."

Syd gasped in surprise when hands grabbed her from behind. A commander held her arms tight and squeezed her biceps. A warning not to try anything. Widje struggled in the grasp of the other commander.

"Take them to the chamber," Furlong said and moved toward the door.

Syd's skin ached, her insides churned. Something just below the surface swirled faster and faster. Energy gathered in her palms.

A loud crack rattled her skull and quick, sharp pain stole her from herself.

CHAPTER TWENTY-FOUR

Syd's back hurt. She took in a sharp inhale, and lightning shot up her spine to the base of her skull. Her eyes flew open.

The room smelled almost medical, like an infirmary. There were no windows, only steel floors and walls. A control panel terminal sat on the far wall. No screens, only buttons.

Old tech, her brain registered through the pain.

She tried to stand and toppled back down. Her wrists were restrained. Twisting carefully, she saw cuffs, but no chains, and pulled again. They wouldn't budge, invisibly tethered to a large, bulbous object in the center of the room.

A magnet.

"Syd? You awake?" A voice from the opposite direction whispered behind her.

"Keal!" Syd turned quickly in the direction of Keal's voice. She immediately saw stars, agony pulsing in the back of her head. Once her vision cleared, she was able to see Keal was restrained in the exact same way with his back to her.

To her left, Widje was slumped forward, her eyes closed and her hands behind her back, too. Syd's heart slowed until she saw Widje's chest move.

"How long was I out? Where are we?" Syd pulled at her restraints again trying to get close to Widje.

"Syd, I'm sorry," Keal said. His voice was quiet, as if he had been crying or would cry soon.

Dread crept along Syd's neck, "For what?" she asked carefully. *What did you do now?*

"It's all my fault. I left my helmet outside the showers. Someone must have picked it up because the next thing I know we are all here."

Her chest deflated in relief, but paranoia replaced her dread. Betrayal was something she could easily rationalize, but that wasn't Keal's style. She looked around the dark room again. The room was lit by a single yellow emergency light by the door. In the corners, red lights blinked. *Cameras.* She took a mental inventory: one door, one light, four cameras. The dark blue from the steel walls and floor engulfed the room, making it impossible to take in any other details.

"It's okay, Keal," Syd said in a hurry. "We need to remain calm. Figure out our next move, figure out where we are. Are we above the academy or below? Can you tell?"

Keal shuffled. "I came here the same way you did. Unconscious."

What was it Furlong had said? *Take them to the...* "Chamber." Syd said aloud. "Furlong said to take us to the chamber." She pulled on her wrists again with a grunt. Panic filled her.

A groan came from her left.

"Widje! Hey! Wake up!" Syd called.

Widje shook her head, colorful hair flaring out in the low light, and she hissed at the pain.

"Syd?" Her eyes focused and then grew wide. She looked around frantically.

"Where—" Widje started.

"We don't know," Keal cut her off.

"Furlong called this the chamber before we were knocked out. Ring any bells?" Syd swept her feet underneath her to get some leverage against the cuffs.

Widje blinked hard. "All I remember is being in the lounge and then being here," she said and trailed off. "Chamber... Chamber..."

"Ever see any chamber in those recon maps?" Keal asked.

Syd rearranged herself. Maybe, if she could concentrate just enough, she'd be able to use her majik to free them. She closed her eyes and caught a thread of gray. It filled her body with soft pinpricks. They trailed along her skin and down her arms like a static charge, but nothing came. No mist or energy at all and the pinpricks fizzled. She tried again. And again. It was like a match that wouldn't spark.

Syd gulped air as her majik failed her over and over. She could barely see straight, and the pain she felt turned to a deep, swollen ache.

"Chamber..." Widje said one more time and shook her head. Then, she looked to Syd and gasped. "Oh—No! Syd!" Her eyes widened. "Syd, stop! We're in Seliss's anti-majik chamber."

Syd slumped against the magnet, putting her whole weight against it. "Great..." she sighed and caught her breath.

"It's really, really old tech," Widje started. "The

magnetic fields interrupt all majik and return it back to its sender. Like a reflection."

Syd's body was now full of energy with nowhere for it to go. She slumped further, and Widje's voice waned in and out of hearing.

"Malvuk used it when he started his experiments," Widje said.

The thought of Villette restrained like this made Syd's chest want to explode. How scared she must have been. But strangely, Syd wasn't scared. She was angry, confused, weak, and frustrated. But not scared.

"Thanks, Widje. That's enough." Syd's jaw clenched, her words spoken like a command.

To Syd's surprise, Widje stopped talking immediately.

Syd looked down to her right arm. "They took our synctrons," she said. "I assume they found your australs, Keal?"

"Full body search it appears," Keal said, and he shuffled again.

They sat in silence for some time. Knowing how long, exactly, was impossible. It could have been five minutes or five hours. The door on the far side of the room swung open, and Furlong stepped in, flanked by two commanders again. A third entered, and Syd caught Gaav's hard eyes, his visor lifted.

Realization slowly expanded in her body, and she lowered her gaze. Any other movement might cause the bile in the back of her throat to come up. Her eyes stung, and Widje struggled in her restraints.

"Now, now…" Furlong clicked her tongue against her teeth. "No need to get so riled up, dear."

Syd heard fingernails clicking on a screen, but still refused to look up. Heeled footsteps walked around and centered themselves at Keal.

"Let's see. Ah, yes. Keal Rhiuld. Son of Jexa Rhiuld. Austral specialist and apprentice to our mutual friend Ivor Malvuk for some time now."

Keal said nothing in return.

Furlong's slow, deliberate steps walked around to Widje but went past her. Shiny, black boots entered Syd's periphery near the single rivet her eyes were locked in on.

"And, the guest of honor, Sydney Orleen. Much more interesting, aren't we? Orphan—oh my, what a tragic event. Parents lost to one of Eichon Wenna's excavation sites. Surely there must be some bad blood there, eh? But no…no." She paused. "Hm. Admitted into Wenna's passion project, ACES Academy, I see. Second incoming class alongside—ah, there we go—Adeline Keylen with whom you've become… Attached? Interesting. Seems you've shown yourself to be an Eheri with rare majik too? My, my… You're an interesting one, indeed."

Something grabbed Syd's face, ripping her concentration from the spot on the floor, and forced her to stare into Furlong's yellow eyes. They were dark, a rich brown in the low light of the room. Her red lips curled into a smile, and she nodded to Gaav.

"Our informant tells us you all came here in the hopes

of finding your beloved hiding with Malvuk somewhere on our campus. You must be almost as disappointed as we are to find her gone."

Syd jerked her head out of Furlongs grip who clicked her tongue again.

"You should still prove useful, though. You're our plan B."

Plan B? What is she even talking about?

Behind Syd, Widje struggled. Furlong chuckled and turned to the door. She stopped at Gaav to whisper something. Gaav saluted her, and she left with the other two commanders. Widje's cuffs continued to rattle; their echoes ricocheted off the metal surfaces of the room.

"Oh, give it a rest, Widje," Gaav said.

"Why would you give us—yourself—away?!"

"Widje, save your strength." Syd said.

The clangs of the restraints died and created silence between Gaav's steps as he paced them in a circle. *What is he waiting for?*

"So," Gaav said. "You know the drill here. Where's Adeline?"

Syd remained quiet and turned her head to follow his circling.

"Where might she have gone?"

Widje's breath grew heavier, angrier. Syd hoped she'd be able to control herself. Keal's boots scraped across the floor. Behind the wall, or maybe from under the floors, pipes creaked faintly.

"Did she give any indication of where else she and Malvuk were going?" Gaav stopped his pacing and motioned to the control panel behind him. He folded his arms.

"I don't want to do this. But, see all these buttons here?" Gaav thumbed to the panel. "Each one sends a message to that magnet behind you and charges it to release a different sort of pain over time, voltage increasing incrementally." He shrugged. "Sure, it's old tech. But it gets the damn job done and typically pretty quickly too. The less I have to dirty my hands with this, the better. But that isn't to say I won't if necessary."

The pipes rattled again, this time seeming to come from the wall directly behind Gaav who just shook his head. He reached into his jacket and threw something on the floor at Syd's feet. *Adeline's journal.*

"It's a boring read, don't you think?" Gaav said.

He walked closer and crouched before Syd, meeting her at eye level. She glanced at the journal, and she felt like she was drowning. She glared at Gaav, seeing past the years and the distance to her oldest friend somewhere still in those flecked hazel eyes. With a blink, his face morphed into the stranger he was now. Her jaw clenched, and he grinned.

"You've always had a tell, Syd, when something was bothering you. Even as kids, your jaw would tense like that, no matter how much you tried to hide what you were feeling."

He stood up and turned to the panel.

"Well that and, if pushed enough, you'd accidentally crush things with your majik. We loved teasing, you know. All of us kids, not just the bullies. We loved seeing how far we could push you, what made you tick."

He found the button he was looking for with a gentle click. Turning around again, he put his hands in his pockets and relaxed against the panel's edge. He shrugged.

"We never did find out. I bet Malvuk can't wait to get you alone."

The hairs on Syd's arms and the back of her neck began to stand on end. Goose bumps rose over every inch of her. A low hum came from the magnet next, slowly but steadily raising into a throbbing whir. She couldn't concentrate on what Gaav was saying over the noise and the static sensation,

All of us kids?
Push me?
Made me tick?

The whirring beat quickened, syncing to a pulse steady with her heartbeat. Her thoughts were drowned out by the electric buzz that filled her eyes, ears, and nose. The pulse's current turned tangible, something full and whole. It overtook her.

Then, nothing.

Silence.

And then, screams.

CHAPTER TWENTY-FIVE

Something cold pressed against Syd's cheek and forehead.

She opened her eyes and grunted, using her core to pull herself upright again and leaving a pool of drool where her face had been on the floor. She wiped her mouth on her shoulder, and she grimaced at the movement. Everything that could possibly ache ached, from her toenails to her eyelashes. Her vision was fuzzy around the edges, and she had to squint to make out shapes. The blue of the steel room came back into focus, and it took her a moment to recognize who was staring down at her.

Gaav had a smug grin on his lips that only came into better focus when he leaned closer. "Have a nice nap? Happen to jog any new information?" Then, in the lowest whisper, "Sorry Syd. Cameras." He pulled away so fast, Syd thought she imagined the faint apology.

She didn't hear any noises from the others, but she refused to break her stare. Carefully, she leaned against the magnet to ease herself.

A hiss echoed around the chamber as a white-hot bolt jolted Syd forward with a cry and pushed her body weight away from the magnet. She hung forward, caught by the tether of her restraints, The burn from the shock sizzled through her lungs. Syd waited for the pain to dull, but it never did.

"Oh, yeah. That." Gaav gave a dry chuckle. "Don't

touch that while it's activated. Gives a nasty shock, doesn't it?"

Syd ran her tongue around her mouth, eyes closed and trying to calm her breath. It all tasted like metal: teeth, gums, cheeks. The icy twang of iron and mineral and earth.

Gaav's footsteps began to circle again and stopped at Widje first, then Keal.

"Well, looks like it's just you and me, Syd," Gaav said. "Like old times. So, c'mon. Think! Where would Adeline possibly run off to?"

Syd did think. It was the only thing she could do to stay conscious. Why did they want Adeline? She didn't know anything more than Gaav already knew.

Gaav sighed and stomped up to Syd. He crouched down in front of her and yanked her hair back. Her neck strained, and she cried out, gasping.

"Really?" Nothing?" He paused, waiting for an answer. Another whisper from the side of his mouth came, "Way see." This confused Syd. Before she could even think about asking, Gaav snarled and gave another loud bark. "Alright then..." He shoved her face away violently, letting go of her hair.

Something poked Syd's hand as Gaav stood and thudded back to the panel. Her fingers twitched at the sensation. Soft, careful, fingers found her palm, and Keal slipped a slender metal canister into her tightened grip. She closed her eyes again before Gaav could notice. Keal's hand silently moved away.

The magnet whirred again, this time in great whooshing sweeps that made Syd's ears pop. The magnets current swelled and released, and the pressure built in the room. In the space between the swells, she thought she heard the pipes creaking again, this time outside the door. She screwed her eyes open and saw Gaav staring at the door too. Red pulsed in the edges of her vision, and she held on. Gaav moved to the door.

The charge in the room swelled again. Syd's head lolled, and her eyes rolled to the back of her head. The sudden loss of control of her body overcame her, and there was a soft reprieve, a calm of letting go.

Her body swayed with the metronome of the magnet's pulse, her ears full and stuffed with white noise. She became weightless for a moment, her body no longer attached, and she slipped away into that peace.

Then, a deafening thunder slammed her back into consciousness. She fell to the floor, her left side stabbed with pain. Her muscles twitched and stretched her neck and back. She convulsed with each electric shock that traveled up and down her spine.

Syd's mouth filled with something wet, something sticky. It expanded in her cheeks, under her tongue, between her teeth, but she couldn't swallow or unclench her jaw. It took every ounce of her strength to open her eyelids between the shockwaves.

She thought she saw Matius and Gaav. They were talking, their movements animated and backlit by the open door. Syd's head slammed into the floor again, and she lost sight for a moment. Through slit eyes, she watched Matius pummel Gaav, and his body slumped to the floor. Her vision went black again, and her neck strained in anticipation of the next shock.

But it didn't come. Her ears rung, and her jaw slowly unclenched itself, frothing saliva spilling from her mouth. Muscles throbbed as they released their tension, and soon, her heartbeat was the only thing she could hear. She kept her eyes shut in the safety of the darkness.

Somewhere, in the back of her slipping consciousness she heard her name.

Then nothing; the cradling tranquility in the black.

Her name again, louder this time.

"Syd!" Matius shouted at her and shook her shoulders roughly. "Wake up! We must go!"

Someone tugged on her restraints. Gasping, life returned to her with a harsh rush. She secured her clutch on the canister in her palm as Matius released her cuffs. He grabbed her arm and helped her to stand without another word. Keal and Widje stood by the door waiting.

Syd used Matius as support and made her way to them, and stopped only to look at Gaav, his body slumped on the floor.

"Come on!" Widje called.

Gunshots from beyond the door met her ears, and she pushed off Matius. The room beyond was a blur. On either side, Avant cadets held off Seliss soldiers and protected the four of them against swords and bullets. Matius led them through a door. The tunnel beyond it was filled with light.

Widje broke into a dash ahead of Syd. Keal stood aside and motioned for Syd to go next. Willing every muscle, she quickened her steps. The tunnel echoed the sounds of fighting the closer she got to the source of light. Behind her, Matius gave the command to retreat.

Syd smelled the outside—grass and humid air. The wind howled past her ears, and her feet carried her faster and faster until she burst through the lighted opening. She stumbled into Widje before she could stop herself. Widje caught Syd and ushered her up a drop rope ladder. Above, the underbelly of an airship hung midair. Below were the training fields and a glass podium behind the ladder.

Avant, in the middle of Seliss. Syd blinked, confusion dawning.

Widje motioned again and grabbed Syd's hand. Syd took a deep breath, and her chest wheezed, but she shook her head. She stood aside. Her hand reached out to Keal to help him up next. She grunted under the weight of him, but he threw his hand on the rung and climbed up quickly. She extended her hand out again, helping whoever came next. One unnamed Avant cadet after another until, finally, Matius appeared. His back was to her, and he shot his gun wildly down the tunnel.

"What are you two waiting for?! Get Sydney on the 'ship!" he shouted.

Widje shook her head, wild hair flying in every direction from the airship's stabilizers. She pointed to Matius and then pointed up.

Matius was out of time to argue. The Seliss soldiers were almost through the tunnel, and their footsteps grew louder over the motors. He jumped, grabbing the highest rung he could and pulled himself up. Widje followed, reaching down and extended her hand to Syd who grabbed on.

The airship engines gathered power to push against the ground. Syd swung on the ladder in midair. Her hair whipped around, stinging her eyes, but the rest of her was numb. Something whizzed near her, and she looked down at the stage covered with Seliss soldiers who shot in her direction. The airship was just out of range, gathering speed. Soldiers littered the training fields, too, faces turned up to her.

Syd opened her palm and looked at the canister Keal had given to her to hide. She glanced down once more and opened the metal clasp. It fell from her fingers, rolling down each joint slowly and silently. The smells of winter and ice filled the air. A snowstorm gathered below as the austral expanded and clouded her view. With no one to command it, it ran wild, and Syd turned to climb, the chill of frost creeping up her back.

"Get her to a bed!" Syd couldn't make out who gave the order.

The door closed behind her, and she immediately collapsed. The adrenaline fled her body, and every muscle screamed at her. The ache pulsed in time to her heartbeat. Hands grabbed under her arms, and she let them, unable to protest or keep her eyes open any longer. They pulled her up, and she tried to help, but her body refused to listen to her. Syd's head slipped to one side as she felt herself being lifted and lowered onto something soft. Only then did she surrender.

There was warmth in her chest. It started small, a single

orange ember, impossibly small, then it slowly expanded burning outward. It caught speed once it filled her torso, her arms, and her legs. All the way to her fingers and toes, and climbed her neck. Syd was held, blanketed in the heat and savored the solace with an inhale, full and strong.

She exhaled, and the warmth left just as quickly.

Her eyes opened, and she feared the oncoming pain from the simple motion. But nothing came. She looked around and found a medic, their back turned, in all white and hunched over a screen. Quietly, she brought her hand in front of her face and flexed her fingers, trying out her toes and legs next. She dared to sit up, and though nothing hurt, she *was* getting annoyed with how many times she'd landed in an infirm lately.

The medic paid her no mind. Syd took in the room: a beige cot set in a bright, enclosed space with secured walls that vibrated with the thrum of engines below. The medic sat in front of a mobile tech station, cables trailing from the wall. Syd swung her legs to the floor and felt the 'ship all around her. They were idling.

"Why have we stopped?" she asked, her mind pushing through everything that happened up to this exact moment. They should be getting as far from Seliss as possible before retaliation.

The white coat turned his attention now on her. He brought a scanner to her cheek and confirmed something, then turned back with a shrug. "Don't ask me. I just clean up around here."

His fingers fiddled with a few keys on the tech station. "You're free to go and ask, though." He waved his hand toward the door impatiently. "The others are down the hall to the left."

Syd nodded slowly and made to move to the door.

"What's your name?" she asked.

"Doren."

"Thank you, Doren."

The hall was bright. One side lined with doors, the other full of windows. She squinted through the sunshine to find trees pushed against the glass, branches broken as if they'd landed on top of the forest and made their own clearing. Her mind automatically calculated the estimated damage to the airship's undercarriage.

To her right, a massive metal door locked in whatever was on the other side. Based on the level of noise in the hall, it was a fair guess those doors led down to the engine room. A glass door sealed away the left side of the airship. Inside, a few people in navy uniforms scurried back and forth in and out of her line of sight.

The infirm door behind her whooshed shut, and she made her way toward what she assumed was the flight deck. The navy uniforms stopped their scurrying and looked at her uneasily. She counted five: a pilot, a co-pilot, and three engineers.

Now is not the time to be shy, something deep inside her said. She nodded to them, looking around the control screens. Instinctively, she noted none of them were showing warning or error alerts. Her eyebrows came together, looking around the room again.

"Excuse me. Where are Matius and the others?" Syd asked.

The co-pilot, indicated by the wings on his uniform, pointed to a heavy door she hadn't noticed. She took in the name of his ID tag: BLANCERE.

"They are in the strategy room, ma'am."

Ma'am? She tilted her head in thanks and made her way through the flight deck, and the others resumed their work. Syd raised her hand to knock, but suddenly felt sheepish and small at the action. She grabbed for the door handle and felt even worse. Shaking herself, she did both before walking in, silently thanking Nova the room was unlocked and saving her from embarrassment.

Keal jumped up and ran to her in a single leap. He grabbed her into a hug before she could even fully enter the room. Her body tensed, bracing for the catch of the recovery majik. Instead, she found herself soft and tender, and her arms clasped around Keal easily.

"I see you're in good condition," Syd said and pulled away with a smile.

Syd looked behind Keal to Widje, who beamed at her. Matius gave his own nod of approval.

"And you!" Keal burst out, leading Syd to a seat at the small table in the center of the room. It sat six perfectly, with Matius at the far end looking toward the door similar to his office in Avant. Keal reclaimed his seat on one side, across from Widje. Syd hesitated, and the swell of companionship in the room dissipated at the two empty chairs. She took her seat at the head of the table, opposite Matius.

"We were just debriefing," Widje said.

Widje adjusted in her seat and leaned forward toward the floating image at the center of the table. She flicked her fingers across the hologram, sending a spinning replica of Seliss in Syd's direction. It zoomed into the area they'd been held captive.

"How long was I out?" Syd asked.

Keal shook his head. "Not long. That medic works quick. We just got the 'ship to safety before you woke up."

"Doren," Syd corrected him.

"What?" Keal asked.

"That medic's name is Doren."

"Okay?" Keal questioned.

Syd's lips thinned. "The people aboard this 'ship are our allies. We should know their names. How long were we held?"

Widje straightened in her chair. "By our estimates, based on when we returned from the mess hall, about six hours."

Syd looked to Matius, a well of gratitude filling inside her. "Thank you," the words escaped her, and a pressure formed behind her eyes. She blinked it away. "Thank you for coming to save us." *You didn't have to. You should be focusing on finding Adeline.*

Matius gave a curt nod, letting the words remain unsaid. "We needed to cut the mission. The quickest way was a direct recovery."

We, Syd noted the word. "How many of Avant's ranks…?" She let the sentence fall and focused her eyes on the spinning hologram.

"Less than we anticipated," Widje said. "Our strategists planned for roughly 100 Seliss cadets and soldiers surrounding the three of us at any given time. Turned out to be a fraction of that, and they were easy to overcome with minimal casualties. Some good guessing by Director Keylen at where we might have been–"

"Minimal casualties?"

Widje nodded. "Two Avant trainees didn't make it back to the 'ship."

Syd's eyes instantly locked onto Matius's. This time, his expression was steeled away. His typical nature sometimes made it so easy to forget that he commanded an army of the most organized and specialized mercenaries and spies. She only knew him as Matius, Adeline's father. The rest of the world knew him as Director Keylen, Avant leader and spouse to Eichon Wenna. How easy it was for her to forget the weight on his shoulders.

How were Avant cadets trained for death? How were their comrades trained on the deaths of others? ACES trained from year one through spiritual means: an entire wing dedicated to the subject twice weekly from a Rhurgari lens. It's the only academy she knew of to prepare their students for the inevitable so that, by year six, all were ready to go out into their specializations as soldiers, commanders, and scholars for the Eichon.

Matius took a breath. "That austral was quite a show there at the end. Where did you get it? It is protocol to search upon capture."

Keal shrugged. "They never check the shoes."

And, though she felt pangs of guilt, Syd couldn't help the tug at the corners of her mouth.

Keal leaned back in his chair, fingers laced behind his head, and gave an exaggerated stretch.

The hologram continued to spin under Widje's control, and Syd stared at the miniature rendering of the chamber, complete with the bulbous magnet and ominous panel. No one at the table spoke for some time. The empty chair did most of that for them. Had Gaav been one of the two casualties they mentioned?

"I've never seen tech like that before," Syd said, to break the silence. "Widje said it was old?"

"Yes," Matius said. "Another of Malvuk's inventions. For better or worse, that man is the inventor of most things we use today. They used devices like this one when he was first starting his experiments early in his career."

Syd's eyes fell again, this time to the grain lines of the wooden table. Thick rivers of brown and tan curving and flowing together.

"They must have trained Gaav while he was undercover," Syd probed.

"Yes," Matius confirmed.

She shifted in her chair, agitated by the lack of explanation. Gaav should be here, sitting next to Widje. Adeline should be here, sitting next to Keal. And where the hell were they, anyway? Why were they just sitting ducks in the middle of a forest somewhere, idling their engines and wasting their fuel? Shouldn't they be doing something, namely finding Adeline? Syd's face flushed with heat.

"I saw you arguing with him," she said and straightened her back. She was losing her patience, and fast. And so what? She was the next Eichon. She could lose her patience whenever she wanted. Yet, she still felt like a small pawn in someone else's game. There were so many questions left un-answered. "What did you say?"

"Look, Sydney…" Matius spread his hands out as if it were an explanation.

She remained silent and held his gaze.

He stuttered and sighed, exasperated. It was only now that Syd realized what she was asking: How could he let one of his own betray him, betray *Wenna*, like that?

Syd's gaze searched the room for an apology. It gave none.

"Sometimes, a specialist goes rogue." The words came from Matius slowly. "Becomes one of the enemies they are reporting on. It's part of the risk of training for espionage the way Avant does, and then dispatching our specialists out into long term assignments. You lose contact, and they lose sight. We do not believe Gaav has gone so far. Yet. He managed to inform us of Seliss's actions in time to rescue you."

Something wasn't adding up. If Gaav knew who she was, why were he and Furlong so concerned about Wenna and Adeline? Why had he apologized? What had he meant when he said *Way see*?

"Why didn't he tell them I was the next Eichon?" Syd asked plainly.

"Enough," Widje said, her voice small but strong. "Gaav made his own choices, and it seems he's playing both sides. Simple as that. We have bigger, more important things to deal with."

Syd couldn't argue that and Matius didn't protest, re-treating into his thoughts. His sunken cheeks made him look gaunt, and his short, dark hair held the grooves of fingers running though it over and over.

When was the last time he'd slept? Syd wondered.

He cleared his throat with a nod. "While we were lucky Seliss wasn't able to attack us in full force," he said, "It was because their army is elsewhere. In Zevir."

CHAPTER TWENTY-SIX

One Year Prior

Even under the bright streetlights, Adeline and Syd had been able to get to Galssop with no problem. Security was always kept at a minimum in the city known for its relaxed atmosphere of technological opulence. Made of money and rich in resources from the land and sea, Galssop had morphed into a neon blur of metal and electric air. The club was no different, a buzzing, searing scene made by and for the trademark population: young, rich cyberpunks with bright hair and brighter clothes from the world over. It was a club made especially for people like Adeline—the elite—and she instantly felt at home.

They'd been able to get the perfect seats at the bar, made from cold metal and cooled by the water conductors that ran under the glass floor. The lights flashed brilliantly off every surface, pulsing in and out of beat to the loud music coming from, seemingly, everywhere. The electricity tickled Adeline's neck and ears.

"I wanna dance!" Adeline shouted in Syd's ear.

Syd nodded toward the dance floor for her to go ahead; she'd protect their seats. She always did. And Adeline had hoped tonight would've been different. This was one of the last time's they'd get to be outside ACES before the transference and graduation. Syd was acting like it was just any other night.

On the dance floor, Adeline swirled her way between

bodies, finding her own little pocket to be lost in the crowd, forgotten for a moment even to her. The music pumped through the crowd of dancers, each swaying and moving to the beats. Just as Adeline slipped away, the song ended. Immediately she looked to find Syd, but instead found the backs of two bright-haired figures towering over Syd on the stool.

Before Adeline realized what she was doing, she grabbed both their collars from behind. They fell away under her yank, her muscles gripped tight.

"Not interested!" Adeline yelled to the two on the ground, eyes locked on Syd's.

Syd stared up to Adeline, mouth gaped but eyes sparkling. And Adeline, in that moment, had never seen anything more beautiful that Syd, lights flashing, bouncing off her from all angles. Pinks, blues, and greens enveloped Syd just as Adeline's hands pulled Syd closer to her, up from the barstool. Eyes locked, too close to back out.

It was the softness of Syd's lips that surprised Adeline the most.

Adeline grabbed Syd's hand, pulling her from the bar and led her back outside where the air was still thick but slightly cooler. Syd's hand were,sweaty but Adeline didn't mind because her palms were so soft. Electricity trailed after them from the club and reflected off the dark streets. Nova and Runar hung overhead, all other stars invisible from the glow of the city.

Syd stopped, taking her hand back and shoving them

in her pockets. She slowed near a weapons shop, windows and doors closed and locked for the night. So, Adeline stopped, too, smoothing out her outfit and catching her breath from the run. She couldn't look at Syd, though. Not yet. The inside of her lip was tender from chewing.

"How long?" Syd asked.

Adeline looked at the ground, at her hands, at anything but Syd. Her face flushed with sudden heat, the reality setting in. If Syd didn't feel the same way, it could jeopardize everything. Or maybe it wouldn't. Maybe they could just ignore this and move on. Maybe they could act like it never happened. Her stomach flipped.

"A few months. A year, maybe?" Adeline said.

Had she really kept her feelings in secret that long? The day she caught the glimmer in Syd's eye, she knew. She started catching herself watching Syd as much as Syd watched her, rushing to meet with Syd as much as Syd rushed to meet her. An anxious energy she had never really known before that created easy smiles and easy laughter. Something Adeline didn't—couldn't—have with anyone else.

Syd coughed and leaned her back against the brick exterior of the shop. She let out a slow breath, and Adeline couldn't meet her eyes just then.

"This can be really, really good or really, really bad," Syd said.

Fear struck Adeline's stomach like lightning. She forced her eyes to find Syd's and for the first time, she couldn't recognize the expression on her best friend's face.

"Syd, I don't wa—" Adeline's voice shook.

"Yeah." Syd cut her off. "I don't want the really, really bad either. So, let's not let it go there."

Syd reached out for Adeline's hand and drew her in close, their bodies radiating heat. Adeline looked at her best friend, really looked at her, with new, fresh eyes. The smallest freckles that liked to hide, the blue and yellow tinge of the streetlights softening her honey eyes.

"When I saw those guys, I couldn't take it anymore," Adeline breathed in a whisper. She leaned her forehead down against Syd's and closed her eyes.

Soft hands slid up Adeline's arms, tingles trailing up her shoulders and to her neck. Then the electricity traveled down, tracing out from Syd's caress making her wish her clothes weren't there at all so she could feel the spark on her skin. Syd's palms gripped at Adeline's waist soft enough that Adeline felt safe, strong enough she felt held. She released her breath and, eyes still closed, Adeline let go.

Present Day

Syd paced the small stretch of carpeting near the strategy room door. Widje, Keal, and Matius sat at the table, each slouched in their own way.

Syd had listened to the report: Zevir was attacked three hours ago. Seliss successfully hacked its Veral system, causing all PRISM to go offline, so to speak. Zevir was staying their ground the best they could, but it was unorganized chaos. Half-human soldiers forgot how to give and take commands when their programming for those commands wasn't being fed directly into their psyche. Seliss might not have the tech, but Zevir was losing ground.

She counted her steps, trying not to lose her own grounding: *one, two, three, four, five, six,* turn. The bigger problem was that the citizenry, including Wenna, were trapped inside the city. *One, two, three, four, five, six,* turn.

"This must have been the 'Plan A' Furlong talked about," Syd said.

"Plan A?" Matius asked.

"Before Gaav took over, in the chamber, Furlong said I was 'Plan B' or something like that. Could our capture have been a distraction?"

"Not likely," Widje said and looked to Matius before continuing. "He'd tipped off Director Keylen of the plans soon after we arrived in Seliss. This 'Plan A'... Sounds like it's to disrupt the transference instead.

"What? Why?" Syd asked.

Widje only shook her head, "Plenty of reasons, I'm sure. But we can't single in on one."

One, two, three, four, five, six, turn.

"Furlong is an Eheri, though, right?" Syd asked, the question surprising even herself. "Why weren't we briefed that Seliss is working *with* an Eheri in their leadership?"

Matius answered easily, "Furlong's majik lineage is recorded, yes. However, her heritage is so diluted that she doesn't actually have any majik left."

One, two, three, four, five, six, turn.

"But, there's gotta be something to that," Syd argued. "Seliss has never worked with Eheris before. And the connection to Adeline—" Syd ignored the others' stares and the growing frustration with herself that she couldn't figure it out. "Hasn't Seliss interrupted transferences before?"

"Yes," this time Keal answered. "But nothing ever came of it, and they haven't tried since Zevir was built and PRISM installed. They were no match."

"We had to pull you three out to guarantee we'd be able to get you to Wenna in time for the ceremony, before Seliss got to her," Matius said.

One, two, three, four, five, six, turn.

"What's the priority here?" Syd asked, giving up on trying to solve the puzzle for now. "What's our next move? What about Adeline?" She stopped herself from stomping her foot like a child.

Matius took a moment. "The last any intel came through, Adeline was alive and left Seliss with Dr. Malvuk. Where, though, we do not know. The more immediate—"

"Way See—Whai Sea!" Syd gasped.

"What?" Keal and Widje asked.

"Before Matius arrived in Seliss, Gaav whispered something to me. He said '*Whai Sea*'."

They all stared at her. Matius's impatience grew right alongside Syd's, the room's tension rising.

"That could be where Adeline is heading with Malvuk!"

Matius stood and leaned over, his hands on the table. "Adeline is alive and that has to be enough for now." His jaw clenched, but he continued. "We must focus on what is in front of us. The more *immediate* priority is to evacuate citizens to the mountains first and foremost, then search for Wenna. These were the last orders we received from her before the airwaves were jammed. Citizens have no protection, save for what PRISM can offer and they are operating on one command: 'attack the enemy', not 'protect civilians'."

Syd frowned and stopped pacing. "What are we doing sitting here in the middle of nowhere, then? Shouldn't we be aiding Zevir? Where even *are* we, anyway?"

"Northern Taams," Matius explained. "We're awaiting Avant reinforcements to meet us here."

Syd's face flushed again. "So, we're just sitting ducks until you feel safe enough to rescue your wife?"

The words left her mouth with such a hiss that even her jaw went slack at their intensity. But Syd was tired of inaction, tired of waiting, tired of no answers and only more questions.

Keal was the first to speak. "Sydney, there are protocols in times of war. That's what this is."

She was also tired of having things explained to her like she was a child. She was a *mostly*-trained soldier, like Keal and Widje and Matius. But deep down, she ultimately knew she feared what she didn't know, of the inner workings and intricacies that led her to this point. That fear was kindling something inside her—an invocation to whatever kept crawling under her skin. She'd mistaken it for her majik before in Seliss, but that hadn't been right. She could control her majik just fine.

Madness.

She thought it had simply grown quiet since training with Villette, but that wasn't it at all. It no longer spoke to her in words and phrases. It flickered inside her and twisted her emotions.

And now it was furious, speaking to her again.

"We'll need two waves," Widje said. "Our reinforcements are heading straight to Zevir to aid in the evacuation efforts. Once we get the signal they've landed, we'll go in behind them to find Wenna."

"Sounds…simple enough," Keal responded, staring off.

"Having second thoughts about all this?" Widje teased with a half-smile.

"Well," Keal started. "Not exactly. It's just…Seliss took all my australs. I'm pretty useless without them. In fact, almost entirely." He slouched deeper into his chair.

Widje stood up, making her way to the door.

"If you think we don't have our own lab on this 'ship," she said, "You're sorely mistaken and as big of a chump as you look. They may not be as strong as the ones you keep at ACES, but our scientists and lab techs are able to come up with some pretty mean austral clones. C'mon."

Keal's face brightened instantly, and he followed Widje out the door without another word.

A swollen silence expanded into the corners of the room. Syd returned to her seat, unsure what else to do. Matius spoke first.

"Syd, you are out of line if you truly think I do not want to rush to Wenna's side this very instant *and* find Adeline."

His voice was low, and his words were calculated.

Somewhere inside of herself, she wanted to reach across the table and comfort him. Somewhere inside, she wanted to cry and tell him to go, now, and fight his way through to Wenna. Somewhere, in the dark, warm depths, she felt herself pound against an invisible prison.

"Your actions speak for you well enough," Syd said before standing again and leaving the room.

It wasn't Syd that explored the airship. More accurately, it was Syd's body that carried her room to room while she looked out from behind her own eyes. Her feet took her out of the flightdeck and back into the main hall, through the metal door, and up the single flight of stairs in the stairwell. Her fingertips felt along the cool surface of the airship's inner walls until she reached the second floor. It was domed and full of light, with a heavy tan carpet and navy accents.

The lounge was empty, and that was strange, Syd's mind thought. Where are Avant's elite who served Matius and helped with the rescue? Her eyes caught on the open library along the wall. Her body moved closer, and she settled on a single title gilded in gold along the spine.

Insurmountable Power: A history of Eichons through the ages by Nervael P. Blouncher.

Her fingers opened the pages, flipping through. *I know this book,* she told herself. It had been assigned in her third year as part of world history. The strange thing about this collection, in particular, was the author categorized each twenty-year reign as stable or unstable, leaving Wenna's short profile at the end of the book with a blank category.

The door to the lounge whooshed open. Syd replaced the book and turned to find Keal plopping down into one of the oversized chairs that was bolted to the floor. He swiveled around to face her.

"Widje was right. Their lab here isn't as advanced as

ours, but I'm definitely well-equipped now. The Avant scientists were so accommodating." He grinned, flashing the inside of a borrowed maroon coat. There, a plethora of canisters were strapped in and tucked away.

Syd looked down at her own body, noticing she was still in a Seliss uniform. Come to think of it, so was Widje. Even Keal, under his new coat.

"I suppose they all know now, don't they?" She waved her hands, the words not syncing up with her thoughts at all. "Who I am, that is and therefore, they know who you are." Her words paused, and her trailing mind caught up. "Tell me, why was it Widje who had to explain to me that you two were my Guard?"

Most of Keal's face dropped, and the smile on Syd's lips told her she enjoyed the reaction, but she didn't believe that. His eyebrows rose, and he shrugged.

"What? I thought it was obvious," he said. "You and I were Adeline's Guard when we all thought she was the next Eichon, at least while at the academy. I assumed there was some kind of unspoken agreement."

Syd's body carried her closer to Keal and into the seat next to him. Her back remained rigid and straight, which made Keal match her body language. Another little pleasure she wasn't sure she fully, actually, enjoyed. He adjusted his posture and looked at her with a face full of questions.

"You okay? Do I need to call the medic or something?"

Syd's head shook. "Just taking in everything. So much has happened in such a short time…and there's still so much yet to come. Do we know when reinforcements will be arriving?"

Keal relaxed, but only a little, and Syd felt delight in being able to manipulate his body language so easily.

"We still have a bit, if you want to rest," Keal said. "We have our own quarters in the lower area of the airship. I can take you down if you'd like."

"No, I'll find my own way." Syd paused. "One last thing. Where are the Avant soldiers who fought today? I haven't seen a single one."

"Ah, while you were in the infirm, we dropped them off at their own airship, which is hiding a few miles away. They will be joining the reinforcements."

Syd nodded, but her mind flared. She stood and left Keal without so much as a goodbye.

Syd's body fell asleep almost instantly. In her dreams, she heard the crashing of waves. She could feel herself on the beach, bottoms of her feet against the warm, rough sand. The waves broke on the low rocks, spraying sea and salt where the sand turned to tall grass. The waves; the rhythm of her breath. The pounding of a drum in the distant field; the pounding on the door.

The pounding on the door! She awoke in a flurry, heart beating hard in her chest. She rubbed her face, eyes still craving sleep. The pounding came again, this time with Widje's voice on the other side.

"Reinforcements have arrived! Meet in the strat room. We begin our flight in five minutes."

Syd looked down at her feet. Just moments ago they were curling in cozy, wet sand. She stretched, testing her muscles, and reaching for her majik. She blinked. Then blinked again to make sure she was back in control.

The four sat at the strategy table again. This time, they were joined by the pilot —ID tag: NEMOU —and co-pilot Blancere as the plan was explained in full. A model of Zevir flashed before them and spun, red and blue circles indicating where Seliss (red) and Avant (blue) soldiers were or would be shortly.

"They are closing in quickly on the city's borders. Seliss has all but taken the outskirts," Matius said

"And the evacuation plan?" Keal asked.

"The soldiers that are there now will carve two paths on either side of the city, on each level." Matius nodded, typing a few commands into a projected keyboard. Two yellow paths lit their way to the central Zevir Tower. "Keal and Widje will be dropped off first at the closer path on Level Five. Your job is to find PRISM soldiers and give them the order to protect and evacuate the citizens. Our troops should keep the Seliss army at bay long enough for the citizens to escape to safety. Assuming Seliss plays by the rules."

Keal and Widje nodded, their faces resolved. The rules of warfare clearly stated no one unarmed should be harmed in times of war. Of course, the rules also stated that the initiator should give intent so the enemy could evacuate its citizens first and Seliss had disregarded that completely.

"And us?" Syd asked, looking at Matius.

He pointed to the other yellow path on the projection. "Our 'ship will swerve around the other side of the city then. Syd, you and I are to head directly to the Tower, find Wenna, and bring her back. We need to ensure you two are not outside of each other's range as we near the transference. Keeping you two separated this long was already a high risk. Once we find Wenna, do *not* leave her side, no matter what. We shouldn't have sent you to Seliss. You needed to be near her this soon to Nova's Eclipse—" He cut himself off.

"Our rendezvous will be at this third exit." Matius clicked a few more keys, and a yellow circle appeared on the northern side of the city. "Because the North end of Zevir butts up against the island's mountains, Seliss isn't focusing its effort there. We estimate that is where they are planning to corner Zevir forces for the final blow. The plan is to force the fighting back to the outskirts, keeping Zevir's streets clear. We should have plenty of time without added reinforcements to get to safety on that edge of the city."

"And if we don't?" Keal asked, breaking Matius's stride.

Matius cleared his throat. "Should either party run out of time, they are to join Avant forces and fight to keep Zevir, its people, and its leader safe. If it becomes a choice, the citizens come first."

Matius's face remained unchanged. It was an order he'd given countless times, the words too effortless. Keal looked to Syd, then back to Matius, and realization dawned on his face as if he finally understood what the failed mission protocol meant. He sighed and ran his fingers through the back of his hair.

"Cheer up, Keal," Widje said. "Odds are better than they were back in Seliss. It was 3 against an entire army."

Widje smiled at him. He smiled back, but Syd could tell his heart wasn't in it.

It was in that moment that Syd understood the difference between Avant and ACES. Where ACES only recruited the best of the best, Avant took in cadets where life-threatening missions were better than whatever life they had before, or would have had otherwise.

She looked at Widje, something swelling inside her. A new respect, maybe. A new honor this person pledged their loyalty to her. Widje was here because she wanted to be here, not because the role fell in her lap or that it was expected of her.

Syd knew very little, she felt, but in this moment she did know one thing. Whatever legacy she was meant to leave behind as Eichon, it was to be a world where alliance and allegiance were a choice.

A column of fire ignited in her chest, flaring adrenaline, and she frowned. *But isn't that what Sevnior wants, too?*

"Syd? Are we ready?" Matius said and shifted the responsibility to her.

To an Eheri orphan, A failed soldier. An Eichon.

She looked to Widje, Keal, Nemou, and Blancere all in turn. They all met her eyes and showed no signs of protest. In the back of her throat, she felt bitter acid, and she swallowed it down. She swallowed it all down.

"Yes."

CHAPTER TWENTY-SEVEN

The emergency lights around the airship flashed red. The pilot and copilot left the strategy room, and, a moment later, the engines below gathered their energy. Syd, curious, followed them into the flight deck.

"A 'ship this size shouldn't take this long to get airborne," she said.

The copilot jumped. "Uh…" He stared at her, and, when she didn't explain herself, continued. "We're conserving fuel, should we need it. Slow build and release… Ma'am?"

Syd nodded to him and looked to the control board. The airship wasn't the newest on the market, but it certainly wasn't the oldest either. All airships, personal, commuters, and fighter, were typically commissioned from Magnate these days, and ACES rarely saw the latter at the shop. Any place that owned fighter airships had their own crews to work on them.

Beeping alarms sounded, alerting all on board to secure themselves as the airship lifted off. Syd grabbed onto the railing above the copilot's chair and watched the two of them work.

"Ma'am, you might want more stability. The chairs in the strategy room are bolted to the floor," the copilot said.

"I learned to fly 'ships at ACES, but never a fighter this size," Syd replied and refused to move.

Her eyes scanned the panels. Two separate screens

flashed numbers, alerting to fuel level, engine speed, cabin pressure, altitude. The engines shook turbulently and the airship lifted itself from the forest landing and above the canopy.

Syd tightened her grip on the railing. The altitude numbers rose, and needles jumped on their gauges. Her stomach flipped with anticipation as the airship lurched forward in the air and gained speed. The beeping stopped, the vibrations dulled, and she loosened her grip.

The center monitor showed the airship as a blinking blip that traveled across the northern reaches of the Taams. Further north, the great Ifor Ridge mountains protected Magnate from the rest of the world, and Syd thought of Saaviana and Reth. Would they still be part of the Council after the transference? Would she want them to be? She couldn't place the uneasiness in her stomach, so she focused on whatever she could—the curiosity that continued to ebb and flow as control panels flashed.

"You have a few vents closed on the under bow. Might want to open those up," she said eventually.

The pilots gave each other a glance, and sadness came over her. She suddenly knew that this wasn't where she was needed, no matter how much this was where she wanted to be. The realization cut, a piece of her fell away. But she was about to become the Eichon—pilot no longer—and she exited the flight deck into the hall.

She stood very still and very quiet, scanning her mind, staring off at the horizon through the windows of the walkway. They were heading southeast and would arrive in thirty minutes or less at their current speed. She sighed and closed her eyes. Even now, she couldn't fully feel the weight of what was going to happen. She knew she should feel something: fear, determination, anger. Anything. And still, nothing.

The door to the infirm opened behind her.

"Oh," Doren said. "Apologies. I wasn't aware that anyone else was out here." He stepped closer to the windows and took a deep breath. "I get airsick in the infirm. No windows."

She turned to him and gave a small smile.

"What did you mean earlier by you being 'clean up around here'? How many patients do you typically see on missions like this?" she asked.

Doren ran his hand over his dark, spikey hair. "I can't give you an answer. There's never been a mission like this, Eichon."

The title hit her like a wave breaking. It rushed through and around her body with such intensity that she was afraid it would knock her to the ground. The weight of that word *Eichon* hung heavy in the air as her silence went on.

"I am sure you and the crew are well equipped for whatever is to come." It sounded as hollow as it tasted.

Doren nodded and continued to stare out the window. Land and trees gave way to ocean and sea. The airship rose higher, avoiding the invisible winds and currents that slid along the water's surface. Wave caps built and broke, becoming tiny, white lines on a blue canvas. She could almost hear them. A flock of seagulls flew under them, in the opposite direction of their destination.

The silence expanded in the hallway, bloated and

bordering on tangible. Syd retreated into herself, and thoughts of the orphanage surfaced. Thoughts of Gaav. *All of us kids*, he'd said. She folded her arms around her midsection, scenes flashing before her: collecting shells on the beach and a young Gaav chasing her inside, tracking sand. Matron Reos had made them sweep the floors for a week straight, but at least they'd been together. At least she'd had someone to talk to as the other kids had run around and out the door to play. The stone tiles on the entry were always colder when doing chores by herself.

That time she found a garden snake in the vegetables and pretended it was her pet. She'd even named it Gareshen, after the great snake beast from their picture books. And when Gaav had found out, he'd captured it and put it in her bed.

Cold stones. Warm sand. Itchy, tickling grass. Soft soil. The sound of laundry flapping in the winds, the smell of soup mixing with salt and earth. Sometimes, she'd hide in the undergrowth of dead shrubs along the sides of the orphanage. There she would find shapes in the clouds under the canopy of branches. Until Gaav would find her and tattle that she was hiding.

The airship vibrated violently for a moment and shook her back to the present. She caught herself on the railing. Maybe Gaav hadn't been the friend she'd thought him to be. Memory was a fuzzy, tricky thing. Maybe, he had simply been the only one to talk to her. Not afraid of her. She frowned, and the flight deck door opened.

"Sir!" Doren saluted Matius.

"At ease, Doren," Matius answered. "I need to speak with the Eichon. Please give us the hall."

There was that word again. Doren nodded and left the hall to the stairwell. Matius moved next to her, hands in his pockets.

"You've instructed them to call me Eichon already," Syd said.

"Yes."

Matius stared out to the ocean, and she studied him, his profile. His strong, angular jaw, just like Adeline's. Her nose, and her ears. Syd's heart sank to her stomach.

"After this, we find Adeline. Right?"

"Yes," Matius said again.

Syd nodded.

Matius coughed. "I know I don't need to impart upon you how critical this mission is."

So don't, she thought. But she let him talk because the more he spoke, the closer she felt to Adeline.

"I trust you value Wenna's life as much as I or Adeline, but I know your heart is elsewhere. This isn't the mission you'd like to be undertaking. I know that. We wanted to tell you sooner, wanted to have you study more closely under Wenna. Take her guidance and use it…. You probably haven't even had time to think about any of this. Everything has gone so quickly.

"Whatever your plans may end up being, whatever your legacy, being able to have Wenna at your side and on your Council, to see Project Nova to its natural completion. Well, that would seem remarkable enough to give it your all when we land."

She listened carefully, dissecting each word as they came and moved together to form meaning. She found small comfort in knowing that Wenna didn't plan to partake in the Resting ritual. She found pleasure in the coded responsibility of his words. It was up to her now, and he knew that.

"My all?" she asked.

"If necessary, do not hold yourself back this time."

This time. The words rang in her ears. What did he know about her and about her powers that she didn't? Syd started to feel small again, shrinking, as if she was a tiny piece to this complicated puzzle that she'd never fully solve. Then, she was sinking again, receding into an echoing dark, a chamber that resounded her heartbeat, her breath—the cacophony of herself.

Syd's body turned to face Matius. "I won't."

He raised an eyebrow.

The lights on the airship began to flash again and indicated to prepare for landing. Her hands gripped the window railing tight, eyes focused on the shimmering cerulean ringed island in the distance.

Scenes of locked battles emerged below as the airship flew overhead. Gunfire and majik sparked along the outskirts of the city's borders. There were no other airships around. They were a giant target, exposed.

"They came by water," Syd heard herself say, but her voice was dulled. It was more a thought, stated aloud. "They aren't planning to retreat. They are planning to occupy."

"When you have Seliss numbers, your soldiers are expendable. Should they call surrender, Avant and Zevir still follow the rules of engagement. We will not attack unless they intend war," Matius said.

"They don't have any 'ships to retreat, though. What happens then?"

Matius tilted his head at her.

"It's simply not realistic." Syd calculated. "To expect enemies to disengage when the opposition has nowhere to go. Will Zevir and her reinforcements aid Seliss in their efforts to retreat?"

"The rules of engagement state—"

"Fuck the rules of engagement. I'm the Eichon, yes? I'm in charge?"

Matius rubbed the back of his neck and reluctantly nodded.

"Zevir and Avant reinforcement *will* aid in Seliss's retreat, *will* aid in getting those men and women to safety should they surrender." Just because their own leadership would view them as expendable, that didn't mean Syd had to.

Matius's jaw clenched, and he shoved his free hand back in his pocket. "Yes, Eichon."

The airship neared the western main pathway leading to Zevir's center: the first drop-off point. The flight deck door flew open again, and Keal and Widje joined them. Alarms sounded, the ascent beginning on the level 5 landing pad. They were coming in quick. Widje saluted Matius as she passed and stopped when Syd turned to them.

"We will see you at 1430 at the rendezvous," Widje

said, her body straight and rigid. Her eyes focused on a distant point somewhere.

Syd looked over to Keal, and his eyes darted nervously. He looked from her to Matius to the outside view, and back again. The airship slowed, and the four of them wobbled in unison at the shift.

These are my Guard. Syd's head nodded to them. "Citizens first, engage only when necessary," her flattened voice said. "The call to evacuate is the highest priority. We will see you at the northern entrance."

Keal's eyes stopped darting, and his face dropped. "Syd…?"

The door to the stairwell opened, and the airship's skeleton crew lined the hall. One of them barked, "It's time! Let's go!"

Footsteps approached. The crew guided Widje and Keal down the hall and through the door. Syd's body turned back to the windows, eyes keeping watch until Keal and Widje were safely on Level Five's outer ring on foot.

The airship was close enough to see blurs of PRISM, Avant, and Seliss uniforms grouped together. Avant forces had created serpentine barriers of themselves against the entrance points to the Tower. Dings reverberated through the airship's metal as stray—or not—bullets found their way to the hull.

A majority of PRISM were using majik and their formation rested behind the Avant reinforcements. Flares of burning fire, distracting whirlwinds and small downpours, and defensive plant life drew the enemy's attention away from Avant. Weapon, no weapon, tactical, offensive, defensive, each Avant soldier embodied their own unique style. That was truly the advantage of their forces. Small numbers meant Avant cadets were individually trained, adding the element of surprise during combat, whereas Seliss trained en masse. Regardless, with each single step the blue and black uniforms gained by pushing the enemy back, upright maroon uniforms would replace fallen ones.

Syd caught a glimpse of a maroon lab coat running to find cover while wild, colorful hair followed close behind. She wasn't expecting Widje to be a gun specialist, but Syd have never asked either. They alternated, Widje with her dual firearms and Keal with cloned australs, until they safely crossed out of sight, hidden under Zevir's outer rings.

Goosebumps raised on Syd's skin. The cabin pressure adjusted, and the airship prepared to take off again.

"We should have less Seliss forces at our drop off," Matius said. "I will disembark first, make sure it is clear, and the crew will help you down when I give the signal. Our last communication with Wenna stated she was in the central Tower in the control room. This is our target. Should we find any citizens along the way, we are to give the order to evacuate as well."

The airship rattled and was piloted away and Matius continued. "We have ten minutes until we land. We are going around the city to hopefully distract the Seliss forces, even if just for a moment."

Syd nodded and continued to survey the scenes below. Each grouping of soldiers was its own microcosm of tension and struggle, of strength and majik and strategy. All of this effort, and for what?

"What is it Seliss is after?" she asked.

Matius took a deep breath. "I assume you mean aside from the obvious. Based on Widje's debrief while you were in the infirm, Sevnior is out to destroy any autocracy associated with the Eichon, including the destruction of the Eichon herself and Zevir's technology."

Syd's mind let the information wash over it, soaking it in, internalizing first and translating second before cognition.

"The city's technology is what keeps an Eichon guarded so well," Matius said. "Without it, the Eichon is vulnerable. A direct attack, to them, could mean hitting two birds with one stone."

The airship's shadow passed over countless squalls below and cascaded over the southern entrance. The distraction had worked. Maroon dots were following the airship to the other side of Level Five.

Syd felt her heartbeat against her rib cage, against all the bones in her body. Her palms were slick with sweat and her breath shallow and quick. But her face didn't react. It gave nothing, unmoving, her eyes focused on the Tower.

"Do we know how many are left inside with Wenna?" Syd asked.

"Our communication was cut off before we could confirm," Matius answered. "Knowing Wenna, she has created a stronghold of just herself and gave the evacuation command to everyone else in the Tower."

The alarms blared again, the descent upon them. Her throat swallowed hard, and her mouth dried. The cheap material of the Seliss uniform brushed against her skin. The crew's boots pounded up the stairs once more, and the door opened. Matius turned, giving her a final nod, and walked past his soldiers who saluted him in turn.

Once he was through the door, the crew turned their collective heads toward Syd. Hands reached out to help her along, to pull her forward, to guide her through, to brace her on the stairs, to lower her to the rope ladder.

Then it was up to her legs to move. The crew stared down at her expectantly. When she looked up, her eyes widened, and a flash of fear overcame her. There was no going back. She lowered one foot and then the other. All she could do was repeat the motion as many times as she had to until her feet found the last rung.

Syd's free foot dangled, and someone grabbed it. Her body whipped around violently, and Matius helped her to the ground, landing with an uncanny clink on Zevir's glass street. The hanging ladder retreated, pulled up by the anonymous crew. She watched it disappear into the emergency hatch, then the hatch closed. The airship's motors whirred and lifted it up and away. The wind swirled around her.

Matius said something she couldn't hear, a deafening ring in her ears. She inhaled hard and sharp, coming back to herself.

Sound returned, too, and the roar of the airship faded.

CHAPTER TWENTY-EIGHT

The air tasted of gunpowder and hot metal. Bullet shells and austral canisters littered the tunnel leading into Zevir from the landing pad. These were the breadcrumbs of battle, their direction indiscernible. In the distance, the sounds of war carried on beyond the settling dust from the airship's ascent.

Syd looked over her shoulder with every other step she took. It wasn't that she felt someone watching her, at least not from the outside. There was that *something* again—that *Madness*—observing, waiting, hunting, and it was always just over her shoulder, darting out of view each time she turned around. For now, though, her breath was her own, her steps were her own, and her heartbeat was her own. She focused on Matius, crouching when he crouched, and waited for him to signal for any movement beyond the entrance.

The outer ring of Zevir's mid-level had never been so desolate. Zevir was a bustling, self-sustained metropolis. People, autos, small airships, and hovercrafts traveled its rings and streets at all hours of the day. Now, all was silent and still. Banners and city flags flapped, and their cracking resounded through the city until it joined the distant backdrop of battle. She looked up at a sudden, dark movement above them through the sea glass of Level Six.

The tall, semi-transparent rings above began to close in, and Syd realized Zevir's inherent design flaw. It was a series of round tunnels stacked on top of each other, all around a single building that reached for the sky. There wasn't anywhere to go.

Her breath caught in her throat, and Matius halted. He put up his fist, signaling to stop. They crouched low again, ducking into an abandoned storefront that advertised fuselage repair. Syd peered over Matius's shoulder and saw nothing. Then, she heard it. A rumbling of footsteps came from the Tower—the very direction they needed to go.

Matius's gloved hands gripped her and broke her thoughts. Silently, they broke into a run in the opposite direction. Friend or foe, she knew it wasn't wise to wait around to find out. Whoever's footsteps those were, meeting them would only delay the mission more at best. The next logical course of action was to find an alternative entrance into the Tower.

Syd's body slipped into autopilot and released her flight instincts to keep pace with Matius. She followed him around the bend, and then another, putting as much distance as they could between them and whoever was trailing. They stopped, hunched low, and listened. Syd couldn't hear anything over the wheezing from her chest. She looked to Matius for what to do next.

He put his finger to his lips. They remained still just long enough for her to catch her breath, and then he nodded, pointing over his shoulder. She straightened her back to see he'd lead them to a Tower side entrance, tucked away between storefronts. Matius set his face and looked for her to confirm.

Syd's face went slack, and her heartbeat faded into the

background, only to be replaced by the rhythmic sound of boots running in unison, of an army trained as one. She couldn't make out how many, no matter how hard she tried. It could have been three or thirty, the echo of the steps growing louder and quicker.

Matius took a quick glance, calculated something, and motioned for her to follow. She slid under the booth of an air travel agency, computer terminals dead silent. Matius leaned in.

"On my ready, you are to make for that Tower entrance," he said and slipped something from his neck, shoving it into Syd's palm. Her fingers instinctively grasped at the small, square, and hard item. "Here's the keycard to get in. It has clearance for every door." He turned quickly to check where the soldiers were.

Syd stared blankly at the keycard in her hand, the weight not registering fully. Something shimmered on the chain just behind the square fob. A ring of Zevir glass. Matius turned back to her, and recognition set in.

"And you will follow?" Syd asked, wishing she didn't need to say the words. Wishing he wouldn't have to confirm her fear.

She took him in, in that long moment between question and answer. The sunken cheeks, the dark circles, the wrinkles that spread out to his temples, the creases in his forehead. Her heart thumped with grief and pushed something bitter to the back of her throat. She swallowed.

Then, she saw it all happen in slow motion. He enfolded her hands over the ring and key, and looked down as he encircled both her hands in his. His dark eyes met her, and he finally answered by shaking his head.

"I will make sure Seliss stays out of the Tower, away from Wenna. Away from you."

Whiplash hit Syd from his words. She slammed into herself, falling deeper inside. The heaviness of the objects in her hands lifted as Matius let go.

"Take care of Wenna and Adeline for me. There's so much—don't hold back."

His words floated down into the vast emptiness Syd found herself locked into once more. Something within her resolved and protested at the same time. A fusion of heartache, longing, and words left unsaid. Missed chances ignited a flame in her belly, and it propelled her to stand. She looked down to the man crouched at her feet. *A knight bent before his Eichon.* Her lips tugged against the spreading, sinister joy she felt.

Matius stood to meet her and grabbed her by the shoulders to embrace her fully. She felt his chest heave as he breathed in and out. She smelled the leather of his jacket. Her hands hung loose at her sides no matter how much she told them to move, to hug him back. She railed against her own mind, taking the only comfort she could from this place. The deep, smokey earth enveloped her but for a moment, then Matius released.

He nodded and turned his back to her. Without another word, he held up three fingers, facing away, and counted down one digit at a time. His ring finger dropped. Two. His middle finger dropped. One. His index finger dropped, and he was gone, disappearing beyond the bend with his blade drawn.

He never looked back. Not once.

Syd's body turned to face the door, and her feet moved toward it step by step.

The door slammed behind her. PRISM soldiers jumped to move forward. She held up her hand automatically.

"Sydney Orleen," her voice called to them, identifying herself.

The soldiers stopped mechanically, waiting.

"You are to evacuate any remaining citizens of Zevir to safety," Syd's voice was strong and commanding. It bounced off the Tower walls and up the central spire.

The half-program, half-human soldiers paused, registering, before they filed together toward the main exit. She watched them as they fled, parting their formation around her like water around a boulder, and placed Matius's chain around her neck.

Nothing stirred in the wake of the new quiet. She squinted. Not even the banners waved, and the lighting was lower than usual. The building was on backup power. Adeline had told her once about Zevir's security. Should the Veral system go offline, the entire city shuts down as a safety measure. What a strange thing to share; Adeline must have truly trusted her. That thought caused Syd's throat to clench, but that meant no elevator and no hovercraft.

Eventually, her feet began to climb one step at a time. The Tower rose three stories above Zevir's seven levels, totaling ten floors she'd have to search should Wenna not be in the command room. Still, Syd's body refused to move quickly, and, instead, looked at the Tower with new eyes, knowing that this would be her home.

Her ears heard nothing but the slow beat of one foot reaching the platform of a step, followed by the next, and next, and next. Her fingertips grazed the handrails. In the middle of active war outside, in here, inside these dark, sturdy walls, she allowed herself a moment of decadent dreams of her reign that sent electric waves of guilty pleasure through her skin. It rippled forth, her cheeks unable to stop smiling.

Or would she return to Darmar? Rebuild and reclaim that land for herself? Now, there was a thought. Or maybe even ACES. As Eichon, she could claim any part of the world she wanted. Even Seliss, with some work. When was the last time an Eichon tried that?

She heard herself exhale a long, annoyed sigh. The decisions would just have to wait. Truthfully, it would be so much easier to just let Seliss take Zevir and build elsewhere, but she needed Wenna. At least until the transference was complete.

The pangs of protest subsided and were replaced by a new electric power that rushed through her body. It, this Madness, was slippery like silk sheets. Easy to slide in and around, slithering like a snake might, wiggling into a comfortable coil wound upon itself. Its spiral deepened with each step Syd took up the Tower.

CHAPTER TWENTY-NINE

Syd's feet stopped climbing at floor six and exited the stairs. Her body followed, the feeling of detachment increasing. She strode the familiar upper hall until she found the door she needed. Her hands removed the chain from her neck and pressed the keycard to the door's scanner. Her fingers refused at first, and she gripped the fob unnaturally, finger joints locking against the motion.

You can't fight it forever. You'll grow tired, very soon, her mind called to her.

The tension in her hand released when the door slid open, and she replaced the chain around her neck. Her head moved from side to side, and her sight followed.

"Wenna?" Syd's tongue and vocal cords worked together against her closed jaw. Annoyance rippled and crawled up her spine. Impatience soon followed. "Wenna, it's Syd. We need to go. The rendezvous is set."

There was no response. Her body moved through the room at a snail's pace, taking in the dead screens, unblinking panels, and unlit keyboards at the center console. Her back bent harshly at the waist, and she peered underneath the counter.

"Where is Matius, Sydney?" Wenna asked, her voice cool.

The temperature dropped severely, wafting breezes in either direction. Syd's body stood upright in its own time and turned to see Wenna's figure silhouetted in the door.

Hooking the ring with her thumb, Syd showed the ring to Wenna.

"Your safety was his primary concern." Syd's lips moved, but her mouth remained locked. She heard her voice splitting in two directions, two tones running alongside one another, a parallel sound in octaves that never touched. Syd found it at once harrowing and luscious. "If he survived, he will meet us at the rendezvous. We must go."

Syd's eyes ached, and she felt them bulging against her sockets. Something was building inside her, swelling. She forced her eyelids to blink to relieve the tension.

"Sydney?" Wenna's voice turned cautious.

Wenna moved aside and let in what little light the outside corridor could offer. Syd's eyelids flew open, and her fingers twitched in impatience. Her body moved forward, closing in on Wenna and the doorway. Wenna stepped aside fully, and their eyes met in passing.

"For now," Syd's echo said and turned toward the stairs. From the platform, her foot stumbled down the first step, followed by the next.

"Stop!" Wenna called after her.

Syd's body stopped and twisted at the waist to look back at Wenna.

"We must go. Get to the rendezvous," Syd's voice said.

Wenna drew herself up. She squinted at Syd, at her form. "The Madness," Wenna said. "It's taken you." The temperature around them rose gradually. "Syd, you're in there. I can still feel you in there." Wenna closed her eyes, inhaling deeply.

The tension behind Syd's eyes flared. Her eyelid twitched, and the corner of her mouth tugged.

"She will be gone soon enough," Syd's two voices sounded against each other.

The temperature continued to rise, and calming warmth spread over Syd's electric skin. Her body tried to shake it off violently, and her eyes glared. Wenna raised her palms slowly, pointing them toward the Tower's peaked ceiling. Syd's arm raised and slashed through the heat that radiated around her.

"Your majik is no longer needed here, Wenna!"

Syd's fists instantly flared, thick fog engulfing them as if it were flames. The mist flicked, withered, rejuvenated itself and swirled as it grew. Wenna's hands poured cascading light from the palms, her arms stretched out before her. The light rushed and fell to the floor like waterfalls. Wenna kept eye contact, unblinking.

"Sydney, you can fight this. You can push through. You're in there. The Madness is locking you away in a small, dark place, but you still hold the key to escape."

Syd's mist hissed, growing and climbing. Thick tendrils of gravity whispered along Syd's arms before flattening into an opaque sleeve.

"Remember, your majik is yours to control," Wenna said.

The gray majik crawled to Syd's neck and descended over her chest and down her stomach. Then, a flicker and Syd's head shook, twitched. Her mouth opened to speak, but a growl came instead.

"No," the duality called.

Wenna raised her palms higher, her light spreading across the floor to where Syd's feet met the stairs. Syd's shadow-covered arms reached for the railing. With a single motion, Wenna flicked her wrists, and the light howled toward Syd.

Syd's arms resisted at first, but her majik's strength broke through. It hoisted her feet up off the ground and pitched her body up and over the railing. She closed her eyes and felt herself fall.

Syd's eyes twitched open. Her mind scanned and found some soreness on her left ankle before her body tightened itself. Wenna pounded down the stairs and rushed to her.

"Sydney! Are you hurt?"

Syd's neck turned slowly, body bending at odd angles to stand up.

"I told you, Wenna," the voice said. "Your majik will do no good here."

Syd's body began to shuffle to the Tower's main door. She extended a hand, and the mist flew forward, bursting the door out and away, into the front courtyard of water fountains and bright imported green grass. *Don't hold back.*

A trail of fog followed her body out through the door, her footprints trapped in its wake. Small tremors shook up her legs with each forward step. She limped, dragging her hurt ankle, though she felt no pain. Wenna's footsteps followed her. *Don't hold back.*

"Remember your training. Remember Keal. Remember Matius." Wenna's voice was steady, only wavering when she picked up speed to catch up. She stood in front of Syd, blocking her way. "Remember Villette."

Syd's eyes widened, and her vision blurred. Her lips stretched into a smile. The mist flicked and licked at her, and her majik held her body like a suit of armor. It cradled and protected her, wrapping her in its safety. Syd blinked the blindness away for a moment and saw the trail of gray flow and expand. The ground shook. *Don't hold back.*

"Remember Matius," Wenna said again, and she looked behind her to the northern entrance. It was a straight shot, and the Avant airship sat at the end of the tunnel roadway. She turned her head to Syd again, a look of shock on her face.

"Remember Keal!" Wenna yelled as a thundcrous clap boomed through the city.

Syd's eyes closed, a flash of lightning behind their lids. A crack shot up through the walls behind her. She did not need to turn to see it. She knew it was there. The wind picked up, her fog reaching and swirling around the skyscraper. She was her body, and she was the fog. She was expansive, like water, like smoke, and moved across the city. The Tower shook. *Don't hold back.*

"Syd! Remember Adeline!" Wenna shouted over the howling, screaming wind and booming thunder.

And she did. In the flow of herself, she found stillness. She found a piece of herself and traced it back to her mind, to her body. She remembered chapped lips and tangled hair, porcelain skin and the rising and falling of Adeline's chest as she slept, the smell of lavender and sweat and glistening skin. She remembered Adeline's resolve and kindness and assuredness against all else, the protection and friendship and fierceness, the embraces of love, the blanket of care. Syd remembered the constant loyalty. The constant faith.

She inhaled, taking it all in. The faith, the loyalty, the care, the love. She inhaled the sureness, the kindness, the resolve; muscles and sweat and lavender.

She inhaled everything. Every moment from the look of betrayal at discovering the truth, the warmth as Adeline held her when she cried, the butterflies in her stomach from their first kiss, Adeline's glistening eyes when Syd agreed to be her Guard, her set jaw when Adeline stuck up for Keal, and her giggle when they'd get in trouble. She remembered it all, chasing Adeline through the stacks of the library, showing her the kitchen and sleeping quarters on the sea-ship. She remembered all the way to Reos pushing Syd toward Adeline all those years ago.

And then, Syd screamed. She screamed from the cage deep within her body. She screamed and cracked her ribs, and her blood boiled as it pounded through her and out of her. She screamed and broke through, violently and quickly. In a single moment, in a single movement, in a single motion, Syd screamed and resurfaced.

The glass walls around them shook and burst, blue glass raining down. Syd raised her arms to shield herself from the spray. Her body collapsed entirely and wavered, and a deep creak came from the Tower behind her.

"Syd." Wenna fell to her knees beside Syd and helped her sit up.

Syd's majik armor crackled at being touched, and Wenna recoiled.

"Syd!" she called again, and the image of Wenna's face flicked in and out of Syd's vision.

She was fog, then she was Syd, then back again.

"Go." Syd grasped for a moment of herself and reached air. Her eyes flew open. "Go!" she sputtered. "I can't call it off, Wenna. I can't control it. It's taking me. It is me. Go."

Syd panicked, and her vision faded again. Then, she was filling the entirety of Zevir's Tower. She was expanding into every corner and crevice.

"Syd," Wenna's voice brought her back. "You must fight it."

Syd could only hold on for a moment longer. In the next, she was bursting through all the doors in the Tower. Then, Wenna was shaking her. And again, Syd plummeted. The weight of herself crashing over and over and her consciousness slipped.

Wenna screamed something, but she was too distant for Syd to hear this time.

Finally, Syd felt it. She slipped, breaking the structure of the building. Gripping and tearing it down. Tearing it all down around her in a single gray swell.

The sounds of motors and smell of engines filled the air. Dust clogged Syd's nose, and she gasped. Debris filled her lungs. Glass screeched under the weight of her sudden consciousness. She couldn't move. Her body was restricted, pinned under something large. Something big. She stretched her eyes toward a sliver of light in the darkness of this heavy place. She pushed her shoulder against the hardness around her and found a space small enough to reach her hand forward, toward the bright thing.

CHAPTER THIRTY

One Week Prior

Her shoulder blades cast shadows like wings down her back from the moonslight. It slipped in through the curtains that framed the bed. Adeline poured over a book, pen in hand, scribbling. Stopped then scribbled again. Taking her time as she recounted the day's events.

A hand reached out from the bedding and trailed its fingertips on her lower back, and she straightened, goosebumps prickling for a moment at the touch. As if on their own, Adeline's lean, slender muscles tensed and relaxed in the same breath.

"Why do you use such old tech?" Syd asked and tossed the sheets aside with a yawn. She looked through the curtains at the two moons and brushed her dark curls from her eyes.

Adeline followed Syd's gaze. Nova was quickly eclipsing her sister, Runar. "I have always liked it better than our issued tablets," she said, barely pausing before returning to her writing. "More personal. Private."

"More private than your mother's archivists logging each one of those journals you fill?"

Adeline heard the grin in Syd's voice and chose to ignore it.

Syd sat up and stretched her arms towards the ceiling. She brought them down, wrapping around Adeline and playfully tugged her to the bed. Adeline finally surrendered herself into a grin of her own, staring into Syd's honey eyes.

"Yeah yeah." Adeline breathed. "You should get back to your room. Full day tomorrow."

Syd groaned dramatically, making a show of sliding off the bed and collecting her clothes. "Oh, right, Visitor's day."

"Don't know what you're complaining about." Adeline sat up on her elbow, watching Syd. "You get out of half your classes."

Syd pulled her shirt over her head and tied her uniform jumper around her waist by its sleeves. She hopped from one foot to the other, slipping on her boots. "Yeah, what could be more fun than a bunch of strangers crowding the halls, all hoping to catch a glimpse of you."

"Oh c'mon." Adeline closed the journal and placed it on the bedside table. "They're here to view the academy, not me."

"Still, it makes my job around here that much harder."

"There you go complaining again…" Adeline grinned, leaning back on the bed on her hands and stared at Syd.

"Mhm," Syd said as her eyes scanned Adeline. She moved in to kiss the tip of her nose quickly. "See you in the morning."

Present Day

Syd paced the room that had become her office. She rung her hands, thick leather gloves squeaking together. The fur that outlined her robe tickled her cheeks. The concrete walls made the space feel like a prison cell. Thin slitted windows didn't help the matter. Though, she couldn't fully blame them.

They had given her some creature comforts: a warm rug, a desk, a tablet. She wasn't truly a prisoner, she knew, but part of her thought she should be. She had stayed hidden in her room since recovery, waiting for the Council to decide if she was still to become the next Eichon. They hadn't gone over what would happen if the answer was no.

Keal relaxed in an armchair beside a roaring fire and tried not to shiver. The flames from the hearth reflected off his new glasses—the right lens clear, the left blackened to help his injury heal.

"You'd think a place like Magnate would have figured out how to heat itself by now," Keal grumbled to no one.

She sat down at the desk, feeling guilty. Syd was, after all, why they were here. Why over half of Zevir's population were suddenly scrambling for space in the mountain academy. Even though Wenna and Villette both had reassured her it wasn't her fault, not truly, Syd was unable to believe it. If only she had been stronger, if only she would have trained a little longer, if only.

Syd's tablet responded to her gloved fingertips, and she tapped back to the public damage report. Her eyes fluttered over the details she'd read at least a thousand times by now: Zevir City destroyed during Seliss's ambush. Zevir's Tower fell whilst Eichon Wenna defended her home against her attackers. Magnate and Avant academies have opened their doors to civilians and PRISM Eheri refugees alike.

There hadn't been any mention of Syd or Adeline. She swiped the screen to the next public report, and it was more of the same. In fact, all of them had the same general text put out by the Council. Syd had only been in recovery for a day, Wenna's healing majik far more potent than Avant's medicine, and the Council had worked quickly to make sure the world had a concise story of what, exactly, happened, however vague.

"Still nothing from Seliss?" Syd asked.

Keal shook his head. "Not a word. I think they're as shocked as the rest of us. Only a matter of time until one of their grunts says something. Probably won't matter, though, once word gets out about our plans with Nova."

Syd chewed the inside of her lip and returned to her tablet. She tapped away from the public reports and searched for Gaav's internal profile. No matter how many times she refreshed the screen, she was met with the same: last point of contact prior to Zevir's fall. Syd frowned and clicked the tablet off.

She'd wanted to go back to ACES immediately, to tuck herself away. To hide. She'd even questioned why Wenna bothered to save her at all, but that was a dangerous thought that she refused to let herself entertain for very long. Ultimately, the Council refused. Magnate was better defensively should Seliss try anything while they were weakened, while they were so close to the transference.

And now, it was upon them. The day Wenna would pass her powers onto the next Eichon. Syd's stomach hadn't stopped flipping since she woke from a dreamless, empty sleep. In fact, so much of her was empty now. Hollowed out, the space within her filled to the brim with guilt.

"Shouldn't you be off convening with the Council?" she asked.

"They know my vote and where I stand. Much rather be here," Keal responded.

"Watching me, you mean."

Keal gave a sigh and turned to her in his chair. "I know it's a lot Syd, but can you trust that I'm actually on your side here? And Widje, too, for that matter? We're your *Guard* for Nova's sake."

Syd looked away, guilt turning to spite. It was true she hadn't been the most welcoming to her friends since recovering. But she hadn't meant to be so rude, not really and not at them. Her shoulders collapsed.

"Sorry, I'm just—" Syd started, but the door opened and cut her off.

Widje walked in, her white fur coat contrasting against her bright hair and brighter eyes. "We have a decision!" she chimed, grinning. "Syd is still to become the next Eichon."

"Alright!" Keal cheered, jumping from his chair. "Congrats, Syd."

Syd didn't know how to take this news. Should she be happy? Relieved? Thankful? Or should she be worried, cautious, and scared? The mix of emotions left her numb, canceling each other out.

"But!" Widje shot Keal a glance, and Syd's eyes snapped to Widje immediately.

"But?" Syd echoed.

"There are a couple stipulations. The Council members will be carried over to your reign, and you will follow through with Project Nova."

"And Adeline?" Syd asked, caring about none of those things more than the fact they still hadn't found Adeline.

"...They didn't mention..." Widje stammered, looking to Keal for help.

"We will find her, Syd. But first, we have to get through the transference." Keal moved to Widje. "Tonight, then?"

Widje nodded. "The eclipse will be visible at 2349 exactly. We are to prepare with the Council until then."

The transference was a solemn affair, and Syd felt grateful the ceremony matched her mood at least. Whereas Keal and Widje had been excited, Syd couldn't allow herself to be. Would the world truly believe Seliss was at fault for the fall of Zevir? Did *she* want the world to believe that? The wind blew the fur of her hood around, and her face itched.

She stood across from Wenna in a gray stone courtyard covered in snow. Wenna wore thick robes of yellow and blue for healing and aura majik, and Syd had been given new clothes of black and silver for gravity majik. Surrounding them in a circle was the Council. Villette gave Syd an encouraging smile in the pale light. Jexa, Reth, and Saaviana stood quietly, their faces like stone in the cold. Matius leaned on a cane the color of ebony, its tip and handle pure silver. Keal and Widje looked to her, beaming through their rosy noses and cheeks.

Snow began to fall; the only other movement were the clouds of breath coming from each of the nine hoods. Syd tried to blink the flakes from her eyelashes, not wanting to miss anything on the off chance she, too, would need to perform this ceremony in twenty years' time.

Wenna raised her hands high above her head and turned her face to Nova. Syd followed her gaze and watched as the Great Moon was overtaken in shadow, outlined finally in the most brilliant white light. That light expanded in all direction, so bright that Syd had to look away. When she blinked her eyes open again, the moon's streams poured in Wenna's palms.

Carefully, Wenna lowered the moonbeams as the light filled her. Her skin glistened and glimmered, and her nostrils and mouth glowed. Otherworldly and terrifying at once. The air surrounding Syd became electric, the fur of her robes standing on their own and her clothes clinging to her skin. The atmosphere turned suffocating, and her breaths grew shallow. Fighting against the restriction in her chest, she watched carefully as Wenna weaved the moonbeams together and brought them down to her.

The beams swirled, and Wenna cupped her arms around them until they formed a ball. Syd found herself transfixed, mesmerized by the dancing shimmering lights. It filled her with a calming wholeness and subtle reassurance. The light wanted her, and she found herself wanting it in return. Her mind emptied, completely, filled with only want and desire for the bright light to call her name. She pined for it and found that it pined for her too. Syd fell to her knees, the thud nothing but a dull echo in her mind. Tears streamed down her face, hot and sticky, as Wenna walked to her with palms full of light.

Wenna cupped Syd's face, and the touch was cold. It

chilled Syd to her bones, but she didn't mind. Wenna bent down and kissed Syd's forehead, a being made of pure light, and Syd's world fell away from her in an instant.

Where she had been kneeling, she was tumbling through nothing head over heels. Then not nothing, the black pocked with a million tiny lights. Then, complete white. Sterile and opulent, and Syd floated there, feeling nothing but love, as if she'd never know any other feeling. Just as she thought she could stay here forever, she was sent tumbling out again, and she flailed, grasping to take the love with her, to keep it and share it.

It forgave her, utterly and completely, for Zevir, for Adeline, for her parents. It forgave her for her doubt, for her guilt, for her Madness. And that light, that brilliance, the heart of the Goddess Gift, turned that forgiveness into grace and divinity within Syd. It filled her with purity and an unshakable adoration of all living things.

Syd fell forward onto her hands and knees on the snow-covered stone. Her eyes poured tears as she looked to Wenna, whose skin had returned to normal. Nova, above, came out from its shadow. Wenna knelt with Syd, and Syd looked at her own gloved palms. She searched deep within her, for even a single thread of the love she'd felt only moments ago.

When she found it hiding there, deep within her core and more solid and strong than anything she'd ever known, she wept into Wenna's arms, and Wenna was there to catch her.

"It's so much," Syd whispered through her tears.

"I know," Wenna said.

CHAPTER THIRTY-ONE

Widje and Keal leaned over Syd's desk, the three of them plotting course. Wenna approached, and they all stood to attention. It had only been a few days since the transference, and old habits were dying hard.

"There's been more volcanic activity across the southern continents, particularly Darmar, since the transference. Our excavation sites there have all but caved in," Wenna said.

Syd just shook her head, looking to Widje and Keal. Syd knew she would be relying on Wenna's guidance more than she should, not only on how to be Eichon but also on what to do. The stipulations were in place for a reason, the biggest of which were to be sure to keep Syd in check should the Madness take over again. But Syd had grown thankful for the closeness and counsel, lost in a sea of choices.

Villette trailed in after Wenna.

"Ah, there you are," Villette said. "Are you two about ready? We need to record the announcement before you leave."

Syd and Wenna had both protested to the public announcement, but the Council had voted in favor. While it was safer to keep Syd's identity hidden, it would lessen the loyalty of the Novari to not know who their new leader was. Not that Syd had any plans to *be* that leader, truthfully.

Tsunamis and earthquakes had increased, too, beyond any of the projected models since the transference. The best way to protect her people was to complete Project Nova. But even before that, the Council hadn't bothered to hold hold a vote on finding Adeline. Wenna, Villette, Keal, and Widje would join in the search. Matius, Reth, and Saaviana would stay behind and organize the relief efforts, as well as reintegrate PRISM. Rhiuld would stay at ACES and help guide Avant while Matius was busy elsewhere.

Magnate staff, black uniforms skintight and detailed in bright orange, brought in an archaic microphone and set it on the desk, followed by a prompter screen that illuminated the first few words of what needed to be said. Wenna joined Syd behind the mic.

"Ready?" Widje looked to them both, relieving the staff of the rest of the recording equipment.

Syd and Wenna nodded in unison.

"And we're still all in agreement this is the best course of action? After this is sent out, everyone will know…" Widje's voice trailed off, more nervous than Syd it seemed. The Eichon's Guard was meant to protect her, help her keep a low profile. This was flying directly in the face of that, and Seliss had still not issued a single statement since Zevir.

"Yes, Widje," Syd said. "We'll need the support of the Novari once Project Nova is underway."

"Okay," Widje said in a sing-song way and stepped behind the recorder. "We're recording in 3…2…1…" She pointed to Wenna.

"People of Terrus, this is Wenna Keylen. By now, the news of Zevir's disastrous fate has likely reached every conceivable corner of our planet. Indeed, Zevir's destruction has resulted in many other cities, towns, and villages to open its homes to refugees of different walks of life. We sincerely thank each and every one of you who have answered that call.

"The day my home collapsed, the home of so many of us, also marked the beginning of the next Eichon's reign. I, Wenna Keylen, am no longer your Eichon. Sydney Orleen, from Darmar, was chosen as Eichon and the transference, like so many before it, was a complete success."

Wenna paused and nodded to Syd, who gave a curt nod.

"Greetings, everyone," she began. "I, Sydney Orleen, begin my reign as your Eichon with a promise." The prompter scrolled and then slowed to meet her pace, but Syd didn't need it. The Council had given her the script to memorize. "A promise to seek resolution and to stop the needless tensions that only take from Terrus's people and serve no one." She hoped the words felt whole, and on some level, she did agree with them. But they tasted hollow and rotten.

"A promise of a new era of understanding and resolve with my personal enemies, in hopes of extinguishing needless, unnecessary wars. In return for this promise, I only ask this of you: trust that this is a new age, a new era that strives toward peace with peaceful means." Syd imagined these words spilling from Sevnior's mouth, just like his speech at the orientation. She closed her eyes for a moment, finding her own resolve in knowing they'd be leaving to search for Adeline shortly.

"This cannot be accomplished without all of us turning

to our friends and our enemies and finding each other's humanity. I ask that you seek kindness and patience within yourself, then to extend that understanding to those around you.

"To lead by example, anyone who seeks refuge in the wake of Zevir's fall will find welcome in Magnate, my new home. Our doors are open."

Syd took a step back, and Widje took over. Widje repeated the message one single time before ending the recording, and the prompter fizzled out.

Turning to the slitted window, Syd stared out at the Ifor Ridge. The snowy mountain tops would take some getting used to once they'd returned. A gust picked up, sending snow flying in a flurry. Syd thought of Adeline, of wherever she was, of whatever she was doing, and imagined her hearing Syd's call to come home.

Behind her, the staff busied with clearing the room of equipment. Villette stepped next to Syd and clasped her hands behind her yellow robes.

"Are we ready to leave, Eichon?" Villette asked.

Syd turned around to find Widje and Keal looking at her expectantly. Keal gave his half grin, and Widje titled her head with a raised eyebrow.

"Yes." Syd said, leading the way to the airship hangar.

Acknowledgements

This book means a lot. It took a decade for me to write, and while I know I will inevitably forget someone in the list below, I'd still like to make the attempt of thanking the folks who knowingly or unknowingly helped in its creation:

Thank you to Brandon, Jared, Elyse, Amita, Tucker, Helen, The Birds, Jacq, Tomm, Michelle, R. Leigh, Jeremy, Kelly, Candace, John, Laura, Kaitlyn, Catherine, Jess, Meeka, Ginger, Ollie, my family for their support, my ever-patient publisher, the Salt & Sage Books team, the Gold Leaf Literary team, Kitase, Nojima, Ishikawa, Yoshida, Mary, Terry, Neil, Brandon (the other one), Micaiah, N.K., Bill, and anyone else who puts up with my general nonsense.

I'm grateful for all the help along the way.

For a list of my teachers and other acknowledgments, visit my website at www.jennstoreybooks.com.

PS – And, of course, the best is for last. Thank you for reading.

About the Author

Jenn Storey, née Treado, (she/they) is a storyteller who uses genre as a framework for exploration. She has studied under faculty from Alverno College, Northwestern University, Texas State University, and holds an M.F.A. in Creative Writing & Poetics from the University of Washington Bothell. Her poetry, essays, and creative nonfiction/ experimental writing have been published in various digital and physical journals. *Tilting Gravity* is her first novel-length work. Learn more at www.jennstoreybooks.com.

More from Dreamsphere Books & Deep Hearts YA

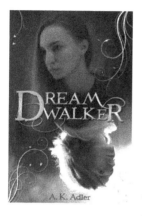

Dreamwalker
A.K. Adler

Luke and Aliya are just figments of each others' dreams. Until the nightmares start, and each needs the other to be real. Fast.

Sixteen-year-old Luke wants to go unnoticed. He doesn't want a girlfriend. He doesn't want to live in his own skin. He definitely doesn't want to have panic attacks whenever he questions his gender identity.

And these problems are nothing compared to the problems he has while he's asleep. When Luke's asleep, he's someone else.

Aliya's options all look bad. Get married as everyone expects...or acknowledge that her strange ability to walk in other people's dreams means she's a shaman. That power might gain her respect, or it might lead to her being feared and driven out of her home. Yet, how can she deny her power when it's the only thing that can save her community from danger?

Her life's about to get a lot more complicated. Curses, epic journeys, battles with the forces of nature, nightmares that can drag you down into death. And a boy from another world who's stuck inside her head.

When Luke's sister develops a terminal illness, his connection to the magic of Aliya's world is her only hope.

But can he come to terms with his secrets in order to claim that magic as his own?

Together, Luke and Aliya will discover that the key to both their problems lies in the same place: through their nightmares to the other side of fear.

The Aziza Chronicles: Awakening
TreVaughn Malik Roach-Carter

Discovering her descent from mythological African warriors called the Aziza was just the beginning of Justice Montgomery's troubles. For not only has she been chosen to be their champion against supernatural evils—a demon is on the loose seeking to manipulate her into misusing her newfound powers.

Determined to do what's right and live up to her heritage, Justice trains and forms a band of allies, both human and supernatural. Yet the demon is determined to lead her astray, in the hope that her power might be used to enact an ancient prophecy.

Should she succeed, Justice might become one of the most legendary Aziza to ever live. But should she fail, she might resurrect a goddess of Hell, and doom the world.

CPSIA information can be obtained
at www.ICGtesting.com
Printed in the USA
BVHW080945230323
661008BV00006B/122